Insane, desperate rage twisted Tanis's face. Somehow he'd make Raistlin listen to reason! Somehow they would all use this strange magic to escape! Tanis started forward, then stopped. From nowhere—seemingly—had come a small silver dagger, long concealed, fastened to the mage's wrist by a cunningly designed leather thong.

"All right," Tanis said, breathing heavily. "You'd kill me without a second thought. But what about your brother? Caramon, stop him!"

Caramon took a step toward his twin. Raistlin raised the silver dagger warningly.

"Don't make him come near me, Tanis," Raistlin said. "I assure you. I am capable of this, truly. What I have sought all my life is within my grasp. I will let nothing stop me. Look at Caramon's face, Tanis! He knows! I killed him once. I can do it again. . . ."

THE WAR OF THE LANCE NEARS ITS END . . .
FOR GOOD . . . OR FOR EVIL. . . .

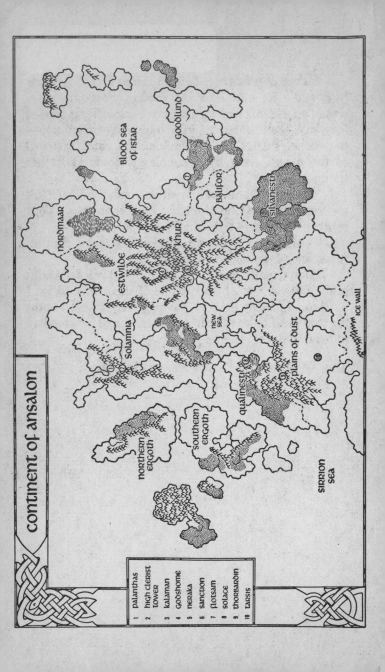

continent of ansalon

1 palanthas
2 high clerist tower
3 kalaman
4 gooshome
5 neraka
6 sanction
7 flotsam
8 solace
9 thorbardin
10 tarsis

blood sea of istar

goodlund

noromaar

estwilde

khur

balifor

silvanesti

solamnia

new sea

northern ergoth

qualinesti

plains of dust

southern ergoth

ice wall

sirrion sea

DragonLance™

CHRONICLES
VOLUME 3
DRAGONS OF SPRING DAWNING

by Margaret Weis and Tracy Hickman

POETRY BY MICHAEL WILLIAMS
COVER ART BY LARRY ELMORE
INTERIOR ART BY JEFFREY BUTLER

TSR, Inc.

To Angel and Curtis, my children, my hope,
and my life—Tracy Raye Hickman

To the Commons Bridge Group, University of Missouri,
1966-1970:
Nancy Olson, Bill Fisher, Nancy Burnett, Ken Randolph,
Ed Bristol, Herb the fry cook,
and in memory of Bob Campbell and John Steele, who
died in Viet Nam,
and to the rest of that wonderful group of mismatched
friends—
this book about friends is fondly dedicated—Margaret Weis

DRAGONLANCE™ CHRONICLES

Volume Three

DRAGONS OF SPRING DAWNING

®Copyright 1985 TSR, Inc.
All Rights Reserved.

First Printing, September, 1985
Printed in the United States of America.
Library of Congress Catalog Card Number: 85-90078

9 8 7 6 5 4 3 2 1

ISBN: 0-88038-175-2

TSR, Inc.
P.O. Box 756
Lake Geneva, WI 53147

TSR UK Ltd.
The Mill, Rathmore Road
Cambridge CB14AD
United Kingdom

Kitiara, of all the days these days
are rocked in dark and waiting, in regret.
The clouds obscure the city as I write this,
delaying thought and sunlight, as the streets
hang between day and darkness. I have waited
past all decision, past the heart in shadows
to tell you this.
                    In absences you grew
more beautiful, more poisonous, you were
an attar of orchids in the swimming night,
where passion, like a shark drawn down a bloodstream,
murders four senses, only taste preserving,
buckling into itself, finding the blood its own,
a small wound first, but as the shark unravels
the belly tatters in the long throat's tunnel.
And knowing this, the night still seems a richness,
a gauntlet of desires ending in peace,
I would still be part of these allurements,
and to my arms I would take in the darkness,
blessed and renamed by pleasure;
                                    but the light,
the light, my Kitiara, when the sun
spangles the rain-gorged sidewalks, and the oil
from doused lamps rises in the sunstruck water,
splintering the light to rainbows! I arise,
and though the storm resettles on the city,
I think of Sturm, Laurana, and the others,
but Sturm the foremost, who can see the sun
straight through the fog and cloudrack. How could I
abandon these?
                And so into the shadow,
and not your shadow but the eager grayness
expecting light, I ride the storm away.

"Why, look, Berem. Here's a path. . . . How strange. All the times we've been hunting in these woods and we've never seen it."

"It's not so strange. The fire burned off some of the brush, that's all. Probably just an animal trail."

"Let's follow it. If it is an animal trail, maybe we'll find a deer. We've been hunting all day with nothing to show for it. I hate to go home empty-handed."

Without waiting for my reply, she turns onto the trail. Shrugging, I follow her. It is pleasant being outdoors today— the first warm day after the bitter chill of winter. The sun is warm on my neck and shoulders. Walking through the fire-ravaged woods is easy. No vines to snag you. No brush to tear at your clothing. Lightning, probably that thunderstorm which struck late last fall.

But we walk for a long time and finally I begin to grow weary. She is wrong—this is no animal trail. It is a man-made path and an old one at that. We're not likely to find any game. Just the same as it's been all day. The fire, then the hard winter. The animals dead or gone. There'll be no fresh meat tonight.

More walking. The sun is high in the sky. I'm tired, hungry. There's been no sign of any living creature.

"Let's turn back, sister. There's nothing here . . ."

She stops, sighing. She is hot and tired and discouraged, I can tell. And too thin. She works too hard, doing women's work and men's as well. Out hunting when she should be home, receiving the pledges of suitors. She's pretty, I think. People say we look alike, but I know they are wrong. It is only that we are so close—closer than other brothers and their sisters. But we've had to be close. Our life has been so hard. . . .

"I suppose you're right, Berem. I've seen no sign . . . Wait, brother . . . Look ahead. What's that?"

I see a bright and shining glitter, a myriad colors dancing in the sunlight—as if all the jewels on Krynn were heaped together in a basket.

Her eyes widen. "Perhaps it's the gates of the rainbow!"

Ha! Stupid girlish notion. I laugh, but I find myself running forward. It is hard to catch up with her. Though I am bigger and stronger, she is fleet as a deer.

We come to a clearing in the forest. If lightning did strike this forest, this must have been where the bolt hit. The land around is scorched and blasted. There was a building here once, I notice. Ruined, broken columns jut up from the blackened ground like broken bones sticking through decaying flesh. An oppressive feeling hangs over the place. Nothing grows here, nor has anything grown here for many springs. I want to leave, but I cannot. . . .

Before me is the most beautiful, wonderful sight I have ever seen in my life, in my dreams. . . . A piece of a stone column, encrusted with jewels! I know nothing about gemstones, but I can tell these are valuable beyond belief! My body begins to shake. Hurrying forward, I kneel down beside the fire-blasted stone and brush away the dirt and filth.

She kneels beside me.

"Berem! How wonderful! Did you ever see anything like it? Such beautiful jewels in such a horrible place." She looks around and I feel her shivering. "I wonder what this used to be? There's such a solemn feeling about it, a holy feeling. But an evil feeling, too. It must have been a temple before the Cataclysm. A temple to the evil gods . . . Berem! What are you doing?"

I have taken out my hunting knife and I begin to chip away the stone around one of the jewels—a radiant green gemstone. It is as big as my fist and sparkles more brilliantly than the sun shining on green leaves. The rock around it comes away easily beneath my knife blade.

"Stop it, Berem!" Her voice is shrill. "It-it's desecration! This place is sacred to some god! I know it!"

I can feel the gemstone's cold crystal, yet it burns with an inner green fire! I ignore her protests.

"Bah! You said before it was the rainbow's gates! You're right! We've found our fortune, as the old story says. If this place was sacred to the gods, they must have abandoned it years ago. Look round, it's nothing but rubble! If they wanted it, they should have taken care of it. The gods won't mind if I take a few of these jewels. . . ."

"Berem!"

An edge of fear in her voice! She's really frightened! Foolish girl. She's beginning to irritate me. The gemstone is almost free. I can wiggle it.

"Look, Jasla." I am shaking with excitement. I can barely talk. "We've nothing to live on, now—what with the fire and the hard winter. These jewels will bring money enough in the market at Gargath for us to move away from this wretched place. We'll go to a city, maybe Palanthas! You know you've wanted to see the wonders there. . . ."

"No! Berem, I forbid it! You are committing sacrilege!"

Her voice is stern. I have never seen her like this! For a moment I hesitate. I draw back, away from the broken stone column with its rainbow of jewels. I, too, am beginning to feel something frightening and evil about this place. But the jewels are so beautiful! Even as I stare at them, they glitter and sparkle in the sunshine. No god is here. No god cares about them. No god will miss them. Embedded in some old column that is crumbling and broken.

I reach down to pry the jewel out of stone with my knife. It is such a rich green, shining as brilliantly as the spring sun shines through the new leaves of the trees. . . .

"Berem! Stop!"

Her hand grasps my arm, her nails dig into my flesh. It hurts . . I grow angry and, as sometimes happens when I grow angry, a haze dims my vision and I feel a suffocating swelling inside of me. My head pounds until it seems my eyes must burst from their sockets.

"Leave me be!" I hear a roaring voice—my own!

I shove her . . .

She falls . . .

It all happens so slowly. She is falling forever. I didn't mean to . . . I want to catch her . . . But I cannot move.

She falls against the broken column.

Blood . . . blood . . .

"Jas!" I whisper, lifting her in my arms.

But she doesn't answer me. Blood covers the jewels. They don't sparkle anymore. Just like her eyes. The light is gone. . . .

And then the ground splits apart! Columns rise from the blackened, blasted soil, spiraling into the air! A great darkness comes forth and I feel a horrible, burning pain in my chest. . . .

"Berem!"

Maquesta stood on the foredeck, glaring at her helmsman.

"Berem, I told you. A gale's brewing. I want the ship battened down. What are you doing? Standing there, staring out to sea. What are you practicing to be—a monument? Get moving, you lubber! I don't pay good wages to statues!"

Berem started. His face paled and he cringed before Maquesta's irritation in such a pitiful manner that the captain of the *Perechon* felt as if she were taking out her anger on a helpless child.

That's all he is, she reminded herself wearily. Even though he must be fifty or sixty years old, even though he was one of the best helmsmen she had ever sailed with—mentally, he was still a child.

"I'm sorry, Berem," Maq said, sighing. "I didn't mean to yell at you. It's just the storm . . . it makes me nervous. There, there. Don't look at me like that. How I wish you could talk! I wish I knew what was going on in that head of yours—if there is anything! Well, never mind. Attend to your duties, then go below. Better get used to lying in your berth for a few days until the gale blows itself out."

Berem smiled at her—the simple, guileless smile of a child.

Maquesta smiled back, shaking her head. Then she hurried away, her thoughts busy with getting her beloved ship prepared to ride out the gale. Out of the corner of her eye, she saw Berem shuffle below, then promptly forgot about him when her first mate came aboard to report that he had found most of the crew and only about one-third of them were so drunk as to be useless . . .

Berem lay in the hammock slung in the crew's quarters of the *Perechon*. The hammock swung back and forth violently as the first winds of the gale struck the *Perechon* as it rode at anchor in the harbor of Flotsam on the Blood Sea of Istar. Putting his hands—the hands that looked too young on the body of a fifty-year-old human—beneath his head, Berem stared up at the lamp swinging from the wooden planks above him.

"Why, look, Berem. Here's a path. . . . How strange. All the

times we've been hunting in these woods and we've never seen it."

"It's not so strange. The fire burned off some of the brush, that's all. Probably just an animal trail."

"Let's follow it. If it is an animal trail, maybe we'll find a deer. We've been hunting all day with nothing to show for it. I hate to go home empty-handed."

Without waiting for my reply, she turns onto the trail. Shrugging, I follow her. It is pleasant being outdoors today—the first warm day after the bitter chill of winter. The sun is warm on my neck and shoulders. Walking through the fire-ravaged woods is easy. No vines to snag you. No brush to tear at your clothing. Lightning, probably that thunderstorm which struck late last fall. . . .

BOOK 1

I

*Flight from darkness
into darkness.*

The dragonarmy officer slowly descended the stairs from the second floor of the Saltbreeze Inn. It was past midnight. Most of the inn's patrons had long since gone to bed. The only sound the officer could hear was the crashing of waves of Blood Bay on the rocks below.

The officer paused a moment on the landing, casting a quick, sharp glance around the Common Room that lay spread out below him. It was empty, except for a draconian sprawled across a table, snoring loudly in a drunken stupor. The dragonman's wings shivered with each snort. The wooden table creaked and swayed beneath it.

The officer smiled bitterly, then continued down the stairs. He was dressed in the steel dragonscale armor copied from the real dragonscale armor of the Dragon Highlords. His helm covered his head and face, making it difficult to see his features. All that was visible beneath the shadow cast by the helm was a reddish brown beard that marked him—racially—as human.

At the bottom of the stairs, the officer came to a sudden halt, apparently nonplussed at the sight of the innkeeper, still awake and yawning over his account books. After a slight nod, the dragon officer seemed about to go on out of the inn without speaking, but the innkeeper stopped him with a question.

"You expecting the Highlord tonight?"

The officer halted and half-turned. Keeping his face averted, he pulled out a pair of gloves and began putting them on. The weather was bitterly chill. The sea city of Flotsam was in the grip of a winter storm the like of which it had not experienced in its three hundred years of existence on the shores of Blood Bay.

"In this weather?" The dragonarmy officer snorted. "Not likely! Not even dragons can outfly these gale winds!"

"True. It's not a fit night out for man or beast," the innkeeper agreed. He eyed the dragon officer shrewdly. "What business do you have, then, that takes you out in this storm?"

The dragonarmy officer regarded the innkeeper coldly. "I don't see that it's any of your business where I go or what I do."

"No offense," the innkeeper said quickly, raising his hands as if ward off a blow. "It's just that if the Highlord comes back and happens to miss you, I'd be glad to tell her where you could be found."

"That won't be necessary," the officer muttered. "I—I've left her a—note . . . explaining my absence. Besides, I'll be back before morning. I—I just need a breath of air. That's all."

"I don't doubt that!" The innkeeper sniggered. "You haven't left her room for three days! Or should I say three nights! Now—don't get mad"—this on seeing the officer flush angrily beneath the helm—"I admire the man can keep *her* satisfied that long! Where was she bound for?"

"The Highlord was called to deal with a problem in the east, somewhere near Solamnia," the officer replied, scowling. "I wouldn't inquire any further into her affairs if I were you."

"No, no," replied the innkeeper hastily. "Certainly not. Well, I bid you good evening—what was your name? She introduced us, but I failed to catch it."

"Tanis," the officer said, his voice muffled. "Tanis Half-Elven. And a good evening to you."

Nodding coldly, the officer gave his gloves a final sharp tug, then, pulling his cloak around him, he opened the door to the inn and stepped out into the storm. The bitter wind swept into the room, blowing out candles and swirling the innkeeper's papers around. For a moment, the officer struggled with the heavy door while the innkeeper cursed fluently and grabbed for his scattered accounts. Finally the officer succeeded in slamming the door shut behind him, leaving the inn peaceful, quiet, and warm once more.

Staring out after him, the innkeeper saw the officer walk past the front window, his head bent down against the wind, his cloak billowing out behind him.

One other figure watched the officer as well. The instant the door shut, the drunken draconian raised its head, its black, reptilian eyes glittering. Stealthily it rose from the table, its steps quick and certain. Padding lightly on its clawed feet, it crept to the window and peered outside. For a few moments, the draconian waited, then it too flung open the door and disappeared into the storm.

Through the window, the innkeeper saw the draconian head in the same direction as the dragonarmy officer. Walking over, the innkeeper peered out through the glass. It was wild and dark outside, the tall iron braziers of flaming pitch that lit the night streets sputtering and flickering in the wind and the driving rain. But the innkeeper thought he saw the dragonarmy officer turn down a street leading to the main part of town. Creeping along behind him, keeping to the shadows, came the draconian. Shaking his head, the innkeeper woke the night clerk, who was dozing in a chair behind the desk.

"I've a feeling the Highlord will be in tonight, storm or no storm," the innkeeper told the sleepy clerk. "Wake me if she comes."

Shivering, he glanced outside into the night once more, seeing in his mind's eye the dragonarmy officer walking the empty streets of Flotsam, the shadowy figure of the draconian slinking after him.

"On second thought," the innkeeper muttered, "let me sleep."

The storm shut down Flotsam tonight. The bars that normally stayed open until the dawn straggled through their grimy windows were locked up and shuttered against the gale. The streets were deserted, no one venturing out into the winds that could knock a man down and pierce even the warmest clothing with biting cold.

Tanis walked swiftly, his head bowed, keeping near the darkened buildings that broke the full force of the gale. His beard was soon rimed with ice. Sleet stung his face painfully. The half-elf shook with the cold, cursing the dragonarmor's cold metal against his skin. Glancing behind him occasionally, he watched to see if anyone had taken an unusual interest in his leaving the inn. But the visibility was reduced to almost nothing. Sleet and rain swirled around him so that he could barely see tall buildings looming up in the darkness, much less anything else. After a while, he realized he better concentrate on finding his way through town. Soon he was so numb with cold that he didn't much care if anyone was following him or not.

He hadn't been in the town of Flotsam long—only four days to be precise. And most of those days had been spent with *her*.

Tanis blocked the thought from his mind as he stared through the rain at the street signs. He knew only vaguely where he was going. His friends were in an inn somewhere on the edge of town, away from the wharf, away from the bars and brothels. For a moment he wondered in despair what he would do if he got lost. He dared not ask about them. . . .

And then he found it. Stumbling through the deserted streets, slipping on the ice, he almost sobbed in relief when he saw the sign swinging wildly in the wind. He hadn't even been able to remember the name, but now he recognized it—the Jetties.

Stupid name for an inn, he thought, shaking so with the cold he could barely grasp the door handle. Pulling the door open, he was blown inside by the force of the wind, and it was with an effort that he managed to shove the door shut behind him.

There was no night clerk on duty—not at this shabby place. By the light of a smoking fire in the filthy grate, Tanis saw a stub of a candle sitting on the desk, apparently for the convenience of guests who staggered in after hours. His hands shook so he could barely strike the flint. After a moment he forced his cold-stiffened fingers to work, lit the candle, and made his way upstairs by its feeble light.

If he had turned around and glanced out the window, he would have seen a shadowy figure huddle in a doorway across the street. But Tanis did not look out the window behind him, his eyes were on the stairs.

"Caramon!"

The big warrior instantly sat bolt upright, his hand reaching reflexively for his sword, even before he turned to look questioningly at his brother.

"I heard a noise outside," Raistlin whispered. "The sound of a scabbard clanking against armor."

Caramon shook his head, trying to clear the sleep away, and climbed out of bed, sword in hand. He crept toward the door until he, too, could hear the noise that had wakened his light-sleeping brother. A man dressed in armor was walking stealthily down the hall outside their rooms. Then Caramon could see the faint glow of candlelight beneath the door. The sound of clanking armor came to halt, right outside their room.

Gripping his sword, Caramon motioned to his brother. Raistlin nodded and melted back into the shadows. His eyes were abstracted. He was calling to mind a magic spell. The twin brothers worked well together, effectively combining magic and steel to defeat their foes.

The candlelight beneath the door wavered. The man must be shifting the candle to his other hand, freeing his sword hand. Reaching out, Caramon slowly and silently slid the bolt on the door. He waited a moment. Nothing happened. The man was hesitating, perhaps wondering if this was the right room. He'll find out soon enough, Caramon thought to himself.

Caramon flung open the door with a sudden jerk. Lunging around it, he grasped hold of the dark figure and dragged him inside. With all the strength of his brawny arms, the warrior flung the armor-clad man to the floor. The candle dropped, its flame extinguishing in melted wax. Raistlin began to chant a magic spell that would entrap their victim in a sticky web-like substance.

"Hold! Raistlin, stop!" the man shouted. Recognizing the voice, Caramon grabbed hold of his brother, shaking him to break the concentration of his spellcasting.

"Raist! It's Tanis!"

Shuddering, Raistlin came out of his trance, arms dropped

limply to his sides. Then he began to cough, clutching his chest.

Caramon cast an anxious glance at his twin, but Raistlin warded him away with a wave of the hand. Turning, Caramon reached down to help the half-elf to his feet.

"Tanis!" he cried, nearly squeezing the breath out of him with an enthusiastic embrace. "Where have you been? We were sick with worry. By all the gods, you're freezing! Here, I'll poke up the fire. Raist"—Caramon turned to his brother—"are you sure you're all right?"

"Don't concern yourself with me!" Raistlin whispered. The mage sank back down on his bed, gasping for breath. His eyes glittered gold in the flaring firelight as he stared at the half-elf, who huddled thankfully beside the blaze. "You better get the others."

"Right." Caramon started out the door.

"I'd put some clothes on first," Raistlin remarked caustically.

Blushing, Caramon hurried back to his bed and grabbed a pair of leather breeches. Pulling these on, he slipped a shirt over his head, then went out into the hallway, softly closing the door behind him. Tanis and Raistlin could hear him knocking gently on the Plainsmen's door. They could hear Riverwind's stern reply and Caramon's hurried, excited explanation.

Tanis glanced at Raistlin—saw the mage's strange hourglass eyes focused on him with a piercing stare—and turned uncomfortably back to gaze into the fire.

"Where *have* you been, Half-Elf?" Raistlin asked in his soft, whispering voice.

Tanis swallowed nervously. "I was captured by a Dragon Highlord," he said, reciting the answer he had prepared. "The Highlord thought I was one of his officers, naturally, and asked me to escort him to his troops, who are stationed outside of town. Of course I had to do as he asked or make him suspicious. Finally, tonight, I was able to get away."

"Interesting." Raistlin coughed the word.

Tanis glanced at him sharply. "What's interesting?"

"I've never heard you lie before, Half-Elf," Raistlin said softly. "I find it . . . quite . . . fascinating."

Tanis opened his mouth, but, before he could reply, Caramon returned, followed by Riverwind and Goldmoon and Tika, yawning sleepily.

Hurrying to him, Goldmoon embraced Tanis swiftly. "My friend!" she said brokenly, holding onto him tightly. "We've been so worried—"

Riverwind clasped Tanis by the hand, his usually stern face relaxed in a smile. Gently he took hold of his wife and removed her from Tanis's embrace, but it was only to take her place.

"My brother!" Riverwind said in Que-shu, the dialect of the Plains people, hugging the half-elf tightly. "We feared you were captured! Dead! We didn't know—"

"What happened? Where were you?" Tika asked eagerly, coming forward to hug Tanis.

Tanis looked over at Raistlin, but he was lying back on his hard pillow, his strange eyes fixed on the ceiling, seemingly uninterested in anything being said.

Clearing his throat self-consciously, intensely aware of Raistlin listening, Tanis repeated his story. The others followed it with expressions of interest and sympathy. Occasionally they asked questions. Who was this Highlord? How big was the army? Where was it located? What were the draconians doing in Flotsam? Were they really searching for them? How had Tanis escaped?

Tanis answered all their question glibly. As for the Highlord, he hadn't seen much of him. He didn't know who he was. The army was not large. It was located outside of town. The draconians were searching for someone, but it was not them. They were looking for a human named Berem or something strange like that.

At this Tanis shot a quick look at Caramon, but the big man's face registered no recognition. Tanis breathed easier. Good, Caramon didn't remember the man they had seen patching the sail on the *Perechon*. He didn't remember or he hadn't caught the man's name. Either way was fine.

The others nodded, absorbed in his story. Tanis sighed in relief. As for Raistlin . . . well, it didn't really matter what the mage thought or said. The others would believe Tanis over Raistlin even if the half-elf claimed day was night. Undoubtedly Raistlin knew this, which was why he didn't cast any doubts on Tanis's story. Feeling wretched, hoping no one would ask him anything else and force him to mire himself deeper and deeper in lies, Tanis yawned and groaned as if exhausted past endurance.

Goldmoon immediately rose to her feet, her face soft with concern. "I'm sorry, Tanis," she said gently. "We've been selfish. You are cold and weary and we've kept you up talking. And we must be up early in the morning to board the ship."

"Damn it, Goldmoon! Don't be a fool! We won't board any ship in this gale!" Tanis snarled.

Everyone stared at him in astonishment, even Raistlin sat up. Goldmoon's eyes were dark with pain, her face set in rigid lines, reminding the half-elf that no one spoke to her in that tone. Riverwind stood beside her, a troubled look on his face.

The silence grew uncomfortable. Finally Caramon cleared his throat with a rumble. "If we can't leave tomorrow, we'll try the next day," he said comfortably. "Don't worry about it, Tanis. The draconians won't be out in this weather. We're safe—"

"I know. I'm sorry," he muttered. "I didn't mean to snap at you, Goldmoon. It's been—nerve-racking—these last few days. I'm so tired I can't think straight. I'll go to my room."

"The innkeeper gave it to someone else," Caramon said, then added hurriedly, "but you can sleep here, Tanis. Take my bed—"

"No, I'll just lie down on the floor." Avoiding Goldmoon's gaze, Tanis began unbuckling the dragonarmor, his eyes fixed firmly on his shaking fingers.

"Sleep well, my friend," Goldmoon said softly.

Hearing the concern in her voice, he could imagine her exchanging compassionate glances with Riverwind. There was the Plainsman's hand on his shoulder, giving him a sympathetic pat. Then they were gone. Tika left, too, closing the door behind her after a murmured goodnight.

"Here, let me help you," Caramon offered, knowing that Tanis—unaccustomed to wearing plate armor—found the intricate buckles and straps difficult to manage. "Can I get you something to eat? Drink? Some mulled wine?"

"No," Tanis said wearily, divesting himself thankfully of the armor, trying not to remember that in a few hours he would have to put it on again. "I just need sleep."

"Here—at least take my blanket," Caramon insisted, seeing that the half-elf was shivering with the cold.

Tanis accepted the blanket gratefully, although he was not certain whether he was shaking with the chill or the violence of his turbulent emotions. Lying down, he wrapped himself in both the blanket and his cloak. Then he closed his eyes and concentrated on making his breathing even and regular, knowing that the mother-hen, Caramon, would never sleep until he was certain Tanis was resting comfortably. Soon he heard

Caramon get into bed. The fire burned low, darkness fell. After a moment, he heard Caramon's rumbling snore. In the other bed, he could hear Raistlin's fitful cough.

When he was certain both the twins were asleep, Tanis stretched out, putting his hands beneath his head. He lay awake, staring into the darkness.

It was near morning when the Dragon Highlord arrived back at the Saltbreeze Inn. The night clerk could see immediately that the Highlord was in a foul temper. Flinging open the door with more force than the gale winds, she glared angrily into the inn, as if its warmth and comfort were offensive. Indeed, she seemed to be at one with the storm outside. It was she who caused the candles to flicker, rather than the howling wind. It was she who brought the darkness indoors. The clerk stumbled fearfully to his feet, but the Highlord's eyes were not on him. Kitiara was staring at a draconian, who sat at a table and who signalled, by an almost imperceptible flicker in the dark reptilian eyes, that something was awry.

Behind the hideous dragonmask, the Highlord's eyes narrowed alarmingly, their expression grew cold. For a moment she stood in the doorway, ignoring the chill wind that blew through the inn, whipping her cloak around her.

"Come upstairs," she said finally, ungraciously, to the draconian.

The creature nodded and followed after her, its clawed feet clicking on the wooden floors.

"Is there anything—" the night clerk began, cringing as the door blew shut with an shattering crash.

"No!" Kitiara snarled. Hand on the hilt of her sword, she stalked past the quivering man without a glance and climbed the stairs to her suite of rooms, leaving the man to sink back, shaken, into his chair.

Fumbling with her key, Kitiara threw open the door. She gave the room a quick sweeping glance.

It was empty.

The draconian waited behind her, standing patiently and in silence.

Furious, Kitiara tugged viciously at the hinges on the dragonmask and yanked it off. Tossing it on the bed, she spoke over her shoulder.

"Come inside and shut the door!"

The draconian did as it was commanded, closing the door softly.

Kitiara did not turn to face the creature. Hands on her hips, she stared grimly at the rumpled bed.

"So—he's gone." It was a statement, not a question.

"Yes, Highlord," lisped the draconian in its hissing voice.

"You followed him, as I ordered?"

"Of course, Highlord." The draconian bowed.

"Where did he go?"

Kitiara ran a hand through her dark, curly hair. She still had not turned around. The draconian could not see her face and he had no idea what emotions—if any—she was keeping hidden.

"An inn, Highlord. Near the edge of town. Called the Jetties."

"Another woman?" The Highlord's voice was tense.

"I think not, Highlord." The draconian concealed a smile. "I believe he has friends there. We had reports of strangers staying in the inn, but since they did not match the description of the Green Gemstone Man, we did not investigate them."

"Someone is there now, watching him?"

"Certainly, Highlord. You will be informed immediately if he—or any inside—leaves the building."

The Highlord stood in silence for a moment, then she turned around. Her face was cold and calm, although extremely pale. But there were a number of factors which could have accounted for her pallor, the draconian thought. It was a long flight from the High Clerist's Tower—rumor had it her armies had been badly defeated there—the legendary dragonlance had reappeared, along with the dragon orbs. Then there was her failure to find the Green Gemstone Man, so desperately sought by the Queen of Darkness, and who was reported to have been seen in Flotsam. The Highlord had a great many things to worry about, the draconian thought with amusement. Why concern herself over one man? She had lovers aplenty, most of them much more charming, much more eager to please than that moody half-elf. Bakaris, for example . . .

"You have done well," Kitiara said finally, breaking in on the draconian's musings. Stripping off her armor with a careless lack of modesty, she waved a negligent hand. She almost seemed herself again. "You will be rewarded. Now leave me."

The draconian bowed again and left, eyes staring at the floor. The creature was not fooled. As it left, the dragonman saw the Highlord's gaze fall upon a scrap of parchment resting on the table. The draconian had seen that parchment upon entering. It was, the creature noted, covered with writing in a delicate elvish script. As the draconian shut the door, there came a crashing sound—the sound of a piece of dragonarmor being hurled full force against a wall.

2

Pursuit.

The gale blew itself out toward morning. The sound of water dripping monotonously from the eaves thudded in Tanis's aching head, almost making him wish for a return of the shrieking wind. The sky was gray and lowering. Its leaden weight pressed down upon the half-elf.

"The seas will be running high," Caramon said sagely. Having listened eagerly to the sea stories told them by William, the innkeeper of the Pig and Whistle in Port Balifor, Caramon considered himself somewhat of an expert on nautical matters. None of the others disputed him, knowing nothing about the

---

sea themselves. Only Raistlin regarded Caramon with a sneering smile when his brother—who had been on small boats only a few times in his life—began talking like an old seadog.

"Maybe we shouldn't even risk going out—" Tika began.

"We're going. Today," Tanis said grimly. "If we have to swim, we're leaving Flotsam."

The others glanced at each other, then looked back at Tanis. Standing, staring out the window, he did not see their raised eyebrows or their shrugging shoulders, though he was aware of them all the same.

The companions were gathered in the brothers' room. It would not be dawn for another hour, but Tanis had awakened them as soon as he heard the wind cease its savage howl.

He drew a deep breath, then turned to face them. "I'm sorry. I know I sound arbitrary," he said, "but there are dangers I know about that I can't explain right now. There isn't time. All I can tell you is this—we have never in our lives been in more dire peril than we are at this moment in this town. We must leave and we must leave now!" He heard an hysterical note creep into his voice and broke off.

There was silence, then, "Sure, Tanis," Caramon said uneasily.

"We're all packed," Goldmoon added. "We can leave whenever you're ready."

"Let's go then," Tanis said.

"I've got to get my things," Tika faltered.

"Go on. Be quick," Tanis told her.

"I-I'll help her," Caramon offered in a low voice.

The big man, dressed, like Tanis, in the stolen armor of a dragonarmy officer, and Tika left quickly, probably hoping to snatch time enough for a last few minutes alone, Tanis thought, fuming in impatience. Goldmoon and Riverwind left to gather their things as well. Raistlin remained in the room, not moving. He had all he needed to carry with him—his pouches with his precious spell components, the Staff of Magius, and the precious marble of the dragon orb, tucked away inside its nondescript bag.

Tanis could feel Raistlin's strange eyes boring into him. It was as if Raistlin could penetrate the darkness of the half-elf's soul with the glittering light from those golden eyes. But still the mage said nothing. Why? Tanis thought angrily. He would almost have welcomed Raistlin's questioning, his accusations.

He would almost welcome a chance to unburden himself and tell the truth—even though he knew what consequences would result.

But Raistlin was silent, except for his incessant cough.

Within a few minutes, the others came back inside the room. "We're ready, Tanis," Goldmoon said in a subdued voice.

For a moment, Tanis couldn't speak. I'll tell them, he resolved. Taking a deep breath, he turned around. He saw their faces, he saw trust; a belief in him. They were following him without question. He couldn't let them down. He couldn't shake this faith. It was all they had to cling to. Sighing, he swallowed the words he had been about to speak.

"Right," he said gruffly and started toward the door.

Maquesta Kar-Thon was awakened from a sound sleep by a banging on her cabin door. Accustomed to having her sleep interrupted at all hours, she was almost immediately awake and reaching for her boots.

"What is it?" she called out.

Before the answer came, she was already getting the feel of the ship, assessing the situation. A glance through the porthole showed her the gale winds had died, but she could tell from the motion of the ship itself that the seas were running high.

"The passengers are here," called out a voice she recognized as that of her first mate.

Landlubbers, she thought bitterly, sighing and dropping the boot she had been dragging on. "Send 'em back," she ordered, lying down again. "We're not sailing today."

There seemed to be some sort of altercation going on outside, for she heard her first mate's voice raised in anger and another voice shouting back. Wearily Maquesta struggled to her feet. Her first mate, Bas Ohn-Koraf, was a minotaur—a race not noted for its easy-going temper. He was exceptionally strong and was known to kill without provocation—one reason he had taken to the sea. On a ship like the *Perechon*, no one asked questions about the past.

Throwing open the door to her cabin, Maq hurried up onto deck.

"What's going on?" she demanded in her sternest voice as her eyes went from the bestial head of her first mate to the bearded face of what appeared to be a dragonarmy officer. But she recognized the slightly slanted brown eyes of the bearded man and fixed him with a cold stare. "I said we're not sailing today, Half-Elf, and I meant—"

"Maquesta," Tanis said quickly, "I've got to talk to you!" He started to push his way past the minotaur to reach her, but Koraf grabbed hold of him and yanked him backwards. Behind Tanis, a larger dragonarmy officer growled and took a step forward. The minotaur's eyes glistened eagerly as he deftly slipped a dirk from the wide, bright-colored sash around his waist.

The crew above decks gathered around immediately, hoping for a fight.

"Caramon—" Tanis warned, holding out his hand restrainingly.

"Kof—!" Maquesta snapped with an angry look meant to remind her first mate that these were paying customers and were not to be handled roughly, at least while in sight of land.

The minotaur scowled, but the dirk disappeared as quickly as it had flashed into the open. Kof turned and walked away disdainfully, the crew muttering in disappointment, but still cheerful. It promised already to be an interesting voyage.

Maquesta helped Tanis to his feet, studying the half-elf with the same intense scrutiny she fixed on a man wanting to sign on as a crew member. She saw at once that the half-elf had changed drastically since she had seen him only four days before, when he and the big man behind him closed the bargain for passage aboard the *Perechon*.

He looks like he's been through the Abyss and back. Probably in some sort of trouble, she decided ruefully. Well I'm not getting him out of it! Not at the risk of my ship. Still, he and his friends had paid for half their passage. And she needed the money. It was hard these days for a pirate to compete with the Highlords. . . .

"Come to my cabin," Maq said ungraciously, leading the way below.

"Stay with the others, Caramon," the half-elf told his companion. The big man nodded. Glancing darkly at the minotaur, Caramon went back over to stand with the rest of the companions who stood silently, huddled around their meager belongings.

Tanis followed Maq down to her cabin and squeezed inside. Even two people in the small cabin were a tight fit. The *Perechon* was a trim vessel, designed for swift sailing and quick maneuvers. Ideal for Maquesta's trade, where it was necessary to slip in and out of harbors quickly, unloading or picking up cargo that wasn't necessarily hers either to pick up or deliver. On occasion, she might enhance her income by catching a fat merchant ship sailing out of Palanthas or Tarsis and slip up on it before it knew what was happening. Then board it quickly, loot it, and make good her escape.

She was adept at outrunning the massive ships of the Dragon Highlords, too, although she made it a point to leave them strictly alone. Too often now, though, the Highlords' ships were seen "escorting" the merchant vessels. Maquesta had lost money on her last two voyages, one reason why she had deigned to carry passengers—something she would never do under normal circumstances.

Removing his helm, the half-elf sat down at the table—or rather fell down, since he was unaccustomed to the motion of the rocking ship. Maquesta remained standing, balancing easily.

"Well, what is you want?" she demanded, yawning. "I told you we can't sail. The seas are—"

"We have to," Tanis said abruptly.

"Look," Maquesta said patiently (reminding herself he was a paying customer), "if you're in some kind of trouble, it's not *my* concern! I'm not risking my ship or my crew—"

"Not me," Tanis interrupted, looking at Maquesta intently, "you."

"Me?" Maquesta said, drawing back, amazed.

Tanis folded his hands on the table and gazed down at them. The pitching and tossing of the vessel at anchor, combined with his exhaustion from the past few days, made him nauseous. Seeing the faint green tinge of his skin beneath his beard and the dark shadows under his hollow eyes, Maquesta thought she'd seen corpses that looked better than this half-elf.

"What do you mean?" she asked tightly.

"I—I was captured by a Dragon Highlord . . . three days ago," Tanis began, speaking in a low voice, staring at his hands. "No, I guess 'captured' is the wrong word. H-He saw me dressed like this and assumed I was one of his men. I had to accompany h-him back to his camp. I've been there—in camp—the last few days, and I—I found out something. I know why the Highlord and the draconians are searching Flotsam. I know what—who—they're looking for."

"Yes?" Maquesta prompted, feeling his fear creep over her

like a contagious disease. "Not the *Perechon*—"

"Your helmsman." Tanis finally looked up at her. "Berem."

"Berem!" Maquesta repeated, stunned. "What for? The man's a mute! A half-wit! A good helmsman, maybe, but nothing more. What could he have done that the Dragon Highlords are looking for him?"

"I don't know," Tanis said wearily, fighting his nausea. "I wasn't able to find out. I'm not sure *they* know! But they're under orders to find him at all costs and bring him alive to"—he closed his eyes to shut out the swaying lamps—"the Dark Queen. . . ."

The breaking light of dawn threw slanted red beams across the sea's rough surface. For an instant it shone on Maq's glistening black skin, a flash like fire came from her golden earrings that dangled nearly to her shoulders. Nervously she ran her fingers through her closely-cropped black hair.

Maquesta felt her throat close. "We'll get rid of him!" she muttered tightly, pushing herself up from the table. "We'll put him ashore. I can find another helmsman—"

"Listen!" Catching hold of Maquesta's arm, Tanis gripped her tightly, forcing her to stop. "They may already know he's here! Even if they don't and they catch him, it won't make any difference. Once they find out he *was* here, on this vessel—and they *will* find out, believe me; there are ways of making even a mute talk—they'll arrest you and everyone on this ship. Arrest you or get rid of you."

He dropped his hand from her arm, realizing he hadn't the strength to hold her. "It's what they've done in the past. I know. The Highlord told me. Whole villages destroyed. People tortured, murdered. Anyone this man comes in contact with is doomed. They fear whatever deadly secret he carries will be passed on, and they can't allow that."

Maquesta sat down. "Berem?" she whispered softly, unbelievingly.

"They couldn't do anything because of the storm," Tanis said wearily, "and the Highlord was called away to Solamnia, some battle there. But sh—the Highlord will be back today. And then—" He couldn't go on. His head sank into his hands as a shudder racked his body.

Maquesta eyed him warily. Could this be true? Or was he making all this up to force her to take him away from some danger? Watching him slump miserably over the table,

Maquesta swore softly. The ship's captain was a shrewd judge of men. She needed to be, in order to control her rough-and-ready crew. And she knew the half-elf wasn't lying. At least, not much. She suspected there were things he wasn't telling, but this story about Berem—as strange as it seemed—had the ring of truth.

It all made sense, she thought uneasily, cursing herself. She prided herself on her judgment, her good sense. Yet she had turned a blind eye to Berem's strangeness. Why? Her lip curled in derision. She liked him—admit it. He was like a child, cheerful, guileless. And so she had overlooked his unwillingness to go ashore, his fear of strangers, his eagerness to work for a pirate when he refused to share in the loot they captured. Maquesta sat a moment, getting the feel of her ship. Glancing outside, she watched the golden sun glint off the white caps, then the sun vanished, swallowed by the lowering gray clouds. It would be dangerous, taking the ship out, but if the wind was right—

"I'd rather be out on the open sea," she murmured, more to herself than to Tanis, "than trapped like a rat on shore."

Making up her mind, Maq rose quickly and started for the door. Then she heard Tanis groan. Turning around, she regarded him pityingly.

"Come on, Half-Elf," Maquesta said, not unkindly. She put her arms around him and helped him stand. "You'll feel better above deck in the fresh air. Besides, you'll need to tell your friends that this isn't going to be what you might call a 'relaxing ocean voyage.' Do you know the risk you're taking?"

Tanis nodded. Leaning heavily on Maquesta, he walked across the heaving deck.

"You're not telling me everything, that's for certain," Maquesta said under her breath as she kicked open the cabin door and helped Tanis struggle up the stairs to the main deck. "I'll wager Berem's not the only one the Highlord's looking for. But I have a feeling this isn't the first bad weather you and your crew have ridden out. I just hope your luck holds!"

The *Perechon* wallowed in the high seas. Riding under short sail, the ship seemed to make little headway, fighting for every inch it gained. Fortunately, the wind backed. Blowing steadily from the southwest, it was taking them straight into the Blood Sea of Istar. Since they were heading for Kalaman, northwest of Flotsam, around the cape of Nordmaar, this was a little out of their way. But Maquesta didn't mind. She wanted to avoid land as much as possible.

There was even the possibility, she told Tanis, that they could sail northeast and arrive in Mithras, homeland of the minotaurs. Although a few minotaurs fought in the armies of the Highlords, the minotaurs in general had not yet sworn allegiance to the Dark Queen. According to Koraf, the minotaurs wanted control of eastern Ansalon in return for their services. And control of the east had just been handed over to a new Dragon Highlord, a hobgoblin called Toede. The minotaurs had no love for humans or elves, but—at this point in time—neither had they any use for the Highlords. Maq and her crew had sheltered in Mithras before. They would be safe there again, at least for a little while.

Tanis was not happy at this delay, but his fate was no longer in his hands. Thinking of this, the half-elf glanced over at the man who stood alone at the center of a whirlwind of blood and flame. Berem was at the helm, guiding the wheel with firm, sure hands, his vacant face unconcerned, unworried.

Tanis, staring hard at the helmsman's shirt front, thought perhaps he could detect a faint glimmer of green. What dark secret beat in the chest where, months ago at Pax Tharkas, he had seen the green glowing jewel embedded in the man's flesh? Why were hundreds of draconians wasting their time, searching for this one man when the war still hung in balance? Why was Kitiara so desperate to find Berem that she had given up command of her forces in Solamnia to supervise the search of Flotsam on just a rumor that he had been seen there?

" 'He is the key!' " Tanis remembered Kitiara's words. " 'If we capture him, Krynn will fall to the might of the Dark Queen. There will be no force in the land able to defeat us then!' "

Shivering, his stomach heaving, Tanis stared at the man in awe. Berem seemed so—so apart from everything, beyond everything—as if the problems of the world affected him not at all. Was he half-witted, as Maquesta said? Tanis wondered. He remembered Berem as he had seen him for those few brief seconds in the midst of the horror of Pax Tharkas. He remembered the look on the man's face as he allowed the traitor Eben to lead him away in a desperate attempt to escape. The look on his face had not been fearful or dull or uncaring. It had been—what? Resigned! That was it! As if he knew the fate that awaited him and went ahead anyway. Sure enough, just as Berem and Eben reached the gates, hundreds of tons of rocks had cascaded down from the gate-blocking mechanism, burying them beneath boulders it would take a dragon to lift. Both bodies were lost, of course.

Or at least Eben's body was lost. Only weeks later, during the celebration of the wedding of Goldmoon and Riverwind, Tanis and Sturm had seen Berem again—alive! Before they could catch him, the man had vanished into the crowd. And they had not seen him again. Not until Tanis found him three— no, four—days ago, calmly sewing a sail on this ship.

Berem steered the ship on its course, his face filled with peace. Tanis leaned over the ship's side and retched.

Maquesta said nothing to the crew about Berem. In explanation of their sudden departure, she said only that she had received word that the Dragon Highlord was a bit too interested in their ship—it would be wise to head for the open seas. None of the crew questioned her. They had no love for the Highlords, and most had been in Flotsam long enough to lose all their money anyway.

Nor did Tanis reveal to his friends the reason for their haste. The companions had all heard the story of the man with the green gemstone and, though they were too polite to say so (with the exception of Caramon), Tanis knew they thought he and Sturm had drunk one too many toasts at the wedding. They did not ask for reasons why they were risking their lives in the rough seas. Their faith in him was complete.

Suffering from bouts of seasickness and torn by gnawing guilt, Tanis hunched miserably upon the deck, staring out to sea. Goldmoon's healing powers had helped him recover somewhat, though there was apparently little even clerics could do for the turmoil in his stomach. But the turmoil in his soul was beyond her help.

He sat upon the deck, staring out to sea, fearing always to see the sails of a ship on the horizon. The others, perhaps because they were better rested, were little affected by the erratic motion of the ship as it swooped through the choppy water, except that all were wet to the skin from an occasional high wave breaking over the side.

Even Raistlin—Caramon was astonished to see—appeared quite comfortable. The mage sat apart from the others, crouched beneath a sail one of the sailors had rigged to help keep the passengers as dry as possible. The mage was not sick. He did not even cough much. He just seemed lost in thought, his golden eyes glittering brighter than the morning sun that flickered in and out of view behind the racing storm clouds.

Maquesta shrugged when Tanis mentioned his fears of pursuit. The *Perechon* was faster than the Highlords' massive ships. They'd been able to sneak out of the harbor safely—the only other ships aware of their going were pirate ships like themselves In that brotherhood, no one asked questions.

The seas grew calmer, flattening out beneath the steady breeze. All day, the storm clouds lowered threateningly, only to be finally blown to shreds by the freshening wind. The night was clear and starlit. Maquesta was able to add more sail. The ship flew over the water. By morning, the companions awakened to one of the most dreadful sights in all of Krynn.

They were on the outer edge of the Blood Sea of Istar.

The sun was a huge, golden ball balanced upon the eastern horizon when the *Perechon* first sailed into the water that was red as the robes the mage wore, red as the blood that flecked his lips when he coughed.

"It is well-named," Tanis said to Riverwind as they stood on deck, staring out into the red, murky water. They could not see far ahead. A perpetual storm hung from the sky, shrouding the water in a curtain of leaden gray.

"I did not believe it," Riverwind said solemnly, shaking his head. "I heard William tell of it and I listened as I listened to his tales of sea dragons that swallow ships and women with the tails of fish instead of legs. But this—" The barbarian Plainsman shook his head, eyeing the blood-colored water uneasily.

"Do you suppose it's true that this is the blood of all those who died in Istar when the fiery mountain struck the Kingpriest's temple?" Goldmoon asked softly, coming to stand beside her husband.

"What nonsense!" Maquesta snorted. Walking across the deck to join them, her eyes flicked constantly around to make certain that she was getting the most out of her ship and her crew.

"You've been listening to Pig-faced William again!" She laughed. "He loves to frighten lubbers. The water gets its color from soil washed up from the bottom. Remember, this is not sand we're sailing over, like the bottom of the ocean. This used to be dry land—the capital city of Istar and the rich countryside around it. When the fiery mountain fell, it split the land apart. The waters from the ocean rushed in, creating a new sea. Now the wealth of Istar lies far beneath the waves."

Maquesta stared over the railing with dreamy eyes, as if she could penetrate the choppy water and see the rumored wealth of the glittering lost city below. She sighed longingly. Goldmoon glanced at the swarthy ship's captain in disgust, her own eyes filled with sadness and horror at the thought of the terrible destruction and loss of life.

"What keeps the soil stirred up?" Riverwind asked, frowning down at the blood-red water. "Even with the motion of the waves and the tides, the heavy soil should settle more than it appears to have."

"Truly spoken, barbarian." Maquesta looked at the tall, handsome Plainsman with admiration. "But then, your people are farmers, or so I've heard, and know a lot about soil. If you put your hand into the water, you can feel the grit of the dirt. Supposedly there is a maelstrom in the center of the Blood Sea that whirls with such force it drags the soil up from the bottom. But whether that is true or another one of Pig-face's stories, I cannot say. I have never seen it, nor have any I've sailed with and I've sailed these waters since I was a child, learning my craft from my father. No one I ever knew was foolish enough to sail into the storm that hangs over the center of the sea."

"How do we get to Mithras, then?" Tanis growled. "It lies on the other side of the Blood Sea, if your charts are correct."

"We can reach Mithras by sailing south, if we are pursued. If not, we can circle the western edge of the Sea and sail up the coast north to Nordmaar. Don't worry, Half-Elven." Maq waved her hand grandly. "At least you can say you've seen the Blood Sea. One of the wonders of Krynn."

Turning to walk aft, Maquesta was hailed from the crow's nest.

"Deck ho! Sail to the west!" the lookout called.

Instantly Maquesta and Koraf both pulled out spyglasses and trained them upon the western horizon. The companions exchanged worried glances and drew together. Even Raistlin left his place beneath the shielding sail and walked across the deck, peering westward with his golden eyes.

"A ship?" Maquesta muttered to Koraf.

"No," the minotaur grunted in his corrupt form of Common. "A cloud, mebbe. But it go fast, very fast. Faster any cloud I ever see."

Now they all could make out the specks of darkness on the horizon, specks that grew larger even as they watched.

Then Tanis felt a wrenching pain inside of him, as if he'd been pierced by a sword. The pain was so swift and so real he gasped, clutching hold of Caramon to keep from falling. The rest stared at him in concern, Caramon wrapping his big arm around his friend to support him.

Tanis knew what flew towards them.

And he knew who led them.

3
Gathering darkness.

"A flight of dragons," said Raistlin, coming to stand beside his brother. "Five, I believe."

"Dragons!" Maquesta breathed. For a moment, she clutched the rail with trembling hands, then she whirled around. "Set all sail!" she commanded.

The crew stared westward, their eyes and minds locked onto the approaching terror. Maquesta raised her voice and shouted her order again, her only thoughts on her beloved ship. The strength and calmness in her voice penetrated the first faint feelings of dragonfear creeping over the crew. Instinctively a few sprang to carry out their orders, then more followed. Koraf with his whip helped as well, striking briskly at any man who didn't move quickly enough to suit him. Within moments, the great sails billowed out. Lines creaked ominously, the rigging sang a whining tune.

"Keep her near the edge of the storm!" Maq yelled to Berem. The man nodded slowly, but it was hard to tell from the vacant expression on his face if he heard or not.

Apparently he did, for the *Perechon* hovered close to the perpetual storm that shrouded the Blood Sea, skimming along on the surface of the waves, propelled by the storm's fog-gray wind.

It was reckless sailing, and Maq knew it. Let a spar be blown away, a sail split, a line break, and they would be helpless. But she had to take the risk.

"Useless," Raistlin remarked coolly. "You cannot outsail dragons. Look, see how fast they gain on us. You were followed, Half-Elf." He turned to Tanis. "You were followed when you left the camp . . . either that"—the mage's voice hissed—"or you led them to us!"

"No! I swear—" Tanis stopped.

The drunken draconian! . . . Tanis shut his eyes, cursing himself. Of course Kit would have had him watched! She didn't trust him any more than she trusted the other men who shared her bed. What a damn egotistical fool he was! Believing he was something special to her, believing she loved him! She loved no one. She was incapable of loving—

"I was followed!" Tanis said through clenched teeth. "You must believe me. I—I may have been a fool. I didn't think they'd follow me in that storm. But I didn't betray you! I swear!"

"We believe you, Tanis," Goldmoon said, coming to stand beside him, glancing at Raistlin angrily out of the corner of her eyes.

Raistlin said nothing, but his lip curled in a sneer. Tanis avoided his gaze, turning instead to watch the dragons. They could see the creatures clearly now. They could see the enormous wingspans, the long tails snaking out behind, the cruel taloned feet hanging beneath the huge blue bodies.

"One has a rider," Maquesta reported grimly, the spyglass to her eye. "A rider with a horned mask."

"A Dragon Highlord," Caramon stated unnecessarily, all of

them knowing well enough what that description meant. The big man turned a somber gaze to Tanis. "You better tell us what's going on, Tanis. If this Highlord thought you were a soldier under his own command, why has he taken the trouble to have you followed and come out after you?"

Tanis started to speak, but his faltering words were submerged in an agonized, inarticulate roar; a roar of mingled fear and terror and rage that was so beastlike, it wrenched everyone's thoughts from the dragons. It came from near the ship's helm. Hands on their weapons, the companions turned. The crew members halted their frantic labors, Koraf came to a dead stop, his bestial face twisted in amazement as the roaring sound grew louder and more fearful.

Only Maq kept her senses. "Berem," she called, starting to run across the deck, her fear giving her sudden horrifying insight into his mind. She leaped across the deck, but it was too late.

A look of insane terror on his face, Berem fell silent, staring at the approaching dragons. Then he roared again, a garbled howl of fear that chilled even the minotaur's blood. Above him, the sails were tight in the wind, the rigging stretched taut. The ship, under all the sail it could bear, seemed to leap over the waves, leaving a trail of white foam behind. But still the dragons gained.

Maq had nearly reached him when, shaking his head like a wounded animal, Berem spun the wheel.

"No! Berem!" Maquesta shrieked.

Berem's sudden move brought the small ship around so fast he nearly sent it under. The mizzenmast snapped with the strain as the ship heeled. Rigging, shrouds, sails, and men plummeted to the deck or fell into the Blood Sea.

Grabbing hold of Maq, Koraf dragged her clear of the falling mast. Caramon caught his brother in his arms and hurled him to the deck, covering Raistlin's frail body with his own as the tangle of rope and splintered wood crashed over them. Sailors tumbled to the deck or slammed up against the bulkheads. From down below, they could hear the sound of cargo breaking free. The companions clung to the ropes or whatever they could grab, hanging on desperately as it seemed Berem would run the ship under. Sails flapped horribly, like dead bird's wings, the rigging went slack, the ship floundered helplessly.

But the skilled helmsman, though seemingly mad with panic,

was a sailor still. Instinctively he held the wheel in a firm grip when it would have spun free. Slowly, he nursed the ship back into the wind with the care of a mother hovering over a deathly sick child. Slowly the *Perechon* righted herself. Sails that had been limp and lifeless caught the wind and filled. The *Perechon* came about and headed on her new course.

It was only then that everyone on board realized that sinking into the sea might have been a quicker and easier death as a gray shroud of wind-swept mist engulfed the ship.

"He's mad! He's steering us into the storm over the Blood Sea!" Maquesta said in a cracked, nearly inaudible voice as she pulled herself to her feet. Koraf started toward Berem, his face twisted in a snarl, a belaying pin in his hand.

"No! Kof!" Maquesta gasped, grabbing hold of him. "Maybe Berem's right! This could be our only chance! The dragons won't dare follow us into the storm. Berem got us into this, he's the only helmsman we've got with a chance of getting us out! If we can just keep on the outskirts—"

A jagged flash of lightning tore through the gray curtain. The mists parted, revealing an gruesome sight. Black clouds swirled in the roaring wind, green lightning cracked, charging the air with the acrid smell of sulphur. The red water heaved and tossed. White caps bubbled on the surface, like froth on the mouth of a dying man. No one could move for an instant. They could only stare, feeling petty and small against the awesome forces of nature. Then the wind hit them. The ship pitched and tossed, dragged over by the trailing, broken mast. Sudden rain slashed down, hail clattered on the wooden deck, the gray curtain closed around them once more.

Under Maquesta's orders, men scrambled aloft to reef the remaining sails. Another party worked desperately to clear the broken mast that was swinging around wildly. The sailors attacked it with axes, cutting away the ropes, letting it fall into the blood-red water. Free of the mast's dragging weight, the ship slowly righted itself. Though still tossed by the wind, under shortened sail, the *Perechon* seemed capable of riding out the storm, even with one mast gone.

The immediate peril had nearly driven all thoughts of dragons from their minds. Now that it seemed they might live a few moments longer, the companions turned to stare through the driving, leaden gray rain.

"Do you think we've lost them?" Caramon asked. The big

warrior was bleeding from a savage cut on his head. His eyes showed the pain. But his concern was all for his brother. Raistlin staggered beside him, uninjured, but coughing so he could barely stand.

Tanis shook his head grimly. Glancing around quickly to see if anyone was hurt, he motioned the group to keep together. One by one, they stumbled through the rain, clinging to the ropes until they were gathered around the half-elf. All of them stared back out over the tossing seas.

At first they saw nothing; it was hard to see the bow of the ship through the rain and wind-tossed seas. Some of the sailors even raised a ragged cheer, thinking they had lost them.

But Tanis, his eyes looking to the west, knew that nothing short of death itself would stop the Highlord's pursuit. Sure enough, the sailor's cheers changed to cries of shock when the head of a blue dragon suddenly cleaved the gray clouds, its fiery eyes blazing red with hatred, its fanged mouth gaping open.

The dragon flew closer still, its great wings holding steady even though buffeted by gusts of wind and rain and hail. A Dragon Highlord sat upon the blue dragon's back. The Highlord held no weapon, Tanis saw bitterly. She needed no weapon. She would take Berem, then her dragon would destroy the rest of them. Tanis bowed his head, sick with the knowledge of what would come, sick with the knowledge that *he* was responsible.

Then he looked up. There was a chance, he thought frantically. Maybe she won't recognize Berem . . . and she wouldn't dare destroy them all for fear of harming him. Turning to look at the helmsman, Tanis's wild hope died at birth. It seemed the gods were conspiring against them.

The wind had blown Berem's shirt open. Even through the gray curtain of rain, Tanis could see the green jewel embedded in the man's chest glow more brilliantly than the green lightning, a terrible beacon shining through the storm. Berem did not notice. He did not even see the dragon. His eyes stared with fixed intensity into the storm as he steered the ship farther and farther into the Blood Sea of Istar.

Only two people saw that glittering jewel. Everyone else was held in thrall by the dragonfear, unable to look away from the huge blue creature soaring above them. Tanis saw the gemstone—as he had seen it before, months ago. And the

Dragon Highlord saw it. The eyes behind the metal mask were drawn to the glowing jewel, then the Highlord's eyes met Tanis's eyes as the half-elf stood upon the storm-tossed deck.

A sudden gust of wind caught the blue dragon. It veered slightly, but the Highlord's gaze never wavered. Tanis saw the horrifying future in those brown eyes. The dragon would swoop down upon them and snatch Berem up in its claws. The Highlord would exult in her victory for a long agonizing moment, then she would order the dragon to destroy them all. . . .

Tanis saw this in her eyes as clearly as he had seen the passion in them only days before when he held her in his arms.

Never taking her eyes from him, the Dragon Highlord raised a gloved hand. It might have been a signal to the dragon to dive down upon them; it might have been a farewell to Tanis. He never knew, because at that moment a shattered voice shouted above the roar of the storm with unbelievable power.

"Kitiara!" Raistlin cried.

Shoving Caramon aside, the magé ran toward the dragon. Slipping on the wet deck, his red robes whipped about him in the wind that was blowing stronger every moment. A sudden gust tore the hood from his head. Rain glistened on his metallic-colored skin, his hourglass eyes gleamed goldén through the gathering darkness of the storm.

The Dragon Highlord grabbed her mount by the spikey mane along his blue neck, pulling the dragon up so sharply that Skie roared in protest. She stiffened in shock, her brown eyes grew wide behind the dragonhelm as she stared down at the frail half-brother she had raised from a baby. Her gaze shifted slightly as Caramon came to stand beside his twin.

"Kitiara?" Caramon whispered in a strangled voice, his face pale with horror as he watched the dragon hovering above them, riding the winds of the storm.

The Highlord turned the masked head once more to look at Tanis, then her eyes went to Berem. Tanis caught his breath. He saw the turmoil in her soul reflected in those eyes.

To get Berem, she would have to kill the little brother who had learned all of what he knew about swordsmanship from her. She would have to kill his frail twin. She would have to kill a man she had—once—loved. Then Tanis saw her eyes grow cold, and he shook his head in despair. It didn't matter. She would kill her brothers, she would kill him. Tanis remembered her words, "Capture Berem and we will have all Krynn at our teet. The Dark Queen will reward us beyond anything we ever dreamed!"

Kitiara pointed at Berem and loosed her hold upon the dragon. With a cruel shriek, Skie prepared to dive. But Kitiara's moment of hesitation proved disastrous. Steadfastly ignoring her, Berem had steered the ship deeper and deeper into the heart of the storm. The wind howled, snapping the rigging. Waves crashed over the bows. The rain slashed down like knives and hailstones began to pile up on the deck, coating it with ice.

Suddenly the dragon was in trouble. A gust of wind hit him, then another. Skie's wings beat frantically as gust after gust pummeled him. The hail drummed upon his head and threatened to tear through the leathery wings. Only the supreme will of his master kept Skie from fleeing this perilous storm and flying to the safety of calmer skies.

Tanis saw Kitiara gesture furiously toward Berem. He saw Skie make a valiant effort to fly closer to the helmsman.

Then a gust of wind hit the ship. A wave broke over them. Water cascaded around them, foaming white, knocking men off their feet and sending them skidding across the deck. The ship listed. Everyone grabbed what they could—ropes, netting, anything—to keep from being washed overboard.

Berem fought the wheel, which was like a living thing, leaping in his hands. Sails split in two, men disappeared into the Blood Sea with terrifying screams. Then, slowly, the ship righted itself again, the wood creaking with the strain. Tanis looked up quickly.

The dragon—and Kitiara—were gone.

Freed from the dragonfear, Maquesta sprang into action, determined once more to save her dying ship. Shouting orders, she ran forward and stumbled into Tika.

"Get below, you lubbers!" Maquesta shouted furiously to Tanis above the storm wind. "Take your friends and get below! You're in our way! Use my cabin."

Numbly, Tanis nodded. Acting by instinct, feeling as if he were in a senseless dream filled with howling darkness, he led everyone below.

The haunted look in Caramon's eyes pierced his heart as the big man staggered past him, carrying his brother. Raistlin's golden eyes swept over him like flame, burning his soul. Then they were past him, stumbling with the others into the small cabin that shivered and rocked, tossing them about like rag dolls.

Tanis waited until everyone was safely inside the tiny cabin, then he slumped against the wooden door, unable to turn around, unable to face them. He had seen the haunted look in Caramon's eyes as the big man staggered past, he had seen the exultant gleam in Raistlin's eyes. He heard Goldmoon weeping quietly and he wished he might die on this spot before he had to face her.

But that was not to be. Slowly he turned around. Riverwind stood next to Goldmoon, his face dark and brooding as he braced himself between ceiling and deck. Tika bit her lip, tears sliding down her cheeks. Tanis stayed by the door, his back against it, staring at his friends mutely. For long moments, no one said a word. All that could be heard was the storm, the waves crashing onto the deck. Water trickled down on them. They were wet and cold and shaking with fear and sorrow and shock.

"I—I'm sorry," Tanis began, licking his salt-coated lips. His throat hurt, he could barely speak. "I—I wanted to tell you—"

"So *that's* where you were these four days," Caramon said in a soft, low voice. "With our *sister*. Our sister, the Dragon Highlord!"

Tanis hung his head. The ship listed beneath his feet, sending him staggering into Maquesta's desk which was bolted to the floor. He caught himself and slowly pushed himself back to face them. The half-elf had endured much pain in his life—pain of prejudice, pain of loss, pain of knives, arrows, swords. But he did not think he could endure this pain. The look of betrayal in their eyes ran straight through his soul.

"Please, you must believe me . . ." What a stupid thing to say! he thought savagely. Why *should* they believe me! I've done nothing but lie to them ever since I returned. "All right," he began again, "I know you don't have any reason to believe me, but at least listen to me! I was walking through Flotsam when an elf attacked me. Seeing me in this get-up"—Tanis gestured at his dragonarmor—"he thought I was a dragon officer. Kitiara saved my life, then she recognized me. She thought I had joined the dragonarmy! What could I say? She"—Tanis swallowed and wiped his hand across his face—"she took me back to the inn and—and—" He choked, unable to continue.

"And you spent four days and nights in the loving embrace

of a Dragon Highlord!" Caramon said, his voice rising in fury. Lurching to his feet, he stabbed an accusing finger at Tanis. "Then after four days, you needed a little rest! So you remembered us and you came calling to make certain we were still waiting for you! And we were! Just like the bunch of trusting lame-brains—"

"All right, so I was with Kitiara!" Tanis shouted, suddenly angry. "Yes, I loved her! I don't expect you to understand—any of you! But I never betrayed you! I swear by the gods! When she left for Solamnia, it was the first chance I had to escape and I took it. A draconian followed me, apparently under Kit's orders. I may be a fool. But I'm not a traitor!"

"Pah!" Raistlin spit on the floor.

"Listen, mage!" Tanis snarled. "If I had betrayed you, why was she so shocked to see you two—her brothers! If I had betrayed you, why didn't I just send a few draconians to the inn to pick you up? I could have, any time. I could have sent them to pick up Berem, too. *He's* the one she wants. *He's* the one the draconians are searching for in Flotsam! I knew he was on this ship. Kitiara offered me the rulership of Krynn if I'd tell her. That's how important he is. All I would've had to do was lead Kit to him and the Queen of Darkness herself would have rewarded me!"

"Don't tell us you didn't consider it!" Raistlin hissed.

Tanis opened his mouth, then fell silent. He knew his guilt was as plain on his face as the beard no true elf could grow. He choked, then put his hand over his eyes to block out their faces. "I—I loved her," he said brokenly. "All these years. I refused to see what she was. And even when I knew—I couldn't help myself. You love"—his eyes went to Riverwind—"and you"— turning to Caramon. The boat pitched again. Tanis gripped the side of the desk as he felt the deck cant away beneath his feet. "What would you have done? For five years, she's been in my dreams!" He stopped. They were quiet. Caramon's face was unusually thoughtful. Riverwind's eyes were on Goldmoon.

"When she was gone," Tanis continued, his voice soft and filled with pain. "I lay in her bed and I *hated* myself. You may hate me now, but you cannot hate me as much as I loathe and despise what I have become! I thought of Laurana and—"

Tanis fell silent, raising his head. Even as he talked, he had become aware of the motion of the ship changing. The rest glanced around, too. It did not take an experienced seaman to notice that they were no longer pitching around wildly. Now they were running in a smooth forward motion, a motion somehow more ominous because it was so unnatural. Before anyone could wonder what it meant, a crashing knock nearly split the cabin door.

"Maquesta she say get up here!" shouted Koraf hoarsely.

Tanis cast one swift glance around at his friends. Riverwind's face was dark; his eyes met Tanis's and held them, but there was no light in them. The Plainsman had long distrusted all who were not human. Only after weeks of danger faced together had he come to love and trust Tanis as a brother. Had all that had been shattered? Tanis looked at him steadily. Riverwind lowered his gaze and, without a word, started to walk past Tanis, then he stopped.

"You are right, my friend," he said, glancing at Goldmoon who was rising to her feet. "I have loved." Without another word, he turned abruptly and went up on deck.

Goldmoon gazed mutely as Tanis as she followed her husband, and he saw compassion and understanding in that silent look. He wished he understood, that he could be so forgiving.

Caramon hesitated, then walked past him without speaking or looking at him. Raistlin followed silently, his head turning, keeping his golden eyes on Tanis every step of the way. Was there a hint of glee in those golden eyes? Long mistrusted by the others, was Raistlin happy to have company in ignominy at last? The half-elf had no idea what the mage might be thinking. Then Tika went past him, giving him a gentle pat on the arm. She knew what it was to love. . . .

Tanis stood a moment alone in the cabin, lost in his own darkness. Then, with a sigh, he followed his friends.

As soon as he set foot on the deck, Tanis realized what had happened. The others were staring over the side, their faces pale and strained. Maquesta paced the foredeck, shaking her head and swearing fluently in her own language.

Hearing Tanis approach, she looked up, hatred in her black flashing eyes.

"You have destroyed us," she said venomously. "You and the god-cursed helmsman!"

Maquesta's words seemed redundant, a repetition of words resounding in his own mind. Tanis began to wonder if she had even spoken, or if it was himself he was hearing.

"We are caught in the maelstrom."

4

"My brother . . ."

T he *Perechon* hurtled for-
ward, skimming along on top of the water as lightly as a bird.
But it was a bird with its wings clipped, riding the swirling tide
of a watery cyclone into a blood-red darkness.

The terrible force pulled the sea waters smooth, until they
looked like painted glass. A hollow, eternal roar swelled from
the black depths. Even the storm clouds circled endlessly above
it, as if all nature were caught in the maelstrom, hurtling to its
own destruction.

Tanis gripped the rail with hands that ached from the tension. Staring into the dark heart of the whirlpool, he felt no fear, no terror—only a strange numb sensation. It didn't matter anymore. Death would be swift and welcome.

Everyone on board the doomed ship stood silently, their eyes wide with the horror of what they saw. They were still some distance from the center; the whirlpool was miles and miles in diameter. Smoothly and swiftly, the water flowed. Above them and around them the winds still howled, the rain still beat upon their faces. But it didn't matter. They didn't notice it anymore. All they saw was that they were being carried relentlessly into the center of the darkness.

This fearsome sight was enough to wake Berem from his lethargy. After the first shock, Maquesta began shouting frantic orders. Dazedly, the men carried them out, but their efforts were useless. Sails rigged against the whirling wind tore apart; ropes snapped, flinging men screaming into the water. Try as he might, Berem could not turn the ship or break it free of the water's fearsome grip. Koraf added his strength to the handling of the wheel, but they might as well have been trying to stop the world from revolving.

Then Berem quit. His shoulders sagged. He stood staring out into the swirling depths, ignoring Maquesta, ignoring Koraf. His face was calm, Tanis saw; the same calm Tanis remembered seeing on Berem's face at Pax Tharkas when he took Eben's hand and ran with him into that deadly wall of cascading boulders. The green jewel in his chest glowed with an eerie light, reflecting the blood red of the water.

Tanis felt a strong hand clutch his shoulder, shaking him out of his rapt horror.

"Tanis! Where's Raistlin?"

Tanis turned. For a moment he stared at Caramon without recognition, then he shrugged.

"What does it matter?" he muttered bitterly. "Let him die where he chooses—"

"Tanis!" Caramon took him by the shoulders and shook him. "Tanis! The dragon orb! His magic! Maybe it can help—"

Tanis came awake. "By all the gods! You're right, Caramon!"

The half-elf looked around swiftly, but he saw no sign of the mage. A cold chill crept over him. Raistlin was capable either of helping them or of helping himself! Dimly Tanis remembered the elven princess, Alhana, saying the dragon orbs had been imbued by their magical creators with a strong sense of self-preservation.

"Below!" Tanis yelled. Leaping for the hatch, he heard Caramon pounding along behind.

"What is it?" called Riverwind from the rail.

Tanis shouted over his shoulder. "Raistlin. The dragon orb. Don't come. Let Caramon and I handle this. You stay here, with them."

"Caramon—" Tika yelled, starting to run after until Riverwind caught her and held her. Giving the warrior an anguished look, she fell silent, slumping back against the rail.

Caramon did not notice. He plunged ahead of Tanis, his huge body moving remarkably fast. Tumbling down the stairway below decks after him, Tanis saw the door to Maquesta's cabin open, swinging on its hinges with the motion of the ship. The half-elf dashed in and came to a sudden stop, just inside the door, as if he had run headlong into a wall.

Raistlin stood in the center of the small cabin. He had lit a candle in a lamp clamped to the bulkheads. The flame made the mage's face glisten like a metal mask, his eyes flared with golden fire. In his hands, Raistlin held the dragon orb, their prize from Silvanesti. It had grown, Tanis saw. It was now the size of child's ball. A myriad colors swirled within it. Tanis grew dizzy watching and wrenched his gaze away.

In front of Raistlin stood Caramon, the big warrior's face as white as Tanis had seen his corpse in the Silvanesti dream when the warrior lay dead at his feet.

Raistlin coughed, clutching at his chest with one hand. Tanis started forward, but the mage looked up quickly.

"Don't come near me, Tanis!" Raistlin gasped through bloodstained lips.

"What are you doing?"

"I am fleeing certain death, Half-Elf!" The mage laughed unpleasantly, the strange laughter Tanis had heard only twice before. "What do you think I am doing?"

"How?" Tanis asked, feeling a strange fear creep over him as he looked into the mage's golden eyes and saw them reflect the swirling light of the orb.

"Using my magic. And the magic of the dragon orb. It is quite simple, though probably beyond your weak mind. I now have the power to harness the energy of my corporeal body and the energy of my spirit into one. I will become pure energy—light, if you want to think of it that way. And, becoming light, I can travel through the heavens like the rays of the sun, returning to this physical world whenever and wherever I choose!"

Tanis shook his head. Raistlin was right—the thought was beyond him. He could not grasp it, but hope sprang into his heart.

"Can the orb do this for all of us?" he demanded.

"Possibly," Raistlin answered, coughing, "but I am not certain. I will not chance it. I know *I* can escape. The others are not my concern. You led them into this blood-red death, Half-Elf. You get them out!"

Anger surged through Tanis, replacing his fear. "At least, your brother—" he began hotly.

"No one," Raistlin said, his eyes narrowing. "Stand back."

Insane, desperate rage twisted Tanis's mind. Somehow he'd make Raistlin listen to reason! Somehow they would all use this strange magic to escape! Tanis knew enough about magic to realize that Raistlin dared not cast a spell now. He would need all his strength to control the dragon orb. Tanis started forward, then saw silver flash in the mage's hand. From nowhere—seemingly—had come a small silver dagger, long concealed on the mage's wrist by a cunningly-designed leather thong. Tanis stopped, his eyes meeting Raistlin's.

"All right," Tanis said, breathing heavily. "You'd kill me without a second thought. But you won't harm your brother. Caramon, stop him!"

Caramon took a step toward his twin. Raistlin raised the silver dagger warningly.

"Don't do it, my brother," he said softly. "Come no closer."

Caramon hesitated.

"Go ahead, Caramon!" Tanis said firmly. "He won't hurt you."

"Tell him, Caramon," Raistlin whispered. The mage's eyes never left his brother's. Their hourglass pupils dilated, the golden light flickered dangerously. "Tell Tanis what I am capable of doing. You remember. So do I. It is in our thoughts every time we look at one another, isn't it, my dear brother?"

"What's he talking about?" Tanis demanded, only half listening. If he could distract Raistlin . . . jump him . . .

Caramon blanched. "The Towers of High Sorcery . . ." He faltered. "But we are forbidden to speak of it! Par-Salian said—"

'That doesn't matter now," Raistlin interrupted in his shattered voice. "There is nothing Par-Salian can do to me. Once I have what has been promised me, not even the great Par-Salian will have the power to face me! But that's none of your concern. This is."

Raistlin drew a deep breath, then began to speak, his strange eyes still on his twin. Only half-listening, Tanis crept closer, his heart pounding in his throat. One swift movement and the frail mage would crumble. . . . Then Tanis found himself caught and held by Raistlin's voice, compelled to stop for a moment and listen, almost as if Raistlin *was* weaving a spell around him.

"The last test in the Tower of High Sorcery, Tanis, was against myself. And I failed. I killed him, Tanis. I killed my brother"—Raistlin's voice was calm—"or at least I thought it was Caramon." The mage shrugged. "As it turned out, it was an illusion created to teach me to learn the depths of my hatred and jealousy. Thus they thought to purge my soul of darkness. What I truly learned was that I lacked self-control. Still, since it was not part of the true Test, my failure did not count against me—except with one person."

"I watched him kill me!" Caramon cried wretchedly. "They made me watch so that I would understand him!" The big man's head dropped in his hands, his body convulsed with a shudder. "I do understand!" he sobbed. "I understood then! I'm sorry! Just don't go without me, Raist! You're so weak! You need me—"

"No longer, Caramon," Raistlin whispered with a soft sigh. "I need you no longer!"

Tanis stared at them both, sick with horror. He couldn't believe this! Not even of Raistlin! "Caramon, go ahead!" he commanded hoarsely.

"Don't make him come near me, Tanis," Raistlin said, his voice gentle, as if he read the half-elf's thoughts. "I assure you—I am capable of this. What I have sought all my life is within my grasp. I will let nothing stop me. Look at Caramon's face, Tanis. He knows! I killed him once. I can do it again. Farewell, my brother."

The mage put both hands upon the dragon orb and held it up to the light of the flaming candle. The colors swirled madly in the orb, flaring brilliantly. A powerful magical aura surrounded the mage.

Fighting his fear, Tanis tensed his body to make a last desperate attempt to stop Raistlin. But he could not move. He heard Raistlin chanting strange words. The glaring, whirling light grew so bright, it pierced his head. He covered his eyes with his hands, but the light burned right through his flesh, searing his brain. The pain was intolerable. He stumbled back against the door frame, hearing Caramon cry out in agony beside him. He heard the big man's body fall to the floor with a thud.

Then all was still, the cabin plunged into darkness. Trembling, Tanis opened his eyes. For a moment he could see nothing but the afterimage of a giant red globe imprinted on his brain. Then his eyes became accustomed to the chill dark. The candle guttered, hot wax dripping onto the wooden floor of the cabin to form a white puddle near where Caramon lay, cold and unmoving. The warrior's eyes were wide open, staring blankly into nothingness.

Raistlin was gone.

Tika Waylan stood on the deck of the *Perechon* staring into the blood-red sea and trying very hard to keep from crying. You must be brave, she told herself over and over. You've learned to fight bravely in battle. Caramon said so. Now you must be brave about this. We'll be together, at least, at the end. He mustn't see me cry.

But the last four days had been unnerving for all of them. Fearful of discovery by the draconians swarming over Flotsam, the companions had remained hidden in the filthy inn. Tanis's strange disappearance had been terrifying. They were helpless, they dared do nothing, not even inquire about him. So for long days they had been forced to stay in their rooms and Tika had been forced to be around Caramon. The tension of their strong attraction to each other—an attraction they were not able to express—was torture. She wanted to put her arms around Caramon, to feel his arms around her, his strong, muscular body pressed against hers.

Caramon wanted the same thing, she was certain. He looked at her, sometimes, with so much tenderness in his eyes that she longed to nestle close to him and share the love that she knew was in the big man's heart.

It could never be, not as long as Raistlin hovered near his twin brother, clinging to Caramon like a frail shadow. Over and over she repeated Caramon's words, spoken to her before they reached Flotsam.

"My commitment is to my brother. They told me, in the Tower of High Sorcery, that his strength would help save the world. I am his strength—his physical strength. He needs me. My first duty is to him and, until that changes, I can't make any other commitments. You deserve someone who puts *you* first, Tika. And so I'll leave you free to find someone like that."

But I don't *want* anyone else, Tika thought sadly. And then the tears did start to fall. Turning quickly, she tried to hide them from Goldmoon and Riverwind. They would misunderstand, think she was crying from fear. No, fear of dying was something she had conquered long ago. Her biggest fear was fear of dying *alone*.

What are they doing? she wondered frantically, wiping her eyes with the back of her hand. The ship was being carried closer and closer into that dreadful dark eye. Where was Caramon? I'll go find them, she decided. Tanis or no Tanis.

Then she saw Tanis come slowly up out of the hatchway, half-dragging, half-supporting Caramon. One look at the big warrior's pale face and Tika's heart stopped beating.

She tried to call out, but she couldn't speak. At her inarticulate scream, however, Goldmoon and Riverwind both turned around from where they had been watching the awesome maelstrom. Seeing Tanis stagger beneath his burden, Riverwind ran forward to help. Caramon walked like a man in drunken stupor, his eyes glazed and sightless. Riverwind caught hold of Caramon just as Tanis's legs gave way completely.

"I'm all right," Tanis said softly in answer to Riverwind's look of concern. "Goldmoon, Caramon needs your help."

"What is it, Tanis?" Tika's fear gave her a voice. "What's the matter? Where's Raistlin? Is he—" She stopped. The half-elf's eyes were dark with the memory of what he had seen and heard below.

"Raistlin's gone," Tanis said briefly.

"Gone? Where?" Tika asked, staring wildly around as if expecting to see his body in the swirling blood-colored water.

"He lied to us," Tanis answered, helping Riverwind ease Caramon down onto a mass of coiled rope. The big warrior said nothing. He didn't seem to see them, or anything for that matter; he just stared sightlessly out over the blood-red sea. "Remember how he kept insisting we had to go to Palanthas, to *learn how* to use the dragon orb? He *knows how* to use the orb already. And now he's gone—to Palanthas, perhaps. I don't suppose it matters." Looking at Caramon, he shook his head in sorrow, then turned away abruptly and walked to the rail.

Goldmoon laid her gentle hands upon the big man, murmuring his name so softly the others could not hear it above the rush of the wind. At her touch, however, Caramon shivered, then began to shake violently. Tika knelt beside him, holding his hand in hers. Still staring straight ahead, Caramon began to cry silently, tears spilling down his cheeks from wide open, staring eyes. Goldmoon's eyes glimmered with her own tears, but she stroked his forehead and kept calling to him as a mother calls a lost child.

Riverwind, his face stern and dark with anger, joined Tanis. "What happened?" the Plainsman asked grimly.

"Raistlin said he— I can't talk about it. Not now!" Tanis shook his head, shuddering. Leaning over the rail, he stared into the murky water below. Swearing softly in elven—a language the half-elf rarely used—he clutched his head with his hands.

Saddened by his friend's anguish, Riverwind laid his hand comfortingly on the half-elf's slumped shoulders.

"So at the end it comes to this," the Plainsman said. "As we foresaw in the dream, the mage has gone, leaving his brother to die."

"And as we saw in the dream, I have failed you," Tanis mumbled, his voice low and trembling. "What have I done? This is my fault! I have brought this horror upon us!"

"My friend," Riverwind said, moved by the sight of Tanis's suffering. "It is not ours to question the ways of the gods—"

"Damn the gods!" Tanis cried viciously. Lifting his head to stare at his friend, he struck his clenched fist on the ship's rail. "It was *me! My choosing!* How often during those nights when she and I were together and I held her in my arms, how often did I tell myself it would be so easy to stay there, with her, forever! I can't condemn Raistlin! We're very much alike, he and I. Both destroyed by an all-consuming passion!"

"You *haven't* been destroyed, Tanis," Riverwind said. Gripping the half-elf's shoulders in his strong hands, the stern-faced Plainsman forced Tanis to face him. "You did not fall victim to your passion, as did the mage. If you had, you would have stayed with Kitiara. You left her, Tanis—"

"I left her," Tanis said bitterly. "I sneaked out like a thief! I should have confronted her. I should have told her the truth about myself! She would have killed me then, but you would have been safe. You and the others could have escaped. How much easier my death would have been— But I didn't have the courage. Now I've brought us to this," the half-elf said, wrenching himself free of Riverwind's grip. "I have failed—not only myself, but all of you."

He glanced around the deck. Berem still stood at the helm, gripping the useless wheel in his hands, that strange look of resignation on his face. Maquesta still fought to save her ship, shrieking commands above the wind's howl and the deep-throated roaring that issued from the depths of the maelstrom. But her crew, stunned by terror, no longer obeyed. Some wept. Some cursed. Most made no sound, but stared in horrid fascination at the gigantic swirl that was pulling them inexorably into the vast darkness of the deep. Tanis felt Riverwind's hand once again touch his shoulder. Almost angrily, he tried to withdraw, but the Plainsman was firm.

"Tanis, my brother, you made your choice to walk this road in the Inn of the Last Home in Solace, when you came to Goldmoon's aid. In my pride, I would have refused your help, and both she and I would have died. Because you could not turn from us in our need, we brought the knowledge of the ancient gods into the world. We brought healing. We brought hope. Remember what the Forestmaster told us? We do not grieve for those who fulfill their purpose in life. We *have* fulfilled our purpose, my friend. Who knows how many lives we have touched? Who knows but that this hope will lead to a great victory? For us, it seems, the battle has ended. So be it. We lay down our swords, only that others may pick them up and fight on."

"Your words are pretty, Plainsman," Tanis snapped, "but tell me truthfully. Can you look on death and not feel bitterness? You have everything to live for—Goldmoon, the children not yet born to you—"

A swift spasm of pain crossed Riverwind's face. He turned his head to hide it, but Tanis, watching him closely, saw the pain and suddenly understood. So he was destroying that, too! The half-elf shut his eyes in despair.

"Goldmoon and I weren't going to tell you. You had enough to worry about." Riverwind sighed. "Our baby would have been born in the autumn," he murmured, "in the time when the leaves on the vallenwoods turn red and golden as they were when Goldmoon and I came into Solace that day, carrying the blue crystal staff. That day the knight, Sturm Brightblade, found us and brought us to the Inn of the Last Home—"

Tanis began to sob, deep racking sobs that tore through his body like knives. Riverwind put his arms around his friend and held him tightly.

"The vallenwoods we know are dead now, Tanis," he continued in a hushed voice. "We could have shown the child only burned and rotted stumps. But now the child will see the vallenwoods as the gods meant them to be, in a land where the trees live forever. Do not grieve, my friend, my brother. You helped bring knowledge of the gods back to the people. You must have faith in those gods."

Gently Tanis pushed Riverwind away. He could not meet the Plainsman's eyes. Looking into his own soul, Tanis saw it twist and writhe like the tortured trees of Silvanesti. Faith? He had no faith. What were the gods to him? *He* had made the decisions. *He* had thrown away everything he ever had of value in his life—his elven homeland, Laurana's love. He had come close to throwing away friendship, too. Only Riverwind's strong loyalty—a loyalty that was badly misplaced—kept the Plainsman from denouncing him.

Suicide is forbidden to the elves. They consider it blasphemy, the gift of life being the most precious of all gifts. But Tanis stared into the blood-red sea with anticipation and longing.

Let death come swiftly, he prayed. Let these blood-stained waters close over my head. Let me hide in their depths. And if there *are* gods, if you *are* listening to me, I ask only one thing: keep the knowledge of my shame from Laurana. I have brought pain to too many. . . .

But even as his soul breathed this prayer he hoped would be his last upon Krynn, a shadow darker than the storm clouds fell across him. Tanis heard Riverwind cry out and Goldmoon scream, but their voices were lost in the roar of the water as the ship began to sink into the heart of the maelstrom. Dully, Tanis looked up to see the fiery red eyes of a blue dragon shining through the black swirling clouds. Upon the dragon's back was Kitiara.

Unwilling to give up the prize that would win them glorious victory, Kit and Skie had fought their way through the storm, and now the dragon—wicked talons extended—dove straight for Berem. The man's feet might have been nailed to the deck. In dream-like helplessness he stared at the diving dragon.

Jolted to action, Tanis flung himself across the heaving deck as the blood-red water swirled around him. He hit Berem full in the stomach, knocking the man backward just as a wave broke over them. Tanis grabbed hold of something; he wasn't sure what, and clung to the deck as it canted away beneath him. Then the ship righted itself. When he looked up, Berem was gone. Above him, he heard the dragon shriek in anger.

And then Kitiara was shouting above the storm, pointing at Tanis. Skie's fiery gaze turned on him. Raising his arm as if he could ward off the dragon, Tanis looked up into the enraged eyes of the beast who was fighting madly to control his flight in the whipping winds.

This is life, the half-elf found himself thinking, seeing the dragon's claws above him. This is life! To live, to be carried out of this horror! For an instant Tanis felt himself suspended in mid-air as the bottom dropped out of his world. He was conscious only of shaking his head wildly, screaming incoherently. The dragon and the water hit him at the same time. All he could see was blood. . . .

Tika crouched beside Caramon, her fear of death lost in her concern for him. But Caramon wasn't even aware of her presence. He stared out into the darkness, tears coursing down his face, his hands clenched into fists, repeating two words over and over in a silent litany.

In agonizing dreamlike slowness, the ship balanced on the edge of the swirling water, as if the very wood of the vessel itself hesitated in fear. Maquesta joined her frail ship in its final desperate struggle for life, lending her own inner strength, trying to change the laws of nature by force of will alone. But it was useless. With a final, heartbreaking shudder, the *Perechon* slipped over the edge into the swirling, roaring darkness.

Timber cracked. Masts fell. Men were flung, screaming, from the listing decks as the blood-red blackness sucked the *Perechon* down into its gaping maw.

After all was gone, two words lingered like a benediction. "My brother. . . ."

5
The chronicler and the mage.

Astinus of Palanthas sat in his study. His hand guided the quill pen he held in firm, even strokes. The bold, crisp writing flowing from that pen could be read clearly, even at a distance. Astinus filled a sheet of parchment quickly, rarely pausing to think. Watching him, one had the impression that his thoughts flowed from his head straight into the pen and out onto the paper, so rapidly did he write. The flow was interrupted only when he dipped the quill in ink, but this, too, had become such an automatic motion to Astinus that it interrupted him as little as the dotting of an "i" or the crossing of a "t."

The door to his study creaked opened. Astinus did not look up from his writing, though the door did not often open while he was engaged in his work. The historian could count the number of times on his fingers. One of those times had been during the Cataclysm. *That* had disturbed his writing, he recalled, remembering with disgust the spilled ink that had ruined a page.

The door opened and a shadow fell across his desk. But there came no sound, though the body belonging to the shadow drew in a breath as though about to speak. The shadow wavered, the sheer enormity of its offense causing the body to tremble.

It is Bertrem, Astinus noted, as he noted everything, filing the information for future reference in one of the many compartments of his mind.

This day, as above Afterwatch Hour falling 29, Bertrem entered my study.

The pen continued its steady advance over the paper. Reaching the end of a page, Astinus lifted it smoothly and placed it on top of similar pieces of parchment stacked neatly at the end of his desk. Later that night, when the historian had finished his work and retired, the Aesthetics would enter the study reverently, as clerics enter a shrine, and gather up the stacks of paper. Carefully they would take them into the great library. Here the pieces of parchment covered with the bold, firm handwriting, were sorted, categorized, and filed in the giant books labeled *Chronicles, A History of Krynn* by Astinus of Palanthas.

"Master . . ." spoke Bertrem in a shivering voice.

This day, as above Afterwatch Hour falling 30, Bertrem spoke, Astinus noted in the text.

"I regret disturbing you, Master," said Bertrem faintly, "but a young man is dying on your doorstep."

This day, as above Restful Hour climbing 29, a young man died on our doorstep.

"Get his name," Astinus said without looking up or pausing in his writing, "so that I may record it. Be certain as to the spelling. And find out where he's from and his age, if he's not too far gone."

"I have his name, Master," Bertrem replied. "It is Raistlin. He comes from Solace township in the land of Abanasinia."

This day, as above Restful Hour climbing 28, Raistlin of Solace died—

Astinus stopped writing. He looked up.

"Raistlin . . . of Solace?"

"Yes, Master," Bertrem replied, bowing at this great honor. It was the first time Astinus had ever looked directly at him, though Bertrem had been with the Order of Aesthetics who lived in the great library for over a decade. "Do you know him, Master? That was why I took the liberty of disturbing your work. He has asked to see you."

"Raistlin. . . ."

A drop of ink fell from Astinus's pen onto the paper.

"Where is he?"

"On the steps, Master, where we found him. We thought, perhaps, one of these new healers we have heard about, the ones who worship the Goddess Mishakal, might aid him. . . ."

The historian glared at the blot of ink in annoyance. Taking a pinch of fine, white sand, he carefully sprinkled it over the ink to dry it so that it would not stain other sheets that would later be set upon it. Then, lowering his gaze, Astinus returned to his work.

"No healer can cure this young man's malady," the historian remarked in a voice that might have come from the depths of time. "But bring him inside. Give him a room."

"Bring him inside the library?" Bertrem repeated in profound astonishment. "Master, no one has ever been admitted except those of our order—"

"I will see him, if I have time at the end of the day," Astinus continued as if he had not heard the Aesthetic's words. "If he is still alive, that is."

The pen moved rapidly across the paper.

"Yes, Master," Bertrem murmured and backed out of the room.

Shutting the door to the study, the Aesthetic hurried through the cool and silent marble halls of the ancient library, his eyes wide with the wonder of this occurrence. His thick, heavy robes swept the floor behind him, his shaved head glistened with sweat as he ran, unaccustomed to such strenuous exertion. The others of his order gazed at him in astonishment as he swept into the library's front entryway. Glancing quickly through the glass pane set in the door, he could see the young man's body upon the stairs.

"We are commanded to bring him inside," Bertrem told the others. "Astinus will see the young man tonight, if the mage is still alive."

One by one, the Aesthetics regarded each other in shocked silence, wondering what doom this portended.

I am dying.

The knowledge was bitter to the mage. Lying in the bed in the cold, white cell where the Aesthetics had placed him, Raistlin cursed his frail and fragile body, he cursed the Tests that shattered it, he cursed the gods who had inflicted it upon him. He cursed until he had no more words to hurl, until he was too exhausted even to think. And then he lay beneath the white linen sheets that were like winding cloths and felt his heart flutter inside his breast like a trapped bird.

For the second time in his life, Raistlin was alone and frightened. He had been alone only once before, and that had been during those three torturous days of Testing in the Tower of High Sorcery. Even then, had he been alone? He didn't think so, although he couldn't remember clearly. The voice . . . the voice that spoke to him sometimes, the voice he could never identify, yet seemed to know . . . He always connected the voice with the Tower. It had helped him there, as it had helped him since. Because of that voice he had survived the ordeal.

But he wouldn't survive this, he knew. The magical transformation he had undergone had placed too great a strain on his frail body. He had succeeded, but at what a cost!

The Aesthetics found him huddled in his red robes, vomiting blood upon their stairs. He managed to gasp out the name of Astinus and his own name when they asked. Then he lost consciousness. When he awoke, he was here, in this cold, narrow monk's cell. And with waking came the knowledge that he was dying. He had asked more of his body than it was capable of giving. The dragon orb might save him, but he had no more strength to work his magic. The words to draw upon its enchantment were gone from his mind.

I am too weak to control its tremendous power anyway, he realized. Let it once know I have lost my strength and it would devour me.

No, there was only one chance remaining to him—the books inside the great library. The dragon orb had promised him that these books held the secrets of the ancient ones, great and powerful mages whose like would never be seen again on Krynn. Perhaps there he could find the means to extend his life. He had to talk to Astinus! He had to gain admittance to the great library, he had shrieked at the complacent Aesthetics. But they only nodded.

"Astinus will see you," they said, "this evening, if he has time."

If *he* has time! Raistlin swore viciously. If *I* have time! He could feel the sands of his life running through his fingers and, grasp at them as he might, he could not stop them.

Gazing at him with pitying eyes, not knowing what to do for him, the Aesthetics brought Raistlin food, but he could not eat. He could not even swallow the bitter herbal medicine that eased his cough. Furious, he sent the idiots away from him. Then he lay back on his hard pillow, watching the sun's light creep across his cell. Exerting all his effort to cling to life, Raistlin forced himself to relax, knowing that this feverish anger would burn him up. His thoughts went to his brother.

Closing his eyes wearily, Raistlin imagined Caramon sitting beside him. He could almost feel Caramon's arms around him, lifting him up so that he could breathe more easily. He could smell his brother's familiar scent of sweat and leather and steel. Caramon would take care of him. Caramon would not let him die. . . .

No, Raistlin thought dreamily. Caramon is dead now. They are all dead, the fools. I must look after myself. Suddenly he realized he was losing consciousness again. Desperately he fought, but it was a losing battle. Making a final, supreme effort, he thrust his shaking hand into a pocket in his robe. His fingers closed around the dragon orb—shrunk to the size of a child's marble—even as he sank into darkness.

He woke to the sound of voices and the knowledge that someone was in the cell with him. Fighting through layers of blackness, Raistlin struggled to the surface of his consciousness and opened his eyes.

It was evening. Lunitari's red light glanced through his window; a shimmering blood stain upon the wall. A candle burned beside his bed and, by its light, he saw two men standing over him. One he recognized as the Aesthetic who had discovered him. The other? He seemed familiar. . . .

"He wakes, Master," said the Aesthetic.

"So he does," remarked the man imperturbably. Bending down, he studied the young mage's face, then smiled and nodded to himself, almost as if someone he had long expected had finally arrived. It was a peculiar look, and it did not go unnoticed by either Raistlin or the Aesthetic.

"I am Astinus," the man spoke. "You are Raistlin of Solace."

"I am." Raistlin's mouth formed the words, his voice was little more than a croak. Gazing up at Astinus, Raistlin's anger returned as he remembered the man's callous remark that he would see him *if he had time*. As Raistlin stared at the man, he felt suddenly chilled. He had never seen a face so cold and unfeeling, totally devoid of human emotion and human passion. A face untouched by time—

Raistlin gasped. Struggling to sit up—with the Aesthetic's help—he stared at Astinus.

Noticing Raistlin's reaction, Astinus remarked, "You look at me strangely, young mage. What do you see with those hourglass eyes of yours?"

"I see . . . a man . . . who is *not* dying. . . ." Raistlin could speak only through painful struggles to draw breath.

"Of course, what did you expect?" the Aesthetic chided, gently propping the dying man against the pillows of his bed. "The Master was here to chronicle the birth of the first upon Krynn and so he will be here to chronicle the death of the last. So we are taught by Gilean, God of the Book."

"Is that true?" Raistlin whispered.

Astinus shrugged slightly. "My personal history is of no consequence compared to the history of the world. Now speak, Raistlin of Solace. What do you want of me? Whole volumes are passing as I waste my time in idle talk with you."

"I ask . . . I beg . . . a favor!" The words were torn from Raistlin's chest and came out stained with blood. "My life . . . is measured . . . in hours. Let me . . . spend them . . . in study . . . in the . . . great library!"

Bertrem's tongue clicked against the roof of his mouth in shock at this young mage's temerity. Glancing at Astinus fearfully, the Aesthetic waited for the scathing refusal which, he felt certain, must flail this rash young man's skin from his bones.

Long moments of silenced passed, broken only by Raistlin's labored breathing. The expression on Astinus's face did not change. Finally he answered coldly. "Do what you will."

Ignoring Bertrem's shocked look, Astinus turned and began

to walk toward the door.

"Wait!" Raistlin's voice rasped. The mage reached out a trembling hand as Astinus slowly came to a halt. "You asked me what I saw when I looked at you. Now I ask you the same thing. I saw that look upon your face when you bent over me. You recognized me! You know me! Who am I? What do you see?"

Astinus looked back, his face cold, blank, and impenetrable as marble.

"You said you saw a man who was not dying," the historian told the mage softly. Hesitating a moment, he shrugged and once again turned away. "I see a man who is."

And, with that, he walked out the door.

It is assumed that You who hold this Book in your Hands have successfully passed the Tests in one of the Towers of High Sorcery, and that You have demonstrated Your Ability to exert Control over a Dragon Orb or some other approved Magical Artifact (see Appendix C) and, further, that You have demonstrated Proven Ability in casting the Spells—

"Yes, yes," muttered Raistlin, hurriedly scanning the runes that crawled like spiders across the page. Reading impatiently through the list of spells, he finally reached the conclusion.

Having completed these Requirements to the Satisfaction of Your Masters, We give into Your Hands this Spellbook. Thus, with the Key, You unlock Our Mysteries.

With a shriek of inarticulate rage, Raistlin shoved the spellbook with its night-blue binding and silver runes aside. His hand shaking, he reached for the next night-blue bound book in the huge pile he had amassed at his side. A fit of coughing forced him to stop. Fighting for breath, he feared for a moment that he could not go on.

The pain was unbearable. Sometimes he longed to sink into oblivion, end this torture he must live with daily. Weak and dizzy, he let his head sink to the desk, cradled in his arms. Rest, sweet, painless rest. An image of his brother came to his mind. There was Caramon in the afterlife, waiting for his little brother. Raistlin could see his twin's sad, doglike eyes, he could feel his pity. . . .

Raistlin drew a breath with a gasp, then forced himself to sit up. Meeting Caramon! I'm getting lightheaded, he sneered at himself. What nonsense!

Moistening his blood-caked lips with water, Raistlin took hold of the next night-blue spellbook and pulled it over to him. Its silver runes flashed in the candlelight, its cover—icy cold to the touch—was the same as the covers of all the other spellbooks stacked around him. Its cover was the same as the spellbook in his possession already—the spellbook he knew by heart and by soul, the spellbook of the greatest mage who ever lived—Fistandantilus.

With trembling hands, Raistlin opened the cover. His fever-ish eyes devoured the page, reading the same requirements—only mages high in the Order had the skill and control necessary to study the spells recorded inside. Those without it who tried to read the spells saw nothing on the pages but gibberish.

Raistlin fulfilled all the requirements. He was probably the only White or Red-Robed mage on Krynn, with the possible exception of the great Par-Salian himself, who could say that. Yet, when Raistlin looked at the writing inside the book, it was nothing more than a meaningless scrawl.

Thus, with the Key, You Unlock our Mysteries—

Raistlin screamed, a thin, wailing sound cut off by a choking sob. In bitter anger and frustration, he flung himself upon the table, scattering the books to the floor. Frantically his hands clawed the air and he screamed again. The magic that he had been too weak to summon came now in his anger.

The Aesthetics, passing outside the doors of the great library, exchanged fearful glances as they heard those terrible cries. Then they heard another sound. A crackling sound followed by a booming explosion of thunder. They stared at the door in alarm. One put his hand upon the handle and turned it, but the door was locked fast. Then one pointed and they all backed up as a ghastly light flared beneath the closed door. The smell of sulphur drifted out of the library, only to be blown away by a great gust of wind that hit the door with such force it seemed it might split in two. Again the Aesthetics heard that bubbling wail of rage, and then they fled down the marble hallway, calling wildly for Astinus.

The historian arrived to find the door to the great library held spellbound. He was not much surprised. With a sigh of resignation, he took a small book from the pocket of his robes and then sat down in a chair, beginning to write in his quick, flowing script. The Aesthetics huddled together near him, alarmed at the strange sounds emanating from within the locked room.

Thunder boomed and rolled, shaking the library's very foundation. Light flared around the closed door so constantly it might have been day within the room instead of the darkest hour of the night. The howling and shrieking of a windstorm blended with the mage's shrill screams. There were thuds and thumps, the rustling sounds of sheaves of paper swirling about in a storm. Tongues of flame flicked from beneath the door.

"Master!" one of the Aesthetics cried in terror, pointing to the flames. "He is destroying the books!"

Astinus shook his head and did not cease his writing.

Then, suddenly, all was silent. The light seen beneath the library door went out as if swallowed by darkness. Hesitantly the Aesthetics approached the door, cocking their heads to listen. Nothing could be heard from within, except a faint rustling sound. Bertrem placed his hand upon the door. It yielded to his gentle pressure.

"The door opens, Master," he said.

Astinus stood up. "Return to your studies," he commanded the Aesthetics. "There is nothing you can do here."

Bowing silently, the monks gave the door a final, scared glance, then walked hurriedly down the echoing corridor, leaving Astinus alone. He waited a few moments to make certain they were gone, then the historian slowly opened the door to the great library.

Silver and red moonlight streamed through the small windows. The orderly rows of shelves that held thousands of bound books stretched into the darkness. Recessed holes containing thousands of scrolls lined the walls. The moonlight shone upon a table, buried under a pile of paper. A guttered candle stood in the center of the table, a night-blue spellbook lay open beside it, the moonlight shining on its bone-white pages. Other spellbooks lay scattered on the floor.

Looking around, Astinus frowned. Black streaks marked the walls. The smell of sulphur and of fire was strong inside the room. Sheets of paper swirled in the still air, falling like leaves after an autumn storm upon a body lying on the floor.

Entering the room, Astinus carefully shut and locked the door behind him. Then he approached the body, wading through the mass of parchment scattered on the floor. He said nothing, nor did he bend down to help the young mage. Standing beside Raistlin, he regarded him thoughtfully.

But, as he drew near, Astinus's robes brushed the metallic-colored, outstretched hand. At that touch, the mage lifted his head. Raistlin stared at Astinus with eyes already darkening with the shadows of death.

"You did not find what you sought?" Astinus asked, staring down at the young man with cold eyes.

"The Key!" Raistlin gasped through white lips flecked with blood. "Lost . . . in time! . . . Fools!" His clawlike hand clenched, anger the only fire that burned in him. "So simple! Everyone knew it . . . no one recorded it! The Key . . . all I need . . . lost!"

"So this ends your journey, my old friend," Astinus said without compassion.

Raistlin raised his head, his golden eyes glittering feverishly. "You *do* know me! *Who am I?*" he demanded.

"It is no longer important," Astinus said. Turning, he started to walk out of the library.

There was a piercing shriek behind him, a hand grasped his robe, dragging him to a halt.

"Don't turn your back on me as you have turned it on the world!" Raistlin snarled.

"Turn my back on the world . . ." the historian repeated softly and slowly, his head moving to face the mage. "Turn my back on the world!" Emotion rarely marred the surface of Astinus's cold voice, but now anger struck the placid calm of his soul like a rock hurled into still water.

"I? Turn my back on the world?" Astinus's voice rolled around the library as the thunder had rolled previously. "I *am* the world, as you well know, old friend! Countless times I have been born! Countless deaths I have died! Every tear shed—mine have flowed! Every drop of blood spilled—mine has drained! Every agony, every joy ever felt has been mine to share!

"I sit with my hand on the Sphere of Time, the sphere *you* made for me, old friend, and I travel the length and breadth of this world chronicling its history. I have committed the blackest deeds! I have made the noblest sacrifices. I am human, elf, and ogre. I am male and female. I have borne children. I have murdered children. I saw you as you were. I see you as you are. If I seem cold and unfeeling, it is because that is how I survive without losing my sanity! My passion goes into my words.

Those who read my books *know* what it is to have lived in any time, in any body that ever walked this world!"

Raistlin's hand loosed its grip on the historian's robes and he fell weakly to the floor. His strength was fading fast. But the mage clung to Astinus's words, even as he felt the coldness of death clutch his heart. I must live, just a moment longer. Lunitari, give me just a moment more, he prayed, calling upon the spirit of the moon from which Red-Robed mages draw their magic. Some word was coming, he knew. Some word that would save him. If only he could hold on!

Astinus's eyes flared as he gazed upon the dying man. The words he hurled at him had been pent up inside the chronicler for countless centuries.

"On the last, perfect day," Astinus said, his voice shaking. "the three gods will come together: Paladine in his Radiance, Queen Takhisis in her Darkness, and lastly Gilean, Lord of Neutrality. In their hands, each bears the Key of Knowledge. They will place these Keys upon the great Altar, and upon the Altar will also be placed my books—the story of every being who has lived upon Krynn throughout time! And then, at last, the world will be complete—"

Astinus stopped, appalled, realizing what he had said, what he had done.

But Raistlin's eyes no longer saw him. The hourglass pupils were dilated, the golden color surrounding them gleamed like flame.

"The Key . . ." Raistlin whispered in exultation. "The Key! I know. . . . I *know!*"

So weak he could scarcely move, Raistlin reached into the small, nondescript pouch that hung from his belt and brought forth the marble-sized dragon orb. Holding it in his trembling hand, the mage stared into it with eyes that were fast growing dim.

"I know who you are," Raistlin murmured with his dying breath. "I know you now and I beseech you—come to my aid as you came to my aid in the Tower and in Silvanesti! Our bargain is struck! Save me, and you save yourself!"

The mage collapsed. His head with its sparse white wispy hair lolled back onto the floor, his eyes with their cursed vision closed. The hand that held the orb went limp, but its fingers did not relax. It held the orb fast in a grip stronger than death.

Little more than a heap of bones garbed in blood-red robes,

Raistlin lay unmoving amid the papers that littered the spell-blasted library.

Astinus stared at the body for long moments, bathed in the garish purplish light of the two moons. Then, his head bowed, the historian left the silent library, closing and locking the door behind him with hands that shook.

Returning to his study, the historian sat for hours, gazing unseeing into the darkness.

6

Palanthas.

"I tell you, it was Raistlin!"

"And I tell you, one more of your furry-elephant, teleporting-ring , plants-living-off-air stories and I'll twist that hoopak around your neck!" Flint snapped angrily.

"It was *too* Raistlin," Tasslehoff retorted, but he said it under his breath as the two walked along the wide, gleaming streets of the beautiful city of Palanthas. The kender knew by long association just how far he could push the dwarf and Flint's threshold for irritation was very low these days.

"And don't go bothering Laurana with your wild tales,

either," Flint ordered, correctly guessing Tas's intentions. "She has enough problems."

"But—"

The dwarf stopped and gazed grimly at the kender from beneath bushy white eyebrows.

"Promise?"

Tas sighed. "Oh, all right."

It wouldn't have been so bad if he didn't feel quite certain he *had* seen Raistlin! He and Flint were walking past the steps of the great library of Palanthas when the kender's sharp eyes caught sight of a group of monks clustered around something lying on the steps. When Flint stopped for a moment to admire some particularly fine piece of dwarven-crafted stonework in a building opposite, Tas took advantage of the opportunity to creep silently up the stairs to see what was going on.

To his amazement, he saw a man that looked just like Raistlin—golden-colored metallic skin, red robes, and all—being lifted up off the stairs and carried inside the library. But by the time the excited kender ran across the street, grabbed Flint, and hauled the grumbling dwarf back again, the group was gone.

Tasslehoff even ran up to the door, banging on it and demanding entrance. But the Aesthetic who answered appeared so horrified at the thought of a kender coming into the great library that the scandalized dwarf hustled Tas off before the monk could open his mouth.

Promises being very nebulous things to kenders, Tas considered telling Laurana anyway, but then he thought of the elf-maid's face as it had appeared lately, wan and drawn from grief, worry, and lack of sleep, and the soft-hearted kender decided maybe Flint was right. If it *was* Raistlin, he was probably here on some secret business of his own and wouldn't thank them for dropping in on him uninvited. Still—

Heaving a sigh, the kender walked on, kicking stones with his feet and looking around the city once more. Palanthas was well-worth the look. The city had been fabled even during the Age of Might for its beauty and grace. There was no other city on Krynn that could compare to it—at least to human thought. Built on a circular pattern like a wheel, the center was, literally, the hub of the city. All the major official buildings were located here, and the great sweeping staircases and graceful columns were breathtaking in their grandeur. From this central circle, wide avenues led off in the directions of the eight major compass points. Paved with fitted stone (dwarven work, of course) and lined with trees whose leaves were like golden lace year-round, these avenues led to the seaport on the north and to the seven gates of the Old City Wall.

Even these gates were masterpieces of architecture, each one guarded by twin minarets whose graceful towers rose over three hundred feet into the air. The Old Wall itself was carved with intricate designs, telling the story of Palanthas during the Age of Dreams. Beyond Old City Wall lay New City. Carefully planned to conform to the original design, New City extended from Old City Wall in the same circular pattern with the same wide, tree-lined avenues. There were, however, no walls around New City. The Palanthians didn't particularly like walls, (walls ruined the over-all design) and nothing in either Old or New City was ever built these days without first consulting the overall design, both within and without. Palanthas's silhouette upon the horizon in the evening was as lovely to the eye as the city itself—with one exception.

Tas's thoughts were rudely interrupted by a poke in the back from Flint.

"What *is* the matter with you?" the kender demanded, facing the dwarf.

"Where are we?" Flint asked surlily, hands on his hips.

"Well, we're . . ." Tas looked around. "Uh . . .that is, I think we're . . . then again, perhaps we're not." He fixed Flint with a cold stare. "How did you get us lost?"

"ME!" The dwarf exploded. "*You're* the guide! *You're* the map reader. *You're* the kender who knows this city like he knows his own house!"

"But *I* was thinking," Tas said loftily.

"What with?" Flint roared.

"I was thinking deep thoughts," Tas said in wounded tones.

"I—oh, never mind," Flint grumbled and began to peer up and down the street. He didn't quite like the looks of things.

"This certainly does seem strange," Tas said cheerfully, echoing the dwarf's thoughts. "It's so empty—not at all like the other streets of Palanthas." He stared longingly down the rows of silent empty buildings. "I wonder—"

"No," said Flint. "Absolutely not. We're going back the way we came—"

"Oh, come on!" Tas said, heading down the deserted street.

"Just a little ways, to see what's down here. You *know* Laurana told us to look around, inspect the forti—forta—the whatch-ma-call-its."

"Fortifications," muttered Flint, stumping reluctantly along after the kender. "And there aren't any around here, you door-knob. This is the center of the city! She meant the walls around the outside of the city."

"There aren't any walls around the outside of the city," Tas said triumphantly. "Not around New City, anyway. And if it's the center, why is it deserted? I think we should find out."

Flint snorted. The kender was beginning to make sense—a fact which caused the dwarf to shake his head and wonder if maybe he shouldn't lie down somewhere out of the sun.

The two walked for several minutes in silence, traveling deeper and deeper into the heart of the city. To one side, only a few blocks away, rose the palatial mansion of the Lord of Palanthas. They could see its towering spires from here. But ahead of them, nothing was visible. It was all lost in shadow. . . .

Tas glanced into windows and stuck his nose into doorways of the buildings they passed. He and Flint proceeded clear to the end of the block before the kender spoke.

"You know, Flint," Tas said uneasily, "these buildings are all empty."

"Abandoned," said Flint in hushed tones. The dwarf laid his hand on his battle-axe, he started nervously at the sound of Tas's shrill voice.

"There's a queer feeling about this place," Tas said, edging closer to the dwarf. "I'm not afraid, mind you—"

"I am," said Flint emphatically. "Let's get out of here!"

Tas looked up at the tall buildings on either side of them. They were well-kept. Apparently the Palanthians were so proud of their city that they even spent money keeping up vacant buildings. There were shops and dwellings of all kinds, obviously structurally sound. The streets were clean and free from litter and garbage. But it was all deserted. This had once been a prosperous area, the kender thought. Right in the heart of the city. Why wasn't it now? Why had everyone left? It gave him an "eerie" feeling and there were not many things in Krynn that gave kender "eerie" feelings.

"There aren't even any rats!" Flint muttered. Taking hold of Tas's arm, he tugged at the kender. "We've seen enough."

"Oh, come on," Tas said. Pulling his arm away, he fought

down the strange eerie sensation and—straightening his small shoulders—started off down the sidewalk once more. He hadn't gone three feet when he realized he was alone. Stopping in exasperation, he looked back. The dwarf was standing on the sidewalk, glowering at him.

"I only want to go as far as that grove of trees at the end of the street," Tas said, pointing. "Look—it's just an ordinary grove of ordinary oak trees. Probably a park or something. Maybe we could have lunch—"

"I don't like this place!" Flint said stubbornly. "It reminds me of . . . of . . . Darken Wood—that place where Raistlin spoke to the spooks."

"Oh, you're the only spook here!" Tas said irritably, determined to ignore the fact that it reminded him of the same thing. "It's broad daylight. We're in the center of a *city*, for the love of Reorx—"

"Then why is it freezing cold?"

"It's winter!" the kender shouted, waving his arms. He hushed immediately, staring around in alarm at the weird way his words echoed through the silent streets. "Are you coming?" he asked in a loud whisper.

Flint drew a deep breath. Scowling, he gripped his battle-axe and marched down the street toward the kender, casting a wary eye at the buildings as though at any moment a spectre might leap out at him.

" 'Tisn't winter," the dwarf muttered out of the corner of his mouth. "Except around here."

"It won't be spring for weeks," Tas returned, glad to have something to argue about and keep his mind off the strange things his stomach was doing—twisting into knots and the like.

But Flint refused to quarrel—a bad sign. Silently, the two crept down the empty street until they reached the end of the block. Here the buildings ended abruptly in a grove of trees. As Tas had said, it seemed just an ordinary grove of oak trees—although they were certainly the tallest oaks either the dwarf or the kender had seen in long years of exploring Krynn.

But as the two approached, they felt the strange chilling sensation become stronger until it was worse than any cold they had ever experienced, even the cold of the glacier in Ice Wall. It was worse because it came from within and it made no sense! Why should it be so cold in just this part of the city? The sun was shining. There wasn't a cloud in the sky. But soon their fin-

72

gers were numb and stiff. Flint could no longer hold his battle-axe and was forced to put it back in its holder with shaking hands. Tas's teeth chattered, he had lost all feeling in his pointed ears, and he shivered violently.

"L-let's g-get out-t of h-here . . ." stammered the dwarf through blue lips.

"W-we're j-just s-standing in a sh-shadow of a building." Tas nearly bit his tongue. "W-when we g-get in the s-s-sunshine, it'll war-warm up."

"No f-fire on K-K-Krynn will w-warm t-this!" Flint snapped visciously, stomping on the ground to get the circulation started in his feet.

"J-just a f-few m-more f-feet. . . ." Tas kept going along gamely, even though his knees knocked together. But he went alone. Turning around, he saw that Flint seemed paralyzed, unable to move. His head was bowed, his beard quivered.

I should go back, Tas thought, but he couldn't. The curiosity that did more than anything in the world to reduce the kender population kept drawing him forward.

Tas came to the edge of the grove of oak trees and—here—his heart almost failed him. Kender are normally immune to the sensation of fear, so only a kender could have come even this far. But now Tas found himself a prey to the most unreasoning terror he had ever experienced. And whatever was causing it was located within that grove of oak trees.

They're ordinary trees, Tas said to himself, shivering. I've talked to spectres in Darken Wood. I've faced three or four dragons. I broke a dragon orb. Just an ordinary grove of trees. I was prisoner in a wizard's castle. I saw a demon from the Abyss. Just a grove of ordinary trees.

Slowly, talking to himself, Tasslehoff inched his way through the oak trees. He didn't go far, not even past the row of trees that formed the outer perimeter of the grove. Because now he could see into the heart of the grove.

Tasslehoff gulped, turned, and ran.

At the sight of the kender running back toward him, Flint knew it was All Over. Something Awful was going to crash out of that grove of trees. The dwarf whirled so rapidly he tripped over his feet and fell sprawling to the pavement. Running up to him, Tas grabbed Flint's belt and pulled him up. Then the two dashed madly down the street, the dwarf running for his very life. He could almost hearing gigantic footsteps thudding along behind him. He did not dare turn around. Visions of a slobbering monster drove him on until his heart seemed about to burst from his body. Finally they reached the end of the street.

It was warm. The sun shone.

They could hear the voices of real live people drifting from the crowded streets beyond. Flint stopped, exhausted, gasping for breath. Glancing fearfully back down the street, he was surprised to see it was still empty.

"What was it?" he managed to ask when he could speak past the thudding of his heart.

The kender's face was pale as death. "A-a t-tower . . ." Tas gulped, puffing.

Flint's eyes opened wide. "A tower?" the dwarf repeated. "I *ran* all that way—nearly killing myself—and I was running from a *tower*! I don't suppose"— Flint's bushy eyebrows came together alarmingly—"that the tower was chasing you?"

"N-no," Tas admitted. "It—it just stood there. But it was the most horrible thing I've ever seen in my life," the kender avowed solemnly, shuddering.

"That would be the Tower of High Sorcery," the Lord of Palanthas told Laurana that evening as they sat in the map room of the beautiful palace on the hill overlooking the city. "No wonder your little friend was terrified. I'm surprised he got as far as the Shoikan Oak Grove."

"He's a kender," Laurana replied, smiling.

"Ah, yes. Well, that explains it. Now that's something I hadn't considered, you know. Hiring kender to do the work around the Tower. We have to pay the most outrageous prices to get men to go into those buildings once a year and keep them in good repair. But then"—the Lord appeared downcast—"I don't suppose the townspeople would be at all pleased to see a sizeable number of kender in the city."

Amothus, Lord of Palanthas, padded across the polished marble floor of the map room, his hands clasped behind his robes of state. Laurana walked next to him, trying to keep from tripping over the hem of the long, flowing gown the Palanthians had insisted she wear. They had been quite charming about the dress, offering it as a gift. But she knew they were horrified to see a Princess of the Qualinesti parading around in blood-stained, battle-scarred armor. Laurana had no choice but to accept it; she could not afford to offend the Palanthians whom she was counting on for help. But she felt naked and fragile and defenseless without her sword at her side and the steel around her body.

And she knew that the generals of the Palanthian army, the temporary commanders of the Solamnic knights, and the other nobles—advisors from the City Senate—were the ones making her feel fragile and defenseless. All of them reminded her with every look that she was—to them—a woman playing at being a soldier. All right, she had done well. She had fought her little war and she had won. Now—back to the kitchen. . . .

"What *is* the Tower of High Sorcery?" Laurana asked abruptly. She had learned after a week of negotiating with the Lord of Palanthas that—although an intelligent man—his thoughts tended to wander into unexplored regions and he needed constant guidance to keep to the central topic.

"Oh, yes. Well, you can see it from the window here, if you really want to—" The Lord seemed reluctant.

"I would like to see it," Laurana said coolly.

Shrugging, Lord Amothus veered from his course and led Laurana to a window she had already noticed because it was covered with thick curtains. The curtains over the other windows of the room were open, revealing a breathtaking view of the city in whatever direction one looked.

"Yes, this is the reason I keep these shut," the Lord said with a sigh in answer to Laurana's question. "A pity, too. This was once the most magnificent view in the city, according to the old records. But that was before the Tower was cursed—"

The Lord drew the curtains aside with a trembling hand, his face dark with sorrow. Startled at such emotion, Laurana looked out curiously, then drew in a breath. The sun was sinking behind the snow-capped mountains, streaking the sky with red and purple. The vibrant colors shimmered in the pure white buildings of Palanthas as the rare, translucent marble from which they were built caught the dying light. Laurana had never imagined such beauty could exist in the world of humans. It rivaled her beloved homeland of Qualinesti.

Then her eyes were drawn to a darkness within the shimmering pearl radiance. A single tower rose up to the sky. It was tall; even though the palace was perched on a hill, the top of the Tower was only slightly below her line of sight. Made of black marble, it stood out in distinct contrast to the white marble of the city around it. Minarets must have once graced its gleaming surface, she saw, though these were now crumbling and broken. Dark windows, like empty eyesockets, stared sightlessly into the world. A fence surrounded it. The fence, too, was black and, on the gate of the fence, Laurana saw something fluttering. For a moment she thought it was a huge bird, trapped there, for it seemed alive. But just as she was about to call the Lord's attention to it, he shut the curtains with a shiver.

"I'm sorry," he apologized. "I can't stand it. Shocking. And to think we've lived with that for centuries. . . ."

"I don't think it's so terrible," Laurana said earnestly, her mind's eye remembering the view of the Tower and the city around it. "The Tower . . . seems right somehow. Your city *is* very beautiful, but sometimes it's such a cold, perfect beauty that I don't notice it anymore." Looking out the other windows, Laurana was once more as enchanted with the view as she had been when she first entered Palanthas. "But after seeing that— that flaw in your city, it makes the beauty stand out in my mind . . . if you understand. . . ."

It was obvious from the bemused expression on the Lord's face that he did *not* understand. Laurana sighed, though she caught herself glancing at the drawn curtains with a strange fascination. "How did the Tower come to be cursed?" she asked instead.

"It was during the—oh, I say, here's someone who can tell the story far better than I," Lord Amothus said, looking up in relief as the door opened. "It isn't a story I enjoy relating, to be perfectly honest."

"Astinus of the Library of Palanthas," announced the herald.

To Laurana's astonishment, every man in the room rose respectfully to his feet—even the great generals and noblemen. All this, she thought, for a libarian? Then, to her even greater astonishment, the Lord of Palanthas and all his generals and all the nobles bowed as the historian entered. Laurana bowed, too, out of confused courtesy. As a member of the royal house of Qualinesti, she was not supposed to bow before anyone on Krynn unless it be her own father, Speaker of the Suns. But when she straightened and studied this man, she felt suddenly that bowing to him had been most fitting and proper.

Astinus entered with an ease and assurance that led her to believe he would stand unabashed in the presence of all the royalty on Krynn and the heavens as well. He seemed middle-aged, but there was an ageless quality about him. His face might have been chiseled out of the marble of Palanthas itself and, at first, Laurana was repelled by the cold, passionless quality of that face. Then she saw that the man's dark eyes literally blazed with life—as though lit from within by the fire of a thousand souls.

"You are late, Astinus," Lord Amothus said pleasantly, though with a marked respect. He and his generals all remained standing until the historian had seated himself, Laurana noticed, as did even the Knights of Solamnia. Almost overcome with an unaccustomed awe, she sank into her seat at the huge, round table covered with maps which stood in the center of the great room.

"I had business to attend to," Astinus replied in a voice that might have sounded from a bottomless well.

"I heard you were troubled by a strange occurrence." The Lord of Palanthas flushed in embarrassment. "I really must apologize. We have no idea how the young man came to be found in such an appalling condition upon your stairs. If only you had let us know! We could have removed the body without fuss—"

"It was no trouble," Astinus said abruptly, glancing at Laurana. "The matter has been properly dealt with. All is now at an end."

"But . . . uh . . . what about the . . . uh . . . remains?" Lord Amothus asked hesitantly. "I know how painful this must be, but there are certain health proclamations that the Senate has passed and I'd like to be sure all has been attended to . . ."

"Perhaps I should leave," Laurana said coldly, rising to her feet, "until this conversation has ended."

"What? Leave?" The Lord of Palanthas stared at her vaguely. "You've only just come—"

"I believe our conversation is distressing to the elven princess," Astinus remarked. "The elves—as you remember, my lord—have a great reverence for life. Death is not discussed in this callous fashion among them."

"Oh, my heavens!" Lord Amothus flushed deeply, rising and taking her hand. "I do beg your pardon, my dear. Absolutely abominable of me. Please forgive me and be seated again. Some wine for the princess—" Amothus hailed a servant, who filled Laurana's glass.

"You were discussing the Towers of High Sorcery as I entered. What do you know of the Towers?" Astinus asked, his eyes staring into Laurana's soul.

Shivering at that penetrating gaze, she gulped a sip of wine, sorry now that she had mentioned it. "Really," she said faintly, "perhaps we should turn to business. I'm certain the generals are anxious to return to their troops and I—"

"What do you know of the Towers?" Astinus repeated.

"I—uh—not much," Laurana faltered, feeling as if she were back in school being confronted by her tutor. "I had a friend— that is, an acquaintance—who took the Tests at the Tower of High Sorcery in Wayreth, but he is—"

"Raistlin of Solace, I believe," Astinus said imperturbably.

"Why, yes!" Laurana answered, startled. "How—"

"I am a historian, young woman. It is my business to know," Astinus replied. "I will tell you the history of the Tower of Palanthas. Do not consider it a waste of time, Lauralanthalasa, for its history is bound up in your destiny." Ignoring her shocked look, he gestured to one of the generals. "You, there, open that curtain. You are shutting out the best view in the city, as I believe the princess remarked before I entered. This, then, is the story of the Tower of High Sorcery of Palanthas.

"My tale must begin with what became known—in hindsight—as the Lost Battles. During the Age of Might, when the Kingpriest of Istar began jumping at shadows, he gave his fears a name—magic-users! He feared them, he feared their vast power. He did not understand it, and so it became a threat to him.

"It was easy to arouse the populace against the magic-users. Although widely respected, they were never trusted— primarily because they allowed among their ranks representatives of all three powers in the universe—the White Robes of Good, the Réd Robes of Neutrality, and the Black Robes of Evil. For they understood—as the Kingpriest did not—that the universe swings in balance among these three and that to disturb the balance is to invite destruction.

"And so the people rose against the magic-users. The five Towers of High Sorcery were prime targets, naturally, for it was in these Towers that the powers of the Order were most concentrated. And it was in these Towers that the young mages came to take the Tests—those who dared. For the Trials are arduous and—worse—hazardous. Indeed, failure means one thing: death!"

"Death?" repeated Laurana, incredulously. "Then Raistlin—"

"Risked his life to take the Test. And he nearly paid the price. That is neither here nor there, however. Because of this deadly penalty for failure, dark rumors were spread about the Towers of High Sorcery. In vain the magic-users sought to explain that these were only centers of learning and that each young mage risking his life did so willingly, understanding the purpose behind it. Here, too, in the Towers, the mages kept their spellbooks and their scrolls, their implements of magic. But no one believed them. Stories of strange rites and rituals and sacrifices spread among the people, fostered by the Kingpriest and his clerics for their own ends.

"And the day came when the populace rose against the magic-users. And for only the second time in the history of the Order, the Robes came together. The first time was during the creation of the dragon orbs which contained the essences of good and evil, bound together by neutrality. After that, they went their separate ways. Now, allied by a common threat, they came together once more to protect their own.

"The magicians themselves destroyed two of the Towers, rather than let the mobs invade them and meddle with that which was beyond their understanding. The destruction of these two Towers laid waste to the countryside around them and frightened the Kingpriest—for there was a Tower of High Sorcery located in Istar and one in Palanthas. As for the third, in the Forest of Wayreth, few cared what became of it, for it was far from any center of civilization.

"And so the Kingpriest approached the magic-users with a show of piety. If they would leave the two Towers standing, he would let them withdraw in peace, removing their books and scrolls and magical implements to the Tower of High Sorcery in Wayreth. Sorrowfully the magic-users accepted his offer."

"But why didn't they fight?" Laurana interrupted. "I've seen Raistlin and . . . and Fizban when they're angry! I can't imagine what truly powerful wizards must be like!"

"Ah, but stop and consider this, Laurana. Your young friend—Raistlin—grew exhausted casting even a few relatively minor spells. And once a spell is cast, it is gone from his memory forever unless he reads his spellbook and studies it once more. This is true of even the highest level mages. It is how the gods protect us from those who might otherwise become too powerful and aspire to godhood itself. Wizards must sleep, they must be able to concentrate, they must spend time in daily study. How could they withstand besieging mobs? And, too, how could they destroy their own people?

"No, they felt they had to accept the Kingpriest's offer. Even the Black Robes, who cared little for the populace, saw that they must be defeated and that magic itself might be lost from the world. They withdrew from the Tower of High Sorcery at Istar—and almost immediately the Kingpriest moved in to occupy it. Then they abandoned the Tower here, in Palanthas. And the story of this Tower is a terrible one."

Astinus, who had been relating this without expression in his voice, suddenly grew solemn, his face darkening.

"Well I remember that day," he said, speaking more to himself than to those around the table. "They brought their books and scrolls to me, to be kept in my library. For there were many, many books and scrolls in the Tower, more than the magic-users could carry to Wayreth. They knew I would guard them and treasure them. Many of the spellbooks were ancient and could no longer be read, since they had been bound with spells of protection—spells to which the Key . . . had been lost. The Key . . ."

Astinus fell silent, pondering. Then, with a sigh, as if brushing away dark thoughts, he continued.

"The people of Palanthas gathered around the Tower as the highest of the Order—the Wizard of the White Robes—closed the Tower's slender gates of gold and locked them with a silver key. The Lord of Palanthas watched him eagerly. All knew the Lord intended to move into the Tower, as his mentor—the Kingpriest of Istar—had done. His eyes lingered greedily on the Tower, for legends of the wonders within—both fair and evil— had spread throughout the land."

"Of all the beautiful buildings in Palanthas," murmured Lord Amothus, "the Tower of High Sorcery was said to be the most splendid. And now. . . ."

"What happened?" asked Laurana, feeling chilled as the darkness of night crept through the room, wishing someone would summon the servants to light the candles.

"The Wizard started to hand the silver key to the Lord," continued Astinus in a deep, sad voice. "Suddenly, one of the Black Robes appeared in a window in the upper stories. As the people stared at him in horror, he shouted, 'The gates will remain closed and the halls empty until the day comes when the master of both the past and the present returns with power!' Then the evil mage leaped out, hurling himself down upon the gates. And as the barbs of silver and of gold pierced the black robes, he cast a curse upon the Tower. His blood stained the ground, the silver and golden gates withered and twisted and turned to black. The shimmering tower of white and red faded to ice gray stone, its black minarets crumbled.

"The Lord and the people fled in terror and, to this day, no one dares approach the Tower of Palanthas. Not even kender"—Astinus smiled briefly—"who fear nothing in this world. The curse is so powerful it keeps away *all* mortals—"

"Until the master of past and present returns," Laurana murmured.

"Bah! The man was mad." Lord Amothus sniffed. "No man is master of past and present—unless it be you, Astinus."

"I am not master!" Astinus said in such hollow, ringing tones that everyone in the room stared at him. "I remember the past, I record the present. I do not seek to dominate either!"

"Mad, like I said." The Lord shrugged. "And now we are forced to endure an eyesore like the Tower because no one can stand to live around it or get close enough to tear it down."

"I think to tear it down would be a shame," Laurana said softly, gazing at the Tower through the window. "It *belongs* here. . . ."

"Indeed it does, young woman," Astinus replied, regarding her strangely.

Night's shadows had deepened as Astinus talked. Soon the Tower was shrouded in darkness while lights sparkled in the rest of the city. Palanthas seemed to be trying to out-glitter the stars, thought Laurana, but a round patch of blackness will remain always in its center.

"How sad and how tragic," she murmured, feeling that she must say something, since Astinus was staring straight at her. "And that—that dark thing I saw fluttering, pinned to the fence—" She stopped in horror.

"Mad, mad," repeated Lord Amothus gloomily. "Yes, that is what's left of the body, so we suppose. No one has been able to get close enough to find out."

Laurana shuddered. Putting her hands to her aching head, she knew that this grim story would haunt her for nights, and she wished she'd never heard it. *Bound up in her destiny!* Angrily she put the thought out of her mind. It didn't matter. She didn't have time for this. Her destiny looked bleak enough without adding nightmarish nursery tales.

As if reading her thoughts, Astinus suddenly rose to his feet and called for more light.

"For," he said coldly, staring at Laurana, "the past is lost. Your future is your own. And we have a great deal of work to do before morning."

Commander of the knights of Solamnia.

"First, I must read a communique I received from Lord Gunthar only a few hours ago." The Lord of Palanthas withdrew a scroll from the folds of his finely woven, woolen robes and spread it on the table, smoothing it carefully with his hands. Leaning his head back, he peered at it, obviously trying to bring it into focus.

Laurana—feeling certain that this must be in reply to a message of her own she had prompted Lord Amothus to send to Lord Gunthar two days earlier—bit her lip in impatience.

"It's creased," Lord Amothus said in apology. "The griffons

the elven lords have so kindly loaned us"—he bowed to Laurana, who bowed back, suppressing the urge to rip the message from his hand—"cannot be taught to carry these scrolls without rumpling them. Ah, now I can make it out. 'Lord Gunthar to Amothus, Lord of Palanthas. Greetings.' Charming man, Lord Gunthar." The Lord looked up. "He was here only last year, during Spring Dawning festival—which, by the way, takes place in three weeks, my dear. Perhaps you would grace our festivities—"

"I would be pleased to, lord, *if* any of us are here in three weeks," Laurana said, clenching her hands tightly beneath the table in an effort to remain calm.

Lord Amothus blinked, then smiled indulgently. "Certainly. The dragonarmies. Well, to continue reading. 'I am truly grieved to hear of the loss of so many of our Knighthood. Let us find comfort in the knowledge that they died victorious, fighting this great evil that darkens our lands. I feel an even greater personal grief in the loss of three of our finest leaders: Derek Crownguard, Knight of the Rose, Alfred MarKenin, Knight of the Sword, and Sturm Brightblade, Knight of the Crown." The Lord turned to Laurana. "Brightblade. He was your close friend, I believe, my dear?"

"Yes, my lord," Laurana murmured, lowering her head, letting her golden hair fall forward to hide the anguish in her eyes. It had been only a short time since they had buried Sturm in the Chamber of Paladine beneath the ruins of the High Clerist's Tower. The pain of his loss still ached.

"Continue reading, Amothus," Astinus commanded coldly. "I cannot afford to take too much time from my studies."

"Certainly, Astinus," the Lord said, flushing. He began to read again hurriedly. " 'This tragedy leaves the knights in unusual circumstances. First, the Knighthood is now made up of— as I understand—primarily Knights of the Crown—the lowest order of knights. This means that—while all have passed their tests and won their shields—they are, however, young and inexperienced. For most, this was their first battle. It also leaves us without any suitable commanders since—according to the Measure—there must be a representative from each of the three Orders of Knights in command.' "

Laurana could hear the faint jingle of armor and the rattle of swords as the knights present shifted uncomfortably. They were temporary leaders until this question of command could be settled. Closing her eyes, Laurana sighed. Please, Gunthar, she thought, let your choice be a wise one. So many have died because of political manuevering. Let this be an end to it!

" 'Therefore I appoint to fill the position of leadership of the Knights of Solamnia, Lauralanthalasa of the royal house of Qualinesti—' " The Lord paused a moment, as if uncertain he had read correctly. Laurana's eyes opened wide as she stared at him in shocked disbelief. But she was not more shocked than the knights themselves.

Lord Amothus peered vaguely at the scroll, rereading it. Then, hearing a murmur of impatience from Astinus, he hurried on—" 'who is the most experienced person currently in the field and the only one with knowledge of how to use the dragonlances. I attest to the validity of this Writ by my seal. Lord Gunthar Uth Wistan, Grand Master of the Knights of Solamnia, and so forth.' " The Lord looked up. "Congratulations, my dear—or perhaps I should say 'general.' "

Laurana sat very still. For a moment she was so filled with anger she thought she might stalk out of the room. Visions swam before her eyes—Lord Alfred's headless corpse, poor Derek dying in his madness, Sturm's peace-filled, lifeless eyes, the bodies of the knights who had died in the Tower laid out in a row. . . .

And now *she* was in command. An elfmaid from the royal household. Not even old enough—by elven standards—to be free of her father's house. A spoiled little girl who had run away from her home to "chase after" her childhood sweetheart, Tanis Half-Elven. That spoiled little girl had grown up. Fear, pain, great loss, great sorrow—she knew that—in some ways—she was older than her father now.

Turning her head, she saw Sir Markham and Sir Patrick exchange glances. Of all the Knights of the Crown, these two had served longest. She knew both men to be valiant soldiers and honorable men. They had both fought bravely at the High Clerist's Tower. Why hadn't Gunthar picked one of them, as she herself had recommended?

Sir Patrick stood up, his face dark. "I cannot accept this," he said in a low voice. "Lady Laurana is a valiant warrior, certainly, but she has never commanded men in the field."

"Have you, young knight?" Astinus asked imperturbably.

Patrick flushed. "No, but that's different. She's a wom—"

"Oh, really, Patrick!" Sir Markham laughed. He was a carefree, easy-going young man—a startling contrast to the stern and serious Patrick. "Hair on your chest doesn't make you a general. Relax! It's politics. Gunthar has made a wise move."

Laurana flushed, knowing he was right. She was a *safe* choice until Gunthar had time to rebuild the Knighthood and entrench himself firmly as leader.

"But there is no precedent for this!" Patrick continued to argue, avoiding Laurana's eyes. "I'm certain that—according to the Measure—women are not permitted in the Knighthood—"

"You are wrong," Astinus stated flatly. "And there *is* precedent. In the Third Dragonwars, a young woman was accepted into the Knighthood following the deaths of her father and her brothers. She rose to Knight of the Sword and died honorably in battle, mourned by her brethren."

No one spoke. Lord Amothus appeared extremely embarrassed—he had almost sunk beneath the table at Sir Markham's reference to hairy chests. Astinus stared coldly at Sir Patrick. Sir Markham toyed with his wine glass, glancing once at Laurana and smiling. After a brief, internal struggle, visible in his face, Sir Patrick sat back down, scowling.

Sir Markham raised his glass. "To our commander."

Laurana did not respond. She was in command. Command of what? she asked herself bitterly. The tattered remnants of the Knights of Solamnia who had been sent to Palanthas; of the hundreds that had sailed, no more than fifty survived. They had won a victory . . . but at what terrible cost? A dragon orb estroyed, the High Clerist's Tower in ruins. . . .

"Yes, Laurana," said Astinus, "they have left you to pick up the pieces."

She looked up startled, frightened of this strange man who spoke her thoughts.

"I didn't want this," she murmured through lips that felt numb.

"I don't believe any of us were sitting around praying for a war," Astinus remarked caustically. "But war has come, and now you must do what you can to win it." He rose to his feet. The Lord of Palanthas, the generals, and the Knights stood up respectfully.

Laurana remained seated, her eyes on her hands. She felt Astinus staring at her, and she stubbornly refused to look at him.

"Must you go, Astinus?" Lord Amothus asked plaintively.

"I must. My studies wait. Already I have been gone too long. You have a great deal to do now, much of it mundane and boring. You do not need me. You have your leader." He made a motion with his hand.

"What?" Laurana said, catching his gesture out of the corner of her eye. Now she looked at him, then her eyes went to the Lord of Palanthas. "Me? You can't mean that! I'm only in command of the Knights—"

"Which makes you commander of the armies of the city of Palanthas, if we so choose," the Lord said. "And if Astinus recommends you—"

"I don't," Astinus said bluntly. "I cannot recommend anyone. I do not shape history—" He stopped suddenly, and Laurana was surprised to see the mask slip from his face, revealing grief and sorrow. "That is, I have endeavored not to shape history. Sometimes, even I fail. . . ." He sighed, then regained control of himself, replacing the mask. "I have done what I came to do, given you a knowledge of the past. It may or may not be relevant to your future."

He turned to leave.

"Wait!" Laurana cried, rising. She started to take a step toward him, then faltered as the cold, stern eyes met hers, forbidding as solid stone. "You—you see—everything that is happening, as it occurs?"

"I do."

"Then you could tell us—where the dragonarmies are, what they are doing—"

"Bah! You know that as well as I do." Astinus turned away again.

Laurana cast a quick glance around the room. She saw the lord and the generals watching her with amusement. She knew she was acting like that spoiled little girl again, but she must have answers! Astinus was near the door, the servants were opening it. Casting a defiant look at the others, Laurana left the table and walked quickly across the polished marble floor, stumbling over the hem of her dress in her haste. Astinus, hearing her, stopped within the doorway.

"I have two questions," she said softly, coming near him.

"Yes," he answered, staring into her green eyes, "one in your head and one in your heart. Ask the first."

"Is there a dragon orb still in existence?"

Astinus was silent a moment. Once more Laurana saw pain

in his eyes as his ageless face appeared suddenly old. "Yes," he said finally. "I can tell you that much. One still exists. But it is beyond your ability to use or to find. Put it out of your thoughts."

"Tanis had it," Laurana persisted. "Does this mean he has lost it? Where"—she hesitated, this was the question in her heart— "where is he?"

"Put it out of your thoughts."

"What do you mean?" Laurana felt chilled by the man's frost-rimed voice.

"I do not predict the future. I see only the present as it becomes the past. Thus I have seen it since time began. I have seen love that, through its willingness to sacrifice everything, brought hope to the world. I have seen love that tried to overcome pride and a lust for power, but failed. The world is darker for its failure, but it is only as a cloud dims the sun. The sun— the love—still remains. Finally I have seen love lost in darkness. Love misplaced, misunderstood, because the lover did not know his—or her—own heart."

"You speak in riddles," Laurana said angrily.

"Do I?" Astinus asked. He bowed. "Farewell, Lauralanthalasa. My advice to you is: concentrate on your duty."

The historian walked out the door.

Laurana stood staring after him, repeating his words: "love lost in darkness." Was it a riddle or did she know the answer and simply refuse to admit it to herself, as Astinus implied?

" 'I left Tanis in Flotsam to handle matters in my absence.' " Kitiara had said those words. Kitiara—the Dragon Highlord. Kitiara—the human woman Tanis loved.

Suddenly the pain in Laurana's heart—the pain that had been there since she heard Kitiara speak those words—vanished, leaving a cold emptiness, a void of darkness like the missing constellations in the night sky. "Love lost in darkness." Tanis was lost. That is what Astinus was trying to tell her. Concentrate on your duties. Yes, she would concentrate on her duties, since that was all she had left.

Turning around to face the Lord of Palanthas and his generals, Laurana threw back her head, her golden hair glinting in the light of the candles. "I will take the leadership of the armies," she said in a voice nearly as cold as the void in her soul.

"Now *this* is stonework!" stated Flint in satisfaction, stamping on the battlements of the Old City Wall beneath his feet "Dwarves built this, no doubt about it. Look how each stone is cut with careful precision to fit perfectly within the wall, no two quite alike."

"Fascinating," said Tasslehoff, yawning. "Did dwarves build that Tower we—"

"Don't remind me!" Flint snapped. "And dwarves did *not* build the Towers of High Sorcery. They were built by the wizards themselves, who created them from the very bones of the world, raising the rocks up out of the soil with their magic."

"That's wonderful!" breathed Tas, waking up. "I wish I could have been there. How—"

"It's nothing," continued the dwarf loudly, glaring at Tas, "compared to the work of the dwarven rockmasons, who spent centuries perfecting their art. Now look at this stone. See the texture of the chisel marks—"

"Here comes Laurana," Tas said thankfully, glad to end his lesson in dwarven architecture.

Flint quit peering at the rock wall to watch Laurana walk toward them from a great dark hallway which opened onto the battlement. She was dressed once more in the armor she had worn at the High Clerist's Tower; the blood had been cleaned off the gold-decorated steel breastplate, the dents repaired. Her long, honey-colored hair flowed from beneath her red-plumed helm, gleaming in Solinari's light. She walked slowly, her eyes on the eastern horizon where the mountains were dark shadows against the starry sky. The moonlight touched her face as well. Looking at her, Flint sighed.

"She's changed," he said to Tasslehoff softly. "And elves never change. Do you remember when we met her in Qualinesti? In the fall, only six months ago. Yet it could be years—"

"She's still not over Sturm's death. It's only been a week," Tas said, his impish kender face unusually serious and thoughtful.

"It's not just that." The old dwarf shook his head. "It had something to do with that meeting she had with Kitiara, up on the wall of the High Clerist's Tower. It was something Kitiara did or said. Blast her!" the dwarf snapped viciously. "I never did trust her! Even in the old days. It didn't surprise *me* to see her in the get-up of a Dragon Highlord! I'd give a mountain of steel coins to know what she said to Laurana that snuffed the light right out of her. She was like a ghost when we brought her down from the wall, after Kitiara and her blue dragon left. I'll bet my beard," muttered the dwarf, "that it had something to do with Tanis."

"I can't believe Kitiara's a Dragon Highlord. She was always . . . always . . ." Tas groped for words, "well fun!"

"Fun?" said Flint, his brows contracting. "Maybe. But cold and selfish, too. Oh, she was charming enough when she wanted to be." Flint's voice sank to a whisper. Laurana was getting close enough to hear. "Tanis never did see it. He always believed there was more to Kitiara beneath the surface. He thought he alone knew her, that she covered herself with a hard shell to conceal her tender heart. Hah! She had as much heart as these stones."

"What's the news, Laurana?" Tas asked cheerfully as the elf-maid came up to them.

Laurana smiled down at her old friends, but—as Flint said—it was no longer the innocent, gay smile of the elfmaid who had walked beneath the aspen trees of Qualinesti. Now her smile was like the bleakness of the sun in a cold winter sky. It gave light but no warmth—perhaps because there was no matching warmth in her eyes.

"I am commander of the armies," she said flatly.

"Congratu—" began Tas, but his voice died at the sight of her face.

"There is nothing to congratulate me about," Laurana said bitterly. "What do I command? A handful of knights, stuck in a ruined bastion miles away in the Vingaard mountains, and a thousand men who stand upon the walls of this city." She clenched her gloved fist, her eyes on the eastern sky that was beginning to show the faintest glimmer of morning light. "We should be out there! Now! While the dragonarmy is still scattered and trying to regroup! We could defeat them easily. But, no, we dare not go out onto the Plains—not even with the dragonlances. For what good are they against dragons in flight? If we had a dragon orb—"

She fell silent for a moment, then drew a deep breath. Her face hardened. "Well, we don't. It's no use thinking about it. So we'll stand here, on the battlements of Palanthas, and wait for death."

"Now, Laurana," Flint remonstrated, clearing his throat gruffly, "perhaps things aren't that dark. There are good solid walls around this city. A thousand men can hold it easily. The gnomes with their catapults guard the harbor. The knights guard the only pass through the Vingaard Mountains and we've sent men to reinforce them. And we *do* have the dragonlances—a few at any rate, and Gunthar sent word more are on the way. So we can't attack dragons in flight? They'll think twice about flying over the walls—"

"That isn't enough, Flint!" Laurana sighed. "Oh, sure, we may hold the dragonarmies off for a week or two weeks or maybe even a month. But then what? What happens to us when they control the land around us? All we can do against the dragons is shut ourselves up in safe little havens. Soon this world will be nothing but tiny islands of light surrounded by vast oceans of darkness. And then—one by one—the darkness will engulf us all."

Laurana laid her head down upon her hand, resting against the wall.

"How long has it been since you've slept?" Flint asked sternly.

"I don't know," she answered. "My waking and sleeping seem mixed together. I'm walking in a dream half the time, and sleeping through reality the other half."

"Get some sleep now," the dwarf said in what Tas referred to as his Grandfather Voice. "We're turning in. Our watch is almost up."

"I can't," Laurana said, rubbing her eyes. The thought of sleep suddenly made her realize how exhausted she was. "I came to tell you—we received reports that dragons were seen, flying westward over the city of Kalaman."

"They're heading this direction then," Tas said, visualizing a map in his head.

"Whose reports?" asked the dwarf suspiciously.

"The griffons. Now don't scowl like that." Laurana smiled slightly at the sight of the dwarf's disgust. "The griffons have been a vast help to us. If the elves contribute nothing more to this war than their griffons, they will have already done a great deal."

"Griffons are dumb animals," Flint stated. "And I trust them about as far as I trust kender. Besides," the dwarf continued, ignoring Tas's indignant glare, "it doesn't make sense. The Highlords don't send dragons to attack without the armies backing them up. . . ."

"Maybe the armies aren't as disorganized as we heard."

Laurana sighed wearily. "Or maybe the dragons are simply being sent to wreak what havoc they can. Demoralize the city, lay waste to the surrounding countryside. I don't know. Look, word's spread."

Flint glanced around. Those soldiers that were off duty, were still in their places, staring eastward at the mountains whose snow-capped peaks were turning a delicate pink in the brightening dawn. Talking in low voices they were joined by others, just waking and hearing the news.

"I feared as much." Laurana sighed. "This will start a panic! I warned Lord Amothus to keep the news quiet, but the Palanthians aren't used to keeping anything quiet! There, what did I tell you?"

Looking down from the wall, the friends could see the streets starting to fill with people—half-dressed, sleepy, frightened. Watching them run from house to house, Laurana could imagine the rumors being spread.

She bit her lip, her green eyes flared in anger. "Now I'll have to pull men off the walls to get these people back into their homes. I can't have them in the streets when the dragons attack! You men, come with me!" Gesturing to a group of soldiers standing nearby, Laurana hurried away. Flint and Tas watched her disappear down the stairs, heading for the Lord's palace. Soon they saw armed patrols fanning out into the streets, trying to herd people back into their homes and quell the rising tide of panic.

"Fine lot of good that's doing!" Flint snorted. The streets were getting more crowded by the moment.

But Tas, standing on a block of stone staring out over the wall, shook his head. "It doesn't matter!" he whispered in despair. "Flint, look—"

The dwarf climbed hurriedly up to stand beside his friend. Already men were pointing and shouting, grabbing bows and spears. Here and there, the barbed silver point of the dragonlance could be seen, glinting in the torchlight.

"How many?" Flint asked, squinting.

"Ten," Tas answered slowly. "Two flights. Big dragons, too. Maybe the red ones, like we saw in Tarsis. I can't see their color against the dawn's light, but I can see riders on them. Maybe a Highlord. Maybe Kitiara . . . Gee," Tas said, struck by a sudden thought, "I hope I get to talk to her this time. It must be interesting being a Highlord—"

His words were lost in the sound of bells ringing from towers all over the city. The people in the streets, stared up at the walls where the soldiers were pointing and exclaiming. Far below them, Tas could see Laurana emerge from the Lord's palace, followed by the Lord himself and two of his generals. The kender could tell from the set of her shoulders that Laurana was furious. She gestured at the bells, apparently wanting them silenced. But it was too late. The people of Palanthas went wild with terror. And most of the inexperienced soldiers were in nearly as bad a state as the civilians. The sound of shrieks and wails and hoarse calls rose up into the air. Grim memories of Tarsis came back to Tas—people trampled to death in the streets, houses exploding in flames.

The kender turned slowly around. "I guess I don't want to talk to Kitiara," he said softly, brushing his hand across his eyes as he watched the dragons fly closer and closer. "I don't want to know what it's like being a Highlord, because it must be sad and dark and horrible. . . . Wait—"

Tas stared eastward. He couldn't believe his eyes, so he leaned far out, perilously close to falling over the edge of the wall.

"Flint!" he shouted, waving his arms.

"What is it?" Flint snapped. Catching hold of Tas by the belt of his blue leggings, the dwarf hauled the excited kender back in with jerk.

"It's like in Pax Tharkas!" Tas babbled incoherently. "Like Huma's tomb. Like Fizban said! They're here! They've come!"

"Who's here!" Flint roared in exasperation.

Jumping up and down in excitement, his pouches bouncing around wildly, Tas turned without answering and dashed off, leaving the dwarf fuming on the stairs, calling out, "Who's here, you rattlebrain?"

"Laurana!" shouted Tas's shrill voice, splitting the early morning air like a slightly off-key trumpet. "Laurana, they've come! They're here! Like Fizban said! Laurana!"

Cursing the kender beneath his breath, Flint stared back out to the east. Then, glancing around swiftly, the dwarf slipped a hand inside a vest pocket. Hurriedly he drew out a pair of glasses and—looking around again to make certain no one was watching him—he slipped them on.

Now he could make out what had been nothing more than a haze of pink light broken by the darker, pointed masses of the

———

mountain range. The dwarf drew a deep, trembling breath. His eyes dimmed with tears. Quickly he snatched the glasses off his nose and put them back into their case, slipping them back into his pocket. But he'd worn the glasses just long enough to see the dawn touch the wings of dragons with a pink light—pink glinting off silver.

"Put your weapons down, lads," Flint said to the men around him, mopping his eyes with one of the kender's handkerchiefs. "Praise be to Reorx. Now we have a chance. Now we have a chance. . . ."

8

The Oath
of the Dragons.

As the silver dragons settled
to the ground on the outskirts of the great city of Palanthas,
their wings filled the morning sky with a blinding radiance.
The people crowded the walls to stare out uneasily at the beautiful, magnificent creatures.

At first the people had been so terrified of the huge beasts,
that they were intent on driving them away, even when
Laurana assured them that these dragons were not evil. Finally
Astinus himself emerged from his library and coldly informed
Lord Amothus that these dragons would not harm them.

Reluctantly the people of Palanthas laid down their weapons.

Laurana knew, however, that the people would have believed Astinus if he told them the sun would rise at midnight. They did *not* believe in the dragons.

It wasn't until Laurana herself walked out of the city gates and straight into the arms of a man who had been riding one of the beautiful silver dragons that the people begin to think there might be something to this children's story after all.

"Who is that man? Who has brought the dragons to us? Why have the dragons come?"

Jostling and shoving, the people leaned over the wall, asking questions and listening to the wrong answers. Out in the valley, the dragons slowly fanned their wings to keep their circulation going in the chill morning.

As Laurana embraced the man, another person climbed down off one of the dragons—a woman whose hair gleamed as silver as the dragon's wings. Laurana embraced this woman, too. Then, to the wonder of the people, Astinus led the three of them to the great library, where they were admitted by the Aesthetics. The huge doors shut behind them.

The people were left to mill about, buzzing with questions and casting dubious glances at the dragons sitting before their city walls.

Then the bells rang out once more. Lord Amothus was calling a meeting. Hurriedly the people left the walls to fill the city square before the Lord's palace as he came out onto a balcony to answer their questions.

"These are silver dragons," he shouted, "good dragons who have joined us in our battle against the evil dragons as in the legend of Huma. The dragons have been brought to our city by—"

Whatever else the Lord intended to say was lost in cheering. The bells rang out again, this time in celebration. People flooded the streets, singing and dancing. Finally, after a futile attempt to continue, the Lord simply declared the day a holiday and returned to his palace.

The following is an excerpt from the Chronicles, A History of Krynn, *as recorded by Astinus of Palanthas. It can be found under the heading: "The Oath of the Dragons."*

As I, Astinus, write these words, I look on the face of the

elflord, Gilthanas, younger son of Solostaran, Speaker of the
Suns, lord of the Qualinesti. Gilthanas's face is very much like
his sister Laurana's face, and not just in family resemblance.
Both have the delicate features and ageless quality of all elves.
But these two are different. Both faces are marked with a sorrow not to be seen on the faces of elves living on Krynn.
Although I fear that, before this war is ended, many elves will
have this same look. And perhaps this is not a bad thing, for it
seems that, finally, the elves are learning that they are part of
this world, not above it.

To one side of Gilthanas sits his sister. To the other sits one of
the most beautiful women I have seen walk on Krynn. She
appears to be an elfmaid, a Wilder elf. But she does not deceive
my eyes with her magic arts. She was never born of woman—
elf or no. She is a dragon—a silver dragon, sister of the Silver
Dragon who was beloved of Huma, Knight of Solamnia. It has
been Silvara's fate to fall in love with a mortal, as did her sister.
But, unlike Huma, this mortal, Gilthanas, cannot accept his
fate. He looks at her . . . she looks at him. Instead of love, I see
a smoldering anger within him that is slowly poisoning both
their souls.

Silvara speaks. Her voice is sweet and musical. The light of
my candle gleams in her beautiful silver hair and in her deep
night-blue eyes.

"After I gave Theros Ironfeld the power to forge the
dragonlances within the heart of the Monument of the Silver
Dragon," Silvara tells me, "I spent much time with the companions before they took the lances to the Council of Whitestone. I
showed them through the Monument, I showed them the paintings of the Dragon War, which picture good dragons—silver
and gold and bronze—fighting the evil dragons.

" 'Where are your people?' the companions asked me.
'Where are the good dragons? Why aren't they helping us in
our time of need?'

"I held out against their questions, as long as I could . . ."

Here Silvara stops speaking and looks at Gilthanas with her
heart in her eyes. He does not meet her gaze but stares at the
floor. Silvara sighs and resumes her story.

"Finally, I could resist his—their—pressure no longer. I told
them about the Oath.

"When Takhisis, the Queen of Darkness, and her evil
dragons were banished, the good dragons left the land to main-

tain the balance between good and evil. Made of the world, we returned to the world, sleeping an ageless sleep. We would have remained asleep, in a world of dreams, but then came the Cataclysm and Takhisis found her way back into the world again.

"Long had she planned for this return, should fate give it to her, and she was prepared. Before Paladine was aware of her, Takhisis woke the evil dragons from their sleep and ordered them to slip into the deep and secret places of the world and steal the eggs of the good dragons, who slept on, unaware. . . .

"The evil dragons brought the eggs of their brethren to the city of Sanction where the dragonarmies were forming. Here, in the volcanoes known as the Lords of Doom, the eggs of the good dragons were hidden.

"Great was the grief of the good dragons when Paladine awoke them from their sleep and they discovered what had occurred. They went to Takhisis to find out what price they would have to pay for the return of their unborn children. It was a terrible price. Takhisis demanded an oath. Each of the good dragons must swear that they would not participate in the war she was about to wage on Krynn. It was the good dragons who had helped bring about her defeat in the last war. This time she meant to insure that they would not become involved."

Here Silvara looks at me pleadingly, as if *I* were to judge them. I shake my head sternly. Far be it from me to judge anyone. I am a historian.

She continues:

"What could we do? Takhisis told us they would murder our children as they slept in their eggs unless we took the Oath. Paladine could not help us. The choice was ours . . . "

Silvara's head droops, her hair hiding her face. I can hear tears choke her voice. Her words are barely audible to me.

"We took the Oath."

She cannot continue, that is obvious. After staring at her for a moment, Gilthanas clears his throat and begins to speak, his voice harsh.

"I—that is—Theros and my sister and I, finally persuaded Silvara that this Oath was wrong. There must be a way, we said, to rescue the eggs of the good dragons. Perhaps a small force of men might be able to steal the eggs back. Silvara was not convinced that I was right, but she did agree—after much talking—to take me to Sanction so that I could see for myself if such a plan might work.

"Our journey was long and difficult. Someday I may relate the dangers we faced, but I cannot now. I am too weary and we do not have time. The dragonarmies are reorganizing. We can catch them offguard, if we attack soon. I can see Laurana burning with impatience, eager to pursue them, even as we are speaking. So I will make our tale short.

"Silvara—in her 'elven form' as you see her now—"

The bitterness in the elflord's voice cannot be expressed.

"—and I were captured outside of Sanction and made prisoners of the Dragon Highlord, Ariakas."

Gilthanas's fist clenches, his face is pale with anger and fear.

"Lord Verminaard was nothing, nothing compared to Lord Ariakas. This man's evil power is immense! And he is as intelligent as he is cruel, for it is *his* strategy that controls the dragonarmies and has led them to victory after victory.

"The suffering we endured at his hands, I cannot describe. I do not believe I can *ever* relate what they did to us!"

The young elflord trembles violently. Silvara starts to reach out a hand to comfort him, but he draws away from her and continues his story.

"Finally—with help—we escaped. We were in Sanction itself—a hideous town, built in the valley formed by the volcanoes—the Lords of Doom. These mountains tower over all, their foul smoke corrupts the air. The buildings are all new and modern, constructed with the blood of slaves. Built into the sides of the mountains is a temple to Takhisis, the Dark Queen. The dragon eggs are held deep within the heart of the volcanoes. It was here, into the temple of the Dark Queen, that Silvara and I made our way.

"Can I describe the temple, except to say it is a building of darkness and of flame? Tall pillars, carved out of the burning rock, soar into the sulphurous caverns. By secret ways, known only to the priests of Takhisis themselves, we traveled, descending lower and lower. You ask who helped us? I cannot say, for her life would be forfeit. I will add only that some god must have been watching over us."

Here Silvara interrupts to murmur, "Paladine," but Gilthanas brushes that aside with a gesture.

"We came to the very bottom chambers and here we found the eggs of the good dragons. At first it seemed all was well. I had . . . a plan. It matters little now, but I saw how we might

---

have been able to rescue the eggs. As I said, it matters little. Chamber after chamber we passed, and the shining eggs, the eggs tinged with silver, gold, and bronze lay gleaming in the fire's light. And then . . ."

The elflord pauses. His face, already paler than death, grows more pallid still. Fearing he might faint, I beckon to one of the Aesthetics to bring him wine. On taking a sip, he rallies and keeps on talking. But I can tell by the far-off look in his eyes that he sees the remembered horror of what he witnessed. As for Silvara—I will write of her in its place.

Gilthanas continues:

"We came to a chamber and found there . . . not eggs . . . nothing but the shells . . . shattered, broken. Silvara cried out in anger, and I feared we might be discovered. Neither of us knew what this portended, but we both felt a chill in our blood that not even the heat of the volcano could warm."

Gilthanas pauses. Silvara begins to sob, very softly. He looks at her and I see—for the first time—love and compassion in his eyes.

"Take her out," he tells one of the Aesthetics. "She must rest." The Aesthetics lead her gently from the room. Gilthanas licks lips that are cracked and dry, then speaks softly.

"What happened next will haunt me, even after death. Nightly I dream of it. I have not slept since but that I waken, screaming.

"Silvara and I stood before the chamber with the shattered eggs, staring at it, wondering . . . when we heard the sound of chanting coming from the flame-lit corridor.

" 'The words of magic!' Silvara said.

"Cautiously we crept nearer, both of us frightened, yet drawn by some horrid fascination. Closer and closer we came—and then we could see . . . "

He shuts his eyes, he sobs. Laurana lays her hand on his arm, her eyes soft with mute sympathy. Gilthanas regains control and goes on.

"Inside a cavern room, at the bottom of the volcano, stands an altar to Takhisis. What it may have been carved to represent, I could not tell, for it was so covered with green blood and black slime that it seemed a horrid growth springing from the rock. Around the altar were robed figures—dark clerics of Takhisis and magic-users wearing the Black Robes. Silvara and I watched in awe as a dark-robed cleric brought forth a shining golden dragon egg and placed it upon that foul altar. Joining hands, the Black Robed magic-users and the dark clerics began a chant. The words burned the mind. Silvara and I clung to each other, fearing we would be driven mad by the evil we could feel but could not understand.

"And then . . . then the golden egg upon the altar began to darken. As we watched, it turned to a hideous green and then to black. Silvara began to tremble.

"The blackened egg upon the altar cracked open . . . and a larva-like creature emerged from the shell. It was loathsome and corrupt to look upon, and I retched at the sight. My only thought was to flee this horror, but Silvara realized what was happening and she refused to leave. Together we watched as the larva split its slime-covered skin and from its body came the evil forms of . . . draconians."

There is a gasp of shock at this statement. Gilthanas's head sinks into his hands. He cannot continue. Laurana puts her arms around him, comforting him, and he holds onto her hands. Finally he draws a shuddering breath.

"Silvara and I . . . were nearly discovered. We escaped Sanction—with help once again—and, more dead than alive, we traveled paths unknown to man or elf to the ancient haven of the good dragons."

Gilthanas sighs. A look of peace comes to his face.

"Compared to the horrors we had endured, this was like sweet rest after a night of feverish nightmares. It was difficult to imagine, amid the beauty of the place, that what we had seen really occurred. And when Silvara told the dragons what was happening to their eggs, they refused at first to believe it. Some even accused Silvara of making it up to try to win their aid. But, deep within their hearts, all knew she spoke truly, and so—at last—they admitted that they had been deceived and that the Oath was no longer binding.

"The good dragons have come to aid us now. They are flying to all parts of the land, offering their help. They have returned to the Monument of the Dragon, to aid in forging the dragonlances just as they came to Huma's aid long ago. And they have brought with them the Greater Lances that can be mounted on the dragons themselves, as we saw in the paintings. Now we may ride the dragons into battle and challenge the Dragon Highlords in the sky."

Gilthanas adds more, a few minor details that I need not

record here. Then his sister leads him from the library to the palace, where he and Silvara may find what rest they can. I fear it will be long before the terror fades for them, if it ever does. Like so much that is beautiful in the world, it may be that their love will fall beneath the darkness that spreads its foul wings over Krynn.

Thus ends the writing of Astinus of Palanthas on the Oath of the Dragons. A footnote reveals that further details of the journey of Gilthanas and Silvara into Sanction, their adventures there, and the tragic history of their love were recorded by Astinus at a later date and may be found in subsequent volumes of his Chronicles.

Laurana sat late at night, writing up her orders for the morrow. Only a day had passed since the arrival of Gilthanas and the silver dragons, but already her plans for pressing the beleaguered enemy were taking shape. Within a few days more, she would lead flights of dragons with mounted riders, wielding the new dragonlances, into battle.

She hoped to secure Vingaard Keep first, freeing the prisoners and slaves held there. Then she planned to push on south and east, driving the dragonarmies before her. Finally she would catch them between the hammer of her troops and the anvil of the Dargaard Mountains that divided Solamnia from Estwilde. If she could retake Kalaman and its harbor, she could cut the supply lines the dragonarmy depended on for its survival on this part of the continent.

So intent was Laurana on her plans that she ignored the ringing challenge of the guard outside her door, nor did she hear the answer. The door opened, but, assuming it was one of her aides, she did not look up from her work until she had completed detailing her orders.

Only when the person who entered took the liberty of sitting down in a chair across from her did Laurana glance up, startled.

"Oh," she said, flushing, "Gilthanas, forgive me. I was so involved. . . . I thought you were . . . but, never mind. How are you feeling? I was worried—"

"I'm all right, Laurana," Gilthanas said abruptly. "I was just more tired than I realized and I—I haven't slept very well since Sanction." Falling silent, he sat staring at the maps she had spread on her table. Absently he picked up a freshly sharpened quill pen and began to smooth the feather with his fingers.

"What is it, Gilthanas?" Laurana asked softly.

Her brother looked up at her and smiled sadly. "You know me too well," he said. "I never could hide anything from you, not even when we were children."

"Is it Father?" Laurana asked fearfully. "Have you heard something—"

"No, I've heard nothing about our people," Gilthanas said, "except what I told you—that they have allied with the humans and are working together to drive the dragonarmies from the Ergoth Isles and from Sancrist."

"It was all because of Alhana," Laurana murmured. "She convinced them that they could no longer live apart from the world. She even convinced Porthios. . . ."

"I gather she has convinced him of more than that?" Gilthanas asked without looking at his sister. He began to poke holes in the parchment with the point of the quill.

"There has been talk of a marriage," Laurana said slowly. "If so, I am certain it would be a marriage of convenience only—to unite our people. I cannot imagine Porthios has it in his heart to love anyone, even a woman as beautiful as Alhana. As for the elven princess herself—"

Gilthanas sighed. "Her heart is buried in the High Clerist's Tower with Sturm."

"How did you know?" Laurana looked at him, astonished.

"I saw them together in Tarsis," Gilthanas said. "I saw his face—and I saw hers. I knew about the Starjewel, too. Since he obviously wanted to keep it secret, I did not betray him. He was a fine man," Gilthanas added gently. "I am proud to have known him, and I never thought I would say that of a human."

Laurana swallowed, brushing her hand across her eyes. "Yes," she whispered huskily, "but that wasn't what you came to tell me."

"No," Gilthanas said, "although perhaps it leads into it." For a moment he sat in silence, as if making up his mind. Then he drew a breath. "Laurana, something happened in Sanction that I did not tell Astinus. I won't tell anyone else, ever, if you ask me not to—"

"Why me?" Laurana said, turning pale. Her hand trembling, she laid down her pen.

Gilthanas seemed not to have heard her. He stared fixedly at the map as he spoke. "When—when we were escaping from Sanction, we had to go back to the palace of Lord Ariakas. I cannot tell you more than that, for to do so would betray the one who saved our lives many times and who lives in danger there still, doing what she can to save as many of her people as possible.

"The night we were there, in hiding, waiting to escape, we overheard a conversation between Lord Ariakas and one of his Highlords. It was a woman, Laurana"—Gilthanas looked up at her now—"a human woman named Kitiara."

Laurana said nothing. Her face was deathly white, her eyes large and colorless in the lamplight.

Gilthanas sighed, then leaned near her and placed his hand on hers. Her flesh was so cold, she might have been a corpse, and he saw, then, that she knew what he was about to say.

"I remembered what you told me before we left Qualinesti, that this was the human woman Tanis Half-Elven loved—sister to Caramon and Raistlin. I recognized her from what I had heard the brothers say about her. I would have recognized her anyway—she and Raistlin, particularly, bear a family resemblance. She—she was talking of Tanis, Laurana." Gilthanas stopped, wondering whether or not he could go on. Laurana sat perfectly still, her face a mask of ice.

"Forgive me for causing you pain, Laurana, but you must know," Gilthanas said at last. "Kitiara laughed about Tanis with this Lord Ariakas and said"—Gilthanas flushed—"I cannot repeat what she said. But they are lovers, Laurana, that much I can tell you. She made it graphically clear. She asked Ariakas's permission to have Tanis promoted to the rank of general in the dragonarmy . . . in return for some sort of information he was going to provide—something about a Green Gemstone Man—"

"Stop," Laurana said without a voice.

"I'm sorry, Laurana!" Gilthanas squeezed her hand, his face filled with sorrow. "I know how much you love him. I—I understand now what it is like to—to love someone that much." He closed his eyes, his head bowed. "I understand what it is like to have that love betrayed. . . ."

"Leave me, Gilthanas," Laurana whispered.

Patting her hand in silent sympathy, the elflord rose and walked softly from the room, shutting the door behind him.

Laurana sat without moving for long moments. Then, pressing her lips firmly together, she picked up her pen and continued writing where she had left off before her brother entered.

9
Victory.

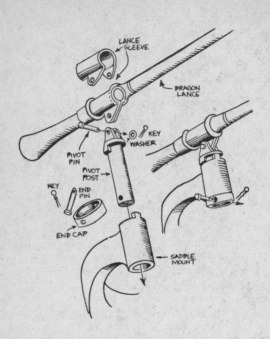

LANCE
SLEEVE

DRAGON
LANCE

KEY
WASHER

PIVOT
PIN

PIVOT
POST

KEY

END
PIN

END CAP

SADDLE
MOUNT

"Let me give you a boost,"
Tas said helpfully.

"I . . . no! Wait!" Flint yelled. But it did no good. The energetic kender had already grabbed hold of the dwarf's boot and heaved, propelling Flint head first right into the hard-muscled body of the young bronze dragon. Hands flailing wildly, Flint caught hold of the harness on the dragon's neck and hung on for dear life, revolving slowly in the air like a sack on a hook.

"What *are* you doing?" Tas asked in disgust, gazing up at Flint. "This is no time to play! Here, let me help—"

"Stop it! Let go!" roared Flint, kicking at Tasslehoff's hands. "Get back! Get back, I say!"

"Get up yourself, then," Tas said, hurt, backing up.

Puffing and red-faced, the dwarf dropped to the ground. "I'll get on in my own good time!" he said, glaring at the kender. "Without help from *you!*"

"Well, you better do it quickly!" Tas shouted, waving his arms. "Because the others are already mounted!"

The dwarf cast a glance back at the big bronze dragon and folded his arms across his chest stubbornly. "I've got to give this some thought—"

"Oh, come on, Flint!" Tas begged. "You're only stalling. I want to *fly!* Please, Flint, hurry!" The kender brightened. "I could go by myself. . . ."

"You'll do no such thing!" The dwarf snorted. "The war's *finally* turning in our favor. Send a kender up on a dragon and that'd be the end. We could just hand the Highlord the keys to the city. Laurana said the only way you'd fly is with me—"

"Then get on!" Tas yelled shrilly. "Or the war will be over! I'll be a grandfather before you move from that spot!"

"You a grandfather," Flint grumbled, glancing once more at the dragon, who was staring at him with a very unfriendly eye—or so the dwarf imagined. "Why, the day you're a grandfather is the day my beard will fall out—"

Khirsah, the dragon, gazed down at the two with amused impatience. A young dragon—as dragons count their time on Krynn—Khirsah agreed with the kender: it was time to fly, time to fight. He had been one of the first to answer the Call that went out to all the gold and silver, bronze and brass dragons. The fire of battle burned hot within him.

Yet, young as he was, the bronze dragon held a great reverence and respect for the elders of the world. Though vastly older than the dwarf in years, Khirsah saw in Flint one who had led a long, full, rich life; one worthy of respect. But, Khirsah thought with a sigh, if I don't do something, the kender's right—the battle *will* be over!

"Pardon me, Respected Sire," Khirsah interrupted, using a term of high respect among dwarves, "may I be of assistance?"

Startled, Flint whirled around to see who spoke.

The dragon bowed its great head. "Honored and Respected Sire," Khirsah said again, in dwarven.

Amazed, Flint stumbled backwards, tripping over Tasslehoff

and sending the kender tumbling to the ground in a heap.

The dragon snaked forth his huge head and, gently taking hold of the kender's fur vest in his great teeth, lifted him to his feet like a new-born kitten.

"Well, I-I don't know," stammered Flint, flushing in pleased embarrassment at being thus addressed by a dragon. "You might . . . and then again you might not." Recovering his dignity, the dwarf was determined not to act overawed. "I've done this a lot, mind you. Riding dragons is nothing new to me. It's just, well, just that I've—"

"You've never ridden a dragon before in your life!" Tasslehoff said indignantly. "And—ouch!"

"Just that I've had more important things on my mind lately," Flint said loudly, punching Tas in the ribs, "and it may take me a while to get the hang of it again."

"Certainly, Sire," Khirsah said without the ghost of a smile. "May I call you Flint?"

"You may," said the dwarf gruffly.

"And I'm Tasslehoff Burrfoot," said the kender, extending his small hand. "Flint never goes anywhere without me. Oh, I guess you haven't any hand to shake with. Never mind. What's your name?"

"My name to mortals is Fireflash." The dragon gracefully bowed his head. "And now, Sir Flint, if you will instruct your squire, the kender—"

"*Squire!*" Tas repeated, shocked. But the dragon ignored him.

"Instruct your squire to come up here; I will help him prepare the saddle and the lance for you."

Flint stroked his beard thoughtfully. Then, he made a grand gesture.

"You, squire," he said to Tas, who was staring at him with his mouth open, "get up there and do as you're told."

"I—you—we—" Tas stuttered. But the kender never finished what he had been about to say because the dragon had lifted him off the ground again. Teeth clamped firmly in the kender's fur vest, Khirsah raised him up and plopped him back onto the saddle that was strapped to the dragon's bronze body.

So enchanted was Tas with the idea of actually being atop a dragon that he hushed up, which is just what Khirsah had intended.

"Now, Tasslehoff Burrfoot," said the dragon, "you were trying to boost your master up into the saddle backwards. The correct position is the one you are in now. The metal lance mounting must be on the front right side of the rider, sitting squarely forward of my right wing joint and above my right fore-shoulder. Do you see?"

"Yes, I see!" called Tas in high excitement.

"The shield, which you see on the ground, will protect you from most forms of dragonbreath—"

"Whoah!" shouted the dwarf, crossing his arms and looking stubborn once more. "What do you mean *most* forms? And how am I supposed to fly and hold a lance *and* a shield all at the same time? Not to mention the fact that the blasted shield's bigger than me and the kender put together—"

"I thought you had done this before, *Sir Flint!*" Tas yelled.

The dwarf's face went red with rage and he let out a bellow, but Khirsah cut in smoothly.

"Sir Flint probably isn't accustomed to this newer model, Squire Burrfoot. The shield fits over the lance. The lance itself fits through that hole and the shield rests on the saddle and slides from side to side on the track. When attacked, you simply duck behind it."

"Hand me the shield, Sir Flint!" the kender yelled.

Grumbling, the dwarf stumped over to where the huge shield lay on the ground. Groaning with the weight, he managed to lift it up and haul it over to the dragon's side. With the dragon's help, the dwarf and the kender between them managed to get the shield mounted. Then Flint went back for the dragonlance. Lugging it back, he thrust the tip of the lance up to Tas, who caught hold of it and—after nearly losing his balance and tumbling overboard—pushed the lance through the hole in the shield. When the pivot locked into position, the lance was counterbalanced and swung lightly and easily, guided by the kender's small hand.

"This is great!" Tas said, experimenting. "Wham! There goes one dragon! Wham! There goes another. I—oh!" Tas stood up on the dragon's back, balanced lightly as the lance itself. "Flint! Hurry! They're getting ready to leave. I can see Laurana! She's riding that big silver dragon and she's flying this way, checking the line. They're going to be signaling in a minute! Hurry, Flint!" Tas began jumping up and down in excitement.

"First, Sir Flint," said Khirsah, "you must put on the padded vest. There . . . that's right. Put the strap through that buckle.

No, not that one. The other—there, you have it."

"You look like a woolly mammoth I saw once." Tas giggled. "Did I ever tell you that story? I—"

"Confound it!" Flint roared, barely able to walk, engulfed in the heavy, fur-lined vest. "This is no time for any of your hare-brained stories." The dwarf came nose-tip to nose-tip with the dragon. "Very well, beast! How do I get up? And mind you—don't you dare lay a tooth on me!"

"Certainly not, Sire," Khirsah said in deep respect. Bowing his head, the dragon extended one bronze wing full length upon the ground.

"Well, that's more like it!" Flint said. Smoothing his beard with pride, he shot a smug glance at the stunned kender. Then, solemnly mounting the dragon's wing, Flint ascended, regally taking his place at the front of the saddle.

"There's the signal!" Tas shrieked, leaping back into the saddle behind Flint. Kicking his heels against the dragon's flanks, he yelled, "Let's go! Let's go!"

"Not so fast," said Flint, coolly testing the workings of the dragonlance. "Hey! How do I steer?"

"You indicate which direction you want me to turn by pulling on the reins," Khirsah said, watching for the signal. There it was.

"Ah, I see," said Flint, reaching down. "After all, I *am* in charge—ulp!"

"Certainly, Sire!" Khirsah leaped into the air, spreading his great wings to catch the rising currents of air that floated up the face of the small cliff they stood upon.

"Wait, the reins—" Flint cried, grasping at them as they slid out of his reach.

Smiling to himself, Khirsah pretended not to hear.

The good dragons and the knights who rode them were gathered on the rolling foothills east of the Vingaard Mountains. Here, the chill winter winds had given way to warm breezes from the north, melting the frost from the ground. The rich smell of growth and renewal perfumed the air as the dragons rose in flashing arcs to take their places in formation.

It was a sight that took the breath away. Tasslehoff knew he would remember it forever—and maybe even beyond that. Bronze and silver, brass and copper wings flared in the morning light. The Greater Dragonlances, mounted on the saddles, glittered in the sun. The knights' armor shone brilliantly. The Kingfisher flag with its golden thread sparkled against the blue sky.

The past few weeks had been glorious. As Flint said, it seemed the tide of war was finally flowing in their direction.

The Golden General, as Laurana came to be called by her troops, had forged an army seemingly out of nothing. The Palanthians, caught up in the excitement, rallied to her cause. She won the respect of the Knights of Solamnia with her bold ideas and firm, decisive actions. Laurana's ground forces surged out of Palanthas, flowing across the plain, pressing the unorganized armies of the Dragon Highlord, known as the Dark Lady, into panic-stricken flight.

Now, with victory after victory behind them and the dragonarmies fleeing before them, the men considered the war as good as won.

But Laurana knew better. They had yet to fight the dragons of the Highlord. Where these were and why they had not fought before was something Laurana and her officers couldn't figure out. Day after day, she held the knights and their mounts in readiness, prepared to take to the air.

And now that day had come. The dragons had been sighted—flights of blues and reds reportedly heading westward to stop the insolent general and her rag-tag army.

In a shimmering chain of silver and bronze, the Dragons of Whitestone, as they were called, soared across the Solamnic Plain. Although all the dragon-mounted knights had been trained in flight as much as time allowed (with the exception of the dwarf who steadfastly refused), this world of wispy, low-hanging clouds and rushing air was still new and foreign to them.

Their banners whipped about wildly. The foot soldiers beneath them seemed no more than bugs crawling across the grasslands. To some of the knights, flying was an exhilarating experience. To others, it was a test of every bit of courage they possessed.

But always before them, leading them in spirit and by example, flew Laurana upon the great silver dragon her brother had ridden from the Dragon Isles. The sunlight itself was not more golden than the hair that streamed out from beneath her helm. She had become a symbol to them like the dragonlance itself— slender and delicate, fair and deadly. They would have followed her to the Gates of the Abyss itself.

Tasslehoff, peering over Flint's shoulder, could see Laurana ahead of them. She rode at the head of the line, sometimes looking back to make certain everyone was keeping up, sometimes bending down to consult with her silver mount. She seemed to have things well under control, so Tas decided he could relax and enjoy the ride. It was truly one of the most wondrous experiences of his life. Tears streaked his wind-blown face as he stared down in absolute joy.

The map-loving kender had found the perfect map.

Below him was spread—in tiny, perfect detail—rivers and trees, hills and valleys, towns and farms. More than anything in the world, Tas wished he could capture the sight and keep it forever.

Why not? he wondered suddenly. Clinging to the saddle with his knees and thighs, the kender let go of Flint and began rummaging around in his pouches. Dragging out a sheet of parchment, he rested it firmly against the dwarf's back and began to draw on it with a piece of charcoal.

"Quit wiggling!" he shouted at Flint, who was still trying to grab the reins.

"What're you doing, you doorknob?" the dwarf yelled, pawing frantically at Tas behind his back like an itch he couldn't scratch.

"I'm making a map!" Tas yelled in ecstasy. "The *perfect* map! I'll be famous. Look! There are our own troops, like little ants. And there's Vingaard Keep! Stop moving! You made me mess up."

Groaning, Flint gave up trying to either grasp the reins or brush away the kender. He decided he better concentrate on keeping a firm grip on both the dragon and his breakfast. He had made the mistake of looking down. Now he stared straight ahead, shivering, his body rigid. The hair from the mane of a griffon that decorated his helm whipped about his face wildly in the rushing wind. Birds wheeled in the skies *beneath* him. Flint decided then and there that dragons were going on his list with boats and horses as Things to Avoid at All Costs.

"Oh!" Tas gasped in excitement. "There are the dragonarmies! It's a battle! And I can see the whole thing!" The kender leaned over in the saddle, peering down. Now and again, through the rushing eddies of air, he thought he could hear the clash of armor and cries and shouts. "Say, could we fly a bit closer? I—whoops! Oh, no! My map!"

Khirsah had made a sudden, swooping dive. The force ripped the parchment from Tas's hands. Forlornly he watched it flutter away from him like a leaf. But he hadn't time to feel sad, for suddenly he felt Flint's body go even more rigid than before.

"What? What is it?" Tas yelled.

Flint was shouting something and pointing. Tas tried desperately to see and hear, but at that moment they flew into a low-hanging cloud and the kender couldn't see his nose in front of his face, as the gully dwarves said.

Then Khirsah emerged from the cloud bank and Tas saw.

"Oh my!" said the kender in awe. Below them, bearing down on the small antlike troops of men, flew line after line of dragons. Their red and blue leathery wings spread like evil banners as they dove down upon the helpless armies of the Golden General.

Tasslehoff could see the solid lines of men waver and break as the terrible dragonfear swept over them. But there was nowhere to run, nowhere to hide on the broad grasslands. This is why the dragons had waited, Tas realized, sick with the thought of the fire and lightning breath exploding among the unprotected troops.

"We've got to stop them—oof!"

Khirsah wheeled so suddenly that Tas nearly swallowed his tongue. The sky flipped over on its side and for an instant the kender had the most interesting sensation of falling *up.* More by instinct than conscious thought, Tas grabbed hold of Flint's belt, remembering suddenly that he was supposed to have strapped himself in as Flint had done. Well, he would do so next time.

If there was a next time. The wind roared around him, the ground spun below him as the dragon spiraled downward. Kenders were fond of new experiences—and this was certainly one of the most exciting—but Tas *did* wish the ground wasn't rushing up to meet them quite so *fast!*

"I didn't mean we had to stop them *right now!*" Tas shouted to Flint. Glancing up—or was it down?—he could see the other dragons far above them, no, below them. Things were getting all muddled. Now the dragons were *behind* them! They were out here in front! Alone! What *was* Flint doing?

"Not so fast! Slow this thing down!" he yelled at Flint. "You've gotten ahead of everybody! Even Laurana!"

The dwarf would have liked nothing better than to slow the dragon down. That last swoop had tossed the reins within his reach and now he was tugging with all his might, shouting "Whoah, beast, whoah!" which he dimly remembered was supposed to work with horses. But it wasn't working with the dragon.

It was no comfort to the terrified dwarf to notice that he wasn't the only one having trouble managing the dragons. Behind him, the delicate line of bronze and silver broke as if by some silent signal, as the dragons veered off into small groups—flights—of twos and threes.

Frantically the knights jerked on the reins, endeavoring to pull the dragons back into straight and orderly cavalry rows. But the dragons knew better—the sky was their domain. Fighting in the air was far different from fighting on the ground. They would show these horse-riders how to fight on dragonback.

Spinning gracefully, Khirsah dove into another cloud, and Tas instantly lost all sense of up or down as the thick fog enveloped him. Then the sunlit sky exploded before his eyes as the dragon burst out. Now he knew which way was up and which was down. *Down* was, in fact, getting uncomfortably close!

Then Flint roared. Startled, Tas looked up and saw that they were heading straight into a flight of blue dragons who—intent upon pursuing a group of panic-stricken foot soldiers—hadn't seen them yet.

"The lance! The lance!" Tas shouted.

Flint grappled with the lance, but he didn't have time to adjust it or set it properly against his shoulder. Not that it mattered. The blue dragons still hadn't seen them. Gliding out of the cloud, Khirsah fell in behind them. Then, like a bronze flame, the young dragon flashed over the group of blues, aiming for their leader—a big blue dragon with a blue-helmed rider. Diving swiftly and silently, Khirsah struck the lead dragon with all four murderously sharp talons.

The force of the impact threw Flint forward in his harness. Tas landed on top of him, flattening the dwarf. Frantically, Flint struggled to sit up, but Tas had one arm wrapped around him tightly. Beating the dwarf on the helm with the other, Tas was shouting encouragement to the dragon.

"That was great! Hit him again!" shrieked the kender, wild with excitement, pounding Flint on the head.

Swearing loudly in dwarven, Flint flung Tas off him. At that moment, Khirsah soared upwards, darting into another cloud before the flight of blues could react to his attack.

Khirsah waited for an instant, perhaps to give his shaken riders time to pull themselves together. Flint sat up and Tas clasped his arms around the dwarf tightly. He thought Flint looked strange, sort of gray-colored and oddly preoccupied. But then this certainly wasn't a normal experience, Tas reminded himself. Before he could ask Flint if he felt all right, Khirsah dove out of the cloud once more.

Tas could see the blue dragons below them. The lead dragon had pulled up in mid-air, hovering on his great wings. The blue was shaken and wounded slightly; there was blood on the rear flanks where Khirsah's sharp talons had punctured the dragon's tough, scaly hide. The dragon and his blue-helmed rider were both scanning the skies, searching for their attacker. Suddenly the rider pointed.

Risking a quick glance behind him, Tas caught his breath. The sight was magnificent. Bronze and silver flashed in the sun as the Whitestone Dragons broke out of the cloud cover and descended screaming upon the flight of blues. Instantly the flight broke as the blues fought to gain altitude and keep their pursuers from attacking them from behind. Here and there battles broke out. Lightning cracked and flared, nearly blinding the kender, as a great bronze dragon to his right screamed in pain and fell from the air, its head blackened and burning. Tas saw its rider helplessly grasping the reins, his mouth opened in a scream the kender could see but not hear as dragon and rider plunged to the ground below.

Tas stared at the ground rushing closer and closer and wondered in a dreamlike haze what it would be like to smash into the grass. But he didn't have time to wonder long, because suddenly Khirsah let out a roar.

The blue leader spotted Khirsah and heard his ringing challenge. Ignoring the other dragons fighting in the skies around him, the blue leader and his rider flew up to continue their duel with the bronze.

"Now it is your turn, dwarf! Set the lance!" Khirsah yelled. Lifting his great wings, the bronze soared up and up, gaining altitude for maneuvering and also giving the dwarf time to prepare.

"I'll hold the reins!" Tas shouted.

———

But the kender couldn't tell if Flint heard him or not. The dwarf's face was rigid and he was moving slowly and mechanically. Wild with impatience, Tas could do nothing but hang onto the reins and watch while Flint fumbled with gray fingers until he finally managed to fix the hilt of the lance beneath his shoulder and brace it as he had been taught. Then he just stared straight ahead, his face empty of all expression.

Khirsah continued rising, then leveled off, and Tas looked around, wondering where their enemies were. He had completely lost sight of the blue and its rider. Then Khirsah suddenly leaped upwards and Tas gasped. *There* was their enemy—right ahead of them!

He saw the blue open his hideous fanged mouth. Remembering the lightning, Tas ducked behind the shield. Then he saw that Flint was still sitting straight-backed, staring grimly out over the shield at the approaching dragon! Reaching around Flint's waist, Tas grabbed hold of the dwarf's beard and yanked his head downward, behind the shield.

Lightning flared and crackled around them. The instant booming thunder nearly knocked both kender and dwarf senseless. Khirsah roared in pain but held true upon his course.

The dragons struck, head-on, the dragonlance speared its victim.

For an instant all Tas could see were blurs of blue and red. The world spun round and round. Once a dragon's hideous, fiery eyes stared at him balefully. Claws flashed. Khirsah shrieked, the blue screamed. Wings beat upon the air. The ground spiraled round and round as the struggling dragons fell.

Why doesn't Fireflash let go? Tas thought frantically. Then he could see—

We're locked together! Tasslehoff realized numbly.

The dragonlance had missed its mark. Striking the wingbone joint of the blue dragon, the lance had bent into his shoulder and was now lodged tight. Desperately the blue fought to free himself, but Khirsah, now filled with battle rage, lashed out at the blue with his sharp fangs and ripping taloned front feet.

Intent upon their own battle, both dragons had completely forgotten their riders. Tas had forgotten the other rider, too, until—glancing up helplessly—he saw the blue helmed dragon officer clinging precariously to his saddle only a few feet away.

Then sky and ground became a blur once more as the dragons whirled and fought. Tas watched in a haze as the blue helm of the officer fell from his head, the officer's blonde hair whipped in the wind. His eyes were cold and bright and not the least afraid. He stared straight into Tasslehoff's eyes.

He looks familiar, thought Tas with an odd sort of detachment, as if this were happening to some other kender while he watched. Where could I have seen him before? Thoughts of Sturm came to his mind.

The dragon officer freed himself from his harness and stood up in the stirrups. One arm—his right arm—hung limply at his side, but his other hand was reaching forward—

Everything became very clear to Tas suddenly. He knew exactly what the officer intended to do. It was as if the man spoke to him, telling him his plans.

"Flint!" cried Tas frantically. "Release the lance! Release it!"

But the dwarf held onto the lance fast, that strange far-away look on his face. The dragons fought and clawed and bit in mid-air; the blue twisting, trying to free himself from the lance as well as fend off its attacker. Tas saw the blue's rider shout something, and the blue broke off its attack for an instant, holding himself steady in the air.

With remarkable agility, the officer leaped from one dragon to the other. Grasping Khirsah around the neck with his good arm, the dragon officer pulled himself upright, his strong legs and thighs clamping themselves firmly onto the struggling dragon's neck.

Khirsah paid the human no attention. His thoughts were fixed totally on his enemy.

The officer cast one quick glance back at the kender and the dwarf behind him and saw that neither was likely to be a threat—strapped, as they must be—into place. Coolly the officer drew his longsword and, leaning down, began to slash at the bronze dragon's harness straps where they crossed across the beast's chest, ahead of the great wings.

"Flint!" pleaded Tas. "Release the lance! Look!" The kender shook the dwarf. "If that officer cuts through the harness, our saddle will fall off! The lance will fall off! *We'll* fall off!"

Flint turned his head slowly, suddenly understanding. Still moving with agonizing slowness, his shaking hand fumbled at the mechanism that would release the lance and free the dragons from their deadly embrace. But would it be in time?

Tas saw the longsword flash in the air. He saw one of the harness straps sag and flutter free. There wasn't time to think or plan. While Flint grappled with the release, Tas—rising up precariously—wrapped the reins around his waist. Then, hanging onto the edge of the saddle, the kender crawled around the dwarf until he was in front of him. Here he lay down flat along the dragon's neck and, wrapping his legs around the dragon's spiney mane, he wormed his way forward and came up silently behind the officer.

The man wasn't paying any attention to the riders behind him, assuming both were safely locked in their harnesses. Intent upon his work—the harness was nearly free—he never knew what hit him.

Rising up, Tasslehoff leaped onto the officer's back. Startled, scrabbling wildly to keep himself balanced, the officer let his sword fall as he clung desperately to the dragon's neck.

Snarling in rage, the officer tried to see what had struck him when suddenly everything went dark! Small arms wrapped themselves around his head, blinding him. Frantically the officer let go of his hold on the dragon in an effort to free himself of what seemed to his enraged mind to be a creature with six legs and arms—all of them clinging to him with a buglike tenacity. But he felt himself start to slide off the dragon and was forced to grab hold of the mane.

"Flint! Release the lance! Flint . . ." Tas didn't even know what he was saying anymore. The ground was rushing up to meet him as the weakened dragons toppled from the skies. He couldn't think. White flashes of light burst in his head as he clung with all his strength to the officer, who was still struggling beneath him.

Then a great metallic bang sounded.

The lance released. The dragons were freed.

Spreading his wings, Khirsah pulled out of his spinning dive and leveled off. The sky and ground resumed their proper, correct positions. Tears streamed down Tas's cheeks. He hadn't been frightened, he told himself, sobbing. But nothing had ever looked so beautiful as that blue, blue sky—back up where it should be!

"Are you all right, Fireflash?" Tas yelled.

The bronze nodded wearily.

"I've got a prisoner," Tas called, suddenly realizing that fact himself. Slowly he let go of the man, who shook his head dizzily, half-choked.

"I guess you're not going anywhere," Tas muttered. Sliding

off the man's back, the kender crawled down the mane toward the dragon's shoulders. Tas saw the officer look up into the skies, and clench his fist in bitter rage as he watched his dragons being slowly driven from the skies by Laurana and her forces. In particular, the officer's gaze fixed on Laurana—and suddenly Tas knew where he had seen him before.

The kender caught his breath. "You better take us down to the ground, Fireflash!" he cried, his hands shaking. "Hurry!"

The dragon arched his head to look around at his riders, and Tas saw that one eye was swollen shut. There were scorch and burn marks all along one side of the bronze head, and blood dripped from a torn nostril. Tas glanced around for the blue. He was nowhere to be seen.

Looking back at the officer, Tas suddenly felt wonderful. It occurred to him what he had done.

"Hey!" he yelled in elation, turning around to Flint. "We *did* it! We fought a dragon and *I* captured a prisoner! Single-handed!"

Flint nodded slowly. Turning back, Tas watched as the ground rose up to meet him, and the kender thought it had never looked so . . . so wonderfully groundlike before!

Khirsah landed. The foot-soldiers gathered around them, yelling and cheering. Someone led the officer away—Tas was not sorry to see him go; noticing that the officer gave him a sharp, penetrating look before he was led off. But then the kender forgot him as he glanced up at Flint.

The dwarf was slumped over the saddle, his face old and tired-looking, his lips blue.

"What's the matter?"

"Nothing."

"But you're holding your chest. Are you wounded?"

"No, I'm not."

"Then why are you holding your chest?"

Flint scowled. "I suppose I'll have no peace until I answer you. Well, if you must know, it's that confounded lance! And whoever designed this stupid vest was a bigger ninny that you are! The shaft of the lance drove right into my collarbone. I'll be black and blue for a week. And as for your prisoner, it's a wonder you weren't both killed, you rattlebrain! Captured, humpf! More like an accident, if you ask me. And I'll tell you something else! I'm never getting on another one of those great beasts as long as I live!"

Flint shut his lips with an angry snap, glaring at the kender so fiercely that Tas turned around and walked quickly away, knowing that when Flint was in *that* kind of mood, it was best to leave him alone to cool off. He'd feel better after lunch.

It wasn't until that night, when Tasslehoff was curled up next to Khirsah, resting comfortably against the dragon's great bronze flank, that he remembered Flint had been clutching the left side of his chest.

The lance had been on the old dwarf's right.

BOOK 2

I

Spring Dawning.

As the day dawned, pink and golden light spreading across the land, the citizens of Kalaman woke to the sound of bells. Leaping out of bed, children invaded parental bedrooms, demanding that mother and father arise so that this special day could get underway. Though some grumbled and feigned to pull the blankets over their heads, most parents laughingly climbed out of bed, not less eager than their children.

Today was a memorable day in the history of Kalaman. Not only was it the annual Spring Dawning festival, it was also a victory celebration for the armies of the Knights of Solamnia. Camped on the plains outside the walled city, the army—led by its now-legendary general, an elf woman—would be making a triumphal entry into the city at noon.

As the sun peeped over the walls, the sky above Kalaman was filled with the smoke of cooking fires, and soon smells of sizzling ham and warm muffins, frying bacon and exotic coffees rousted even the sleepiest from warm beds. They would have been roused soon enough anyway, for almost immediately the streets were filled with children. All discipline was relaxed on the occasion of Spring Dawning. After a long winter of being cooped up indoors, children were allowed to "run wild" for a day. By nightfall there would be bruised heads, skinned knees, and stomach aches from too many sweets. But all would remember it as a glorious day.

By mid-morning the festival was in full swing. Vendors hawked their wares in gaily colored booths. The gullible lost their money on games of chance. Dancing bears capered in the streets, and illusionists drew gasps of amazement from young and old.

Then at noon the bells rang out again. The streets cleared. People lined the sidewalks. The city gates were flung open, and the Knights of Solamnia prepared to enter Kalaman.

An expectant hush came over the crowd. Peering ahead eagerly, they jostled to get a good view of the Knights, particularly the elfwoman of whom they had heard so many stories. She rode in first, alone, mounted on a pure white horse. The crowd—prepared to cheer—found themselves unable to speak, so awed were they by the woman's beauty and majesty. Dressed in flashing silver armor decorated with beaten gold work, Laurana guided her steed through the city gates and into the streets. A delegation of children had been carefully rehearsed to strew flowers in Laurana's path, but so overcome were the children at the sight of the lovely woman in the glittering armor that they clutched their flowers and never threw a single one.

Behind the golden-haired elfmaiden rode two who caused not a few in the crowd to point in wonder—a kender and a dwarf, mounted together on a shaggy pony with a back as broad as a barrel. The kender seemed to be having a wonderful time, yelling and waving to the crowds. But the dwarf, sitting behind him, grasping him around the waist with a deathlike grip, was sneezing so badly he seemed likely to sneeze himself right off the back of the animal.

Following the dwarf and kender rode an elflord, so like the elfmaiden that no one in the crowd needed his neighbor to tell him they were brother and sister. Beside the elflord rode another elfmaid with strange silver hair and deep blue eyes, who seemed shy and nervous among the crowd. Then came the the Knights of Solamnia, perhaps seventy-five strong, resplendent in gleaming armor. The crowd began to cheer, waving flags in the air.

A few of the Knights exchanged grim glances at this, all of them thinking that if they had ridden into Kalaman only a month before, they would have received a far different reception. But now they were heroes. Three hundred years of hatred and bitterness and unjust accusations were wiped from the minds of the public as they cheered those who had saved them from the terrors of the dragonarmies.

Marching after the Knights were several thousand the footmen. And then, to the great delight of the crowd, the sky above the city filled with dragons—not the dreaded flights of red and blue the people had feared all winter. Instead, the sun flashed off wings of silver and bronze and gold as the awesome creatures circled and dove and pivoted in their well-organized flights. Knights sat in the dragonsaddles, the barbed blades of dragonlances sparkling in the morning light.

After the parade, the citizens gathered to hear their Lord speak a few words in honor of the heroes. Laurana blushed to hear it told that she alone was responsible for the discovery of the dragonlances, the return of the good dragons, and the tremendous victories of the armies. Stammering, she tried to deny this, gesturing to her brother and to the Knights. But the yells and cheers of the crowd drowned her out. Helplessly Laurana looked at Lord Michael, Grand Master Gunthar Uth Wistan's representative, who had lately arrived from Sancrist. Michael only grinned.

"Let them have their hero," he said to her above the shouting. "Or heroine I should say. They deserve it. All winter they lived in fear, waiting for the day the dragons would appear in the skies. Now they have a beautiful heroine who rides out of children's tales to save them."

"But it's not true!" Laurana protested, edging nearer Michael to make herself heard. Her arms were filled with winter roses.

Their fragrance was cloying, but she dared not offend anyone by setting them aside. "I didn't ride out of a children's story. I rode out of fire and darkness and blood. Putting me in command was a political stratagem of Lord Gunthar's—we both know that. And if my brother and Silvara hadn't risked their lives to bring the good dragons, we'd be parading down these streets in chains behind the Dark Lady."

"Bah! This is good for them. Good for us, too," Michael added, glancing at Laurana out of the corner of his eye as he waved to the crowd. "A few weeks ago we couldn't have begged the Lord to give us a crust of stale bread. Now—because of the Golden General—he's agreed to garrison the army in the town, provide us with supplies, horses, anything we want. Young men are flocking to join up. Our ranks will be swelled by a thousand or more before we leave for Dargaard. And you've lifted the morale of our own troops. You saw the Knights as they were in the High Clerist's Tower—look at them now."

Yes, thought Laurana bitterly. I saw them. Split by dissension among their own ranks, fallen into dishonor, bickering and plotting among themselves. It took the death of a fine and noble man to bring them to their senses. Laurana closed her eyes. The noise, the smell of the roses—which always brought Sturm to her mind—the exhaustion of battle, the heat of the noonday sun, all crashed over her in a stifling wave. She grew dizzy and feared she might faint. The thought was mildly amusing. How would that look—for the Golden General to keel over like a wilted flower?

Then she felt a strong arm around her.

"Steady, Laurana," said Gilthanas, supporting her. Silvara was beside her, taking the roses from her arms. Sighing, Laurana opened her eyes and smiled weakly at the Lord, who was just concluding his second speech of the morning to thunderous applause.

I'm trapped, Laurana realized. She would have to sit here the rest of the afternoon, smiling and waving and enduring speech after speech praising her heroism when all she wanted was to lie down in some dark, cool place and sleep. And it was all a lie, all a sham. If only they knew the truth. What if she stood up and told them she was so frightened during the battles that she could remember details only in her nightmares? Told them that she was nothing but a gamepiece for the Knights? Told them that she was here only because she had run away from her home—a spoiled little girl chasing after a half-elven man who didn't love her. What would they say?

"And now"—the Lord of Kalaman's voice rang out above the noise of the crowd—"it is my honor and my very great privilege to present to you the woman who has turned the tide of this war, the woman who has sent the dragonarmies fleeing for their lives over the plains, the woman who has driven the evil dragons from the sky, the woman whose armies captured the evil Bakaris, commander of the Dragon Highlord's armies, the woman whose name is even now being coupled with the great Huma's as the most valiant warrior on Krynn. Within a week, she will be riding to Dargaard Keep to demand the surrender of the Dragon Highlord known as the Dark Lady. . . ."

The Lord's voice was drowned in cheering. He paused dramatically, then—reaching behind him—caught hold of Laurana and nearly dragged her forward. "Lauralanthalasa of the Royal House of Qualinesti!"

The noise was deafening. It reverberated off the tall stone buildings. Laurana looked out over the sea of open mouths and wildly waving flags. They don't want to hear about *my* fear, she realized wearily. They've fears enough of their own. They don't want to hear about darkness and death. They want children's tales about love and rebirth and silver dragons.

Don't we all.

With a sigh, Laurana turned to Silvara. Taking the roses back, she held them up into the air, waving to the jubilant crowd. Then she began her speech.

Tasslehoff Burrfoot was having a splendid time. It had been an easy task to evade Flint's watchful gaze and slip off the platform where he had been told to stand with the rest of the dignitaries. Melting into the crowd, he was now free to explore this interesting city again. Long ago, he'd come to Kalaman with his parents and he cherished fond memories of the open-air bazaar, the seaport where the white-winged ships lay at anchor, and a hundred other wonders.

Idly he wandered among the festive crowd, his keen eyes seeing everything, his hands busy stuffing objects into his pouches. Really, Tas thought, the people of Kalaman were extremely careless! Purses had the most uncanny habit of falling from people's belts into Tas's hands. The streets might be paved with jewels the way he discovered rings and other fascinating trinkets.

Then the kender was transported into realms of delight when he came across a cartographer's stall. And, as fortune would have it, the cartographer had gone to watch the parade. The stall was locked and shuttered, with a large "CLOSED" sign hanging on a hook.

"What a pity," thought Tas. "But I'm sure he wouldn't mind if I just looked at his maps." Reaching out, he gave the lock an expert twitch, then smiled happily. A few more "twitches" and it would open easily. "He mustn't really mean for people to keep out if he puts on such a simple-minded lock. I'll just pop in and copy a few of his maps to update my collection."

Suddenly Tas felt a hand on his shoulder. Irritated that someone should bother him at a time like this, the kender glanced around to see a strange figure that seemed vaguely familiar. It was dressed in heavy cloaks and robes, though the spring day was warming rapidly. Even its hands were wrapped in cloth, like bandages. Bother—a cleric, thought the kender, annoyed and preoccupied.

"I beg your pardon," said Tas to the cleric who had hold of him, "I don't mean to be rude, but I was just—"

"Burrfoot?" interrupted the cleric in a cold, lisping voice. "The kender who rides with the Golden General?"

"Why, yes," Tas said, flattered that someone had recognized him. "That's me. I've ridden with Laura—the, er—Golden General—for a long time now. Let's see, I think it was in the late fall. Yes, we met her in Qualinesti right after we escaped from the hobgoblin's prison wagons which was a short time after we killed a black dragon in Xak Tsaroth. That's the most wonderful story—" Tas forgot about the maps. "You see we were in this old, old city that had fallen into a cavern and it was filled with gully dwarves. We met one named Bupu, who had been charmed by Raistlin—"

"Shut up!" The cleric's wrapped hand went from Tasslehoff's shoulder to the collar of his shirt. Gripping it expertly, the cleric twisted it with a sudden jerk of its hand and lifted the kender off his feet. Although kender are generally immune to the emotion of fear, Tas found that being unable to breathe was an extremely uncomfortable sensation.

"Listen to me carefully," the cleric hissed, shaking the frantically struggling kender as a wolf shakes a bird to break its neck.

"That's right. Hold still and it hurts less. I've got a message for the Golden General." Its voice was soft and lethal. "It's here—" Tas felt a rough hand stuffing something into his vest pocket. "See that you deliver it some time tonight when she's alone. Understand?"

Choked by the cleric's hand, Tas couldn't speak or even nod, but he blinked his eyes twice. The cloaked head nodded, dropped the kender back to the ground, and walked rapidly off down the street.

Gasping for breath, the shaken kender stared at the figure as it walked away, its long robes fluttering in the wind. Tas absently patted the scroll that had been thrust into his pocket. The sound of that voice brought back very unpleasant memories: the ambush on the road from Solace, heavily cloaked figures like clerics . . . only they weren't clerics! Tas shuddered. A draconian! Here! In Kalaman!

Shaking his head, Tas turned back to the cartographer's stall. But the pleasure had gone out of the day. He couldn't even feel excited when the lock fell open into his small hand.

"Hey, you!" shrieked a voice. "Kender! Get away from there!"

A man was running up to him, puffing and red in the face. Probably the cartographer himself.

"You shouldn't have run," Tas said listlessly. "You needn't bother opening up for me."

"Opening!" The man's jaw sagged. "Why, you little thief! I got here just in time—"

"Thanks all the same." Tas dropped the lock into the man's hand and walked off, absentmindedly evading the enraged cartographer's effort to grab him. "I'll be going now. I'm not feeling very well. Oh, by the way, did you know that lock's broken? Worthless. You should be more careful. You never know who could sneak in. No, don't thank me. I haven't got time. Goodbye."

Tasslehoff wandered off. Cries of "Thief! Thief!" rang out behind him. A town guardsman appeared, forcing Tas to duck into a butcher's shop to avoid being run over. Shaking his head over the corruption of the world, the kender glanced about, hoping for a glimpse of the culprit. Seeing no one interesting in sight, he kept going, and suddenly wondered irritably how Flint had managed to lose him again.

Laurana shut the door, turned the key in the lock, and leaned thankfully against it, reveling in the peace and quiet and welcome solitude of her room. Tossing the key on a table, she walked wearily over to her bed, not even bothering to light a candle. The rays of the silver moon streamed in through the leaded glass panes of the long, narrow window.

Downstairs, in the lower rooms of the castle, she could still hear the sounds of merrymaking she had just left. It was nearly midnight. She had been trying for two hours to escape. It finally took Lord Michael's intercession on her behalf— pleading her exhaustion from the battles—that induced the lords and ladies of the city of Kalaman to part with her.

Her head ached from the stuffy atmosphere, the smell of strong perfume, and too much wine. She shouldn't have drunk so much, she knew. She had a weak head for wine and, anyway, she didn't really like it. But the pain in her head was easier to bear than the pain in her heart.

Throwing herself down on the bed, she thought hazily about getting up and closing the shutters, but the moon's light was comforting. Laurana detested lying in the darkness. Things lurked in the shadows, ready to spring out at her. I should get undressed, she thought, I'll wrinkle this dress . . . and it's borrowed. . . .

There was a knock at her door.

Laurana woke with a start, trembling. Then she remembered where she was. Sighing, she lay very still, closing her eyes again. Surely they'd realize she was alseep and go away.

There was another knock, more insistent than the first.

"Laurana . . ."

"Tell me in the morning, Tas," Laurana said, trying to keep the irritation from her voice.

"It's important, Laurana," Tas called. "Flint's with me."

Laurana heard a scuffling sound outside the door.

"Come on, tell her—"

"I will not! This was your doing!"

"But he said it was important and I—"

"All right, I'm coming!" Laurana sighed. Stumbling out of bed, she fumbled for the key on the table, unlocked the door, and flung it open.

"Hi, Laurana!" Tas said brightly, walking inside. "Wasn't that a wonderful party? I've never eaten roast peacock before—"

"What is it, Tas?" Laurana sighed, shutting the door behind them.

Seeing her pale, drawn face, Flint poked the kender in the back. Giving the dwarf a reproachful look, Tas reached into the pocket of his fleecy vest and drew forth a rolled scroll of parchment, tied with a blue ribbon.

"A-a cleric—sort of—said to give this to you, Laurana," Tas said.

"Is that all?" Laurana asked impatiently, snatching the scroll from the kender's hand. "It's probably a marriage proposal. I've had twenty in the last week. Not to mention proposals of a more unique nature."

"Oh, no," said Tas, suddenly serious. "It's not anything like that, Laurana. It's from—" He stopped.

"How do you know who it's from?" Laurana fixed the kender with a piercing gaze.

"I—uh—guess I—sort of—glanced at it—" Tas admitted. Then he brightened. "But it was only because I didn't want to bother you with anything that wasn't important."

Flint snorted.

"Thank you," Laurana said. Unrolling the scroll, she walked over to stand by the window where the moonlight was bright enough to read by.

"We'll leave you alone," Flint said gruffly, herding the protesting kender toward the door.

"No! Wait!" Laurana choked. Flint turned, staring at her in alarm.

"Are you all right?" he said, hurrying over to her as she sank down into a nearby chair. "Tas—get Silvara!"

"No, no. Don't bring anyone. I'm . . . all right. Do you know what this says?" she asked in a whisper.

"I tried to tell him," Tasslehoff said in an injured voice, "but he wouldn't let me."

Her hand shaking, Laurana handed the scroll to Flint.

The dwarf opened it and read aloud.

"Tanis Half-Elven received a wound in the battle of Vingaard Keep. Although at first he believed it was slight, it has worsened so that he is past even the help of the dark clerics. I ordered that he be brought to Dargaard Keep, where I could care for him. Tanis knows the gravity of his injury. He asks that he be allowed to be with you when he dies, that he may explain matters to you and so rest with an easy spirit.

"I make you this offer. You have as your captive my officer, Bakaris, who was captured near Vingaard Keep. I will exchange Tanis Half-Elven for Bakaris. The exchange will take place at dawn tomorrow in a grove of trees beyond the city walls. Bring Bakaris with you. If you are mistrustful, you may also bring Tanis's friends, Flint Fireforge and Tasslehoff Burrfoot. But no one else! The bearer of this note waits outside the city gate. Meet him tomorrow at sunrise. If he deems all is well, he will escort you to the half-elf. If not, you will never see Tanis alive.

"I do this only because we are two women who understand each other.

"Kitiara"

There was an uneasy silence, then, "Humpf," Flint snorted, and rolled up the scroll.

"How can you be so calm!" Laurana gasped, snatching the scroll from the dwarf's hand. "And you"—her gaze switched angrily to Tasslehoff—"why didn't you tell me before now? How long have you known? You *read* he was dying, and you're so—so—"

Laurana put her head in her hands.

Tas stared at her, his mouth open. "Laurana," he said after a moment, "surely you don't think Tanis—"

Laurana's head snapped up. Her dark, stricken eyes went to Flint, then to Tas. "You don't believe this message is real do you?" she asked incredulously.

"Of course not!" Flint said.

"No," scoffed Tas. "It's a trick! A *draconian* gave it to me! Besides Kitiara's a Dragon Highlord now. What would Tanis be doing with her—"

Laurana turned her face away abruptly. Tasslehoff stopped and glanced at Flint, whose own face suddenly seemed to age.

"So that's it," the dwarf said softly. "We saw you talking to Kitiara on the wall of the High Clerist's Tower. You were discussing more than Sturm's death, weren't you?"

Laurana nodded, wordlessly, staring at her hands in her lap.

"I never told you," she murmured in a voice barely audible, "I couldn't . . . I kept hoping. . . . Kitiara said . . . said she'd left Tanis in—some place called Flotsam . . . to look after things while she was gone."

"Liar!" said Tas promptly.

"No." Laurana shook her head. "When she says we are two

women who understand each other, she's right. She wasn't lying. She was telling the truth, I know. And at the Tower she mentioned the dream." Laurana lifted her head. "Do you remember the dream?"

Flint nodded uncomfortably. Tasslehoff shuffled his feet.

"Only Tanis could have told her about the dream we all shared," Laurana continued, swallowing a choking feeling in her throat. "I saw him with her in the dream, just as I saw Sturm's death. The dream's coming true . . ."

"Now wait a minute," Flint said gruffly, grabbing hold of reality as a drowning man grabs a piece of wood. "You said yourself you saw your own death in the dream, right after Sturm's. And you didn't die. And nothing hacked up Sturm's body, either."

"I haven't died yet, like I did in the dream," Tas said helpfully. "And I've picked lots of locks, well, not lots, but a few here and there, and none were poisoned. Besides, Laurana, Tanis wouldn't—"

Flint shot Tas a warning glance. The kender lapsed into silence. But Laurana had seen the glance and understood. Her lips tightened.

"Yes, he would. You both know it. He loves her." Laurana was quiet a moment, then, "I'm going. I'll exchange Bakaris."

Flint heaved a sigh. He had seen this coming. "Laurana—"

"Wait a minute, Flint," she interrupted. "If Tanis received a message saying you were dying, what would he do?"

"That's not the point," Flint mumbled.

"If he had to go into the Abyss itself, past a thousand dragons, he'd come to you—"

"Perhaps and perhaps not," said Flint gruffly. "Not if he was leader of an army. Not if he had responsibilities, people depending on him. He'd know I'd understand—"

Laurana's face might have been carved of marble, so impassive and pure and cold was her expression. "I never asked for these responsibilities. I never wanted them. We can make it look as if Bakaris escaped—"

"Don't do it, Laurana!" Tas begged. "He's the officer who brought back Derek and Lord Alfred's body at the High Clerist's Tower, the officer you shot in the arm with the arrow. He hates you, Laurana! I—I saw the way he looked at you the day we captured him!"

Flint's brows drew together. "The lords and your brother are still below. We'll discuss the best way to handle this—"

"I'm not discussing anything," Laurana stated, lifting her chin in the old imperious gesture the dwarf knew so well. "*I'm* the general. It's my decision."

"Maybe you should ask someone's advice—"

Laurana regarded the dwarf with bitter amusement. "Whose?" she asked. "Gilthanas's? What would I say? That Kitiara and I want to exchange lovers? No, we'll tell no one. What would the knights have done with Bakaris anyway? Execute him according to knightly ritual. They owe me something for all I've done. I'll take Bakaris as payment."

"Laurana"— Flint tried desperately to think of some way to penetrate her frozen mask—"there is a protocol that must be followed in prisoner exchange. You're right. You *are* the general, and you must know how important this is! You were in your father's court long enough—" *That* was a mistake. The dwarf knew it as soon as he opened his mouth and he groaned inwardly.

"I am no longer in my father's court!" Laurana flashed. "And to the Abyss with protocol!" Rising to her feet, she regarded the Flint coldly, as if he were someone she had just met. The dwarf was, in fact, strongly reminded of her as he had seen her in Qualinesti, the evening she had run away from her home to follow after Tanis in childish infatuation.

"Thank you for bringing this message. I have a great deal to do before morning. If you have any regard for Tanis, please return to your rooms and say nothing to anyone."

Tasslehoff cast Flint an alarmed glance. Flushing, the dwarf tried hastily to undo the damage.

"Now, Laurana," he said gruffly, "don't take my words to heart. If you've made your decision, I'll support you. I'm just being an old crotchety grandfather, that's all. I worry about you, even if you are a general. And you should take me with you—like the note says—"

"Me, too!" cried Tas indignantly.

Flint glared at him, but Laurana didn't notice. Her expression softened. "Thank you, Flint. You too, Tas," she said wearily. "I'm sorry I snapped at you. But I really believe I should go alone."

"No," Flint said stubbornly. "I care about Tanis as much as you. If there's any chance he is dy—" The dwarf choked and wiped his hand across his eyes. Then he swallowed the lump in his throat. "I want to be with him."

"Me, too," mumbled Tas, subdued.

"Very well." Laurana smiled sadly. "I can't blame you. And I'm sure he'd want you to be there."

She sounded so certain, so positive she would see Tanis. The dwarf saw it in her eyes. He made one final effort. "Laurana, what if it's a trap. An ambush—"

Laurana's expression froze again. Her eyes narrowed angrily Flint's protest was lost in his beard. He glanced at Tas. The kender shook his head.

The old dwarf sighed.

2

The penalty of failure.

"There it is, sir," said the dragon, a huge red monster with glistening black eyes and a wing span that was like the shadows of night. "Dargaard Keep. Wait, you can see it clearly in the moonlight . . . when the clouds part."

"I see it," replied a deep voice. The dragon, hearing the dagger-edged anger in the man's tone, began his descent swiftly, spiraling round and round as he tested the shifting air currents among the mountains. Nervously eyeing the keep surrounded by the rocky crags of the jagged mountains, the dragon looked for a place to make a smooth and easy landing. It would never do to jounce Lord Ariakas.

At the far northern end of the Dargaard Mountains stood their destination—Dargaard Keep, as dark and dismal as its legends. Once—when the world was young—Dargaard Keep had graced the mountain peaks, its rose-colored walls rising in graceful sweeping beauty up from the rock in the very likeness of a rose itself. But now, thought Ariakas grimly, the rose has died. The Highlord was not a poetic man, nor was he much given to flights of fancy. But the fire-blackened, crumbling castle atop the rock looked so much like a decayed rose upon a withering bush that the image struck him forcibly. Black latticework, stretching from broken tower to broken tower, no longer formed the petals of the rose. Instead, mused Ariakas, it is the web of the insect whose poison had killed it.

The great red dragon wheeled a final time. The southern wall surrounding the courtyard had fallen a thousand feet to the base of the cliff during the Cataclysm, leaving a clear passage to the gates of the keep itself. Breathing a heartfelt sigh of relief, the red saw smooth tiled pavement beyond, broken only here and there by rents in the stonework, suitable for a smooth landing. Even dragons—who feared few things on Krynn—found it healthier to avoid Lord Ariakas's displeasure.

In the courtyard below, there was a sudden fever of activity, looking like an anthill disturbed by the approach of a wasp. Draconians shrieked and pointed. The captain of the night watch came hurrying to the battlements, looking over the edge into the courtyard. The draconians were right. A flight of red dragons were indeed landing in the courtyard, one of them bearing an officer, too, by the armor. The captain watched uneasily as the man leaped from the dragon saddle before his mount had come to halt. The dragon's wings beat furiously to avoid striking the officer, sending dust billowing about him in moonlit clouds as he strode purposefully across the stones of the courtyard toward the door. His black boots rang on the pavement, sounding like a death knell.

And—with that thought—the captain gasped, suddenly recognizing the officer. Turning, nearly stumbling over the draconian in his haste, he cursed the soldier and ran through the keep in search of Acting Commander, Garibanus.

Lord Ariakas's mailed fist fell upon the wooden door with a thunderous blow that sent splinters flying. Draconians scrambled to open it, then shrank back abjectly as the Dragon Highlord stalked inside, accompanied by a blast of cold wind that extinguished the candles and caused torch flames to waver.

Casting a swift glance from behind the gleaming mask of the dragonhelm as he entered, Ariakas saw a large circular hallway spanned by a vaulted, domed ceiling. Two giant curved staircases rose from either side of the entryway, leading up to a balcony on the second level. As Ariakas looked around, ignoring the groveling draconians, he saw Garibanus emerge from a doorway near the top of the stairs, hastily buttoning his trousers and pulling a shirt over his head. The captain of the watch stood—quaking—next to Garbanias, pointing down at the Dragon Highlord.

Ariakas guessed in a moment whose company the acting commander had been enjoying. Apparently he was filling in for the missing Bakaris in more ways than one!

"So *that's* where she is!" Lord Ariakas thought in satisfaction. He strode across the hallway and up the stairs, taking them two at a time. Draconians scuttled out of his path like rats. The captain of the guard disappeared. Ariakas was fully halfway up the stairs before Garibanus had collected himself enough to address him.

"L-Lord Ariakas," he stammered, stuffing his shirt into his pants and hurrying down the stairs. "This is an—er—unexpected honor."

"Not *unexpected,* I believe?" Arkiakas said smoothly, his voice sounding strangely metallic coming from the depths of the dragonhelm.

"Well, perhaps not," Garibanus said with a weak laugh.

Ariakas continued climbing, his eyes fixed on a doorway above him. Realizing the lord's intended destination, Garibanus interposed himself between Ariakas and the door.

"My lord," he began apologetically, "Kitiara is dressing. She—"

Without a word, without even pausing in his stride, Lord Ariakas swung his gloved hand. The blow caught Garibanus in the ribcage. There was a whooshing sound, like a bellows deflating, and the sound of bones cracking, then a wet soggy splatter as the force of the blow sent the young man's body into the wall opposite the stairs some ten yards distant. The limp body slid to the floor below, but Ariakas never noticed. Without a backward glance, he resumed his climb, his eyes on the door at the top of the stairs.

Lord Ariakas, commander-in-chief of the dragonarmies, reporting directly to the Dark Queen herself, was a brilliant man, a military genius. Ariakas had nearly held the rulership of the Ansalon continent in his grasp. Already he was styling himself "Emperor." His Queen was truly pleased with him, his rewards from her were many and lavish.

But now he saw his beautiful dream slipping through his fingers like smoke from autumn fires. He had received reports of his troops fleeing wildly across the Solamnic plains, falling back from Palanthas, withdrawing from Vingaard Keep, abandoning plans for the siege of Kalaman. The elves had allied with human forces in Northern and Southern Ergoth. The mountain dwarves had emerged from their subterranean home of Thorbardin and, it was reported, allied with their ancient enemies, the hill dwarves and a group of human refugees in an attempt to drive the dragonarmies from Abanasinia. Silvanesti had been freed. A Dragon Highlord had been killed in Ice Wall. And, if rumor was to be believed, a group of gully dwarves held Pax Tharkas!

Thinking of this as he swept up the stairs, Ariakas worked himself into a fury. Few survived Lord Ariakas's displeasure. None survived his furies.

Ariakas inherited his position of authority from his father, who had been a cleric in high standing with the Queen of Darkness. Although only forty, Ariakas had held his position almost twenty years—his father having met an untimely death at the hands of his own son. When Ariakas was two, he had watched his father brutally murder his mother, who had been attempting to flee with her little son before the child became as perverted with evil as his father.

Though Ariakas always treated his father with outward shows of respect, he never forgot his mother's murder. He worked hard and excelled in his studies, making his father inordinately proud. Many wondered whether that pride was with the father as he felt the first thrusts of the knife-blade his nineteen-year-old son plunged into his body in revenge for his mother's death—and with an eye to the throne of Dragon Highlord.

Certainly it was no great tragedy to the Queen of Darkness, who quickly found young Ariakas more than made up for the loss of her favorite cleric. The young man had no clerical talents himself, but his considerable skills as a magic-user won him the Black Robes and the commendations of the evil wizards who instructed him. Although he passed the dreadful Tests in the Tower of High Sorcery, magic was not his love. He practiced it infrequently, and never wore the Black Robes which marked his standing as a wizard of evil powers.

Ariakas's true passion was war. It was he who had devised the strategy that had enabled the Dragon Highlords and their armies to subjugate almost all of the continent of Ansalon. It was he who had insured that they met with almost no resistance, for it had been Ariakas's brilliant strategy to move swiftly, striking the divided human, elf, and dwarven races before they had time to unite, and snap them up piecemeal. By summer, Ariakas's plan called for him to rule Ansalon unchallenged. Other Dragon Highlords on other continents of Krynn were looking to him with undisguised envy—and fear. For one continent could never satisfy Ariakas. Already his eyes were turning westward, across the Sirrion Sea.

But now—disaster.

Reaching the door of Kitiara's bedchamber, Ariakas found it locked. Coldly he spoke one word in the language of magic and the heavy wooden door blew apart. Ariakas strode through the shower of sparks and blue flame that engulfed the door into Kitiara's chamber, his hand on his sword.

Kit was in bed. At the sight of Ariakas she rose, her hand clutching a silken dressing gown around her lithe body. Even through his raging fury, Ariakas was still forced to admire the woman who, of all his commanders, he had come to rely on most. Though his arrival must have caught her off-guard, though she must know she had forfeited her life by allowing herself to be defeated, she faced him coolly and calmly. Not a spark of fear lit her brown eyes, not a murmur escaped her lips.

This only served to enrage Ariakas further, reminding him of his extreme disappointment in her. Without speaking, he yanked off the dragonhelm and hurled it across the room where it slammed into an ornately carved wooden chest, shattering it like glass.

At the sight of Ariakas's face, Kitiara momentarily lost control and shrank back in her bed, her hand nervously clasping the ribbons of her gown.

Few there were who could look up Ariakas's face without blenching. It was a face devoid of any human emotion. Even his anger showed only in the twitching of a muscle along his jaw. Long black hair swept down around his pallid features. A day's growth of beard appeared blue on his smooth-shaven skin. His eyes were black and cold as an ice-bound lake.

Ariakas reached the side of the bed in a bound. Ripping down the curtains that hung around it, he reached out and grabbed hold of Kitiara's short, curly hair. Dragging her from her bed, he hurled her to the stone floor.

Kitiara fell heavily, an exclamation of pain escaping her. But she recovered quickly, and was already starting to twist to her feet like a cat when Ariakas's voice froze her.

"Stay on your knees, Kitiara," he said. Slowly and deliberately he removed his long, shining sword from its scabbard. "Stay on your knees and bow your head, as the condemned do when they come to the block. For I am your executioner, Kitiara. Thus do my commanders pay for their failure!"

Kitiara remained kneeling, but she looked up at him. Seeing the flame of hatred in her brown eyes, Ariakas felt a moment's thankfulness that he held his sword in his hand. Once more he was compelled to admire her. Even facing imminent death, there was no fear in her eyes. Only defiance.

He raised his blade, but the blow did not fall.

Bone-cold fingers wrapped around the wrist of his sword-arm.

"I believe you should hear the Highlord's explanation," said a hollow voice.

Lord Ariakas was a strong man. He could hurl a spear with force enough to drive it completely through the body of a horse. He could break a man's neck with one twist of his hand. Yet he found he could not wrench himself loose from the chill grasp that was slowly crushing his wrist. Finally, in agony, Ariakas dropped the sword. It fell to the floor with a clatter.

Somewhat shaken, Kitiara rose to her feet. Making a gesture, she commanded her minion to release Ariakas. The Lord whirled around, raising a hand to call forth the magic that would reduce this creature to cinders.

Then he stopped. Sucking in his breath, Ariakas stumbled backwards, the magic spell he had been prepared to cast slipping from his mind.

Before him stood a figure no taller than himself, clad in armor so old it predated the Cataclysm. The armor was that of a Knight of Solamnia. The symbol of the Order of the Rose was traced upon the front, barely visible and worn with age. The armored figure wore no helm, it carried no weapon. Yet Ariakas—staring at it—fell back another step. For the figure he stared at was not the figure of a living man.

The being's face was transparent. Ariakas could see right through it to the wall beyond. A pale light flickered in the cavernous eyes. It stared straight ahead, as if it, too, could see right through Ariakas.

"A death knight!" he whispered in awe.

The Lord rubbed his aching wrist, numb with the cold of those who dwell in realms far removed from the warmth of living flesh. More frightened than he dared admit, Ariakas bent down to retrieve his sword, muttering a charm to ward off the aftereffects of such a deadly touch. Rising, he cast a bitter glance at Kitiara, who was regarding him with a crooked smile.

"This—this creature serves you?" he asked hoarsely.

Kitiara shrugged. "Let us say, we agree to serve each other."

Ariakas regarded her in grudging admiration. Casting a sidelong glance at the death knight, he sheathed his sword.

"Does he always frequent your bedroom?" He sneered. His wrist ached abominably.

"He comes and goes as he chooses," Kitiara replied. She gathered the folds of the gown casually around her body, reacting apparently more from the chill in the early spring air than out of a desire for modesty. Shivering, she ran her hand through her curly hair and shrugged. "It's *his* castle, after all."

Ariakas paused, a faraway look in his eyes, his mind running back over ancient legends. "Lord Soth!" he said suddenly, turning to the figure. "Knight of the Black Rose."

The Knight bowed in acknowledgment.

"I had forgotten the ancient story of Dargaard Keep," Ariakas murmured, regarding Kitiara thoughtfully. "You have more nerve than even *I* gave you credit for, lady—taking up residence in this accursed dwelling! According to legend, Lord Soth commands a troop of skeletal warriors—"

"An effective force in a battle," Kitiara replied, yawning. Walking over to a small table near a fireplace, she picked up a cut-glass carafe. "Their touch alone"—she regarded Ariakas with smile—"well, you know what their touch is like to those who lack the magic skills to defend against it. Some wine?"

"Very well," Ariakas replied, his eyes still on the transparent face of Lord Soth. "What about the dark elves, the banshee women who reputedly follow him?"

"They're here . . . somewhere." Kit shivered again, then lifted her wine glass. "You'll probably hear them before long. Lord Soth doesn't sleep, of course. The ladies help him pass the long hours in the night." For an instant, Kitiara paled, holding the wine glass to her lips. Then she set it down untouched, her hand shaking slightly. "It is not pleasant," she said briefly. Glancing around, she asked, "What have you done with Garibanus?"

Tossing off the glass of wine, Ariakas gestured negligently. "I left him . . . at the bottom of the stairs."

"Dead?" Kitiara questioned, pouring the Highlord another glass.

Ariakas scowled. "Perhaps. He got in my way. Does it matter?"

"I found him . . . entertaining," Kitiara said. "He filled Bakaris's place in more than one respect."

"Bakaris, yes." Lord Ariakas drank another glass. "So your commander managed to get himself captured as your armies went down to defeat!"

"He was an imbecile," Kitiara said coldly. "He tried riding dragonback, even though he is still crippled."

"I heard. What happened to his arm?"

"The elf woman shot him with an arrow at the High Clerist's Tower. It was his own fault, and he now has paid for it. I had removed him from command, making him my bodyguard. But he insisted on trying to redeem himself."

"You don't appear to be mourning his loss," Ariakas said, eyeing Kitiara. The dressing gown, tied together only by two ribbons at the neck, did little to cover her lithe body.

Kit smiled. "No, Garibanus is . . . quite a good replacement. I hope you haven't killed him. It will be a bother getting someone else to go to Kalaman tomorrow."

"What are you doing at Kalaman—preparing to surrender to the elf woman and the knights?" Lord Ariakas asked bitterly, his anger returning with the wine.

"No," Kitiara said. Sitting down in a chair opposite Ariakas, she regarded him coolly. "I'm preparing to accept *their* surrender."

"Ha!" Ariakas snorted. "They're not insane. They know they're winning. And they're right!" His face flushed. Picking up the carafe, he emptied it into his glass. "You owe your death knight your life, Kitiara. Tonight at least. But he won't be around you forever."

"My plans are succeeding much better than I had hoped," Kitiara replied smoothly, not in the least disconcerted by Ariakas's flickering eyes. "If I fooled you, my lord, I have no doubt that I have fooled the enemy."

"And how have you fooled me, Kitiara?" Ariakas asked with lethal calm. "Do you mean to say that you are *not* losing on all fronts? That you are *not* being driven from Solamnia? That the dragonlances and the good dragons have *not* brought about ignominious defeat?" His voice rose with each word.

"They have not!" Kitiara snapped, her brown eyes flashing. Leaning across the table, she caught hold of Ariakas's hand as he was about to raise the wine glass to his lips. "As for the good dragons, my lord, my spies tell me their return was due to an elflord and a silver dragon breaking into the temple at Sanction where they discovered what was happening to the good dragon eggs. Whose fault was that? Who slipped up there? Guarding that temple was *your* responsibility—"

Furiously, Ariakas wrenched his hand free of Kitiara's grip. Hurling the wine glass across the room, he stood and faced her.

"By the gods, you go too far!" he shouted, breathing heavily.

"Quit posturing," Kitiara said. Coolly rising to her feet, she turned and walked across the room. "Follow me to my war room, and I will explain my plans."

Ariakas stared down at the map of northern Ansalon. "It might work," he admitted.

"Of course, it will work," Kit said, yawning and stretching languidly. "My troops have run before them like frightened rabbits. Too bad the knights weren't astute enough to notice that we always drifted southward, and they never wondered why my forces just seemed to melt away and vanish. Even as we speak, my armies are gathering in a sheltered valley south of these mountains. Within a week, an army several thousand strong will be ready to march on Kalaman. The loss of their 'Golden General' will destroy their morale. The city will probably capitulate without a fight. From there, I regain all the land we appear to have lost. Give me command of that fool Toede's armies to the south, send the flying citadels I've asked for, and Solamnia will think it's been hit by another Cataclysm!"

"But the elfwoman—"

"Need not concern us," Kitiara said.

Ariakas shook his head. "This seems the weak link in your plans, Kitiara. What about Half-Elven? Can you be certain he won't interfere?"

"It doesn't matter about him. *She* is the one who counts and she is a woman in love." Kitiara shrugged. "She trusts me, Ariakas. You scoff, but it's true. She trusts me too much and Tanis Half-Elven too little. But that's always the way of lovers. The ones we love most are those we trust least. It proved quite that fortunate Bakaris fell into their hands."

Hearing a change in her voice, Ariakas glanced at Kitiara sharply, but she had turned from him, keeping her face averted. Immediately he realized she was not as confident as she seemed, and then he knew she had lied to him. The half-elf! What about him? Where *was* he, for that matter. Ariakas had heard a great deal about him, but had never met him. The Dragon Highlord considered pressing her on this point, then abruptly changed his mind. Much better to have in his possession this knowledge that she had lied. It gave him a power over this dangerous woman. Let her relax in her supposed complacency.

Yawning elaborately, Ariakas feigned indifference. "What will you do with the elfwoman?" he asked as she would expect him to ask. Ariakas's passion for delicate blonde women was well-known.

Kitiara raised her eyebrows, giving him a playful look. "Too bad, my lord," she said mockingly, "but Her Dark Highness has asked for the lady. Perhaps you could have her when the Dark Queen is finished."

Ariakas shivered. "Bah, she'll be no use to me then. Give her to your friend, Lord Soth. He liked elfwomen once upon a time, if I remember correctly."

"You do," murmured Kitiara. Her eyes narrowed. She held up her hand. "Listen," she said softly.

Ariakas fell silent. At first he heard nothing, then he gradually became aware of a strange sound—a wailing keen, as if a hundred women mourned their dead. As he listened, it grew louder and louder, piercing the stillness of the night.

The Dragon Highlord set down his wine glass, startled to see his hand trembling. Looking at Kitiara, he saw her face pale beneath its tan. Her large eyes were wide. Feeling his eyes upon her, Kitiara swallowed and licked her dry lips.

"Awful, isn't it?" she asked, her voice cracking.

"I faced horrors in the Towers of High Sorcery," said Ariakas softly, "but that was nothing compared to this. What *is* it?"

"Come," Kit said, standing up. "If you have the nerve, I'll show you."

Together, the two left the war room, Kitiara leading Ariakas through the winding corridors of the castle until they came back to Kit's bedroom above the circular entry way with the vaulted ceiling.

"Stay in the shadows," Kitiara warned.

An unnecessary warning, Ariakas thought as they crept softly out onto the balcony overlooking the circular room. Looking down over the edge of the balcony, Ariakas was overcome with sheer horror at the sight below him. Sweating, he drew back swiftly in the shadows of Kitiara's bedroom.

"How can you stand that?" he asked her as she entered and shut the door softly behind her. "Does that go on every night?"

"Yes," she said, trembling. She drew a deep breath and closed her eyes. Within a moment she was back in control. "Sometimes I think I'm used to it, then I make the mistake of looking down there. The song isn't so bad. . . ."

"It's ghastly!" Ariakas muttered, wiping cold sweat from his face. "So Lord Soth sits down there on his throne every night, surrounded by his skeletal warriors, and the dark hags sing that horrible lullaby!"

"And it is the same song, always," Kitiara murmured. Shivering, she absently picked up the empty wine carafe, then set it back down on the table. "Though the past tortures him, he cannot escape it. Always he ponders, wondering what he might have done to avoid the fate that dooms him to walk forever upon the land without rest. The dark elven women, who were part of his downfall, are forced to relive his story with him. Nightly they must repeat it. Nightly he must hear it."

"What are the words?"

"I know them, now, almost as well as he does." Kitiara laughed, then shuddered. "Call for another carafe of wine and I'll tell you his tale, if you have the time."

"I have time," Ariakas said, settling back in his chair. "Though I must leave in the morning if I am to send the citadels."

Kitiara smiled at him, the charming, crooked smile that so many had found so captivating.

"Thank you, my lord," she said. "I will not fail you again."

"No," said Ariakas coolly, ringing a small silver bell, "I can promise you that, Kitiara. If you do, you will find *his* fate"—he motioned downstairs where the wailing had reached a shivering pitch—"a pleasant one compared to your own."

The Knight of the Black Rose

"As you know," began Kitiara, "Lord Soth was a true and noble knight of Solamnia. But he was an intensely passionate man, lacking in self-discipline, and this was his downfall.

"Soth fell in love with a beautiful elfmaid, a disciple of the Kingpriest of Istar. He was married at the time, but thoughts of his wife vanished at the sight of the elfmaid's beauty. Forsaking both his sacred marriage vows and his knightly vows, Soth gave in to his passion. Lying to the girl, he seduced her and brought her to live at Dargaard Keep, promising to marry her. His wife disappeared under sinister circumstances."

Kitiara shrugged, then continued:

"According to what I've heard of the song, the elfmaid remained true to the knight, even after she discovered his terrible misdeeds. She prayed to the Goddess Mishakal that the knight be allowed to redeem himself and, apparently, her prayers were answered. Lord Soth was given the power to prevent the Cataclysm, though it would mean sacrificing his own life.

"Strengthened by the love of the girl he had wronged, Lord Soth left for Istar, fully intending to stop the Kingpriest and restore his shattered honor.

"But the knight was halted in his journey by elven women, disciples of the Kingpriest, who knew of Lord Soth's crime and threatened to ruin him. To weaken the effects of the elfmaid's love, they intimated that she had been unfaithful to him in his absence.

"Soth's passions took hold of him, destroying his reason. In a jealous rage he rode back to Dargaard Keep. Entering his door, he accused the innocent girl of betraying him. Then the Cataclysm struck. The great chandelier in the entryway fell to the floor, consuming the elfmaid and her child in flames. As she died, she called down a curse upon the knight, condemning him to eternal, dreadful life. Soth and his followers perished in the fire, only to be reborn in hideous form."

"So this is what he hears," Ariakas murmured, listening.

And in the climate of dreams
When you recall her, when the world of the dream
expands, wavers in light,
when you stand at the edge of blessedness and sun,

Then we shall make you remember,
shall make you live again
through the long denial of body

For you were first dark in the light's hollow,
    expanding like a stain, a cancer

For you were the shark in the slowed water
    beginning to move

For you were the notched head of a snake,
    sensing forever warmth and form

For you were inexplicable death in the crib,
    the long house in betrayal

And you were more terrible than this
    in a loud alley of visions,
    for you passed through unharmed, unchanging

As the women screamed, unraveling silence,
    halving the door of the world,
    bringing forth monsters

As a child opened in parabolas of fire
    There at the borders
    of two lands burning

As the world split, wanting to swallow you back
    willing to give up everything
    to lose you in darkness.

You passed through these unharmed, unchanging,
but now you see them
strung on our words—on your own conceiving
as you pass from night—to awareness of night
to know that hatred is the calm of philosophers
that its price is forever
that it draws you through meteors
through winter's transfixion

through the blasted rose
through the sharks' water
through the black compression of oceans
through rock—through magma
to yourself—to an abscess of nothing
that you will recognize as nothing
that you will know is coming again and again
under the same rules.

3
The trap . . .

Bakaris slept fitfully in his jail cell. Though haughty and insolent during the day, his nights were tortured by erotic dreams of Kitiara and fearful dreams of his execution at the hands of the Knights of Solamnia. Or perhaps it was his execution at Kitiara's hands. He was never certain, when he woke in a cold sweat, which it had been. Lying in his cold cell in the still hours of the night when he could not sleep, Bakaris cursed the elven woman who had been the cause of his downfall. Over and over he plotted his revenge upon er—if only she would fall into his hands.

Bakaris was thinking of this, hovering between sleep and wakefulness, when the sound of a key in the lock of his cell door brought him to his feet. It was near dawn, near the hour of execution! Perhaps the knights were coming for him!

"Who is it?" Bakaris called harshly.

"Hush!" commanded a voice. "You are in no danger, if you keep quiet and do as you are told."

Bakaris sat back down on his bed in astonishment. He recognized the voice. How not? Night after night it had spoken in his vengeful thoughts. The elf woman! And the commander could see two other figures in the shadows, small figures. The dwarf and the kender, most likely. They always hung around the elf woman.

The cell door opened. The elf woman glided inside. She was heavily cloaked and carried another cloak in her hand.

"Hurry," she ordered coldly. "Put this on."

"Not until I know what this is about," Bakaris said suspiciously, though his soul sang for joy.

"We are exchanging you for . . . for another prisoner," Laurana replied.

Bakaris frowned. He mustn't seem too eager.

"I don't believe you," he stated, lying back down on his bed. "It's a trap—"

"I don't care what you believe!" Laurana snapped impatiently. "You're coming if I have to knock you senseless! It won't matter whether you are conscious or not, just so long as I'm able to exhibit you to Kiti—the one wants you!"

Kitiara! So that was it. What was she up to? What game was she playing? Bakaris hesitated. He didn't trust Kit any more than she trusted him. She was quite capable of using him to further her own ends, which is undoubtedly what she was doing now. But perhaps he could use her in return. If only he knew what was going on! But looking at Laurana's pale, rigid face, Bakaris knew that she was quite prepared to carry out her threat. He would have to bide his time.

"It seems I have no choice," he said. Moonlight filtered through a barred window into the filthy cell, shining on Bakaris's face. He'd been in prison for weeks. How long he didn't know, he'd lost count. As he reached for the cloak, he caught Laurana's cold green eyes, which were fixed on him intently, narrow slightly in disgust.

Self-consciously, Bakaris raised his good hand and scratched the new growth of beard.

"Pardon, your ladyship," he said sarcastically, "but the servants in your establishment have not thought fit to bring me a razor. I know how the sight of facial hair disgusts you elves!"

To his surprise, Bakaris saw his words draw blood. Laurana's face turned pale, her lips chalk-white. Only by a supreme effort did she control herself. "Move!" she said in a strangled voice.

At the sound, the dwarf entered the room, hand on his battle-axe. "You heard the general," Flint snarled. "Get going. Why your miserable carcass is worth trading for Tanis—"

"Flint!" said Laurana tersely.

Suddenly Bakaris understood! Kitiara's plan began to take shape in his mind.

"So—Tanis! He's the one I'm being exchanged for." He watched Laurana's face closely. No reaction. He might have been speaking of a stranger instead of a man Kitiara had told him was this woman's lover. He tried again, testing his theory. "I wouldn't call him a prisoner, however, unless you speak of a prisoner of love. Kit must have tired of him. Ah, well. Poor man. I'll miss him. He and I have much in common—"

Now there was a reaction. He saw the delicate jaws clench, the shoulders tremble beneath the cloak. Without a word, Laurana turned and stalked out of the cell. So he was right. This had something to do with the bearded half-elf. But what? Tanis had left Kit in Flotsam. Had she found him again? Had he returned to her? Bakaris fell silent, wrapping the cloak around him. Not that it mattered, not to him. He would be able to use this new information for his own revenge. Recalling Laurana's strained and rigid face in the moonlight, Bakaris thanked the Dark Queen for her favors as the dwarf shoved him out the cell door.

The sun had not risen yet, although a faint pink line on the eastern horizon foretold that dawn was an hour or so away. It was still dark in the city of Kalaman—dark and silent as the town slept soundly following its day and night of revelry. Even the guards yawned at their post or, in some cases, snored as they slept soundly. It was an easy task for the four heavily cloaked figures to flit silently through the streets until they came to a small locked door in the city wall.

"This used to lead to some stairs that led up to the top of the wall, across it, then back down to the other side," whispered

Tasslehoff, fumbling in one of his pouches until he found his lock-picking tools.

"How do you know?" Flint muttered, peering around nervously.

"I used to come to Kalaman when I was little," Tas said. Finding the slender piece of wire, his small, skilled hands slipped it inside the lock. "My parents brought me. We always came in and out this way."

"Why didn't you use the front gate, or would that have been too simple?" Flint growled.

"Hurry up!" ordered Laurana impatiently.

"We would have used the front gate," Tas said, manipulating the wire. "Ah, there." Removing the wire, he put it carefully back into his pouch, then quietly swung the old door open. "Where was I? Oh, yes. We would have used the front gate, but kender weren't allowed in the city."

"And your parents came in anyway!" Flint snorted, following Tas through the door and up a narrow flight of stone stairs. The dwarf was only half-listening to the kender. He kept his eye on Bakaris, who was, in Flint's view, behaving himself just a bit too well. Laurana had withdrawn completely within herself. Her only words were sharp commands to hurry.

"Well, of course," Tas said, prattling away cheerfully. "They always considered it an oversight. I mean, why should we be on the same list as goblins? Someone must have put us there accidentally. But my parents didn't consider it was polite to argue, so we just came in and out by the side door. Easier for everyone all around. Here we are. Open that door—it's not usually locked. Oops, careful. There's a guard. Wait until he's gone."

Pressing themselves against the wall, they hid in the shadows until the guard had stumbled wearily past, nearly asleep on his feet. Then they silently crossed the wall, entered another door, ran down another flight of stairs, and were outside the city walls.

They were alone. Flint, looking around, could see no sign of anybody or anything in the half-light before dawn. Shivering, he huddled in his cloak, feeling apprehension creep over him. What if Kitiara was telling the truth? What if Tanis was with her? What if he *was* dying?

Angrily Flint forced himself to stop thinking about that. He almost hoped it was a trap! Suddenly his mind was wrenched from its dark thoughts by a harsh voice, speaking so near that he started in terror.

"Is that you, Bakaris?"

"Yes. Good to see you again, Gakhan."

Shaking, Flint turned to see a dark figure emerge from the shadows of the wall. It was heavily cloaked and swathed in cloth. He remembered Tas's description of the draconian.

"Are they carrying any other weapons?" Gakhan demanded, his eyes on Flint's battle-axe.

"No," Laurana answered sharply.

"Search them," Gakhan ordered Bakaris.

"You have my word of honor," Laurana said angrily. "I am a princess of the Qualinesti—"

Bakaris took a step toward her. "Elves have their own code of honor," he sneered. "Or so you said the night you shot me with your cursed arrow."

Laurana's face flushed, but she made no answer nor did she fall back before his advance.

Coming to stand in front of her, Bakaris lifted his right arm with his left hand, then let it fall. "You destroyed my career, my life."

Laurana, holding himself rigid, watched him without moving. "I said I carry no weapons."

"You can search me, if you like," offered Tasslehoff, interposing himself—accidentally—between Bakaris and Laurana. "Here!" He dumped the contents of a pouch onto Bakaris's foot.

"Damn you!" Bakaris swore, cuffing the kender on the side of the head.

"Flint!" Laurana cautioned warningly through clenched teeth. She could see the dwarf's face red with rage. At her command, the dwarf choked back his anger.

"I'm s-sorry, truly!" Tas snuffled, fumbling around the ground after his things.

"If you delay much longer, we won't have to alert the guard," Laurana said coldly, determined not to tremble at the man's foul touch. "The sun will be up and they will see us clearly."

"The elfwoman is right, Bakaris," Gakhan said, an edge in his reptilian voice. "Take the dwarf's battle-axe and let's get out of here."

Looking at the brightening horizon—and at the cloaked and hooded draconian—Bakaris gave Laurana a vicious glance, then snatched the battle-axe away from the dwarf.

"He's no threat! What's an old man like him going to do, anyway?" Bakaris muttered.

"Get moving," Gakhan ordered Laurana, ignoring Bakaris. "Head for that grove of trees. Keep hidden and don't try alerting the guard. I am a magic-user and my spells are deadly. The Dark Lady said to bring you safely, 'general.' I have no instructions regarding your two friends."

They followed Gakhan across the flat, open ground outside the city gates to a large grove of trees, keeping in the shadows as much as possible. Bakaris walked beside Laurana. Holding her head high, she resolutely refused to even acknowledge his existence. Reaching the trees, Gakhan pointed.

"Here are our mounts," he said.

"We're not going anywhere!" Laurana said angrily, staring at the creatures in alarm.

At first Flint thought they were small dragons, but as he drew nearer, the dwarf caught his breath.

"Wyvern!" he breathed.

Distantly related to dragons, wyvern are smaller and lighter and were often used by the Highlords to relay messages, as the griffons were used by the elven lords. Not nearly as intelligent as dragons, the wyvern are noted for their cruel and chaotic natures. The animals in the grove peered at the companions with red eyes, their scorpionlike tails curled menacingly. Tipped with poison, the tail could sting an enemy to death within seconds.

"Where is Tanis?" Laurana demanded.

"He grew worse," Gakhan answered. "If you want to see him, you must come to Dargaard Keep."

"No," Laurana drew back, only to feel Bakaris's hand close over her arm in a firm grip.

"Don't call for help," he said pleasantly, "or one of your friends will die. Well, it seems we're taking a little trip to Dargaard Keep. Tanis is a *dear* friend. I'd hate for him to miss seeing you." Bakaris turned to the draconian. "Gakhan, go back to Kalaman. Let us know the reaction of the people when they discover their 'general' missing."

Gakhan hesitated, his dark reptilian eyes regarding Bakaris warily. Kitiara had warned him something like this might occur. He guessed what Bakaris had in mind—his own private revenge. Gakhan could stop Bakaris, that was no problem. But there was the chance that—during the unpleasantness—one of the prisoners might escape and go for help. They were too near the city walls for comfort. Blast Bakaris anyway! Gakhan scowled, then realized there was nothing he could do but hope Kitiara had provided for this contingency. Shrugging, Gakhan comforted himself with the thought of Bakaris's fate when he returned to the Dark Lady.

"Certainly, Commander," the draconian replied smoothly. Bowing, Gakhan faded back into the shadows. They could see his cloaked figure darting from tree to tree, heading for Kalaman. Bakaris's face grew eager, the cruel lines around the bearded mouth deepened.

"Come on, General." Bakaris shoved Laurana toward the wyvern.

But instead of advancing, Laurana whirled to face the man. "Tell me one thing," she said through pale lips. "Is it true? Is Tanis with . . . with Kitiara? Th-the note said he was wounded at Vingaard Keep . . . dying!"

Seeing the anguish in her eyes—anguish not for herself, but for the half-elf, Bakaris smiled. He had never dreamed revenge could be so satisfying. "How should I know? I've been locked in your stinking prison. But I find it difficult to believe he'd be wounded. Kit never allowed him near a fight! The only battles he wages are those of love. . . ."

Laurana's head drooped. Bakaris laid a hand on her arm in mocking sympathy. Angrily Laurana shook free, turning to keep her face hidden.

"I don't believe you!" Flint growled. "Tanis would never allow Kitiara do this—"

"Oh, you're right there, dwarf," Bakaris said, realizing quickly just how far his lies would be believed. "He knows nothing of this. The Dark Lady sent him to Neraka weeks ago, to prepare for our audience with the Queen."

"You know, Flint," Tas said solemnly. "Tanis *was* really fond of Kitiara. Do you remember that party at the Inn of the Last Home? It was Tanis's Day of Life Gift party. He'd just 'come of age' by elven standards and—boy! Was that some party! Do you remember? Caramon got a tankard of ale dumped over his head when he grabbed Dezra. And Raistlin drank too much wine and one of his spells misfired and burned up Otik's apron, and Kit and Tanis were together in that corner next to the firepit. and they were—"

Bakaris glanced at Tas in annoyance. The commander disliked being reminded of how close Kitiara really was to the half-elf.

"Tell the kender to keep quiet, General," Bakaris growled, "or I'll let the wyvern have him. Two hostages would suit the Dark Lady just as well as three."

"So it is a trap," Laurana said softly, looking around in a daze. "Tanis isn't dying . . . he's not even there! I've been a fool—"

"We're not going anywhere with you!" Flint stated, planting his feet on the ground firmly.

Bakaris regarded him coolly. "Have you ever seen a wyvern sting anyone to death?"

"No," said Tas with interest, "but I saw a scorpion once. Is it like that? Not that I'd want to try it, mind you," the kender faltered, seeing Bakaris's face darken.

"The guards on the walls of the city might well hear your screams," Bakaris said to Laurana, who stared at him as if he were speaking a language she didn't comprehend. "But, by then, it would be too late."

"I've been a fool," Laurana repeated softly.

"Say the word, Laurana!" Flint said stubbornly. "We'll fight—"

"No," she said in a small voice, like a child's. "No. I won't risk your lives, not you and Tas. It was my folly. I will pay. Bakaris, take me. Let my friends go—"

"Enough of this!" Bakaris said impatiently. "I'm not letting anyone go!" Climbing onto the back of a wyvern, he extended his hand to Laurana. "There's only two, so we'll have to double up."

Her face expressionless, Laurana accepted Bakaris's help and climbed onto the wyvern. Putting his good arm around her, he held her close, grinning.

At his touch, Laurana's face regained some of its color. Angrily, she tried to free herself from his grip.

"You are much safer this way, General," Bakaris said harshly in her ear. "I would not want you to fall."

Laurana bit her lip and stared straight ahead, forcing herself not to cry.

"Do these creatures *always* smell so awful," Tas said, regarding the wyvern with disgust as he helped Flint mount. "I think you should convince them to bathe—"

"Watch the tail," Bakaris said coldly. "The wyvern will generally not kill unless I give them the command, but they are highstrung. Little things upset them."

"Oh." Tas gulped. "I'm sure I didn't mean to be insulting. Actually, I suppose one could get used to the smell, after a bit—"

At a signal from Bakaris, the wyvern spread their leathery wings and soared into the air, flying slowly under the unaccustomed burden. Flint gripped Tasslehoff tightly and kept his eyes on Laurana, flying ahead of them with Bakaris. Occasionally the dwarf saw Bakaris lean close to Laurana and he saw Laurana pull away from him. The dwarf's face grew grim.

"That Bakaris is up to no good!" the dwarf muttered to Tas.

"What?" said Tas, turning around.

"I said that Bakaris is up to no good!" the dwarf shouted. "And I'll wager he's acting on his own and not following orders, either. That Gakhan-character wasn't at all pleased about being ordered off."

"What?" Tas yelled. "I can't hear! All this wind—"

"Oh, never mind!" The dwarf felt dizzy all of a sudden. He was finding it hard to breath. Trying to take his mind off himself, he stared gloomily down at the tree tops emerging from the shadows as the sun began to rise.

After flying for about an hour, Bakaris made a motion with his hand and the wyvern began slowly circling, searching for a clear place to land on the heavily forested mountainside. Pointing at a small clearing just barely visible among the trees, Bakaris shouted instructions to the lead beast. The wyvern landed as ordered and Bakaris climbed down.

Flint glanced around, his fears growing. There was no sign of any fortress. No sign of life of any kind. They were in a small cleared area, surrounded by tall pine trees whose ancient limbs were so thick and tangled that they effectively shut out most of the sun's light. Around them, the forest was dark and filled with moving shadows. At one end of the clearing Flint saw a small cave, carved out of the cliff face.

"Where are we?" Laurana asked sternly. "This can't possibly be Dargaard Keep. Why are we stopping?"

"Astute observation, 'general,' " Bakaris said pleasantly. "Dargaard Keep is about a mile farther up the mountain. They're not expecting us yet. The Dark Lady probably hasn't even had her breakfast. We wouldn't want to be impolite and disturb her, would we?" He glanced over at Tas and Flint. "You two—stay put," he instructed as the kender seemed about to jump down. Tas froze.

Moving to stand near Laurana, Bakaris placed his hand on the neck of the wyvern. The beast's lidless eyes followed his every move as expectantly as a dog waiting to be fed.

"You get down, Lady Laurana," Bakaris said with lethal softness, coming quite near her as she sat upon the wyvern's back, regarding him scornfully. "We've time for a little . . . breakfast ourselves. . . ."

Laurana's eyes flashed. Her hand to her sword with such conviction she almost convinced herself it was there. "Stand away from me!" she commanded with such presence that, for a moment, Bakaris halted. Then, grinning, he reached up and grabbed hold of her wrist.

"No, lady. I wouldn't struggle. Remember the wyvern—and your friends over there. One word from me, and they will die very nasty deaths!"

Cringing, Laurana looked over to see the wyvern's scorpion tail poised above Flint's back. The beast quivered with anticipation of the kill.

"No! Laurana—" Flint began in agony, but she cast a sharp glance at him, reminding him that she was still the general. Her face drained of life, she allowed Bakaris to help her down.

"There, I thought you looked hungry," Bakaris said, grinning.

"Let them go!" Laurana demanded. "It's me you want—"

"You're right there," Bakaris said, grabbing hold of her around her waist. "But their presence seems to insure your good behavior."

"Don't you worry about us, Laurana!" Flint roared.

"Shut up, dwarf!" Bakaris cried in a rage. Shoving Laurana back against the body of the wyvern, he turned to stare at the dwarf and the kender. Flint's blood chilled as he saw the wild madness in the man's eyes.

"I—I think we better do as he says, Flint," Tas said, swallowing. "He'll hurt Laurana—"

"Hurt her? Oh, not much," Bakaris said, laughing. "She will still be useful to Kitiara for whatever purpose she may have in mind. But don't move, dwarf. I may forget myself!" Bakaris warned, hearing Flint choke in anger. He turned back to Laurana. "As it is, Kitiara won't mind if I have a little fun with the lady first. No, don't faint—"

It was an old elven self-defense technique. Flint had seen it done often and he tensed, ready to act as Laurana's eyes rolled up, her body sagged, and her knees seemed to give way.

Instinctively, Bakaris reached to catch her.

"No, you don't! I like my women lively—oof!"

Laurana's fist slammed into his stomach, knocking the breath from his body. Doubling over in pain, he fell forward. Bringing her knee up, Laurana caught him directly under the chin. As Bakaris pitched into the dirt, Flint grabbed the startled kender and slid off the wyvern.

"Run, Flint! Quickly!" Laurana gasped, leaping away from the wyvern and the man groaning on the ground. "Get into the woods!"

But Bakaris, his face twisted with rage, reached out his hand and grabbed Laurana's ankle. She stumbled and fell flat, kicking frantically at him. Wielding a tree limb, Flint leaped at Bakaris as the commander was struggling to his feet. Hearing Flint's roar, Barkaris spun around and struck the dwarf in the face with the back of his hand. In the same motion, he caught hold of Laurana's arm and dragged her to her feet. Then, turning, he glared at Tas, who had run up beside the unconscious dwarf.

"The lady and I are going into the cave . . . " Bakaris said, breathing heavily. He gave Laurana's arm a wrench, causing her to cry out in pain. "Make one move, kender, and I'll break her arm. Once we get into the cave, I don't want to be disturbed. There's a dagger in my belt. I'll be holding it to the lady's throat. Do you understand, little fool?"

"Yes, s-sir," stammered Tasslehoff. "I—I wouldn't dream of interfering. I—I'll just stay here with—with Flint."

"Don't go into the woods." Bakaris began to drag Laurana toward the cave. "Draconians guard the forest."

"N-no, sir," stuttered Tas, kneeling down beside Flint, his eyes wide.

Satisfied, Bakaris glared once more at the cowering kender, then shoved Laurana toward the entrance to the cave.

Blinded by tears, Laurana stumbled forward. As if to remind her she was trapped, Bakaris twisted her arm again. The pain was excruciating. There was no way to break free of the man's powerful grip. Cursing herself for falling into this trap, Laurana tried to battle her fear and think clearly. It was hard, the man's hand was strong, and his smell—the human smell—

reminded her of Tanis in a horrifying way.

As if guessing her thoughts, Bakaris clutched her close to him, rubbing his bearded face against her smooth cheek.

"You will be one more woman the half-elf and I have shared—" he whispered hoarsely, then his voice broke off in a bubble of agony.

For an instant, Bakaris's grip on Laurana's arm tightened almost past endurance. Then it loosened. His hand slipped from her arm. Laurana tore free of his grip, then spun around to face him.

Blood oozed between Bakaris's fingers as he clutched at his side where Tasslehoff's little knife still protruded from the wound. Drawing his own dagger, the man lunged at the defiant kender.

Something snapped in Laurana, letting loose a wild fury and hatred she had not guessed lurked inside her. No longer feeling any fear, no longer caring if she lived or died, Laurana had one thought in mind—she would kill this human male.

With a savage shriek, she flung herself at him, knocking him to the ground. He gave a grunt, then lay still beneath her. Desperately Laurana fought, trying to grab his knife. Then she realized his body was not moving. Slowly she rose to her feet, shaking in reaction.

For a moment she could see nothing through the red mist before her eyes. When it cleared, she saw Tasslehoff roll the body over. Bakaris lay dead. His eyes stared up at the sky, a look of profound shock and surprise on his face. His hand still clutched the dagger he had driven into his own gut.

"What happened?" Laurana whispered, quivering with anger and revulsion.

"You knocked him down and he fell on his knife," Tas said calmly.

"But before that—"

"Oh, I stuck him," Tas said. Plucking his knife from the man's side, he looked at it proudly. "And Caramon told me it wouldn't be of any use unless I met a vicious rabbit! Wait until I tell him!

"You know, Laurana," he continued, somewhat sadly, "everyone always underestimates us kender. Bakaris really should have searched my pouches. Say, that was a neat fainting trick you pulled. Did you—"

"How's Flint?" Laurana interrupted, not wanting to remember those last few horrible moments. Without quite knowing what she was doing or why, she pulled her cape from her shoulders and threw it down over the bearded face. "We've got to get out of here."

"He'll be all right," Tas said, glancing over at the dwarf, who was groaning and shaking his head. "What about the wyvern? Do you think they'll attack us?"

"I don't know," Laurana said, eyeing the animals. The wyvern stared around uneasily, uncertain as to what had happened to their master. "I've heard they're not very smart. They generally won't act on their own. Maybe—if we don't make any sudden moves—we can escape into the forest before they figure out what's happened. Help Flint."

"Come on, Flint," Tas said urgently, tugging at the dwarf. "We've got to esc—"

The kender's voice was cut off by a wild cry, a cry of such fear and terror that it made Tas's hair stand on end. Looking up, he saw Laurana staring at a figure that had—apparently—emerged from the cave. At the sight of the figure, Tasslehoff felt the most terrible sensation sweep over his body. His heart raced, his hands went cold, he couldn't breathe.

"Flint!" he managed to gasp before his throat closed completely.

The dwarf, hearing a tone in the kender's voice he'd never heard before, struggled to sit up. "What—"

Tas could only point.

Flint focused his bleary vision in the direction Tas indicated.

"In the name of Reorx," the dwarf said, his voice breaking, "what is that?"

The figure moved relentlessly toward Laurana, who—held spellbound at its command—could do nothing but stare at it. Dressed in antique armor, it might have been a Knight of Solamnia. But the armor was blackened as if it had been burned by fire. An orange light flared beneath its helm, while the helm itself seemed perched on empty air.

The figure reached out an armored arm. Flint choked in horror. The armored arm did not end in a hand. The knight seemingly grasped hold of Laurana with nothing but air. But she screamed in pain, falling to her knees in front of the ghastly vision. Her head slumped forward, she collapsed, senseless from the chill touch. The knight released his grip, letting the inert body slip to the ground. Bending down, the knight lifted her in his arms.

Tas started to move, but the knight turned his flaring orange gaze upon him and the kender was held fast, gazing into the orange flame of the creature's eyes. Neither he nor Flint could look away, though the horror was so great that the dwarf feared he might lose his reason. Only his love and concern for Laurana kept him clinging to consciousness. Over and over he told himself he must do something, he must save her. But he couldn't make his trembling body obey. The knight's flickering gaze swept over the two.

"Go back to Kalaman," said a hollow voice. "Tell them we have the elfwoman. The Dark Lady will arrive tomorrow at noon, to discuss terms of surrender."

Turning, the knight walked over Bakaris's body, the figure's shimmering armor passing right through the corpse as if it no longer existed. Then the knight vanished into the dark shadows of the woods, carrying Laurana in his arms.

With the knight's departure, the spell was lifted. Tas, feeling weak and sick, began to shiver uncontrollably. Flint struggled to his feet.

"I'm going after it—" the dwarf muttered, though his hands shook so he could barely lift his helm from the dirt.

"N-no," stammered Tasslehoff, his face strained and white as he stared after the knight. "Whatever that thing was, we can't fight it. I—I was scared, Flint!" The kender shook his head in misery. "I—I'm sorry, but I can't face that—that thing again! We've got to go back to Kalaman. Maybe we can get help—"

Tas started off into the woods at a run. For a moment Flint stood angry and irresolute, staring after Laurana. Then his face crumpled in agony. "He's right," he mumbled. "I can't go after that thing either. Whatever it was, it wasn't of this world."

Turning away, Flint caught a glimpse of Bakaris, lying beneath Laurana's cloak. Swift pain cramped the dwarf's heart. Ignoring it, Flint said to himself with sudden certainty, "He was lying about Tanis. And so was Kitiara. He's not with her, I know it!" The dwarf clenched his fist. "I don't know where Tanis is, but someday I'll have to face him and I'll have to tell him . . . I let him down. He trusted me to keep her safe, and I failed!" The dwarf closed his eyes. Then he heard Tas shout. Sighing, he stumbled blindly after the kender, rubbing his left arm as he ran. "How will I ever tell him?" he moaned. "How?"

4

A peaceful interlude.

"All right," said Tanis, glaring at the man who sat so calmly in front of him. "I want answers. You deliberately took us into the maelstrom! Why? Did you know this place was here? Where are we? Where are the others?"

Berem sat before Tanis in a wooden chair. It was ornately carved with figures of birds and animals in a style popular among the elves. In fact, it reminded Tanis strongly of Lorac's throne in the doomed elven kingdom of Silvanesti. The likeness did nothing to calm Tanis's spirits, and Berem flinched under the half-elf's angry stare. The hands that were too young for the middle-aged man's body plucked at his shabby trousers. He shifted his gaze to glance nervously around their strange surroundings.

"Damn it! Answer me!" Tanis raved. Flinging himself at Berem, he gripped the man's shirt and yanked him up from his chair. Then his clenching hands moved to the man's throat.

"Tanis!" Swiftly Goldmoon rose and laid a restraining hand on Tanis's arm. But the half-elf was beyond reason. His face was so twisted with fear and anger that she didn't recognize him. Frantically she tore at the hands that gripped Berem. "Riverwind, make him stop!"

The big Plainsman grasped Tanis by the wrists and wrenched him away from Berem, holding the half-elf in his strong arms. "Leave him alone, Tanis!"

For a moment, Tanis struggled, then went limp, drawing a deep, shuddering breath.

"He's a mute," Riverwind said sternly. "Even if he wanted to tell you, he couldn't. He can't talk—"

"Yes, I can."

The three stopped, startled, staring at Berem.

"I can talk," he said calmly, speaking Common. Absently he rubbed his throat where the marks of Tanis's fingers stood out red against his tan skin.

"Then why pretend you can't?" Tanis asked, breathing heavily.

Berem rubbed his neck, his eyes on Tanis. "People don't ask questions of a man who can't talk. . . . "

Tanis forced himself to calm down, to think about this a moment. Glancing at Riverwind and Goldmoon, he saw Riverwind scowl and shake his head. Goldmoon shrugged slightly. Finally Tanis dragged another wooden chair over to sit in front of Berem. Noticing that the back of the chair was split and cracked, he sat down carefully. "Berem," Tanis spoke slowly, curbing his impatience, "you're talking to us. Does that mean you'll answer our questions?"

Berem stared at Tanis, then nodded his head, once.

"Why?" Tanis asked.

Berem licked his lips, glancing around. "I—You must help me—get out of here—I-I can't stay here—"

Tanis felt chilled, despite the warm stuffiness of the room. "Are you in danger? Are we in danger? What is this place?"

"I don't know!" Berem looked around helplessly. "I don't know where we are. I only know I cannot stay here. I must get back!"

"Why? The Dragon Highlords are hunting for you. One of th-the Highlords—" Tanis coughed, then spoke huskily. "One of them told me that *you* were the key to complete victory for the Dark Queen. Why, Berem? What do you have that they want?"

"I don't know!" Berem cried, clenching his fist. "I only know that they have been chasing me . . . I have been fleeing them for-for years! No peace . . . no rest!"

"How long, Berem?" Tanis asked softly. "How long have they been chasing you?"

"Years!" Berem said in a strangled voice. "Years . . . I don't know how long." Sighing, he seemed to sink back into his calm complacency. "I am three hundred and twenty-two years old. Twenty-three? Twenty-four?" He shrugged. "For most of those years, the Queen has been seeking me."

"Three hundred and twenty-two!" Goldmoon said in astonishment. "But—but you're human! That's not possible!"

"Yes, I am human," Berem said, his blue eyes focusing on Goldmoon. "I know it is impossible. I have died. Many times." His gaze switched to Tanis. "You saw me die. It was in Pax Tharkas. I recognized you when you first came on the ship."

"You did die when the rocks fell on you!" Tanis exclaimed. "But we saw you *alive* at the wedding feast, Sturm and I—"

"Yes. I saw you, too. That's why I fled. I knew . . . there would be more questions." Berem shook his head. "How could I explain my survival to you? I do not know myself how I survive! All I know is that I die and then I'm alive again. Again and again." His head sank into his hands. "All I want is peace!"

Tanis was completely mystified. Scratching his beard, he stared at the man. That he was lying was almost certain. Oh, not about dying and coming back to life. Tanis had seen that himself. But he knew for a fact that the Queen of Darkness was exerting almost all forces she could spare from the war to search for this man. Surely he must know why!

"Berem, how did the green gemstone get, uh, into your flesh?"

"I don't know," Berem answered in such a low voice they could barely hear him. Self-consciously, his hand clutched his breast as if it pained him. "It is part of my body, like my bones and my blood. I—I think *it* is what brings me back to life."

"Can you remove it?" Goldmoon asked gently, sinking down onto a cushion next to Berem, her hand on his arm.

Berem shook his head violently, his gray hair falling over his eyes. "I've tried!" he muttered, "Many times I've tried to rip it out! I might as well try to tear out my own heart!"

Tanis shivered, then sighed in exasperation. This was no help! He still had no idea where they were. He'd hoped Berem could tell them . . . Once more, Tanis looked around their strange surroundings. They were in a room of an obviously ancient building, lit with a soft eerie light that seemed to come from the moss that covered the walls like tapestry. The furniture was as old as the building and in battered, shabby condition, though it must have been rich once. There were no windows. Nothing could be heard outside. They had no idea how long they'd been here. Time had grown confused, broken only by eating some of the strange plants and sleeping fitfully.

Tanis and Riverwind had explored the building but could find no exit and no other signs of life. Tanis wondered, in fact, if some magical spell had not been laid over the whole thing, a spell designed to keep them inside. For every time they ventured forth, the narrow, dimly lit hallways always led them inexplicably back to this room.

They remembered little about what happened after the ship sank into the maelstrom. Tanis recalled hearing the wooden planks shattering. He remembered seeing the mast fall, the sails rip. He heard screams. He saw Caramon washed overboard by a gigantic wave. He remembered seeing Tika's red curls swirling in the water, then she, too, was gone. There had been the dragon . . . and Kitiara. . . . The scratches of the dragon's talons remained on his arm. Then there was another wave . . . he remembered holding his breath until he knew he would die from the pain in his lungs. He remembered thinking that death would be easy and welcome, even as he fought to grab hold of a piece of wood. He remembered surfacing in the rushing water, only to be sucked down again and knowing it was the end. . . .

And then he had awakened in this strange place, his clothes wet with sea water, to find Riverwind and Goldmoon and Berem here with him.

At first Berem had seemed terrified of them, crouching in a corner, refusing to let them come near. Patiently Goldmoon spoke to him and brought him food. Gradually, her gentle ministrations won him over. That and—Tanis recognized now—his intense desire to leave this place.

Tanis had supposed, when he first began to question Berem, that the man had steered the ship into the maelstrom because he knew this place existed, that he had brought them here on purpose.

But now the half-elf wasn't so certain. It was apparent from the confused and frightened look on Berem's face that he had no idea where they were either. The mere fact that he was even talking to them gave an indication that what he said was true. He was desperate. He wanted out of here. Why?

"Berem—" Tanis began, getting up and pacing about the room. He felt Berem's gaze follow him. "If you are running from the Queen of Darkness, this seems like it might be an ideal place to hide—"

"No!" Berem shouted, half-rising.

Tanis spun around. "Why not? Why are you so determined to get out of here? Why do you want to go back to where *she* will find you?"

Berem cringed, huddling back down in his chair. "I-I don't know anything about this place! I swear it! I-I m-must get back. . . . There's someplace I must go . . . I'm hunting for something. . . . Until I find it, there'll be no rest."

"Find it! Find what?" Tanis shouted. He felt Goldmoon's hand on his and he knew he was raving like a maniac, but it was so frustrating! To have what the Queen of Darkness would give the world to acquire and not know why!

"I can't tell you!" Berem whimpered.

Tanis sucked in his breath, closing his eyes, trying to calm himself. His head throbbed. He felt as if he might fly into a thousand pieces. Goldmoon rose to her feet. Putting both her hands on his shoulders, she whispered soothing words he could not comprehend, except for the name of Mishakal. Slowly the terrible feeling passed, leaving him drained and exhausted.

"All right, Berem." Tanis sighed. "It's all right. I'm sorry. We won't talk about it anymore. Tell me about yourself. Where are you from?"

Berem hesitated a moment, his eyes narrowed and he grew tense. Tanis was struck by Berem's peculiar manner. "I'm from Solace. Where are you from?" he repeated casually.

Berem regarded him warily. "You—you would never have heard of it. A-A small village outside of . . . outside of . . ." He swallowed, then cleared his throat. "Neraka."

"Neraka?" Tanis looked at Riverwind.

The Plainsman shook his head. "He's right. I have never heard of it."

"Nor I," Tanis muttered. "Too bad Tasslehoff and his maps aren't here . . . Berem, why—"

"Tanis!" Goldmoon cried.

The half-elf rose at the sound of her voice, his hand going reflexively to the sword that wasn't there. Dimly he remembered struggling with it in the water, its weight dragging him down. Cursing himself for not setting Riverwind to guard the door, he could do nothing now but stare at the red-robed man who stood framed in its opening.

"Hello," the man said pleasantly, speaking Common.

The red robes brought Raistlin's image back to Tanis with such force that the half-elf's vision blurred. For a moment he thought it *was* Raistlin. Then he saw clearly. This mage was older—much older, and his face was kind.

"Where are we?" Tanis demanded harshly. "Who are you? Why were we brought here?"

"*KreeaQUEKH*" the man said in disgust. Turning, he walked away.

"Damn!" Tanis jumped forward, intent on grabbing the man and dragging him back. But he felt a firm hand on his shoulder.

"Wait," Riverwind counseled. "Calm down, Tanis. He's a magic-user. You couldn't fight him even if you had a sword. We'll follow him, see where he goes. If he laid a spell on this place, perhaps he'll have to lift it to get out himself."

Tanis drew a deep breath. "You're right, of course." He gasped for air. "I'm sorry. I don't know what's wrong with me. I feel tight and stretched, like the skin over a drum. We'll follow him. Goldmoon, you stay here with Berem—"

"No!" Berem shouted. Throwing himself out of the chair, he clutched at Tanis with such force he nearly knocked him down. "Don't leave me here! Don't!"

"We're not going to leave you!" Tanis said, trying to extricate himself from Berem's deathlike grip. "Oh, all right. Maybe we'd all better stay together anyway."

Hurrying out into the narrow corridor, they started down the bleak, deserted hallway.

"There he goes!" Riverwind pointed.

In the dim light, they could just see a bit of red robe whisking around a corner. Walking softly, they followed after it. The hallway led down another hallway with other rooms branching off it.

"This was never here before!" Riverwind exclaimed. "There was always solid wall."

"Solid illusion," Tanis muttered. Stepping into the hallway, they looked around curiously. Rooms filled with the same ancient, mismatched furniture as in their room opened from the empty corridor. These rooms, too, were empty, but all lit with the same strange glowing lights. Perhaps it was an inn. If so, they appeared to be its only customers and might have been its only customers for a hundred years.

They made their way through broken corridors and vast pillared halls. There wasn't time to investigate their surroundings, not while trailing the red-robed man, who was proving remarkably quick and elusive. Twice they thought they had lost him, only to catch a glimpse of the red robes floating down a circular stairway beneath them, or flitting through an adjacent hallway.

It was at one such juncture that they stood for a moment, glancing down two divergent hallways, feeling lost and frustrated.

"Split up," Tanis said after a moment. "But don't go far. We'll meet back here. If you see any sign of him, Riverwind, whistle once. I'll do the same."

Nodding, the Plainsman and Goldmoon slipped down one hallway while Tanis—with Berem practically tripping on his heels—searched the other one.

He found nothing. The hallway led to a large room, eerily lit as was everything else in this strange place. Should he look in it or turn back? After hesitating a moment, Tanis decided to take a quick glance inside. The room was empty, except for a huge round table. And on the table, he saw as he drew closer, was a remarkable map!

Tanis bent quickly over the map, hoping for a clue as to where and what this mysterious place was. The map was a miniature replica of the city! Protected by a dome of clear crystal, it was so exact in detail that Tanis had the strange feeling the city beneath the crystal was more real than the one where he stood.

"Too bad Tas isn't here," he thought to himself wistfully, picturing the kender's delight.

The buildings were constructed in the ancient style; delicate spires rose into the crystal sky, light sparkled off the white domes. Stone archways spanned garden boulevards. The streets were laid out like a great spider web, leading directly into the heart of the city itself.

Tanis felt Berem pluck nervously at his sleeve, gesturing that they should leave. Even though he could talk, it was obvious that the man had grown accustomed to, and perhaps even preferred, silence.

"Yes, just a moment," Tanis said, reluctant to go. He had heard nothing from Riverwind and there was every possibility this map might lead them out of this place.

Bending over the glass, he stared at the miniature more closely. Around the center of the city stood great pavilions and columned palaces. Domes made of glass cradled summer flowers amid the winter snows. In the exact center of the city itself rose a building that seemed familiar to Tanis, though he knew he had never been in this city in his life. Still, he recognized it. Even as he studied it, searching his memory, the hair prickled on the back of his neck.

It seemed to be a temple to the gods. And it was the most beautiful structure he had ever seen, more beautiful than the Towers of the Sun and the Stars in the elven kingdoms. Seven towers rose to the heavens as if praising the gods for their creation. The center tower soared into the skies far above the rest, as if it did not praise the gods, but rivaled them. Confused memories of his elven teachers came back to him, telling him stories of the Cataclysm, stories of the Kingpriest—

Tanis drew back from the miniature, his breath catching in his throat. Berem stared at him in alarm, the man's face going white.

"What is it?" he croaked in fear, clutching at Tanis.

The half-elf shook his head. He could not speak. The terrible implications of where they were and what was going on were breaking over him like red waters of the Blood Sea.

In confusion, Berem looked at the center of the map. The man's eyes widened, then he shrieked, a scream unlike any Tanis had heard before. Suddenly Berem threw himself bodily upon the crystal dome, beating at it as if he would tear it apart.

"The City of Damnation!" Berem moaned. "The City of Damnation."

Tanis started forward to calm him, then he heard

Riverwind's shrill whistle. Grabbing Berem, Tanis hauled him away from the crystal. "I know," he said. "Come on, we've got to get out of here."

But how? How did you get out of a city that was supposed to have been blasted off the face of Krynn? How did you get out of a city that must lie at the very bottom of the Blood Sea? How did you get out of—

As he shoved Berem through the door of the map room, Tanis glanced above the doorway. Word were carved in its crumbling marble. Word that had once spoken of one of the wonders of the world. Words whose letters were now cracked and covered with moss. But he could read them.

Welcome, O noble visitor, to our beautiful city.
Welcome to the city beloved of the gods.
Welcome, honored guest, to
Istar.

5

"I killed him once. . . ."

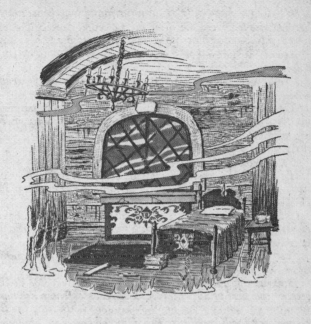

"*I*'ve seen what you're doing
to him! You're trying to murder him!" Caramon shouted at Par-
Salian. Head of the Tower of High Sorcery—the last Tower of
High Sorcery, located in the weird, alien forests of Wayreth—
Par-Salian was the highest ranking in the Order of magic-users
currently living on Krynn.

To the twenty-year-old warrior, the withered old man in the
snowy white robes was a thing he might have broken with his
bare hands. The young warrior had put up with a good deal the
last two days, but now his patience had run out.

———

"We are not in the business of murder," Par-Salian said in his soft voice. "Your brother knew what he faced when he agreed to undergo these Trials. He knew death was the penalty for failure."

"He didn't, not really," Caramon mumbled, brushing his hand across his eyes. "Or if he did, he didn't care. Sometimes his . . . his love for his magic clouds his thinking."

"Love? No." Par-Salian smiled sadly. "I do not think we could call it love."

"Well, whatever," Caramon muttered. "He didn't realize what you were going to do to him! It's all so damn serious—"

"Of course," Par-Salian said mildly. "What would happen to you, warrior, if you went into battle without knowing how to use your sword?"

Caramon scowled. "Don't try to weasel out—"

"What would happen?" Par-Salian persisted.

"I'd be killed," Caramon said with the elaborate patience one uses when speaking to an elderly person who is growing a bit childish. "Now—"

"Not only would you die," Par-Salian continued, "but your comrades, those who depend on you, might they also die because of your incompetence?"

"Yes," Caramon said impatiently, starting to continue his tirade. Then, pausing, he fell silent.

"You see my point," Par-Salian said gently. "We do not require this Test of all who would use magic. There are many with the gift who go through life, content with using the first elementary spells taught by the schools. These are enough to help them in their day-to-day lives, and that is all they want. But sometimes there comes a person like your brother. To him, the gift is more than a tool to help him through life. To him, the gift is life. He aspires higher. He seeks knowledge and power that can be dangerous—not only to the user but to those around him as well. Therefore we force all magic-users who would enter into those realms where true power can be attained to take the Test, to submit themselves to the Trials. Thus we weed out the incompetent. . . ."

"You've done your best to weed out Raistlin!" Caramon snarled. "He's not incompetent, but he's frail and now he's hurt, maybe dying!"

"No, he isn't incompetent. Quite the contrary. Your brother has done very well, warrior. He has defeated all of his enemies.

He has handled himself like a true professional. Almost too professional." Par-Salian appeared thoughtful. "I wonder if someone hasn't taken an interest in your brother."

"I wouldn't know." Caramon's voice hardened with resolve. "And I don't care. All I know is that I am putting a stop to it. Right now."

"You cannot. You will not be permitted. He isn't dying—"

"You can't stop me!" Caramon stated coldly. "Magic! Tricks to keep kids amused! True power! Bah! It's not worth getting killed over—"

"Your brother believes it is," Par-Salian said softly. "Shall I show you how much he believes in his magic? Shall I show you true power?"

Ignoring Par-Salian, Caramon took a step forward, determined to end his brother's suffering. That step was his last—at least for some time. He found himself immobilized, frozen in place as surely as if his feet were encased in ice. Fear gripped Caramon. It was the first time he had ever been spellbound, and the helpless feeling of being totally under another's control was more terrifying than facing six axe-wielding goblins.

"Watch." Par-Salian began to chant strange words. "I am going to show you a vision of what might have been. . . ."

Suddenly Caramon saw himself entering the Tower of High Sorcery! He blinked in astonishment. He was walking through the doors and down the eerie corridors! The image was so real that Caramon looked down at his own body in alarm, half-afraid he might find he wasn't really there. But he was. He seemed to be in two places at the same time. True power. The warrior began to sweat, then shivered with a chill.

Caramon—the Caramon in the Tower—was searching for his brother. Up and down empty corridors he wandered, calling Raistlin's name. And finally he found him.

The young mage lay on the cold stone floor. Blood trickled from his mouth. Near him was the body of a dark elf, dead—by Raistlin's magic. But the cost had been terrible. The young mage himself seemed near death.

Caramon ran to his brother and lifted the frail body in his strong arms. Ignoring Raistlin's frantic pleas to leave him alone, the warrior began to carry his twin from this evil Tower. He would take Raistlin from this place if it was the last thing he did.

But—just as they came near the door that led out of the

Tower—a wraith appeared before them. Another test, Caramon thought grimly. Well, this will be one test Raistlin won't have to handle. Gently laying his brother down, the warrior turned to meet this final challenge.

What happened then made no sense. The watching Caramon blinked in astonishment. He saw himself cast a magic spell! Dropping his sword, he held strange objects in his hands and began to speak words he didn't understand! Lightning bolts shot from his hands! The wraith vanished with a shriek.

The real Caramon looked wildly at Par-Salian, but the mage only shook his head and—wordlessly—pointed back to the image that wavered before Caramon's eyes. Frightened and confused, Caramon turned back to watch.

He saw Raistlin rise slowly.

"How did you do that?" Raistlin asked, propping himself up against the wall.

Caramon didn't know. How could he do something that took his brother years of study! But the warrior saw himself rattling off a glib explanation. Caramon also saw the look of pain and anguish on his brother's face.

"No, Raistlin!" the real Caramon cried. "It's a trick! A trick of this old man's! I can't do that! I'd never steal your magic from you! Never!"

But the image Caramon—swaggering and brash—went over to "rescue" his "little" brother, to save him from himself.

Raising his hands, Raistlin held them out toward his brother. But not to embrace him. No. The young mage, sick and injured and totally consumed with jealousy, began to speak the words of the one spell, the last spell he had strength to cast.

Flames flared from Raistlin's hands. The magical fire billowed forth—and engulfed his brother.

Caramon watched in horror, too stunned to speak, as his own image was consumed in fire. . . . He watched as his brother collapsed onto the cold stone floor.

"No! Raist—"

Cool, gentle hands touched his face. He could hear voices, but their words were meaningless. He could understand, if he chose. But he didn't want to understand. His eyes were closed. He could open them, but he refused. Opening his eyes, hearing those words, would only make the pain real.

"I must rest," Caramon heard himself say, and he sank back into darkness.

He was approaching another Tower, a different Tower. The Tower of the Stars in Silvanesti. Once more Raistlin was with him, only now his brother wore the Black Robes. And now it was Raistlin's turn to help Caramon. The big warrior was wounded. Blood pulsed steadily from a spear-wound that had nearly taken off his arm.

"I must rest," Caramon said again.

Gently Raistlin laid him down, making him comfortable, his back propped up against the cold stone of the Tower. And then Raistlin started to leave.

"Raist! Don't—" Caramon cried. "You can't leave me here!"

Looking around, the injured, defenseless warrior saw hordes of the undead elves who had attacked them in Silvanesti waiting to leap upon him. Only one thing held them back, his brother's magical power.

"Raist! Don't leave me!" he screamed.

"How does it feel to be weak and alone?" *Raistlin asked him softly.*

"Raist! My brother . . ."

"I killed him once, Tanis, I can do it again!"

"Raist! No! Raist!"

"Caramon, please . . ." Another voice. This one gentle. Soft hands touched him. "Caramon, please! Wake up! Come back, Caramon. Come back to me. I need you."

No! Caramon pushed away that voice. He pushed away the soft hands. No, I don't want to come back. I won't. I'm tired. I hurt. I want to rest.

But the hands, the voice, wouldn't let him rest. They grabbed him, pulling him from the depths where he longed to sink.

And now he was falling, falling into a horrible red darkness. Skeletal fingers clutched at him, eyeless heads whirled past him, their mouths gaping in silent cries. He drew a breath, then sank into blood. Struggling, smothering, he finally fought his way back to the surface and gasped for air once more. Raistlin! But no, he's gone. His friends. Tanis. Gone, too. He saw him swept away. The ship. Gone. Cracked in half. Sailors cut apart, their blood mingling with the blood-red sea.

Tika! She was near him. He pulled her close. She was gasping for air. But he could not hold onto her. The swirling water tore her from his arms and swept him under. This time he could not find the surface. His lungs were on fire, bursting. Death . . .

---

rest . . . sweet, warm. . . .

But always those hands! Dragging him back to the gruesome surface. Making him breathe the burning air. No, let me go!

And then other hands, rising up from the blood-red water. Firm hands, they took him down from the surface. He fell down . . . down . . . into merciful darkness. Whispered words of magic soothed him, he breathed . . . breathed water . . . and his eyes closed . . . the water was warm and comforting . . . He was a child once more.

But not complete. His twin was missing.

No! Waking was agony. Let him float in that dark dream forever. Better than the sharp, bitter pain.

But the hands tugged at him. The voice called to him.

"Caramon, I need you . . ."

Tika.

"I'm no cleric, but I believe he'll be all right now. Let him sleep awhile."

Tika brushed away her tears quickly, trying to appear strong and in control.

"What . . . what was wrong?" she made herself ask calmly, though she was unable to restrain a shudder. "Was he hurt when the ship . . . went into th-the whirlpool. He's been like this for days! Ever since you found us."

"No, I don't think so. If he had been injured, the sea elves would have healed him. This was something within himself. Who is this 'Raist' he talks about?"

"His twin brother," Tika said hesitantly.

"What happened? Did he die?"

"No-no. I-I'm not quite sure what happened. Caramon loved his brother very much and he . . . Raistlin betrayed him."

"I see." The man nodded solemnly. "It happens, up there. And you wonder why I choose to live down here."

"You saved his life!" Tika said. "And I don't know you . . . your name."

"Zebulah," the man answered, smiling. "And I didn't save his life. He came back for love of you."

Tika lowered her head, her red curls hid her face. "I hope so," she whispered. "I love him so much. I would die myself, if it would save him."

Now that she was certain Caramon would be all right, Tika focused her attention on this strange man. She saw he was middle-aged, clean-shaven, his eyes as wide and frank as his smile. Human, he was dressed in red robes. Pouches dangled from his belt.

"You're a magic-user," Tika said suddenly. "Like Raistlin!"

"Ah, that explains it." Zebulah smiled. "Seeing me, in his semi-conscious state, made this young man think of his brother."

"But what are you doing here?" Tika glanced around at her strange surroundings, seeing them for the first time.

She had seen them, of course, when the man brought her here, but she hadn't noticed them in her worry. Now she realized she was in a chamber of a ruined, crumbling building. The air was warm and stifling. Plants grew lushly in the moist air.

There was some furniture, but it was as ancient and ruined as the room in which it was haphazardly placed. Caramon lay on a three-legged bed—the fourth corner being held up by a stack of old, moss-covered books. Thin rivulets of water, like small, glistening snakes, trickled down a stone wall that gleamed with moisture. Everything gleamed with moisture, in fact, reflecting the pale, eerie, green light that glowed from the moss growing on the wall. The moss was everywhere, of every different color and variety. Deep green, golden yellow, coral red—it climbed the walls and crawled across the domed ceiling.

"What am I doing here?" she murmured. "And where is here?"

"Here is— Well, I suppose you could say here," Zebulah answered pleasantly. "The sea elves saved you from drowning and I brought you here."

"Sea elves? I never heard of sea elves," Tika said, glancing around curiously, as if she might see one hiding in a closet. "And I don't remember elves saving me. All I remember is some sort of huge, gentle fish. . . ."

"Oh, you needn't look around for the sea elves. You won't see them. They fear and distrust KreeaQUEKH—'air-breathers' in their language. And those fish were the sea elves, in the only shape they let KreeaQUEKH see them. Dolphins, you call them."

Caramon stirred and moaned in his sleep. Laying her hand upon his forehead, Tika brushed back his damp hair, soothing him.

"Why did they save our lives, then?" she asked.

"Do you know any elves, land elves?" Zebulah asked.

"Yes," Tika answered softly, thinking of Laurana.

"Then you know that to all elves, life is sacred."

"I understand." Tika nodded. "And like the land elves, they renounce the world rather than help it."

"They are doing what they can to help," Zebulah rebuked her severely. "Do not criticize what you do not understand, young woman."

"I'm sorry," Tika said, flushing. She changed the subject. "But you, you're human. Why—"

"Why am I here? I have neither the time nor the inclination to relate my story to you, for it is obvious you would not understand me either. None of the others do."

Tika caught her breath. "There are others? Have you seen any more from our ship. . . our friends?"

Zebulah shrugged. "There are *always* others down here. The ruins are vast, and many hold small pockets of air. We take those we rescue to the nearest dwellings. As for your friends, I couldn't say. If they were on the ship with you, they were most likely lost. The sea elves have given the dead the proper rituals and sent their souls upon their way." Zebulah stood up. "I'm glad your young man survived. There's lots of food around here. Most of the plants you see are edible. Wander about the ruins if you like. I've laid a magic spell on them so you can't get into the sea and drown. Fix the place up. You'll find more furniture—"

"But wait!" Tika cried. "We can't stay here! We must return to the surface. Surely there must be some way out?"

"They all ask me that," Zebulah said with a touch of impatience. "And, frankly, I agree. There *must* be some way out. People seem to find it on occasion. Then, there are those who simply decide that—like me—they don't want to leave. I have several old friends who have been around for years. But, see for yourself. Look around. Just be careful you stay in the parts of the ruins we've arranged." He turned toward the door

"Wait! Don't go!" Jumping up, tipping over the rickety chair she sat upon, Tika ran after the red-robed magic-user. "You might see my friends. You could tell them—"

"Oh, I doubt it," Zebulah replied. "To tell you the truth—and no offense, young woman—I'm fed up with your conversation. The longer I live here, the more *KreeaQUEKH* like you irritate me. Always in a hurry. Never satisfied to stay in one place. You and your young man would be much happier down here in this world than up there in that one. But no, you'll kill yourselves trying to find your way back. And what do you face up there? Betrayal!" He glanced back at Caramon.

"There is a war up there!" Tika cried passionately. "People are suffering. Don't you care about that?"

"People are always suffering up there," Zebulah said. "Nothing *I* can do about it. No, I don't care. After all, where does caring get you? Where did it get him?" With a angry gesture at Caramon, Zebulah turned and left, slamming the ramshackle door behind him.

Tika stared after the man uncertainly, wondering if she shouldn't run out and and grab him and hang onto him. He was apparently their only link to the world *up there*. Wherever *down here* was. . . .

"Tika . . ."

"Caramon!" Forgetting Zebulah, Tika ran to the warrior, who was struggling to sit up.

"Where in the name of the Abyss are we?" he asked, looking around with wide eyes. "What happened? The ship—"

"I'm—I'm not sure," Tika faltered. "Do you feel well enough to sit? Perhaps you should lie down. . . ."

"I'm all right," Caramon snapped. Then, feeling her flinch at his harshness, he reached out and pulled her in his arms. "I'm sorry, Tika. Forgive me. It's just . . , I . . ." He shook his head.

"I understand," Tika said softly. Resting her head on his chest, she told him about Zebulah and the sea elves. Caramon listened, blinking in confusion as he slowly absorbed all he heard. Scowling, he looked at the door.

"I wish I'd been conscious," he muttered. "That Zebulah character knows the way out, more than likely. I'd have made him show us."

"I'm not so sure," Tika said dubiously. "He's a magic-user like—" She broke off hurriedly. Seeing the pain in Caramon's face, she nestled closer to him, reaching up to stroke his face.

"Do you know, Caramon," she said softly, "he's right in a way. We *could* be happy here. Do you realize, this is the first time we've ever been alone. I mean really and truly alone together? And it's so still and peaceful and beautiful in a way. The glowing light from the moss is so soft and eerie, not harsh and glaring like sunlight. And listen to the water murmuring, its singing to us. Then there's this old, old furniture, and this funny bed . . ."

Tika stopped talking. She felt Caramon's arms tighten around her. His lips brushed her hair. Her love for him surged through her, making her heart stand still with pain and longing. Swiftly she put her arms around him, holding him close, feeling his heart beat against hers.

"Oh, Caramon!" she whispered breathlessly. "Let's be happy! Please! I—I know that—that sometime we'll have to leave. We'll have to find the others and return to the world above. But for now, let's be alone—together!"

"Tika!" Caramon clasped her, crushing her to him as if he would mold their bodies into one, single, living being. "Tika, I love you! I-I told you once that I couldn't make you mine until I could commit myself to you completely. I can't do that—not yet."

"Yes, you can!" Tika said fiercely. Pushing away from him, she looked into his eyes. "Raistlin's gone, Caramon! You can make your own life!"

Caramon shook his head gently. "Raistlin's still a part of me. He always will be, just as I'll always be a part of him. Can you understand?"

No, she couldn't, but she nodded anyway, her head drooping.

Smiling, Caramon drew a quivering breath. Then he put his hand beneath her chin and raised her head. Her eyes were beautiful, he thought. Green with flecks of brown. They shimmered now with tears. Her skin was tan from living outdoors and more freckled than ever. Those freckles embarrassed her. Tika would have given seven years of her life for creamy skin like Laurana's. But Caramon loved every freckle, he loved the crisp, curling red hair that clung to his hands.

Tika saw the love in his eyes. She caught her breath. He drew her near. His heart beating faster, he whispered, "I'll give you what I can of myself, Tika, if you'll settle for that. I wish, for your sake, it was more."

"I love you!" was all she said, clasping him around the neck.

He wanted to be certain she understood. "Tika—" he began.

"Hush, Caramon . . ."

6

Apoletta.

After a long chase through the streets of a city whose crumbling beauty seemed a horror to Tanis, they entered one of the lovely palaces in the center. Running through a dead garden and into a hall, they rounded a corner and came to a halt. The red-robed man was nowhere to be seen.

"Stairs!" Riverwind said suddenly. His own eyes growing accustomed to the strange light, Tanis saw they were standing at the top of a flight of marble stairs that descended so steeply they had lost sight of their quarry. Hurrying to the landing, they could once more see the red robes fluttering down them.

"Keep in the shadows near the wall," Riverwind cautioned, motioning them to the side of the stairway that was big enough for fifty men to walk down it abreast.

Faded and cracked murals on the walls were still so exquisite and life-like that Tanis had the fevered impression the people portrayed there were more alive than he was. Perhaps some of them had been standing in this very spot when the fiery mountain struck the Temple of the Kingpriest. . . . Putting the thought out of his mind, Tanis kept going.

After running down about twenty steps, they came to a broad landing, decorated with life-size statues of silver and gold. From here, the stairs continued down, leading to another landing, leading to more steps, and so on until they were all exhausted and breathless. Still the red robes fluttered ahead of them.

Suddenly Tanis noticed a change in the air. It was becoming more humid, the smell of the sea was strong. Listening, he could hear the faint sounds of water lapping against stone. He felt Riverwind touch his arm, pulling him back into the shadows. They were near the bottom of the steps. The red-robed man was in front of them, standing at the very bottom, peering into a pool of dark water that stretched out before him into a vast, shadowy cavern.

The red-robed man knelt by the side of the water. And then Tanis was aware of another figure; this one in the water! He could see hair shining in the torchlight—it had a faint greenish cast. Two slender white arms rested on the stone steps, the rest of the figure was submerged. The figure's head lay cradled on its arms, in a state of complete relaxation. The red-robed man reached out a hand and gently touched the figure in the water. The figure raised its head.

"I have been waiting," a woman's voice said, sounding reproachful.

Tanis gasped. The woman spoke elven! Now he could see her face, the large, luminous eyes, pointed ears, delicate features. . . .

A sea elf!

Confused tales from his childhood came back to Tanis as he tried to follow the conversation of the red-robed man and the elven woman, who was smiling at him fondly.

"I'm sorry, beloved," the red-robed man said soothingly, in elven, sitting down beside her. "I went to see how the young man you were concerned about was doing. He'll be all right, now. It was a close one, though. You were correct. He was certainly intent on dying. Something about his brother—a magic-user—betraying him."

"Caramon!" Tanis murmured. Riverwind looked at him questioningly. The Plainsman could not, of course, follow the elven conversation. Tanis shook his head, not wanting to miss what else was said.

"*QueaKI'ICHKeecx,*" said the woman in scorn. Tanis was puzzled, that word was certainly not elven!

"Yes!" The man frowned. "After I made sure those two were safe, I went to see some of the others. One of them—a bearded fellow, a half-elf, leaped at me as if he would swallow me whole! The others we managed to save are doing well."

"We laid out the dead with ceremony," said the woman, and Tanis could hear the ages-old sorrow in her voice, the sorrow of the elves for the loss of life.

"I would have liked to ask them what they were doing in the Blood Sea of Istar. I've never known a ship's captain foolish enough to dare the maelstrom. The girl told me there's war going on above. Maybe they had no choice."

The elven woman playfully splashed water on the red-robed man. "There's *always* war going on above! You are too curious, my beloved. Sometimes I think you might leave me and return to your world. Especially after you talk with these *KreeaQUEKH.*"

Tanis heard a note of true concern in the woman's voice, though she was still playfully splashing the man.

The red-robed man leaned down and kissed her on the wet, greenish hair shining in the light of the sputtering torch on the wall above them. "No, Apoletta. Let them have their wars and their brothers who betray brothers. Let them have their impetuous half-elves and their foolish sea captains. As long as my magic serves me, I will live below the waves—"

"Speaking of impetuous half-elves," Tanis interrupted in elven as he strode rapidly down the stairs. Riverwind, Goldmoon, and Berem followed, though they had no idea what was being said.

The man turned his head in alarm. The elven woman disappeared into the water so swiftly that Tanis wondered for a moment if he might have imagined her existence. Not a ripple on the dark surface betrayed where she had been. Reaching the bottom of the steps, Tanis caught hold of the magic-user's hand just as he was about to follow the sea elf into the water.

"Wait! I'm *not* going to swallow you!" Tanis pleaded. "I'm sorry I acted the way I did back there. I know this looks bad, sneaking around after you like this. But we had no choice! I know I can't stop you if you're going to cast a spell or something. I know you could engulf me in flames or put me to sleep or wrap me in cobweb or a hundred other things. I've been around magic-users. But won't you please listen to us? Please help us. I heard you talking about two of our friends—a big man and a pretty red-haired girl. You said the man nearly died—his brother betrayed him. We want to find them. Won't you tell us where they are?"

The man hesitated.

Tanis went on hurriedly, losing coherence in his efforts to keep hold of this man who might be able to help them. "I saw the woman here with you. I heard her speak. I know who she is. A sea elf, isn't she? You are right. I am half-elven. But I was raised among the elves, and I've heard their legends. I thought that's all they were, legends. But then I thought dragons were legends, too. There *is* a war being fought in the world above. And you're right. There always seems to be a war being fought somewhere. But this war won't stay up above. If the Queen of Darkness conquers, you can be certain she'll find out the sea elves are down here. I don't know if there are dragons below the ocean, but—"

"There are sea dragons, half-elf," said a voice, and the elven woman reappeared in the water once more. Moving with a flash of silver and green, she glided through the dark sea until she reached the stone steps. Then, resting her arms on them, she gazed up at him with brilliant green eyes. "And we have heard rumors of their return. We did not believe them, though. We did not know the dragons had awakened. Whose fault was that?"

"Does it matter?" asked Tanis wearily. "They have destroyed the ancient homeland. Silvanesti is a land of nightmares now. The Qualinesti were driven from their homes. The dragons are killing, burning. Nothing, no one is safe. The Dark Queen has one purpose—to gain dominance over every living being. Will you be safe? Even down here? For I presume we are below the sea?"

"You are right, half-elf," said the red-robed man, sighing.

"You are below the sea, in the ruins of the city of Istar. The sea elves saved you and brought you here, as they bring all those whose ships are wrecked. I know where your friends are and I can take you there. Beyond that, I don't see what more I can do for you."

"Get us out of here," Riverwind said flatly, understanding the conversation for the first time. Zebulah had spoken in Common. "Who is this woman, Tanis? She looks elven."

"She is a sea elf. Her name is . . ." Tanis stopped.

"Apoletta," said the elven woman, smiling. "Forgive me for not extending a formal greeting, but we do not clothe our bodies as do you *KreeaQUEKH*. Even after all these years, I cannot persuade my husband to quit covering his body in those ridiculous robes when he goes onto the land. Modesty, he calls it. So I will not embarrass either you or him by getting out of the water to greet you as is proper."

Flushing, Tanis translated the elven woman's words to his friends. Goldmoon's eyes widened. Berem did not seem to hear, he was lost in some sort of inner dream, only vaguely aware of what was happening around him. Riverwind's expression did not change. Apparently nothing he heard about elves could surprise him anymore.

"Anyway, the sea elves are the ones who rescued us," Tanis went on. "Like all elves, they consider life sacred and will help anyone lost at sea or drowning. This man, her husband—"

"Zebulah," he said, extending his hand.

"I am Tanis Half-Elven, Riverwind and Goldmoon of the Que-shu tribe, and Berem, uh—" Tanis faltered and fell silent, not quite knowing where to go from here.

Apoletta smiled politely, but her smile quickly faded. "Zebulah," she said, "find the friends the half-elf speaks of and bring them back here."

"We should go with you," Tanis offered. "If you thought I was going to swallow you, there's no telling what Caramon might do—"

"No," said Apoletta, shaking her head. The water glistened on her hair and sparkled on her smooth green-tinged skin. "Send the barbarians, half-elf. You stay here. I would talk with you and learn more of this war you say could endanger us. It saddens me to hear the dragons have awakened. If that is true, I fear you might be right. Our world will no longer be safe."

"I will be back soon, beloved," Zebulah said.

Apoletta reached out her hand to her husband. Taking it, he raised it to his lips, kissing it gently. Then he left. Tanis quickly translated for Riverwind and Goldmoon, who readily agreed to go in search of Caramon and Tika.

As they followed Zebulah back through the eerie, broken streets, he told them tales of the fall of Istar, pointing out various landmarks as they went along.

"You see—" he explained, "when the gods hurled the fiery mountain onto Krynn, it struck Istar, forming a giant crater in the land. The sea water rushed in to fill up the void, creating what came to be known as the Blood Sea. Many of the buildings in Istar were destroyed, but some survived and, here and there, retained small pockets of air. The sea elves discovered that this was an excellent place to bring mariners they rescued from capsized ships. Most of them soon feel quite at home."

The mage spoke with a hint of pride which Goldmoon found amusing, though she kindly did not allow her amusement to show. It was the pride of ownership, as if the ruins belonged to Zebulah and he had arranged to display them for the public's enjoyment.

"But you are human. You are not a sea elf. How did you come to live here?" Goldmoon asked.

The magic-user smiled, his eyes looking back across the years. "I was young and greedy," he said softly, "always in hopes of finding a quick way to make my fortune. My magic arts took me down into the depths of the ocean, searching for the lost wealth of Istar. I found riches all right, but not gold or silver.

"One evening I saw Apoletta, swimming among the sea forests. I saw her before she saw me, before she could change her shape. I fell in love with her . . . and long I worked to make her mine. She could not live up above and, after I had existed so long in the peace and tranquil beauty down here, I knew I no longer had a life in the world above either. But I enjoy talking to your kind occasionally, so I wander among the ruins now and then, to see who the elves have brought in."

Goldmoon looked around the ruins as Zebulah paused to catch his breath between stories. "Where is the fabled temple of the Kingpriest?" she asked.

A shadow passed over the mage's face. The look of pleasure he had worn was replaced by an expression of deep sorrow tinged with anger.

"I'm sorry," Goldmoon said quickly. "I did not mean to cause you pain. . . ."

"No, it's all right," Zebulah said with a brief, sad smile. "In fact, it is good for me to remember the darkness of that dreadful time. I tend to forget—in my daily ramblings here—that this used to be a city of laughing, crying, living, and breathing beings. Children played in these streets—they were playing that terrible evening when the gods cast the fiery mountain down."

He was silent for a moment then, with a sigh, continued.

"You ask where the temple stands. It stands no longer. In the place where the Kingpriest stood, shouting his arrogant demands to the gods, there is a dark pit. Although it is filled with sea water, nothing lives within it. None know its depth, for the sea elves will not venture near it. I have looked into its dark, still waters as long as I could bear the terror, and I do not believe there is an end to its darkness. It is as deep as the heart of evil itself."

Zebulah stopped in one of the sea-dark streets and peered at Goldmoon intently. "The guilty were punished. But why the innocent? Why did they have to suffer? You wear the medallion of Mishakal the Healer. Do you understand? Did the goddess explain it to you?"

Goldmoon hesitated, startled by the question, searching within her soul for the answer. Riverwind stood beside her, stern and silent as always, his thoughts hidden.

"Often I myself have questioned," Goldmoon faltered. Moving nearer Riverwind, she touched his arm with her hand as though to reassure herself he was near. "In a dream, once, I was punished for my questioning, for my lack of faith. Punished by losing the one I love." Riverwind put his strong arm around her and held her close. "But whenever I feel ashamed of my questioning, I am reminded that it was my questioning that led me to find the ancient gods."

She was silent a moment. Riverwind stroked her silver-gold hair and she glanced up at him with a smile. "No," she said softly to Zebulah, "I do not have the answer to this great riddle. I still question. I still burn with anger when I see the innocent suffer and the guilty rewarded. But I know now that my anger can be as a forging fire. In its heat, the raw lump of iron that is my spirit is tempered and shaped to form the shining rod of steel that is my faith. That rod supports my weak flesh."

Zebulah studied Goldmoon silently as she stood amid the ruins of Istar, her silver-golden hair shining like the sunlight that would never touch the crushed buildings. The classic beauty of her face was marked by the effects of the dark roads she had traveled. Far from marring that beauty, the lines of suffering and despair had refined it. There was wisdom in her eyes, enhanced now by the great joy that came from the knowledge of the new life she carried within her body.

The mage's gaze went to the man who held the woman so tenderly. His face, too, bore the marks of the long, tortuous path he had walked. Although stern and stoic that face would always be, his deep love for this woman showed clearly in the man's dark eyes and the gentleness of his touch.

Perhaps I have made a mistake staying beneath the waters so long, Zebulah thought, suddenly feeling very old and sad. Perhaps I could have helped, if I had stayed above and used my anger as these two used theirs—to help them find answers. Instead, I let my anger gnaw at my soul until it seemed easiest to hide it down here.

"We should delay no longer," said Riverwind abruptly. "Caramon will soon get it into his head to come looking for us, if he has not already."

"Yes," said Zebulah, clearing his throat. "We should go, although I do not think the young man and woman will have left. He was very weak—"

"Was he injured?" Goldmoon asked in concern.

"Not in body," Zebulah replied as they entered a tumbledown building on a crumbling side-street. "But he has been injured in his soul. I could see that even before the girl told me about his twin brother."

A dark line appeared between Goldmoon's finely drawn brows, her lips tightened.

"Pardon me, Lady of the Plains," Zebulah said with a slight smile, "but I see that forging fire you spoke of blaze in your eyes."

Goldmoon flushed. "I told you I was still weak. I should be able to accept Raistlin and what he did to his brother without questioning. I should have faith that it is all part of the greater good I cannot envision. But I'm afraid I can't. All I can do is pray that the gods keep him out of my path."

"Not me," said Riverwind suddenly, his voice harsh. "Not me," he repeated grimly.

Caramon lay staring into the darkness. Tika, cradled in his arms, was fast asleep. He could feel her heart beating, he could hear her soft breathing. He started to run his hand through the tangle of red curls that lay upon his shoulder, but Tika stirred at his touch and he stopped, fearful of waking her. She should rest. The gods alone knew how long she had been awake, watching over him. She would never tell him, he knew that. When he had asked, she had only laughed and teased him about his snoring.

But there had been a tremor in her laughter, she had been unable to look into his eyes.

Caramon patted her shoulder reassuringly and she nestled close. He felt comforted as he realized she slept soundly, and then he sighed. Only a few weeks ago, he had vowed to Tika that he would never take her love unless he could commit himself to her body *and* soul. He could still hear his words, "My first commitment is to my brother. I am his strength."

Now Raistlin was gone, he had found his own strength. As he had told Caramon, "I need you no longer."

I should be glad, Caramon told himself, staring into the darkness. I love Tika and I have her love in return. And now we are free to express that love. I can make that commitment to her. She can come first in all my thoughts now. She is loving, giving. She *deserves* to be loved.

Raistlin never did. At least that's what they all believe. How often have I heard Tanis ask Sturm when he thought I couldn't hear why I put up with the sarcasm, the bitter recriminations, the imperious commands. I've seen them look at me with pity. I know they think I'm slow-thinking sometimes and I am—compared to Raistlin. I am the ox, lumbering along, bearing the burden without complaint. That's what they think of me.

They don't understand. They don't *need* me. Even Tika doesn't *need* me—not like Raist needed me. They never heard him wake screaming in the night when he was little. We were left alone so much, he and I. There was no one there in the darkness to hear him and comfort him but me. He could never remember those dreams, but they were awful. His thin body shook with fear. His eyes were wild with the sight of terrors only he could see. He clutched at me, sobbing. And I'd tell him stories or make funny shadow-pictures on the wall to drive away the horror.

"Look, Raist," I'd say, "bunnies . . ." and I'd hold up two fingers and wiggle them like a rabbit's ears.

After awhile, he'd stop trembling. He wouldn't smile or laugh. He never did either, much, even when he was little. But he would relax.

"I must sleep. I am so tired," he'd whisper, holding my hand fast. "But you stay awake, Caramon. Guard my sleep. Keep them away. Don't let them get me."

"I'll stay awake. I won't let anything hurt you, Raist!" I'd promise.

Then he would smile—almost—and, exhausted, his eyes would close. I kept my promise. I would stay awake while he slept. And it was funny. Maybe I did keep *them* away, because as long as I was awake and watching, the nightmares never came to him.

Even when he was older, sometimes he'd still cry out in the night and reach out to me. And I'd be there. But what will he do now? What will he do without me when he's alone, lost, and frightened in the darkness?

What will I do without him?

Caramon shut his eyes and, softly, fearful of waking Tika, he began to cry.

7

Berem.
Unexpected help.

"**And** that's our story," said Tanis simply.

Apoletta had listened attentively to him, her green eyes intent upon his face. She had not interrupted. When he was finished, she remained silent. Resting her arms on the side of the steps leading into the still water, she seemed lost in thought. Tanis did not disturb her. The feeling of peace and serenity present beneath the sea soothed and comforted him. The thought of returning to the harsh, glaring world of sunlight and blaring noise seemed suddenly frightening. How easy it would be to ignore everything and stay here, beneath the sea, hidden forever in this silent world.

"What about him?" she asked finally, nodding her head at Berem.

Tanis came back to reality with a sigh.

"I don't know," he said, shrugging, glancing at Berem. The man was staring into the darkness of the cavern. His lips were moving, as if repeating a chant over and over.

"He is the key, according to the Queen of Darkness. Find him, she said, and victory is hers."

"Well," Apoletta said abruptly, "you've got him. Does that make victory yours?"

Tanis blinked. The question caught him by surprise. Scratching his beard, he pondered. It was something that had not occurred to him.

"True . . . we have got him," he murmured, "but what do we do with him? What is there about him that grants victory—to either side?"

"Doesn't he know?"

"He claims he doesn't."

Apoletta regarded Berem, frowning. "I would say he was lying," she said after a moment, "but then he is human, and I know little of the strange workings of the human mind. There is a way you can find out, however. Journey to the Temple of the Dark Queen at Neraka."

"Neraka!" repeated Tanis, startled. "But that's—" He was interrupted by a cry of such wild fear and terror that he nearly leaped into the water. His hand went to his empty scabbard. With a curse, he whirled around expecting nothing less than a horde of dragons.

There was only Berem, staring at him with wide eyes.

"What is it, Berem?" Tanis asked irritably. "Did you see something?"

"He didn't see anything, Half-Elf," Apoletta said, studying Berem with interest. "He reacted that way when I said Neraka—"

"Neraka!" Berem repeated, shaking his head wildly. "Evil! Great evil! No . . . no . . ."

"That's where you came from," Tanis told him, stepping nearer.

Berem shook his head firmly.

"But you told me—"

———

"A mistake!" Berem muttered. "I didn't mean Neraka. I m-meant . . . Takar . . . Takar! That's what I meant . . ."

"You meant Neraka. You know the Dark Queen has her great Temple there, in Neraka!" Apoletta said sternly.

"Does she?" Berem looked directly at her, his blue eyes wide and innocent. "The Dark Queen, a Temple in Neraka? No, there's nothing there but a small village. My village . . ." Suddenly he grasped his stomach and doubled over, as if in pain. "I don't feel good. Leave me alone—" he mumbled like a child and slumped to the marble floor near the edge of the water. Sitting there, clutching his stomach, he stared into the darkness.

"Berem!" said Tanis in exasperation.

"Don't feel good . . ." Berem muttered sullenly.

"How old did you say he was?" Apoletta asked.

"Over three hundred years, or so he *claims*," Tanis said in disgust. "If you believe only half of what he says, that cuts it down to one hundred and fifty, which doesn't seem too plausible either, not for a human."

"You know," replied Apoletta thoughtfully, "the Queen's Temple at Neraka is a mystery to us. It appeared suddenly, after the Cataclysm, so far as we have been able to determine. Now we find this man who would trace his own history to that same time and place."

"It is strange . . ." said Tanis, glancing again at Berem.

"Yes. It may be nothing more than coincidence, but follow coincidence far enough and you'll find it tied to fate, so my husband says." Apoletta smiled.

"Coincidence or not, I don't see myself walking into the Temple of the Queen of Darkness and asking why she's searching the world for a man with a green gemstone buried in his chest," Tanis said wryly, sitting down near the water's edge again.

"I suppose not," Apoletta admitted. "It's hard to believe though, from what you say, that she has grown so powerful. What have the good dragons been doing all this time?"

"Good dragons!" Tanis repeated, astounded. "What good dragons?"

Now it was Apoletta's turn to look amazed. "Why, the *good* dragons. The silver dragons and gold dragons. Bronze dragons. And the dragonlances. Surely the silver dragons gave you those that were in their keeping. . . ."

"I never heard of silver dragons," Tanis replied, "except in some old song about Huma. The same with dragonlances.

We've been searching for them so long without a trace, I was beginning to believe they didn't exist except in children's stories."

"I don't like this." Apoletta rested her chin on her hands, her face drawn and pale. "Something's wrong. Where are the good dragons? Why aren't they fighting? At first I discounted rumors of the sea dragons' return, for I knew the good dragons would never permit it. But if the good dragons have disappeared, as I must believe from talking with you, Half-Elf, then I fear my people truly are in danger." She lifted her head, listening. "Ah, good, here comes my husband with the rest of your friends." She pushed away from the edge. "He and I can go back to my people and discuss what we must do—"

"Wait!" Tanis said, hearing footsteps coming down the marble stairs. "You've got to show us the way out! We can't stay here!"

"But I don't know the way out," Apoletta said, her hands making circles in the water as she kept herself afloat. "Neither does Zebulah. It was never our concern."

"We could wander through these ruins for weeks!" Tanis cried. "Or maybe forever! You're not certain people *do* escape from this place, are you? Maybe they just die!"

"As I said," Apoletta repeated coldly, "it was never our concern."

"Well, make it your concern!" Tanis shouted. His voice echoed back eerily across the water. Berem looked up at him and shrank away in alarm. Apoletta's eyes narrowed in anger. Tanis drew in a deep breath, then bit his lip, suddenly ashamed.

"I'm sorry—" he began, but then Goldmoon came up to him, placing her hand on his arm.

"Tanis? What is it?" she asked.

"Nothing that can be helped." Sighing, he glanced past her. "Did you find Caramon and Tika? Are they all right?"

"Yes, we found them," Goldmoon answered, her gaze following Tanis's. Together they watched the two come slowly down the stairs behind Riverwind and Zebulah. Tika was staring around in wonder. Caramon, Tanis noticed, kept his eyes focused straight ahead. Seeing the man's face, Tanis looked back at Goldmoon.

"You didn't answer my second question?" he said softly.

"Tika's all right," Goldmoon answered. "As for Caramon—" She shook her head.

Tanis looked back at Caramon and could barely restrain an exclamation of dismay. He would not have recognized the jovial, good-natured warrior in this man with the grim, tear-streaked face, the haunted, shadowed eyes.

Seeing Tanis's shocked look, Tika drew near Caramon and slipped her hand through his arm. At her touch, the warrior seemed to awaken from his dark thoughts. He smiled down at her. But there was something in Caramon's smile—a gentleness, a sorrow—that had never been there before.

Tanis sighed again. More problems. If the ancient gods *had* returned, what were they trying to do to them? See how heavy the burden could get before they collapsed beneath it? Did they find this amusing? Trapped beneath the sea . . . Why not just give up? Why not just stay down here? Why bother searching for a way out? Stay down here and forget everything. Forget the dragons . . . forget Raistlin . . . forget Laurana . . . Kitiara. . . .

"Tanis . . ." Goldmoon shook him gently.

They were all standing around him now. Waiting for him to tell them what to do.

Clearing his throat, he started to speak. His voice cracked and he coughed. "You needn't look at me!" he said finally, harshly. "I don't have any answers. We're trapped, apparently. There's no way out."

Still they watched him, with no dimming of the faith and trust in their eyes. Tanis glared at them angrily. "Quit looking at me to lead you! I *betrayed* you! Don't you realize that! It's my fault. Everything's my fault! Find someone else—"

Turning to hide tears he could not stop, Tanis stared out across the dark water, wrestling with himself to regain control. He did not realize, until she spoke, that Apoletta had been watching him.

"Perhaps I can help you, after all," the sea elf said slowly.

"Apoletta, what are you saying?" Zebulah said fearfully, hurrying to the edge of the water. "Consider—"

"I have considered," Apoletta replied. "The half-elf said we should be concerned about what happens in the world. He is right. The same thing could happen to us that happened to our Silvanesti cousins. They renounced the world and allowed dark and evil things to creep into their land. We have been warned in time. We can still fight the evil. Your coming here may have saved us, Half-Elf," she said earnestly. "We owe you something in return."

"Help us get back to our world," Tanis said.

Apoletta nodded gravely. "I will do so. Where would you go?"

Sighing, Tanis shook his head. He couldn't think. "I suppose one place is as good as another," he said wearily.

"Palanthas," Caramon said suddenly. His deep voice echoed across the still water.

The others glanced at him in uncomfortable silence. Riverwind frowned darkly.

"No," said Apoletta, swimming to the edge once more, "I cannot take you to Palanthas. Our borders extend only as far as Kalaman. Beyond that, we dare not venture. Especially if what you say is true, for beyond Kalaman lies the ancient home of the sea dragons."

Tanis wiped his eyes and nose, then turned back around to face his friends. "Well? Any more suggestions?"

They were silent, watching him. Then Goldmoon stepped forward.

"Shall I tell you a story, Half-Elf?" she said, resting her gentle hand upon his arm. "A story of a woman and man, lost and alone and frightened. Bearing a great burden, they came to an inn. The woman sang a song, a blue crystal staff performed a miracle, a mob attacked them. One man stood up. One man took charge. One man—a stranger—said, 'We'll go out through the kitchen.'" She smiled. "Do you remember, Tanis?"

"I remember," he whispered, caught and held by her beautiful, sweet expression.

"We're waiting, Tanis," she said simply.

Tears dimmed his vision again. Tanis blinked rapidly, then glanced around. Riverwind's stern face was relaxed. Smiling a half-smile, he laid his hand on Tanis's arm. Caramon hesitated a moment, then—striding forward—embraced Tanis in one of his bearlike hugs.

"Take us to Kalaman," Tanis told Apoletta when he could breathe again. "It's where we were headed anyway."

The companions slept at the edge of the water, getting what rest they could before the journey, which Apoletta told them would be long and strenuous.

"How will we travel? By boat?" Tanis asked, watching as Zebulah stripped off his red robes and dove into the water.

Apoletta glanced at her husband, treading water easily beside her. "You will swim," she said. "Didn't you wonder how we brought you down here? Our magic arts, and those of my husband, will give you the ability to breathe water as easily as you now breathe air."

"You're going to turn us into fish?" Caramon asked, horrified.

"I suppose you could look at it that way," Apoletta replied. "We will come for you at the ebb tide."

Tika clasped Caramon's hand. He held onto her tightly, and Tanis, seeing them share a secret look between them, suddenly felt his burden lighten. Whatever turmoil surged in Caramon's soul, he had found a strong anchor to keep him from being swept out into dark waters.

"We'll never forget this beautiful place," Tika said softly.

Apoletta only smiled.

8

Dark tidings.

"Papa! Papa!"

"What is it, Little Rogar?" The fisherman, accustomed to the excited cries of his small son, who was just big enough to begin discovering the wonders of the world, did not raise his head from his work. Expecting to hear about anything from a star-fish stranded on the bank to a lost shoe found stuck in the sand, the fisherman kept on restringing his net as the little boy dashed up to him.

"Papa," said the tow-haired child, eagerly grabbing his father's knee and getting himself entangled in the net in the process, "a pretty lady. Drown dead."

"Eh?" the fisherman asked absently.

"A pretty lady. Drown dead," the little boy said solemnly, pointing with a chubby finger behind him.

The fisherman stopped his work now to stare at his son. This was something new.

"A pretty lady? Drowned?"

The child nodded and pointed again, down the beach.

The fisherman squinted his eyes against the blazing noon sun and peered down the shoreline. Then he looked back at his son and his brows came together in a stern expression.

"Is this more of Little Rogar's stories?" he asked severely. "Because if it is, you'll be taking yer dinner standing up."

The child shook his head, his eyes wide. "No," he said, rubbing his small bottom in memory. "I promised."

The fisherman frowned, looking out to sea. There'd been a storm last night, but he hadn't heard anything that sounded like a ship smashing up on the rocks. Perhaps some of the town's people with their fool pleasure boats had been out yesterday and been stranded after dark. Or worse, murder. This wouldn't be the first body washed up ashore with a knife in its heart.

Hailing his oldest son, who was sluicing out the bottom of the dingy, the fisherman put his work aside and stood up. He started to send the small boy in to his mother, then remembered he needed the child to guide them.

"Take us to the pretty lady," the fisherman said in a heavy voice, giving his other son a meaningful glance.

Tugging his father along eagerly, Little Rogar headed back down the beach while his parent and his older brother followed more slowly, fearing what they might find.

They had gone only a short distance before the fisherman saw a sight that caused him to break into a run, his older son pounding along behind.

"A shipwreck. No doubt!" the fisherman puffed. "Blasted landlubbers! Got no business going out in those eggshell boats."

There was not just one pretty lady lying on the beach, but two. Near them were four men. All were dressed in fine clothes. Broken timbers lay scattered around, obviously the remains of a small pleasure craft.

"Drown dead," said the little boy, bending to pat one of the pretty ladies.

"No, they're not!" grunted the fisherman, feeling for the life-beat in the woman's neck. One of the men was already beginning to stir—an older man, seemingly about fifty, he sat up and stared around in confusion. Seeing the fisherman, he started in terror and crawled over on his hands and knees to shake one of his unconscious companions.

"Tanis, Tanis!" the man cried, rousing a bearded man, who sat up suddenly.

"Don't be afraid," the fisherman said, seeing the bearded man's alarm. "We're going to help, if we can. Davey, run back and get yer ma. Tell her to bring blankets and that bottle of brandy I saved from Yuletide. Here, mistress," he said gently, helping one of the women to sit up. "Take it easy. You'll be all right. Strange sort of business—" the fisherman muttered to himself, holding the woman in his arms and patting her soothingly. "For being near drowned, none of them seems to have swallowed any water. . . ." Wrapped in blankets, the castaways were escorted back to the fisherman's small house near the beach. Here they were given douses of brandy and every other remedy the fisherman's wife could think of for drowning. Little Rogar regarded them all with pride, knowing that his "catch" would be the talk of the village for the next week.

"Thank you again for your help," Tanis said gratefully.

"Glad to be there," the man said gruffly. "Just be wary. Next time you go out in one of them small boats, head for shore the first sign of a storm."

"Er, yes, I'll—we'll do that," Tanis said in some confusion. "Now, if you could just tell us where we are. . . ."

"Yer north of the city," the fisherman said, waving a hand. "About two-three miles. Davey can give ye a lift in the cart."

"That's very kind of you," Tanis said, hesitating and glancing at the others. They returned his look, Caramon shrugging. "Uh, I know this sounds strange, but we—we were blown off course. What city are we north of?"

"Why, Kalaman, to be sure," the fisherman said, eyeing them suspiciously.

"Oh!" said Tanis. Laughing weakly, he turned to Caramon. "What did I tell you? We—uh—weren't blown as far off course as you thought."

"We weren't?" Caramon said, his eyes open wide. "Oh, we weren't," he amended hastily as Tika dug her elbow into his ribs. "Yeah, I guess I was wrong, as usual. You know me, Tanis, never could get my bearings—"

"Don't overdo it!" Riverwind muttered, and Caramon fell silent.

The fisherman gave them all a dark look. "Yer a strange bunch, no doubt," he said. "You can't remember how you came to smash up. Now you don't even know where you are. I reckon you was all drunk, but that's not my concern. If you'll take my advice, you'll none of you set foot in a boat again, drunk or sober. Davey, bring round the cart."

Giving them a final, disgusted glance, the fisherman lifted his small son on his shoulder and went back to work. His older son disappeared, presumably going to fetch the cart.

Tanis sighed, looking around at his friends.

"Can any of you know how we got here?" he asked quietly. "Or why we're dressed like this?"

One by one, they all shook their heads.

"I remember the Blood Sea and the maelstrom," Goldmoon said. "But then the rest seems like something I dreamed."

"I remember Raist . . ." Caramon said softly, his face grave. Then, feeling Tika's hand slip through his, he looked down at her. His expression softened. "And I remember—"

"Hush," Tika said, blushing, laying her cheek against his arm. Caramon kissed her red curls. "It wasn't a dream," she murmured.

"I remember a few things, too," Tanis said grimly, looking at Berem. "But it's disjointed, fragmented. None of it seems to go together right in my mind. Well, it's no good looking back. We've got to look forward. We'll go to Kalaman and find out what's been happening. I don't even know what day it is! Or month for that matter. Then—"

"Palanthas," Caramon said. "We'll go to Palanthas."

"We'll see," Tanis said, sighing. Davey was returning with the cart, drawn by a boney horse. The half-elf looked at Caramon. "Are you really certain you want to find that brother of yours?" he asked quietly.

Caramon did not answer.

The companions arrived in Kalaman about mid-morning.

"What's going on?" Tanis asked Davey as the young man drove the cart through the city streets. "Is there a festival?"

The streets were crowded with people. Most of the shops were closed and shuttered. Everyone stood around in small clumps, talking together in excited tones.

"It looks more like a funeral," Caramon said. "Someone important must have died."

"That—or war," Tanis muttered. Women were weeping, men looked sorrowful or angry, children stood about, staring fearfully at their parents.

"Can't be war, sir," Davey said, "and Spring Dawning festival was two days ago. Don't know what's the matter. Just a minute. I can find out if you want," he said, pulling the horse to a stop.

"Go ahead," Tanis said. "Just a minute, though. Why can't it be war?"

"Why, we've won the war!" Davey said, staring at Tanis in astonishment. "By the gods, sir, you *musta* been drunk if you don't remember. The Golden General and the good dragons—"

"Oh, yes," Tanis said hastily.

"I'll stop in here, at the fish market," Davey said, hopping down. "They'll know."

"We'll come with you." Tanis motioned the others.

"What's the news?" Davey called, running up to a knot of men and women standing before a shop redolent with the odor of fresh fish.

Several men turned immediately, all speaking at once. Coming up behind the boy, Tanis caught only parts of the excited conversation. "Golden General captured! . . . City doomed . . . people fleeing . . . evil dragons . . ."

Try as they might, the companions could make nothing out of this. The people seemed reluctant to talk around strangers— giving them dark, mistrustful glances, especially seeing their rich clothing.

The companions thanked Davey once more for the ride into town, then left him among his friends. After a brief discussion, they decided to head for the marketplace, hoping to find out more details of what had happened. The crowds grew denser as they walked until they practically had to fight their way through the packed streets. People ran here and there, asking for the latest rumors, shaking their heads in despair. Occasionally they saw some citizens, their belongings hastily packed in bundles, heading for the city gates.

"We should buy weapons," Caramon said grimly. "The news doesn't sound good. Who do you suppose this 'Golden General' is, anyway? The people seem to think a lot of him if his disappearance throws them into this much turmoil."

"Probably some Knight of Solamnia," Tanis said. "And you're right, we should buy weapons." He put his hand to his belt. "Damn! I had a purse of funny-looking old gold coins, but it's gone now! As if we didn't have enough trouble. . . ."

"Wait a minute!" Caramon grunted, feeling his belt. "Why! What the— My purse was here a second ago!" Whirling around, the big warrior caught a glimpse of small figure disappearing among the crush of people, a worn leather pouch in its hand. "Hey! You! That's mine!" Caramon roared. Scattering people like straws in the wind, he leaped after the small thief. Reaching out a huge hand, he caught hold of a fleecy vest and plucked the squirming figure up off the street. "Now give me back—" The big warrior gasped. "Tasslehoff!"

"Caramon!" Tasslehoff cried.

Caramon dropped him in astonishment. Tasslehoff stared around wildly. "Tanis!" he shouted, seeing the half-elf coming through the crowd. "Oh, Tanis!" Running forward, Tas threw his arms around his friend. Burying his face in Tanis's belt, the kender burst into tears.

The people of Kalaman lined the walls of their city. Just a few days before they had done the same thing, only then their mood had been festive as they watched the triumphant procession of knights and silver and golden dragons. Now they were quiet, grim with despair. They looked out over the plain as the sun rose to its zenith in the sky. Nearly noon. They waited silently.

Tanis stood next to Flint, his hand on the dwarf's shoulder. The old dwarf had nearly broken down at the sight of his friend.

It was a sad reunion. In hushed and broken voices, Flint and Tasslehoff took turns telling their friends what had happened since they were parted in Tarsis months ago. One would talk until overcome, then the other would carry on the story. Thus the companions heard of the discovery of the dragonlances, the destruction of the dragon orb, and Sturm's death.

Tanis bowed his head, overwhelmed with sorrow at this news. For a moment, he couldn't imagine the world without this noble friend. Seeing Tanis's grief, Flint's gruff voice went on to tell of Sturm's great victory and the peace he had found in death.

"He is a hero in Solamnia now," Flint said. "Already they're telling stories of him, like they do of Huma. His great sacrifice saved the Knighthood, or so it is said. He would have asked for nothing more, Tanis."

The half-elf nodded wordlessly. Then, trying to smile, "Go on," he said. "Tell me what Laurana did when she arrived in Palanthas. And is she still there? If so, we were thinking about going—"

Flint and Tas exchanged glances. The dwarf's head bowed. The kender looked away, snuffling and wiping his small nose with a handkerchief.

"What is it?" Tanis asked in a voice he didn't recognize as his own. "Tell me."

Slowly, Flint related the story. "I'm sorry, Tanis," the dwarf said, wheezing. "I let her down—"

The old dwarf began to sob so pitifully that Tanis's heart ached with sorrow. Clasping his friend in his arms, he held him tightly.

"It wasn't your fault, Flint," he said, his voice harsh with tears. "It's mine, if anyone's. It was for me she risked death and worse."

"Start placing blame and you will end cursing the gods," said Riverwind, laying his hand on Tanis's shoulder. "Thus do my people say."

Tanis was not comforted. "What time is the—the Dark Lady to come?"

"Noon," said Tas softly.

Now it was nearly noon and Tanis stood with the rest of the citizens of Kalaman, waiting for the arrival of the Dark Lady. Gilthanas stood some distance from Tanis, pointedly ignoring him. The half-elf couldn't blame him. Gilthanas knew why Laurana had left, he knew what bait Kitiara had used to snare his sister. When he asked Tanis coldly if it was true that he had been with the Dragon Highlord, Kitiara, Tanis could not deny it.

"Then I hold you responsible for whatever happens to Laurana," Gilthanas said, his voice shaking in rage. "And I will pray to the gods nightly that whatever cruel fate befalls her, you will meet the same thing—only a hundred times worse!"

"Don't you think I'd accept that if it would bring her back!" Tanis cried in anguish. But Gilthanas only turned away.

Now the people began to point and murmur. A dark shadow was visible in the sky—a blue dragon.

"That's her dragon," Tasslehoff said solemnly. "I saw it at the High Clerist's Tower."

The blue dragon circled lazily above the city in slow spirals, then landed leisurely within bow-shot of the city walls. A deathly hush fell upon the city as the dragon's rider stood up in the stirrups. Removing her helm, the Dark Lady began to speak, her voice ringing through the clear air.

"By now you have heard that I have captured the elf woman you call the 'Golden General!'" Kitiara shouted. "In case you need proof, I have this to show you." She raised her hand. Tanis saw the flash of sunlight on a beautifully crafted silver helm "In my other hand, though you cannot see it from where you stand, I have a lock of golden hair. I will leave both these here, on the plain, when I depart, that you may have something to remember your 'general' by."

There was a harsh murmur from the people lining the walls. Kitiara stopped speaking a moment, regarding them coldly. Watching her, Tanis dug his nails into his flesh to force himself to remain calm. He had caught himself contemplating a mad scheme to leap from the wall and attack her where she stood.

Goldmoon, seeing the wild, desperate look on his face, moved near and laid her hand on his arm. She felt his body shaking, then he stiffened at her touch, bringing himself under control. Looking down at his clenched hands, she was horrified to see blood trickling down his wrists.

"The elfmaid, Lauralanthalasa, has been taken to the Queen of Darkness at Neraka. She will remain as hostage with the Queen until the following conditions are met. First, the Queen demands that a human called Berem, the Everman, be turned over to her immediately. Second, she demands that the good dragons return to Sanction, where they will give themselves up to Lord Ariakas. Finally, the elflord, Gilthanas, will call for the Knights of Solamnia and the elves of both the Qualinesti and Silvanesti tribes to lay down their arms. The dwarf, Flint Fireforge, will require of his people that they do the same."

"This is madness!" Gilthanas called out in answer, stepping forward to the edge of the wall and staring down at the Dark Lady. "We cannot agree to these demands! We have no idea who this Berem is, or where to find him. I cannot answer for my people, nor can I answer for the good dragons. These demands are totally unreasonable!"

"The Queen is not unreasonable," Kitiara replied smoothly. "Her Dark Majesty has foreseen that these demands will need time to be acted upon. You have three weeks. If, within that time, you have not found the man, Berem, whom we believe to be in the area around Flotsam, and if you have not sent away the good dragons, I will return and, this time, you will find more than a lock of your 'general's hair before the gates of Kalaman."

Kitiara paused.

"You will find her head."

With that, she tossed the helm down onto the ground at her dragon's feet, then, at a word, Skie lifted his wings and rose into the air.

For long moments, no one spoke or moved. The people stared down at the helm lying before the wall. The red ribbons fluttering bravely from the top of the silver helm seemed the only movement, the only color. Then someone cried out in terror, pointing.

Upon the horizon appeared an incredible sight. So awful was it that no one believed it at first, each thinking privately he must be going mad. But the object drifted closer and all were forced to admit its reality, though that did not diminish the horror.

Thus it was that the people of Krynn had their first glimpse of Lord Ariakas's most ingenious war machine—the flying citadels.

Working in the depths of the temples of Sanction, the black-robed magic-users and dark clerics ripped a castle from its foundations and set it in the skies. Now, floating upon dark gray storm clouds, lit by jagged barbs of white lightning, surrounded by a hundred flights of red and black dragons, the citadel loomed over Kalaman, blotting out the noon sun, casting its dreadful shadow over the city.

The people fled the walls in terror. Dragonfear worked its horrible spell, causing panic and despair to fall upon all who dwelt in Kalaman. But the citadel's dragons did not attack. Three weeks, their Dark Queen had ordered. They would give these wretched humans three weeks. And they would keep watch to see that, during this time, the Knights and the good dragons did not take the field.

Tanis turned to the rest of the companions who stood huddled upon the walls, staring bleakly at the citadel. Accustomed to the effects of dragonfear, they had been able to withstand it and were not fleeing in panic as were the rest of the citizens of Kalaman. Consequently they stood alone together upon the walls.

"Three weeks," Tanis said clearly, and this friends turned to him.

For the first time since they had left Flotsam, they saw that his face was free of its self-condemning madness. There was peace in his eyes, much as Flint has seen peace in Sturm's eyes after the knight's death.

"Three weeks," Tanis repeated in a calm voice that sent shivers up Flint's spine, "we have three weeks. That should be time enough. I'm going to Neraka, to the Dark Queen." His eyes went to Berem, who stood silently nearby. "You're coming with me."

Berem's eyes opened wide in stark terror. "No!" he whimpered, shrinking backwards. Seeing the man about to run, Caramon's huge hand reached out and caught hold of him.

"You will go with me to Neraka," Tanis said in a soft voice, "or I will take you right now and give you to Gilthanas. The elf lord loves his sister dearly. He would not hesitate to hand you over to the Queen of Darkness if he thought that would buy Laurana's freedom. You and I know differently. We know that giving you up wouldn't change matters a bit. But he doesn't. He is an elf, and he would believe she would keep her bargain."

Berem stared at Tanis warily. "You won't give me up?"

"I'm going to find out what's going on," Tanis stated coldly, avoiding the question. "At any rate, I'll need a guide, someone who knows the area . . ."

Wrenching himself free of Caramon's grip, Berem regarded them with a hunted expression. "I'll go," he wimpered. "Don't give me to the elf . . ."

"All right," Tanis said coldly. "Quit sniveling. I'll be leaving before dark and I've got a lot to do—"

Turning abruptly, he was not surprised to feel a strong hand grip his arm. "I know what you're going to say, Caramon." Tanis did not turn around. "And the answer is no. Berem and I are going alone."

"Then you'll go to your deaths alone," Caramon said quietly, holding onto Tanis firmly.

"If so, then that's what I'll do!" Tanis tried without success to break free of the big man. "I'm not taking any of you with me."

"And you'll fail," Caramon said. "Is that what you want? Are you going just to find a way to die that will end your guilt? If so, I can offer you my sword right now. But if you truly want to free Laurana then you're going to need help."

"The gods have reunited us," Goldmoon said gently. "They have brought us together again in our time of greatest need. It is a sign from the gods, Tanis. Don't deny it."

The half-elf bowed his head. He could not cry, there were no tears left. Tasslehoff's small hand slipped into his.

"Besides," said the kender cheerfully, "think how much trouble you'd get into without me!"

9
A single candle.

The city of Kalaman was
deathly silent the night after the Dark Lady issued her ultima-
tum. Lord Calof declared a State of War, which meant all taverns were closed, the city gates were locked and barred, no one
allowed to leave. The only people permitted to enter were families from the small farming and fishing villages near Kalaman.
These refugees began arriving near sundown, telling fearful
tales of draconians swarming over their land, looting and burning.

Although some of the noblemen of Kalaman had been

---

opposed to such a drastic measure as a declared State of War, Tanis and Gilthanas—united for once—had forced the Lord to make this decision. Both of them painted vivid and horrifying pictures of the burning of the city of Tarsis. These proved extremely convincing. Lord Calof made his declaration, but then stared at the two men helplessly. It was obvious he had no idea what to do in regard to the defense of the city. The horrifying shadow of the floating citadel hovering above had completely unnerved the lord, and most of his military leaders were in little better shape. After listening to some of their wilder ideas, Tanis rose to his feet.

"I have a suggestion, my lord," he said respectfully. "You have a person here, well-qualified to take over the defense of this city—"

"You, Half-Elf?" interrupted Gilthanas with a bitter smile.

"No," said Tanis gently. "You, Gilthanas."

"An elf?" said Lord Calof in amazement.

"He was in Tarsis. He has had experience fighting the draconians and the dragons. The good dragons trust him and will follow his judgment."

"That's true!" Calof said. A look of vast relief crossed his face as he turned to Gilthanas. "We know how elves feel about humans, my lord, and—I must admit—most humans feel the same about elves. But we would be eternally grateful if you could help us in this time of peril."

Gilthanas stared at Tanis, puzzled for a moment. He could read nothing in the half-elf's bearded face. It was almost, he thought, the face of a dead man. Lord Calof repeated his question, adding something about "reward," apparently thinking Gilthanas's hesitation was due to a reluctance to accept the responsibility.

"No, my lord!" Gilthanas came out of his reverie with a start. "No reward is necessary or even wanted. If I can help save the people of this city, that will be reward enough. As for being of different races"—Gilthanas looked once more at Tanis—"perhaps I have learned enough to know that doesn't make any difference. It never did."

"Tell us what to do," Calof said eagerly.

"First, I would like a word with Tanis," Gilthanas said, seeing the half-elf preparing to depart.

"Certainly. There is a small room through the door to your right where you may talk in private." The lord gestured.

Once inside the small, luxuriously appointed room, both men stood in uncomfortable silence for long moments, neither looking at the other directly. Gilthanas was the first to break the silence.

"I have always despised humans," the elflord said slowly, "and now I find myself preparing to take on the responsibility of protecting them." He smiled. "It is a good feeling," he added softly, looking directly at Tanis for the first time.

Tanis's eyes met Gilthanas's and his grim face relaxed for a moment, though he did not return the elflord's smile. Then his gaze fell, his grave expression returned.

"You're going to Neraka, aren't you?" Gilthanas said after another long pause.

Tanis nodded, wordlessly.

"Your friends? They're going with you?"

"Some of them," Tanis replied. "They all want to go, but—" He found he could not continue, remembering their devotion. He shook his head.

Gilthanas stared down at an ornately carved table, absently running his hand over the gleaming wood.

"I must leave," Tanis said heavily, starting for the door. "I have a lot yet to do. We plan to leave at midnight, after Solinari's set—"

"Wait." Gilthanas put his hand on the half-elf's arm. "I—I want to tell you I'm sorry . . . about what I said this morning. No, Tanis, don't leave. Hear me out. This isn't easy for me." Gilthanas paused a moment. "I've learned a great deal, Tanis—about myself. The lessons have been hard ones. I forgot them . . . when I heard about Laurana. I was angry and frightened and I wanted to hit someone. You were the closest target. What Laurana did, she did out of love for you. I'm learning about love, too, Tanis. Or I'm trying to learn." His voice was bitter. "Mostly I'm learning about pain. But that's my problem."

Tanis was watching him now. Gilthanas's hand was still on his shoulder.

"I know now, after I've had time to think," Gilthanas continued softly, "that what Laurana did was right. She *had* to go, or her love would have been meaningless. She had faith in you, believed in you enough to go to you when she heard you were dying, even though it meant going to that evil place—"

Tanis's head bowed. Gilthanas gripped him tightly, both hands on his shoulders.

"Theros Ironfeld said once that—in all the years he had lived—he had never seen anything done out of love come to evil. We have to believe that, Tanis. What Laurana did, she did out of love. What you do now, you do out of love. Surely the gods will bless that."

"Did they bless Sturm?" Tanis asked harshly. "He loved!"

"Didn't they? How do you know?"

Tanis's hand closed over Gilthanas's. He shook his head. He wanted to believe. It sounded wonderful, beautiful . . . just like tales of dragons. As a child, he'd wanted to believe in dragons, too. . . .

Sighing, he walked away from the elflord. His hand was on the doorknob when Gilthanas spoke again.

"Farewell . . . brother."

The companions met by the wall, at the secret door Tasslehoff had found that led up and over the walls, out into the plains beyond. Gilthanas could, of course, have given them permission to leave by the front gates, but the fewer people who knew of this dark journey the better as far as Tanis was concerned.

Now they were gathered inside the small room at the top of the stairs. Solinari was just sinking behind the distant mountains. Tanis, standing apart from the others, watched the moon as its last silvery rays touched the battlements of the horrible citadel hovering above them. He could see lights in the floating castle. Dark shapes moved around. Who lived in that dreadful thing? Draconians? The black-robed mages and dark clerics whose power had torn it from the soil and now kept it drifting among masses of thick gray clouds?

Behind him, he heard the others talking in soft voices—all except for Berem. The Everman—watched over closely by Caramon—stood apart, his eyes wide and fearful.

For long moments Tanis watched them, then he sighed. He faced another parting, and this one grieved him so that he wondered if he had the strength to make it. Turning slightly, he saw the last beaming rays of Solinari's fading light touch Goldmoon's beautiful silver-gold hair. He saw her face, peaceful and serene—even though she contemplated a journey into darkness and danger. And he knew he had the strength.

With a sigh, he walked away from the window to rejoin his friends.

"Is it time?" Tasslehoff asked eagerly.

Tanis smiled, his hand reaching out fondly to stroke Tas's ridiculous topknot of hair. In a changing world, kenders remained constant.

"Yes," Tanis said, "it is time." His eyes went to Riverwind. "For *some* of us."

As the Plainsman met the half-elf's steady, unwavering gaze, the thoughts in his mind were reflected in his face, as clear to Tanis as clouds flitting across the night sky. First Riverwind was uncomprehending, perhaps he had not even heard Tanis's words. Then the Plainsman realized what had been said. Now he understood, and his stern, rigid face face flushed, the brown eyes flared. Tanis said nothing. He simply shifted his gaze to Goldmoon.

Riverwind looked at his wife, who stood in a pool of silvery moonlight, waiting, her own thoughts far away. There was a sweet smile on her lips. A smile Tanis had seen only recently. Perhaps she was seeing her child playing in the sun.

Tanis looked back at Riverwind. He saw the Plainsman's inner struggle, and Tanis knew that the Que-shu warrior would offer—no, he would insist—on accompanying them, even though it meant leaving Goldmoon behind.

Walking to him, Tanis put his hands on the tall man's shoulders, looking into the Plainsman's dark eyes.

"Your work is done, my friend," Tanis said. "You have walked winter's path far enough. Here our roads separate. Ours leads into a bleak desert. Yours wends its way through green and blossoming trees. You have a responsibility to the son or daughter you are bringing into the world." He put his hand on Goldmoon's shoulder now, drawing her near, seeing her about to protest.

"The baby will be born in the autumn," Tanis said softly, "when the vallenwoods are red and golden. Don't cry, my dear." He gathered Goldmoon into his arms. "The vallenwoods will grow again. And you will take the young warrior or the young maiden into Solace, and you will tell them a story of two people who loved each other so much they brought hope into a world of dragons."

He kissed her beautiful hair. Then Tika, weeping softly, took his place, bidding Goldmoon farewell. Tanis turned to Riverwind. The Plainsman's stern mask was gone, his face showed plainly the marks of his grief. Tanis himself could barely see through his tears.

"Gilthanas will need help, planning the defense of the city."
Tanis cleared his throat. "I wish to the gods this was truly the
end of your dark winter, but I'm afraid it must last a little
longer."

"The gods are with us, my friend, my brother," Riverwind
said brokenly, embracing the half-elf. "May they be with you,
as well. We will wait here for your return."

Solinari dipped behind the mountains. The only lights in the
night sky were the cold and glittering stars and the hideous
gleam of windows in the citadel, watching them with yellow
eyes. One by one, the companions bid the Plainsmen good-
bye. Then, following Tasslehoff, they silently crossed the wall,
entered another door, and crept down another staircase. Tas
shoved open the door at the bottom. Moving cautiously, hands
on their weapons, the companions stepped out onto the plain.

For a moment, they stood huddled together, staring out
across the plain where—even in the deep darkness—it seemed
to them they would be visible to thousands of eyes watching
from the citadel above.

Standing next to Berem, Tanis could feel the man shivering
with fear and he felt glad he had assigned Caramon to watch
him. Ever since Tanis had stated they were going to Neraka, the
half-elf had seen a frantic, haunted look in the man's blue
eyes—much like the look of a trapped animal. Tanis caught
himself pitying the man, then hardened his heart. Too much
was at stake. Berem was the key, the answer lay within him and
within Neraka. Just how they were going to go about discovering the answer, Tanis hadn't decided yet, although the begin-
nings of a plan stirred in his brain.

Far away, the blaring noise of horns split the night air. An
orange light flared on the horizon. Draconians, burning a village. Tanis gripped his cloak around him. Though Spring
Dawning had come and past, the chill of winter was still in the
air.

"Move out," he said softly.

One by one, he watched them run across the strip of open
grassland, racing to reach the shelter of the grove of trees
beyond. Here small, fast-flying brass dragons waited to carry
them into the mountains.

This might all end tonight, Tanis though nervously, watching
Tasslehoff scamper into the darkness like a mouse. If the

dragons were discovered, if the watching eyes in the citadel saw them—it would be all over. Berem would fall into the hands of the Queen. Darkness would cover the land.

Tika followed Tas, running lightly and surely. Flint ran close behind, wheezing. The dwarf looked older. The thought that he was unwell crossed Tanis's mind, but he knew Flint would never agree to stay behind. Now Caramon ran through the darkness, his armor clanking. One hand was fixed firmly on Berem, tugging him along beside him.

My turn, Tanis realized, seeing the others safely sheltered within the grove. This is it. For good or for evil, the story is drawing near its end. Glancing up, he saw Goldmoon and Riverwind watching them from the small window in the tower room.

For good or for evil.

What if it does end in darkness, Tanis wondered for the first time. What will become of the world? What will become of those I'm leaving behind?

Steadily he looked up at these two people who were as dear to him as the family he'd never known. And, as he watched, he saw Goldmoon light a candle. For a brief instant the flame illuminated her face and Riverwind's. They raised their hands in parting, then extinguished the flame lest unfriendly eyes see it.

Taking a deep breath, Tanis turned and tensed himself to run.

The darkness might conquer, but it could never extinguish hope. And though one candle—or many—might flicker and die, new candles would be lit from the old.

Thus hope's flame always burns, lighting the darkness until the coming of day.

BOOK 3

I

An old man and a golden dragon.

He was an ancient gold dragon, the oldest of his kind. In his day, he had been a fierce warrior. The scars of his victories were visible on his wrinkled golden skin. His name had once been as shining as his glories, but he had forgotten it long ago. A few of the younger, irreverent gold dragons referred to him affectionately as Pyrite—Fool's Gold—due to his not infrequent habit of mentally fading out of the present and reliving his past.

Most of his teeth were gone. It had been eons since he had munched up a nice bit of deer meat or torn apart a goblin. He was able to gum a rabbit now and then, but mostly he lived on oatmeal.

When Pyrite lived in the present, he was an intelligent, if irrascible, companion. His vision was dimming, though he refused to admit it, and he was as deaf as a doorknob. His mind was quick. His conversation was still sharp as a tooth—so the saying went among dragons. It was just that he rarely discussed the same topic as anyone else in his company.

But when he was back in his past, the other golds took to their caves. For when he remembered them, he could still throw spells remarkably well, and his breath weapons were as effective as ever.

On this day, however, Pyrite was neither in past nor in present. He lay on the Plains of Estwilde, napping in the warm spring sunshine. Next to him sat an old man doing the same thing, his head pillowed on the dragon's flank.

A battered and shapeless pointed hat rested over the old man's face to shield his eyes from the sun. A long white beard flowed out from under the hat. Booted feet stuck out from beneath long, mouse-colored robes.

Both slept soundly. The gold dragon's flanks heaved and thrummed with his wheezing breath. The old man's mouth was wide open, and he sometimes woke himself with a prodigious snore. When this happened, he would sit bolt upright—sending his hat rolling onto the ground (which did not help its appearance) and look around in alarm. Seeing nothing, he would grunt to himself in annoyance, replace his hat (after he found it), poke the dragon irritably in the ribs, then go back to his nap.

A casual passerby might have wondered what in the name of the Abyss these two were doing calmly sleeping on the Plains of Estwilde, even though it *was* a fine, warm spring day. The passerby might have supposed the two were waiting for someone, for the old man would occasionally awaken, remove his hat, and peer solemnly up into the empty sky.

A passerby might have wondered—had there been any passersby. There were not. At least no friendly ones. The Plains of Estwilde were crawling with draconian and goblin troops. If the two knew they were napping in a dangerous place, they did not seem to mind.

Awakening from a particularly violent snore, the old man was just about to scold his companion sternly for making such terrible noises when a shadow fell across them.

"Ha!" the old man said angrily, staring up. "Dragonriders! A whole passel of 'em. Up to no good, too, I suppose." The old man's white eyebrows came together in a V-shape above his nose. "I've had about enough of this. Now they have the nerve to come and cut off my sunshine. Wake up!" he shouted, poking at Pyrite with a weather-beaten old wooden staff.

The gold dragon grumbled, opened one golden eye, stared at the old man (seeing only a mouse-colored blur), and calmly shut his eye again.

The shadows continued to pass over—four dragons with riders.

"Wake up, I say, you lazy lout!" the old man yelled. Snoring blissfully, the gold rolled over on his back, his clawed feet in the air, his stomach turned to the warm sun.

The old man glared at the dragon for a moment, then, in sudden inspiration, ran around to the great head. "War!" he shouted gleefully, directly into one of the dragon's ears. "It's war! We're under attack—"

The effect was startling. Pyrite's eyes flared open. Rolling over onto his stomach, his feet dug into the ground so deeply he nearly mired himself. His head reared up fiercely, his golden wings spread and began to beat, sending clouds of dust and sand a mile high.

"War!" he trumpeted. "War! We're called. Gather the flights! Mount the attack!"

The old man appeared rather taken aback by this sudden transformation, and he was also rendered momentarily speechless by the accidental inhalation of a mouthful of dust. Seeing the dragon start to leap into the air, however, he ran forward, waving his hat.

"Wait!" he yelled, coughing and choking. "Wait for me!"

"Who are you that I should wait?" Pyrite roared. The dragon stared through the billowing sand. "Are you my wizard?"

"Yes, yes," the old man called hastily. "I'm—uh—your wizard. Drop your wing a bit so I can climb on. Thanks, there's a good fellow. Now I . . . oh! Whoah! I'm not strapped in! . . . Look out! My hat! Confound it, I didn't tell you to take off yet!"

"We've got to reach the battle in time," Pyrite cried fiercely. "Huma's fighting alone!"

"Huma!" The old man snorted. "Well, you're not going to

arrive in time for *that* battle! Few hundred years late. But that's not the battle I had in mind. It's those four dragons there, to the east. Evil creatures! We've got to stop them—"

"Dragons! Ah, yes! I see them!" roared Pyrite, swooping up in hot pursuit of two extremely startled and highly insulted eagles.

"No! No!" yelled the old man, kicking the dragon in the flanks. "East, you ninny! Fly two more points to the east!"

"Are you sure you're my wizard?" Pyrite asked in a deep voice. "My wizard never spoke to me in that tone."

"I'm—uh, sorry, old fellow," the old man said quickly, "just a bit nervous. Upcoming conflict and all that."

"By the gods, there *are* four dragons!" Pyrite said in astonishment, having just caught a blurred glimpse of them.

"Take me in close so I can get a good shot at them," the old man shouted. "I have a really wonderful spell—Fireball. Now," he muttered, "if I can just remember how it goes."

Two dragonarmy officers rode among the flight of four brass dragons. One rode at the front. A bearded man, his helm seemed slightly large for him and was worn pulled well down over his face, shadowing his eyes. The other officer rode behind the group. He was a huge man, nearly splitting out of his black armor. He wore no helm—there probably wasn't one large enough—but his face was grim and watchful, particularly over the prisoners who rode the dragons in the center of the flight.

It was an odd assortment of prisoners—a woman dressed in mismatched armor, a dwarf, a kender, and a middle-aged man with long, unkempt gray hair.

The same passerby who had observed the old man and his dragon might have noticed that the officers and their prisoners went out of their way to avoid detection by any ground troops of the Dragon Highlord. Indeed, when one group of draconians spotted them and began to shout, trying to attract their attention, the dragonarmy officers studiously ignored them. A truly sharp observer might also have wondered what brass dragons were doing in the Dragon Highlord's service.

Unfortunately, neither the old man nor his decrepit golden dragon was a sharp observer.

Keeping in the clouds, they sneaked up on the unsuspecting group.

"Whiz down out of here at my command," the old man said, cackling to himself in high glee over the prospect of a fight. "We'll attack 'um from the rear."

"Where's Sir Huma?" the gold asked, peering blearily through the cloud.

"Dead," muttered the old man, concentrating on his spell.

"Dead!" roared the dragon in dismay. "Then we're too late?"

"Oh, never mind!" snapped the old man irritably. "Ready?"

"Dead," repeated the dragon sadly. Then his eyes blazed. "But we'll avenge him!"

"Yes, quite," said the old man. "Now . . . at my signal— No! Not yet! You—"

The old man's words were lost in a rush of wind as the gold dove out of the cloud, plummeting down on the four smaller dragons beneath him like a spear shooting from the sky.

The big dragonarmy officer in the back caught a glimpse of movement above him and glanced up. His eyes widened.

"Tanis!" he yelled in alarm at the officer in the front.

The half-elf turned. Alerted by the sound of Caramon's voice, he was ready for trouble, but at first he couldn't see anything. Then Caramon pointed.

Tanis looked up.

"What in the name of the gods—" he breathed.

Streaking down out of the sky, diving straight for them, was a golden dragon. Riding on the dragon was on old man, his white hair flying out behind him (he'd lost his hat), his long white beard blowing back over his shoulders. The dragon's mouth was bared in a snarl that would have been vicious if it hadn't been toothless.

"I think we're under attack," Caramon said in awe.

Tanis had come to the same conclusion. "Scatter!" he yelled, swearing under his breath. Down below them, an entire division of draconians watched the aerial battle with intense interest. The last thing he had wanted to do was call attention to the group, now some crazy old man was ruining everything.

The four dragons, hearing Tanis's command, broke instantly from formation—but not soon enough. A brilliant fireball burst right in their midst, sending the dragons reeling in the sky.

Momentarily blinded by the brilliant light, Tanis dropped the reins and threw his arms around the creature's neck as it went rolling about out of control.

Then he heard a familiar voice.

"That got'em! Wonderful spell, Fireball—"

"Fizban!" Tanis groaned.

Blinking his eyes, he fought desperately to bring his dragon under control. But it seemed the beast knew how to handle himself better than the inexperienced rider, for the brass soon righted himself. Now that Tanis could see, he flashed a glance around at the others. They appeared unhurt, but they were scattered all over the sky. The old man and his dragon were pursuing Caramon—the old man had his hand outstretched, apparently all set to cast another devastating spell. Caramon was yelling and gesturing—he, too, had recognized the befuddled old mage.

Racing toward Fizban from behind came Flint and Tasslehoff, the kender shrieking in glee and waving his hands, Flint hanging on for dear life. The dwarf looked positively green.

But Fizban was intent upon his prey. Tanis heard the old man shout several words and extend his hand. Lightning shot from his fingertips. Fortunately his aim was off. The lightning streaked past Caramon's head, forcing the big man to duck but otherwise not injuring him.

Tanis swore an oath so vile he startled himself. Kicking his dragon in the flanks, he pointed at the old man.

"Attack!" he commanded the dragon. "Don't hurt him, just drive him out of here."

To his amazement, the brass refused. Shaking his head, the dragon began to circle, and it suddenly occurred to Tanis that the creature intended to land!

"What? Are you mad?" Tanis swore at the dragon. "You're taking us down into the dragonarmies!"

The dragon seemed deaf, and now Tanis saw that all the other brass dragons were circling, preparing to land.

In vain Tanis pleaded with his dragon. Berem, sitting behind Tika, clutched the woman so desperately she could barely breathe. The Everman's eyes were on the draconians, who were swarming over the plains toward where the dragons were going to land. Caramon was flailing about wildly, trying to avoid the lightning bolts that zapped all around him. Flint had even come to life, tugging frantically at his dragon's reins, roaring in anger, while Tas was still yelling wildly at Fizban. The old man followed after them all, herding the brass dragons before him like sheep.

They landed near the foothills of the Khalkist Mountains. Looking quickly across the plains, Tanis could see draconians swarming toward them.

We might bluff our way out of this, Tanis thought feverishly, though their disguises had been intended only to get them into Kalaman, not deceive a party of suspicious draconians. However, it was worth a shot. If only Berem would remember to stay in the background and keep quiet.

But before Tanis could say a word, Berem leaped from the back of his dragon and took off, running frantically into the foothills. Tanis could see the draconians pointing at him, yelling.

So much for keeping in the background. Tanis swore again. The bluff might still work. . . . they could always claim a prisoner was trying to escape. No, he realized in despair, the draconians would simply chase after Berem and catch him. According to what Kitiara had told him, all the draconians in Krynn had descriptions of Berem.

"In the name of the Abyss!" Tanis forced himself to calm down and think logically, but the situation was fast getting out of control. "Caramon! Go after Berem. Flint, you— No, Tasslehoff, get back here! Damn it! Tika, go after Tas. No, on second thought, stay with me. You, too, Flint—"

"But Tasslehoff's gone after that crazy old—"

"And if we're lucky, the ground will open and swallow them both!" Tanis glanced back over his shoulder and swore savagely. Berem—driven by fear—was clambering over rocks and scrub bushes with the lightness of a mountain goat, while Caramon—hampered by the dragon armor and his own arsenal of weapons—slipped down two feet for every foot he gained.

Looking back across the Plains, Tanis could see the draconians clearly. Sunlight gleamed off their armor and their swords and spears. Perhaps there was still a chance, if the brass dragons would attack—

But just as he started to order them into battle, the old man came running up from where he had landed his ancient gold dragon. "Shoo!" said the old man to the brass dragons. "Shoo—get away! Go back to wherever you came from!"

"No! Wait!" Tanis nearly tore out his beard in frustration, watching as the old man ran among the brass dragons, waving his arms like a farmer's wife driving her chickens to shelter.

Then the half-elf stopped swearing for—to his astonishment—the brass dragons prostrated themselves flat on the ground before the old man in his mouse-colored robes. Then, lifting their wings, they soared gracefully into the air.

In a rage, forgetting he was dressed in captured dragonarmy armor, Tanis ran across the trampled grass toward the old man, following Tas. Hearing them coming, Fizban turned around to face them.

"I've a good mind to wash your mouth out with soap," the old mage snapped, glowering at Tanis. "You're my prisoners now, so just come along quietly or you'll taste my magic—"

"Fizban!" cried Tasslehoff, throwing his arms around the old man.

The old mage peered down at the kender hugging him, then staggered backwards in amazement.

"It's Tassle—Tassle—" he stammered.

"Burrfoot," Tas said backing off and bowing politely. "Tasslehoff Burrfoot."

"Great Huma's ghost!" Fizban exclaimed.

"This is Tanis Half-Elven. And that is Flint Fireforge. You remember him?" Tasslehoff continued, waving a small hand at the dwarf.

"Uh, yes, quite," Fizban muttered, his face flushing.

"And Tika . . . and that's Caramon up there . . . oh, well, you can't see him now. Then there's Berem. We picked *him* up in Kalaman and—oh, Fizban!—he's got a green gem—ugh, ouch, Tanis, that hurt!"

Clearing his throat, Fizban cast a bleak look around.

"You're—uh—*not* with the—er—uh—dragonarmies?"

"No," said Tanis grimly, "we're not! Or at least we weren't." He gestured behind them. "That's likely to change any moment now, though."

"Not with the dragonarmies at all?" Fizban pursued hopefully. "You're sure you haven't converted? Been tortured? Brainwashed?"

"No, damn it!" Tanis yanked off his helm. "I'm Tanis Half-Elven, remember—"

Fizban beamed. "Tanis Half-Elven! So pleased to see you again, sir." Grabbing Tanis's hand, he shook it heartily.

"Confound it!" Tanis snapped in exasperation, snatching his hand out of the old man's grip.

"But you were riding dragons!"

"Those were *good* dragons!" Tanis shouted. "They've come back!"

"No one told *me!*" The old man gasped indignantly.

"Do you know what you've done?" Tanis continued, ignoring the interruption. "You've blown us out of the skies! Sent back our only means to get to Neraka—"

"Oh, I know what I've done," Fizban mumbled. He glanced back over his shoulder. "My, my. Those fellows seem to be gaining. Mustn't be caught by them. Well, what are we doing standing around?" He glared at Tanis. "Some leader *you* are! I suppose I'll have to take charge. . . . Where's my hat?"

"About five miles back," stated Pyrite with a great yawn.

"You still here?" Fizban said, glaring at the gold dragon in annoyance.

"Where else would I be?" the dragon asked gloomily.

"I told you to go with the others!"

"I didn't want to." Pyrite snorted. A bit of fire flared from his nose, making it twitch. This was followed by a tremendous sneeze. Sniffing, the dragon continued peevishly. "No respect for age, those brass dragons. They talk constantly! And giggle. Gets on my nerves, that silly giggle. . . ."

"Well, you'll just have to go back by yourself then!" Fizban stalked up to stare the dragon in its bleary eye. "We're going on a long journey into dangerous country—"

"*We're* going?" Tanis cried. "Look, old man, Fizban, whatever your name is, why don't you *and* your—uh—friend here go back. You're right. It's going to be a long, dangerous journey. Longer, now, that we've lost our dragons and—"

"Tanis . . . " said Tika warningly, her eyes on the draconians.

"Into the hills quick," Tanis said, drawing a deep breath, trying to control his fear and his anger. "Go on, Tika. You and Flint. Tas—" He grabbed the kender.

"No, Tanis! We can't leave him here!" Tas wailed.

"Tas!" Tanis said in a voice that warned the kender the halfelf had plainly had enough and wasn't going to stand for anything further. Apparently the old man understood the same thing.

"I've got to go with these folks," he said to the dragon. "They need me. You can't go back on your own. You'll just have to sallyforth—"

"Polymorph!" the dragon said indignantly. "The word is 'polymorph!' You never get that right—"

"Whatever!" the old man yelled. "Quickly! We'll take you with us."

"Very well," the dragon said. "I *could* use the rest."

"I don't think—" Tanis began, wondering what they would do with a large gold dragon, but it was too late.

While Tas watched, fascinated, and Tanis fumed in impatience, the dragon spoke a few words in the strange language of magic. There was a bright flash and then, suddenly, the dragon vanished.

"What? Where?" Tasslehoff looked all around.

Fizban leaned over to pick up something out of the grass.

"Get moving! Now!" Tanis hustled Tas and the old man into the foothills, following after Tika and Flint.

"Here," Fizban said to Tas as they ran. "Hold out your hand."

Tas did as instructed. Then the kender caught his breath in awe. He would have come to a dead stop to examine it, except Tanis caught him by the arm and dragged him forward.

In the palm of Tas's hand gleamed a tiny golden figure of a dragon, carved in exquisite detail. Tas imagined he could even see the scars on the wings. Two small red jewels glittered in the eyes, then—as Tas watched—the jewels winked out as golden eyelids closed over them.

"Oh, Fizban, it—it's—beautiful! Can I truly keep it?" Tas yelled over his shoulder to the old man, who was puffing along behind.

"Sure, my boy!" Fizban beamed. "At least until this adventure's ended."

"Or it ends us," Tanis muttered, climbing rapidly over the rocks. The draconians were drawing nearer and nearer.

2

The golden span.

Up and up into the hills they climbed, the draconians in pursuit of the group, who now appeared to them to be spies.

The group had lost the trail Caramon used chasing after Berem, but could not take time to search for it. They were considerably startled, therefore, when they suddenly came across Caramon, sitting calmly on a boulder, Berem—unconscious—stretched out beside him.

"What happened?" Tanis asked, breathing heavily, exhausted after the long climb.

"I caught up with him, finally." Caramon shook his head. "And he put up a fight. He's strong for an old guy, Tanis. I had to clunk him. I'm afraid I was a bit too hard, though," he added, staring down at the comatose figure remorsefully.

"Great!" Tanis was too tired even to swear.

"I'll handle this," Tika said, reaching into a leather pouch.

"The draconians are coming up past that last big rock," Flint reported as he stumbled into view. The dwarf seemed about done in. He collapsed onto a rock, mopping his sweating face with the end of his beard.

"Tika—" Tanis began.

"Found it!" she said triumphantly, pulling out a small vial. Kneeling down beside Berem, she took the stopper from the vial and waved it under his nose. The unconscious man drew a breath, then immediately began to cough.

Tika slapped him on the cheeks. "On your feet!" she said in her barmaid voice. "Unless you want the draconians to catch you."

Berem's eyes flew open in alarm. Clutching his head, he sat up dizzily. Caramon helped him stand.

"That's wonderful, Tika!" Tas said in excitement. "Let me—" Before she could stop him, Tas grabbed the vial and held it up to his own nose, inhaling deeply.

"Eeee Ahhhh!" The kender gagged, staggering back into Fizban, who had come up the path after Flint. "Ugh! Tika! That's . . . awful!" He could barely speak. "What is it?"

"Some concoction of Otik's," Tika said, grinning. "All of us barmaids carried it. Came in handy in lots of instances, if you take my meaning." Her smile slipped. "Poor Otik," she said softly. "I wonder what's become of him. And the Inn—"

"No time for that now, Tika." Tanis said impatiently. "We've got to go. On your feet, old man!" This to Fizban, who was just sitting down comfortably.

"I've got a spell," Fizban protested as Tas tugged and prodded him up. "Take care of those pests instantly. Poof!"

"No!" Tanis said. "Absolutely not. With my luck, you'd turn them all into trolls."

"I wonder if I could . . ." Fizban's face brightened.

The afternoon sun was just beginning to slide down the rim of the sky when the trail they had been following ever higher into the mountains suddenly branched off into two different directions. One led into the mountain peaks, the other seemed to wind around the side. There might be a pass among the peaks, Tanis thought; a pass they could defend, if necessary.

But before he could say a word, Fizban started off on the trail that wound around the mountain. "This way," the old mage announced, leaning on his staff as he tottered forward.

"But—" Tanis started to protest.

"Come on, come on. This way!" said Fizban insistently, turning around and glaring at them from beneath his bushy white eyebrows. "That way leads to a dead end—in more ways than one. I know. I've been here before. This leads around the side of a mountain to a great gorge. Bridge over the gorge. We can get across, then fight the draconians when they try to come after us."

Tanis scowled, unwilling to trust the crazy old mage.

"It *is* a good plan, Tanis," Caramon said slowly. "It's obvious we're going to have to fight them sometime." He pointed to the draconians climbing up the mountain trails after them.

Tanis glanced around. They were all exhausted. Tika's face was pale, her eyes glazed. She leaned on Caramon, who had even left his spears back on the trail to lighten his burden.

Tasslehoff grinned at Tanis cheerfully. But the kender was panting like a small dog and he was limping on one foot.

Berem looked the same as always, sullen and frightened. It was Flint that worried Tanis most. The dwarf had not said a word during their flight. He had kept up with them without faltering, but his lips were blue and his breath came in short gasps. Every once in a while—when he thought no one was looking—Tanis had seen him put his hand over his chest or rub his left arm as if it pained him.

"Very well." The half-elf decided. "Go on, old mage. Though I'm probably going to regret this," he added, under his breath as the rest hurried along after Fizban.

Near sundown, the companions came to a halt. They stood on a small rocky ledge about three-quarters of the way up the side of the mountain. Before them was a deep, narrow gorge. Far below they could see a river winding its way through the bottom of the gorge like a glistening snake.

It must be a four-hundred-foot drop, Tanis calculated. The trail they stood on hugged the side of the mountain, with sheer cliff on one side and nothing but air on the other. There was only one way across the gorge.

"And that bridge," said Flint—the first words he had spoken in hours, "is older than I am . . . and in worse shape."

"That bridge has stood for years!" Fizban said indignantly. "Why, it survived the Cataclysm!"

"I believe it," Caramon said sincerely.

"At least it's not too long," Tika tried to sound hopeful, though her voice faltered.

The bridge across the narrow gorge was of a unique construction. Huge vallenwood limbs were driven into the sides of the mountain on either side of the gorge. These limbs formed an X-shape that supported the wooden plank platform. Long ago, the structure must have been an architectural marvel. But now the wooden planks were rotted and splitting. If there had been a railing, it had long since fallen down into the chasm below. Even as they watched, the timbers creaked and shuddered in the chill wind of evening.

Then, behind them, they heard the sound of guttural voices and the clash of steel on rock.

"So much for going back," Caramon muttered. "We should cross over one by one."

"No time," Tanis said, rising to his feet. "We can only hope the gods are with us. And—I hate to admit it—but Fizban's right. Once we get across, we can stop the draconians easily. They'll be excellent targets, stuck out there on that bridge. I'll go first. Keep behind me, single-file. Caramon, you're rear guard. Berem, stay behind me."

Moving as swiftly as he dared, Tanis set foot on the bridge. He could feel the planks quiver and shake. Far below, the river flowed swiftly between the canyon walls; sharp rocks jutted up from its white, foaming surface. Tanis caught his breath and looked away quickly.

"Don't look down," he said to the others, feeling a chill emptiness where his stomach had been. For an instant he couldn't move, then, getting a grip on himself, he edged his way forward. Berem came right behind him, fear of the dragonmen completely obliterating any other terrors the Everman might have experienced.

After Berem came Tasslehoff, walking lightly with kender skill, peering over the edge in wonder. Then the terrified Flint, supported by Fizban. Finally Tika and Caramon set foot on the shivering planks, keeping nervous watch behind them.

Tanis was nearly halfway across when part of the platform

---

gave way, the rotten wood splintering beneath his feet.

Acting instinctively, in a paraxoysm of terror, he clutched desperately at the planking and caught hold of the edge. But the rotten wood crumbled in his grasp. His fingers slipped and—

—a hand closed over his wrist.

"Berem!" Tanis gasped. "Hold on!" He forced himself to hang limply, knowing that any movement on his part would only make Berem's hold on him harder to maintain.

"Pull him up!" he heard Caramon roar, then, "Don't anybody move! The whole thing's liable to give way!"

His face tight with the strain, sweat beading on his forehead, Berem pulled. Tanis saw the muscles on the man's arm bulge, the veins nearly burst from the skin. With what seemed like agonizing slowness, Berem dragged the half-elf up over the edge of the broken bridge. Here Tanis collapsed. Shaking with fright, he lay clinging to the wood, shivering.

Then he heard Tika cry out. Raising his head, he realized with grim amusement that he had probably just gained his life only to lose it. About thirty draconians appeared on the trail behind them. Tanis turned to look across the gaping hole in the center of the bridge. The other side of the platform was still standing. He might jump across the huge hole to safety, and so might Berem and Caramon—but not Tas, not Flint, not Tika, or the old mage.

"Excellent targets, you said," Caramon murmured, drawing his sword.

"Cast a spell, Old One!" Tasslehoff said suddenly.

"What?" Fizban blinked.

"A spell!" Tas cried, pointing at the draconians, who—seeing the companions trapped on the bridge—hurried up to finish them off.

"Tas, we're in enough trouble," Tanis began, the bridge creaking beneath his feet. Moving warily, Caramon stationed himself squarely in front of them, facing the draconians.

Fitting an arrow to his bowstring, Tanis fired. A draconian clutched its chest and fell, shrieking, off the cliff. The half-elf fired again and hit again. The draconians in the center of the line hesitated, milling about in confusion. There was no cover, no way to escape the half-elf's deadly barrage. The draconians in the front of the line surged forward toward the bridge.

At that moment, Fizban began to cast his spell.

Hearing the old mage chant, Tanis felt his heart sink. Then he reminded himself bitterly that they really couldn't be in a worse position. Berem, next to him, was watching the draconians with a stoic composure that Tanis found startling until he remembered that Berem didn't fear death; he would always return to life. Tanis fired again and another draconian howled in pain. So intent was he on his targets, that he forgot Fizban until he heard Berem gasp in astonishment. Glancing up, Tanis saw Berem staring into the sky. Following Berem's gaze, the half-elf was so astonished he nearly dropped his bow.

Descending from the clouds, glittering brightly in the dying rays of the sun—was a long golden bridge span. Guided by motions of the old mage's hand, the golden span dropped down out of the heavens to close the gap in the bridge.

Tanis came to his senses. Looking around, he saw that—for the moment—the draconians were also transfixed—staring at the golden span with glittering reptilian eyes.

"Hurry!" Tanis yelled. Gripping Berem by the arm, he dragged the Everman after him and jumped up onto the span as it hovered just about a foot above the gap. Berem followed, stumbling up clumsily. Even as they stood on it, the span kept dropping, slowing a bit under Fizban's guidance.

The span was still about eight inches above the platform when Tasslehoff, shrieking wildly, leaped onto it, pulling the awestruck dwarf up after him. The draconians—suddenly realizing their prey was going to escape—howled in rage and surged onto the wooden bridge. Tanis stood on the golden span, near its end, firing his arrows at the lead draconians. Caramon remained behind, driving them back with his sword.

"Get on across!" Tanis ordered Tika as she hopped onto the span beside him. "Stay beside Berem. Keep an eye on him. You, too, Flint, go with her. Go on!" he snarled viciously.

"I'll stay with you, Tanis," Tasslehoff offered.

Casting a backward glance at Caramon, Tika reluctantly obeyed orders, grabbing hold of Berem and shoving him along before her. Seeing the draconians coming, he needed little urging. Together they dashed across the span onto the remaining half of the wooden bridge. It creaked alarmingly beneath their weight. Tanis only hoped it would hold, but he couldn't spare a glance. Apparently it was, for he heard Flint's thick boots clumping across it.

"We made it!" Tika yelled from the side of the canyon.

"Caramon!" Tanis shouted, firing another arrow, trying to

keep his footing on the golden span.

"Go ahead!" Fizban snapped at Caramon irritably. "I'm concentrating. I have to set the span down in the right place. A few more centimeters to the left, I think—"

"Tasslehoff, go on across!" Tanis ordered.

"I'm not leaving Fizban!" said the kender stubbornly as Caramon stepped up onto the golden span. The draconians, seeing the big warrior leaving, surged forward again. Tanis fired arrows as fast as he could; one draconian lay on the bridge in a pool of green blood, another toppled over the edge. But the half-elf was growing tired. Worse, he was running out of arrows. And the draconians kept coming. Caramon came to a stop beside Tanis on the span.

"Hurry, Fizban!" pleaded Tasslehoff, wringing his hands.

"There!" Fizban said in satisfaction. "Perfect fit. And the gnomes said I was no engineer."

Just as he spoke, the golden span carrying Tanis, Caramon, and Tasslehoff dropped firmly into place between the two sections of the broken bridge.

And at that moment, the other half of the wooden bridge— the half still standing, the half that led to safety on the other side of the canyon—creaked, crumbled, and fell into the canyon.

"In the name of the gods!" Caramon gulped in fear, catching hold of Tanis and dragging him back just as the half-elf had been about to set foot on the wooden planking.

"Trapped!" Tanis said hoarsely, watching the logs tumble end over end into the ravine, his soul seeming to plummet with them. On the other side, he could hear Tika scream, her cries blending with the exultant shouts of the draconians.

There was a rending, snapping sound. The draconian's cries of exultation changed at once to horror and fear.

"Look! Tanis!" Tasslehoff cried in wild excitement. "Look!"

Tanis glanced back in time to see the other part of the wooden bridge tumble into the ravine, carrying with it most of the draconians. He felt the golden span shudder.

"We'll fall, too!" Caramon roared. "There's nothing to support—"

Caramon's tongue froze to the roof of his mouth. With a strangled gulp, he looked slowly from side to side.

"I don't believe it—" he muttered.

"Somehow, I do. . . ." Tanis drew a shuddering breath.

In the center of the canyon, suspended in midair, hung the magical golden span, glittering in the light of the setting sun as the wooden bridge on either side of it plunged into the ravine. Upon the span stood four figures, staring down at the ruins beneath them—and across the great gaps between them and the sides of the gorge.

For long moments, there was complete, absolute, deathly silence. Then Fizban turned triumphantly to Tanis.

"Wonderful spell," said the mage with pride. "Got a rope?"

It was well after dark by the time the companions finally got off the golden span. Flinging a rope to Tika, they waited while she and the dwarf fastened it securely to a tree. Then—one by one—Tanis, Caramon, Tas, and Fizban swung off the span and were hauled up the side of the cliff by Berem. When they were all across, they collapsed, exhausted from fatigue. So tired were they that they didn't even bother to find shelter, but spread their blankets in a grove of scrubby pine trees and set the watch. Those not on duty fell instantly asleep.

The next morning, Tanis woke, stiff and aching. The first thing he saw was the sun shining brightly off the sides of the golden span—still suspended solidly in mid-air.

"I don't suppose you can get rid of that thing?" he asked Fizban as the old mage helped Tas hand out a breakfast of quith-pa.

"I'm afraid not," the old man said, eyeing the span wistfully.

"He tried a few spells this morning," Tas said, nodding in the direction of a pine tree completely covered with cobwebs and another that was burned to a crisp. "I figured he better quit before he turned us all into crickets or something."

"Good idea," muttered Tanis, staring gloomily out at the gleaming span. "Well, we couldn't leave a clearer trail if we painted an arrow on the side of the cliff." Shaking his head, he sat down beside Caramon and Tika.

"They'll be after us, too, you can bet," Caramon said, munching half-heartedly on quith-pa. "Have dragons bring 'em across." Sighing, he stuck most of the dried fruit back in his pouch.

"Caramon?" said Tika. "You didn't eat much. . . ."

"I'm not hungry," he mumbled as he stood up. "Guess I'll scout ahead a ways." Shouldering his pack and his weapons, he started off down the trail.

Her face averted, Tika began busily packing away her things, avoiding Tanis's gaze.

"Raistlin?" Tanis asked.

Tika stopped. Her hands dropped into her lap.

"Will he always be like this, Tanis?" she asked helplessly, looking fondly after him. "I don't understand!"

"I don't either," Tanis said quietly, watching the big man disappear into the wilderness. "But, then, I never had a brother or a sister."

"*I* understand!" said Berem. His soft voice quivered with a passion that caught Tanis's attention.

"What do you mean?"

But—at his question—the eager, hungry look on the Everman's face vanished.

"Nothing—" he mumbled, his face a blank mask.

"Wait!" Tanis rose quickly. "Why do you understand Caramon?" He put his hand on Berem's arm.

"Leave me alone!" Berem shouted fiercely, flinging Tanis backward.

"Hey, Berem," Tasslehoff said, looking up and smiling as if he hadn't heard a thing. "I was sorting through my maps and I found one that has the most interesting story—"

Giving Tanis a hunted glance, Berem shuffled over to where Tasslehoff sat cross-legged on the ground, his sheaf of maps spread out all around him. Hunching down over the maps, the Everman soon appeared lost in wonder, listening to one of Tas's tales.

"Better leave him alone, Tanis," Flint advised. "If you ask me, the only reason he understands Caramon is that he's as crazy as Raistlin."

"I didn't ask you, but that's all right," Tanis said, sitting down beside the dwarf to eat his own ration of quith-pa. "We're going to have to be going soon. With luck, Tas will find a map—"

Flint snorted. "Humpf! A lot of good *that* will do us. The last map of his we followed took us to a sea port without a sea!"

Tanis hid his smile. "Maybe this will be different," he said. "At least it's better than following Fizban's directions."

"Well, you're right there," the dwarf admitted grumpily. Giving Fizban a sideways glance, Flint leaned over near Tanis. "Didn't you ever wonder how he managed to live through that fall at Pax Tharkas?" he asked in a loud whisper.

"I wonder about a lot of things," Tanis said quietly. "Like—

how are you feeling?"

The dwarf blinked, completely taken aback by the unexpected question. "Fine!" he snapped, his face flushing.

"It's just, sometimes I've seen you rub your left arm," Tanis continued.

"Rheumatism," the dwarf growled. "You know it always bothers me in the spring. And sleeping on the ground doesn't help. I thought you said we should be moving along." The dwarf busied himself with packing.

"Right." Tanis turned away with a sigh. "Found anything, Tas?"

"Yes, I think so," the kender said eagerly. Rolling up his maps, he stashed them in his map case, then slipped the case into a pouch, taking a quick peek at his golden dragon while he was at it. Although seemingly made of metal, the figurine changed position in the oddest way. Right now, it was curled around a golden ring—Tanis's ring, one Laurana had given him and he had returned to her, when he told her he was in love with Kitiara. Tasslehoff became so absorbed in staring at the dragon and the ring that he nearly forgot Tanis was waiting.

"Oh," he said, hearing Tanis cough impatiently. "Map. Right. Yes, you see, once when I was just a little kender, my parents and I traveled through the Khalkist Mountains—that's where we are now—on our way to Kalaman. Usually, you know, we took the northern, longer route. There was a fair, every year, at Taman Busuk, where they sold the most marvelous things, and my father never missed it. But one year—I think it was the year after he'd been arrested and put in the stocks over a misunderstanding with a jeweler—we decided to go through the mountains. My mother'd always wanted to see Godshome, so we—"

"The map?" interrupted Tanis.

"Yes, the map." Tas sighed. "Here. It was my father's, I think. Here's where we are, as near as Fizban and I can figure. And here's Godshome."

"What's that?"

"An old city. It's in ruins, abandoned during the Cataclysm—"

"And probably crawling with draconians," Tanis finished.

"No, not *that* Godshome," Tas continued, moving his small finger over into the mountains near the dot that marked the city. "*This* place is also called Godshome. In fact, it was called that long before there was a city, according to Fizban."

Tanis glanced at the old mage, who nodded.

"Long ago, people believed the gods lived there," he said solemnly. "It is a very holy place."

"And it's hidden," added Tas, "in a bowl in the center of these mountains. See? No one ever goes there, according to Fizban. No one knows about the trail except him. And there *is* a trail marked on my map, at least into the mountains. . . ."

"No one ever goes there?" Tanis asked Fizban.

The old mage's eyes narrowed in irritation. "No."

"No one except you?" Tanis pursued.

"I've been lots of place, Half-Elven!" The mage snorted. "Got a year? I'll tell you about them!" He shook a finger at Tanis. "You don't appreciate me, young man! Always suspicious! And after everything I've done for you—"

"Uh, I wouldn't remind him about *that!*" Tas said hurriedly, seeing Tanis's face darken. "Come along, Old One."

The two hurried off down the trail, Fizban stomping along angrily, his beard bristling.

"Did the gods really live in this place we're going to?" Tas asked him to keep him from bothering Tanis.

"How should I know?" Fizban demanded irritably. "Do I look like a god?"

"But—"

"Did anyone ever tell you that you talk entirely too much?"

"Almost everyone," Tas said cheerfully. "Did I ever tell you about the time I found a woolly mammoth?

Tanis heard Fizban groan. Tika hurried past him, to catch up with Caramon.

"Coming, Flint?" Tanis called.

"Yes," the dwarf answered, sitting down suddenly on a rock. "Give me a moment. I've dropped my pack. You go on ahead."

Occupied in studying the kender's map as he walked, Tanis did not see Flint collapse. He did not hear the odd note in the dwarf's voice, or see the spasm of pain that briefly contracted the dwarf's face.

"Well, hurry up," Tanis said absently. "We don't want to leave you behind."

"Aye, lad," Flint said softly, sitting on the rock, waiting for the pain to subside—as it always did.

Flint watched his friend walk down the trail, still moving somewhat clumsily in the dragonarmor. *We don't want to leave you behind.*

"Aye, lad," Flint repeated to himself. Brushing his gnarled hand quickly across his eyes, the dwarf stood up and followed his friends.

3
Godshome.

It was a long and weary day
spent wandering through the mountains aimlessly as near as
the impatient half-elf could tell.

The only thing that kept him from throttling Fizban—after
they had walked into the second box canyon in less than four
hours—was the undeniable fact that the old man kept them
headed in the right direction. No matter how lost and turned
around they seemed to get, no matter how often Tanis could
have sworn they'd passed the same boulder three times, whenever he caught a glimpse of the sun they were still traveling

unerringly to the southeast.

But as the day wore on, he saw the sun less and less frequently. Winter's bitter chill had gone from the air and there was even the faint smell of green and growing things borne on the wind. But soon the sky darkened with lead-gray clouds and it began to rain, a dull, drumming drizzle that penetrated the heaviest cloak.

By mid-afternoon, the group was cheerless and dispirited—even Tasslehoff, who had argued violently with Fizban over directions to Godshome. This was all the more frustrating to Tanis since it was that obvious neither of them knew where they were. (Fizban, in fact, was caught holding the map upside down.) The fight resulted in Tasslehoff stuffing his maps back in his pouch and refusing to get them out again while Fizban threatened to cast a spell that would turn Tasslehoff's topknot into a horse's tail.

Fed up with both of them, Tanis sent Tas to the back of the line to cool off, mollified Fizban, and nursed secret thoughts of sealing them both up in a cave.

The calmness that the half-elf had felt in Kalaman was slowly vanishing on this dismal journey. It had been a calmness, he realized now, brought about by activity, the need to make decisions, the comforting thought that he was finally doing something tangible to help Laurana. These thoughts kept him afloat in the dark waters that surrounded him, much as the sea elves had aided him in the Blood Sea of Istar. But now he felt the dark waters begin to close over his head once more.

Tanis's thoughts were constantly with Laurana. Over and over, he heard Gilthanas's accusing words—*She did this for you!* And though Gilthanas had, perhaps, forgiven him, Tanis knew he could never forgive himself. What was happening to Laurana in the Dark Queen's Temple? Was she still alive? Tanis's soul shrank from that thought. Of course she was alive! The Dark Queen would not kill her, not as long as she wanted Berem—

Tanis's eyes focused on the man walking ahead of him, near Caramon. I will do anything to save Laurana, he swore beneath his breath, clenching his fist. Anything! If it means sacrificing myself or—

He stopped. Would he really give up Berem? Would he really trade the Everman to the Dark Queen, perhaps plunge the world into a darkness so vast it would never see light again?

No, Tanis told himself firmly. Laurana would die before she would be part of such a bargain. Then—after he'd walked a few more steps—he'd change his mind. Let the world take care of itself, he thought gloomily. We're doomed. We can't win, no matter what happens. Laurana's life, that's the only thing that counts . . . the only thing . . .

Tanis was not the only gloomy member of the group. Tika walked beside Caramon, her red curls a bright spot of warmth and light in the gray day. But the light was only in the vibrant red of her hair, it had gone out of her eyes. Although Caramon was unfailingly kind to her, he had not held her since that wonderful, brief moment beneath the sea when his love had been hers. This made her angry in the long nights—he had used her, she decided, simply to ease his own pain. She vowed she would leave him when this was over. There was a wealthy young nobleman in Kalaman who had not been able to take his eyes off her. . . . But those were night thoughts. During the day, when Tika glanced at Caramon, and saw him plodding along next to her, his head bowed, her heart melted. Gently she touched him. Looking up at her quickly, he smiled. Tika sighed. So much for wealthy young noblemen.

Flint stumped along, rarely speaking, never complaining. If Tanis had not been wrapped up in his own inner turmoil, he would have noted this as a bad sign.

As for Berem, no one knew what he was thinking—if anything. He seemed to grow more nervous and wary the farther they traveled. The blue eyes that were too young for his face darted here and there like those of a trapped animal.

It was on the second day in the mountains that Berem vanished.

Everyone had been more cheerful in the morning, when Fizban announced that they should arrive in Godshome soon. But gloom quickly followed. The rain grew heavier. Three times in one hour the old mage led them plunging through the brush with excited cries of "This is it! Here we are!" only to find themselves in a swamp, a gorge, and—finally—staring at a rock wall.

It was this last time—the dead end—that Tanis felt his soul start to rip from his body. Even Tasslehoff fell back in alarm at the sight of the half-elf's rage-distorted face. Desperately Tanis fought to hold himself together, and it was then he noticed.

"Where's Berem?" he asked, a sudden chill freezing his anger.

Caramon blinked, seemingly coming back from some distant world. The big warrior looked around hastily, then turned to face Tanis, his face flushed with shame. "I—I dunno, Tanis. I—I thought he was next to me."

"He's our only way into Neraka," the half-elf said through clenched teeth, "and he's the only reason they're keeping Laurana alive. If they catch him—"

Tanis stopped, sudden tears choking him. Desperately he tried to think, despite the blood pounding in his head.

"Don't worry, lad," Flint said gruffly, patting the half-elf on the arm. "We'll find him."

"I'm sorry, Tanis," Caramon mumbled. "I was thinking about—about Raist. I—I know I shouldn't—"

"How in the name of the Abyss does that blasted brother of yours work mischief when he's not even here!" Tanis shouted. Then he caught himself. "I'm sorry, Caramon," he said, drawing a deep breath. "Don't blame yourself. I should have been watching, too. We all should have. We've got to backtrack anyway, unless Fizban can take us through solid rock . . . no, don't even consider it, old man. . . . Berem can't have gone far and his trail should be easy to pick up. He's not skilled in wood-lore."

Tanis was right. After an hour tracing back their own footsteps, they discovered a small animal trail none of them had noticed in passing. It was Flint who saw the man's tracks in the mud. Calling excitedly to the others, the dwarf plunged into the brush, following the clearly marked trail easily. The rest hurried after him, but the dwarf seemed to have experienced an unusual surge of energy. Like a hunting hound who knows the prey is just ahead of him, Flint trampled over tangleshoot vines and hacked his way through the undergrowth without pause. He quickly outdistanced them.

"Flint!" Tanis shouted more than once. "Wait up!"

But the group fell farther and farther behind the excited dwarf until they lost sight of him altogether. Flint's trail proved even clearer than Berem's, however. They had little difficulty following the print of the dwarf's heavy boots, not to mention the broken tree limbs and uprooted vines that marked his passing.

Then suddenly they were brought to a halt.

They had reached another rock cliff, but this time there was a way through—a hole in the rock formed a narrow tunnel-like opening. The dwarf had entered easily—they could see his tracks—but it was so narrow that Tanis stared at it in dismay.

"Berem got through it," Caramon said grimly, pointing at a smear of fresh blood the rock.

"Maybe," Tanis said dubiously. "See what's on the other side, Tas," he ordered, reluctant to enter until he was certain he was not being led a merry chase.

Tasslehoff crawled through with ease, and soon they heard his shrill voice exclaiming in wonder over something, but it echoed so they had trouble understanding his words.

Suddenly Fizban's face brightened. "This is it!" cried the old mage in high glee. "We've found it! Godshome! The way in—through this passageway!"

"There's no other way?" Caramon asked, staring at the narrow opening gloomily.

Fizban appeared thoughtful. "Well, I seem to recall—"

Then, "Tanis! Hurry!" came through quite clearly from the other side.

"No more dead ends. We'll get through this way," Tanis muttered, "somehow."

Crawling on hands and knees, the companions crept into the narrow opening. The way did not become easier; sometimes they were forced to flatten themselves and slither through the mud like snakes. Broad-shouldered Caramon had the worst time, and for a while Tanis thought perhaps they might have to leave the big man behind. Tasslehoff waited for them on the other side, peering in at them anxiously as they crawled. "I heard something, Tanis," he kept saying. "Flint shouting. Up ahead. And wait until you see this place, Tanis! You won't believe it!"

But Tanis couldn't take time to listen or look around, not until everyone was safely through the tunnel. It took all of them, pulling and tugging, to drag Caramon through and when he finally emerged, the skin on his arms and back was cut and bleeding.

"This is it!" Fizban stated. "We're here."

The half-elf turned around to see the place called Godshome.

"Not exactly the place I'd choose to live if I were a god," Tasslehoff remarked in a subdued voice.

Tanis was forced to agree.

They stood at the edge of a circular depression in the center of a mountain. The first thing that struck Tanis when he looked upon Godshome was the overwhelming desolation and emptiness of the place. All along the path up into the mountains, the companions had seen signs of new life: trees budding, grass greening, wild flowers pushing their way through the mud and remnants of snow. But here there was nothing. The bottom of the bowl was perfectly smooth and flat, totally barren, gray and lifeless. The towering peaks of the mountain surrounding the bowl soared above them. The jagged rock of the peaks seemed to loom inward, giving the observer the impression of being pressed down into the crumbling rock beneath his feet. The sky above them was azure, clear, and cold, devoid of sun or bird or cloud, though it had been raining when they entered the tunnel. It was like an eye staring down from gray, unblinking rims. Shivering, Tanis quickly withdrew his gaze from the sky to look once more within the bowl.

Below that staring eye, within the center of the bowl itself, stood a circle of huge, tall, shapeless boulders. It was a perfect circle made up of imperfect rocks. Yet they matched so nearly and stood so close together that when Tanis tried to look between them, he could not make out from where he was standing what the strange stones guarded so solemnly. These boulders were all that was visible in the rock-strewn and silent place.

"It makes me feel so terribly sad," Tika whispered. "I'm not frightened—it doesn't seem evil, just so sorrowful! If the gods *do* come here, it must be to weep over the troubles of the world."

Fizban turned to regard Tika with a penetrating look and seemed about to speak, but before he could comment, Tasslehoff shouted. "There, Tanis!"

"I see!" The half-elf broke into a run.

On the other side of the bowl, he could see the vague outline of what appeared to be two figures—one short and the other tall—struggling.

"It's Berem!" screamed Tas. The two were plainly visible to his keen kender eyes. "And he's doing something to Flint! Hurry, Tanis!"

Bitterly cursing himself for letting this happen, for not keeping closer watch on Berem, for not forcing the man to reveal those secrets he was so obviously holding back, Tanis ran across the stony ground with a speed born of fear. He could hear the others calling to him, but he paid no attention. His eyes were on the two in front of him and now he could see them clearly. Even as he watched, he saw the dwarf fall to the ground. Berem stood over him.

"Flint!" Tanis screamed.

His heart was pounding so that blood dimmed his vision. His lungs ached, there didn't seem air enough to breath. Still he ran faster, and now he could see Berem turn to look at him. He seemed to be trying to say something—Tanis could see the man's lips moving—but the half-elf couldn't hear through the surge of blood beating in his ears. At Berem's feet lay Flint. The dwarf's eyes were closed, his head lolled over to one side, his face was ashen gray.

"What have you done?" Tanis shrieked at Berem. "You've killed him!" Grief, guilt, despair, and rage exploded within Tanis like one of the old mage's fireballs, flooding his head with unbearable pain. He could not see, a red tide blurred his sight.

His sword was in his hand, he had no idea how. He felt the cold steel of the hilt. Berem's face swam within a blood-red sea; the man's eyes filled—not with terror—but with deep sorrow. Then Tanis saw the eyes widen with pain, and it was only then he knew he had plunged the sword into Berem's unresisting body, plunged it so deeply that he felt it cleave through flesh and bone and scrape the rock upon which the Everman was leaning.

Warm blood washed over Tanis's hands. A horrible scream burst in his head, then a heavy weight fell on him, nearly knocking him down.

Berem's body slumped over him, but Tanis didn't notice. Frantically he struggled to free his weapon and stab again. He felt strong hands grab him. But in his madness, the half-elf fought them off. Finally pulling his sword free, he watched Berem fall to the ground, blood streaming from the horrible wound just below the green gemstone that glittered with an unholy life in the man's chest.

Behind him, he heard a deep, booming voice and a woman's sobbing pleas and a shrill wail of grief. Furious, Tanis spun around to face those who had tried to thwart him. He saw a big man with a grief-stricken face, a red-haired girl with tears streaming down her cheeks. He recognized neither of them. And then there appeared before him an old, old man. His face was calm, his ageless eyes filled with sorrow. The old man smiled gently at Tanis and, reaching out, laid his hand on the half-elf's shoulder.

His touch was like cool water to a fevered man. Tanis felt reason return. The bloody haze cleared from his vision. He dropped the blood-stained sword from his red hands and collapsed, sobbing, at Fizban's feet. The old man leaned down and gently patted him.

"Be strong, Tanis," he said softly, "for you must say good-bye to one who has a long journey before him.

Tanis remembered. "Flint!" he gasped.

Fizban nodded sadly, glancing at Berem's body. "Come along. There's nothing more you can do here."

Swallowing his tears, Tanis staggered to his feet. Shoving aside the mage, he stumbled over to where Flint lay on the rocky ground, his head resting on Tasslehoff's lap.

The dwarf smiled as he saw the half-elf approach. Tanis dropped down on his knees beside his oldest friend. Taking Flint's gnarled hand in his, the half-elf held it fast.

"I almost lost him, Tanis," Flint said. With his other hand he tapped his chest. "Berem was just about to slip out through that other hole in the rocks over there when this old heart of mine finally burst. He—he heard me cry out, I guess, because the next thing I knew he had me in his arms and was laying me down on the rocks."

"Then he didn't—he didn't—harm you . . ." Tanis could barely speak.

Flint managed a snort. "Harm me! He couldn't harm a mouse, Tanis. He's as gentle as Tika." The dwarf smiled up at the girl, who also knelt beside him. "You take care of that big oaf, Caramon, you hear?" he said to her. "See he comes in out of the rain."

"I will, Flint." Tika wept.

"At least you won't be trying to drown me anymore," the dwarf grumbled, his eyes resting fondly on Caramon. "And if you see that brother of yours, give him a kick in the robes for me."

Caramon could not speak. He only shook his head. "I—I'll go look after Berem," the big man mumbled. Taking hold of Tika, he gently helped her stand and led her away.

"No, Flint! You can't go off adventuring without me!" Tas wailed. "You'll get into no end of trouble, you know you will!"

"It'll be the first moment of peace I've had since we met," the dwarf said gruffly. "I want you to have my helm—the one with the *griffon's* mane." He glared at Tanis sternly, then turned his gaze back to the sobbing kender. Sighing, he patted Tas's hand. "There, there, lad, don't take on so. I've had a happy life, blessed with faithful friends. I've seen evil things, but I've seen a lot of good things, too. And now hope has come into the world. I hate to leave you"—his rapidly dimming vision focused on Tanis—"just when you need me. But I've taught you all I know, lad. Everything will be fine. I know . . . fine . . ."

His voice sank, he closed his eyes, breathing heavily. Tanis held tightly to his hand. Tasslehoff buried his face in Flint's shoulder. Then Fizban appeared, standing at Flint's feet.

The dwarf opened his eyes. "I know you, now," he said softly, his eyes bright as he looked at Fizban. "You'll come with me, won't you? At least at the beginning of the journey . . . so I won't be alone? I've walked with friends so long, I feel . . . kind of funny . . . going off like this . . . by myself."

"I'll come with you," Fizban promised gently. "Close your eyes and rest now, Flint. The troubles of this world are yours no longer. You have earned the right to sleep."

"Sleep," the dwarf said, smiling. "Yes, that's what I need. Wake me when you're ready . . . wake me when it's time to leave—" Flint's eyes closed. He drew in a smooth easy breath, then let it out . . .

Tanis pressed the dwarf's hand to his lips. "Farewell, old friend," the half-elf whispered, and he placed the hand on the dwarf's still chest.

"No! Flint! No!" Screaming wildly, Tasslehoff flung himself across the dwarf's body. Gently Tanis lifted the sobbing kender in his arms. Tas kicked and fought, but Tanis held him firmly, like a child, and finally Tas subsided—exhausted. Clinging to Tanis, he wept bitterly.

Tanis stroked the kender's topknot, then—glancing up—stopped.

"Wait! What are you doing, old man?" he cried.

Setting Tas back down on the ground, Tanis rose quickly to his feet. The frail old mage had lifted Flint's body in his arms and, as Tanis watched in shock, began walking toward the strange circle of stones.

"Stop!" Tanis ordered. "We must give him a proper ceremony, build a cairn."

Fizban turned to face Tanis. The old man's face was stern. He held the heavy dwarf gently and with ease.

"I promised him he would not travel alone," Fizban said simply.

Then, turning, he continued to walk toward the stones. Tanis, after a moment's hesitation, ran after him. The rest stood as if transfixed, staring at Fizban's retreating figure.

It had seemed an easy thing to Tanis to catch up with an old man bearing such a burden. But Fizban moved incredibly fast, almost as if he and the dwarf were as light as the air. Suddenly aware of the weight of his own body, Tanis felt as if he were trying to catch a wisp of smoke soaring heavenward. Still he stumbled after them, reaching them just as the old mage entered the ring of boulders, carrying the dwarf's body in his arms.

Tanis squeezed through the circle of rocks without thinking, knowing only that he must stop this crazed old mage and recover his friend's body.

Then he stopped within the circle. Before him spread what he first took to be a pool of water, so still that nothing marred its smooth surface. Then he saw that it wasn't water—it was a pool of glassy black rock! The deep black surface was polished to a gleaming brilliance. It stretched before Tanis with the darkness of night and, indeed, looking down into its black depths, Tanis was startled to see stars! So clear were they that he looked up, half-expecting to see night had fallen, though he knew it was only mid-afternoon. The sky above him was azure, cold and clear, no stars, no sun. Shaken and weak, Tanis dropped to his knees beside the pool and stared once more into its polished surface. He saw the stars, he saw the moons, he saw *three* moons, and his soul trembled, for the black moon visible only to those powerful mages of the Black Robes was now visible to him—like a dark circle cut out of blackness. He could even see the gaping holes where the constellations of the Queen of Darkness and the Valiant Warrior had once wheeled in the sky.

Tanis recalled Raistlin's words, "Both gone. She has come to Krynn, Tanis, and he has come to fight her. . . ."

Looking up, Tanis saw Fizban step onto the black rock pool, Flint's body in his arms.

The half-elf tried desperately to follow, but he could no more force himself to crawl out upon that cold rock surface than he could have made himself leap into the Abyss. He could only watch as the old mage, walking softly as if unwilling to waken a sleeping child in his arms, move out into the center of glistening black surface.

———

"Fizban!" Tanis called.

The old man did not stop or turn but walked on among the glittering stars. Tanis felt Tasslehoff creep up next to him. Reaching out, Tanis took his hand and held it fast, as he had held Flint's

The old mage reached the center of the rock pool . . . and then disappeared.

Tanis gasped. Tasslehoff leaped past him, starting to run out onto the mirrorlike surface. But Tanis caught him.

"No, Tas," the half-elf said gently. "You can't go on this adventure with him. Not yet. You must stay with me awhile. *I* need you now."

Tasslehoff fell back, unusually obedient, and as he did so, he pointed.

"Look, Tanis!" he whispered, his voice quivering. "The constellation! It's come back!"

As Tanis stared into the surface of the black pool, he saw the stars of the constellation of the Valiant Warrior return. They flickered, then burst into light, filling the dark pool with their blue-white radiance. Swiftly Tanis looked upward—but the night sky above was dark and still and empty.

4
Everman's story.

"Tanis!" called Caramon's voice.

"Berem!" Suddenly remembering what he had done, Tanis turned and stumbled over the rock-strewn ground toward Caramon and Tika, who were staring in horror at the blood-smeared rock where Berem's body lay. As they watched, Berem began to stir, groaning—not in pain—but as if with remembered pain. Plucking Tanis's sword from his chest, Berem rose slowly to his feet. The only sign of his hideous injury were traces of blood upon his skin, and these vanished as Tanis watched.

"He is called the Everman, remember?" Tanis said to the ashen-faced Caramon. "Sturm and I saw him die in Pax Tharkas, buried under a ton of rock. He's died countless deaths, only to rise again. And he claims he doesn't know why." Tanis came forward to stand very close to Berem, staring at the man, who watched him approach with sullen, wary eyes.

"But you do know, don't you, Berem?" Tanis said. The half-elf's voice was soft, his manner calm. "You know," he repeated, "and you're going to tell us. The lives of more may hang in balance."

Berem's gaze lowered. "I'm sorry . . . about your friend," he mumbled. "I—I tried to help, but there was nothing—"

"I know." Tanis swallowed. "I'm sorry . . . about what I did, too. I—I couldn't see. . . . I didn't understand—"

But as he said the words, Tanis realized he was lying. He *had* seen, but he had seen only what he wanted to see. How much of what happened in his life was like that? How much of what he saw was distorted by his own mind? He hadn't understood Berem because he didn't *want* to understand Berem! Berem had come to represent for Tanis those dark and secret things within himself he hated. He had killed Berem, the half-elf knew; but in reality, he had driven that sword through himself.

And now it was as if that sword wound had spewed out the foul, gangrenous poison corrupting his soul. Now the wound could heal. The grief and sorrow of Flint's death was like a soothing balm poured inside, reminding him of goodness, of higher values. Tanis felt himself freed at last of the dark shadows of his guilt. Whatever happened, he had done his best to try and help, to try and make things right. He had made mistakes, but he could forgive himself now and go on.

Perhaps Berem saw this in Tanis's eyes. Certainly he saw grief, he saw compassion. Then, "I am tired, Tanis," Berem said suddenly, his eyes on the half-elf's tear-reddened eyes. "I am so very tired." His glance went to the black pool of rock. "I—I envy your friend. He is at rest now. He has found peace. Am I never to have that?" Berem's fist clenched, then he shuddered and his head sank into his hands. "But I am afraid! I see the end—it is very close. And I am frightened!"

"We're all frightened." Tanis sighed, rubbing his burning eyes. "You're right—the end is near, and it seems fraught with darkness. You hold the answer, Berem."

"I'll—I'll tell you—what I can," Berem said haltingly, as if the words were being dragged out of him. "But you've got to help me!" His hand clutched Tanis's. "You must promise to help me!"

"I cannot promise," Tanis said grimly, "not until I know the truth."

Berem sat down, leaning his back against the blood-stained rock. The others settled around him, drawing their cloaks close as the wind rose, whistling down the sides of the mountains, howling among the strange boulders. They listened to Berem's tale without interruption, though Tas was occasionally seized by a fit of weeping and snuffled quietly, his head resting on Tika's shoulder.

At first Berem's voice was low, his words spoken reluctantly. Sometimes they could see him wrestling with himself, then he would blurt forth the story as if it hurt. But gradually he began speaking faster and faster, the relief of finally telling the truth after all these years flooding his soul.

"When—when I said I understood how you"—he nodded at Caramon—"felt about—about losing your brother, I spoke the truth. I—I had a sister. We—we weren't twins, but we were probably as close as twins. She was just a year younger. We lived on a small farm, outside of Neraka. It was isolated. No neighbors. My mother taught us to read and write at home, enough to get by. Mostly we worked on the farm. My sister was my only companion, my only friend. And I was hers.

"She worked hard—too hard. After the Cataclysm, it was all we could to do to keep food on the table. Our parents were old and sick. We nearly starved that first winter. No matter what you have heard about the Famine Times, you cannot imagine." His voice died, his eyes dimmed. "Ravenous packs of wild beasts and wilder men roamed the land. Being isolated, we were luckier than some. But many nights we stayed awake, clubs in our hands, as the wolves prowled around the outside of the house—waiting. . . . I watched my sister—who was a pretty little thing—grow old before she was twenty. Her hair was gray as mine is now, her face pinched and wrinkled. But she never complained.

"That spring, things didn't improve much. But at least we had hope, my sister said. We could plant seeds and watch them grow. We could hunt the game that returned with the spring. There would be food on the table. She loved hunting. She was a good shot with a bow, and she enjoyed being outdoors. We often went together. That day—"

Berem stopped. Closing his eyes, he began to shake as if chilled. But, gritting his teeth, he continued.

"That day, we'd walked farther than usual. A lightning fire had burned away the brush and we found a trail we'd never seen before. It had been a bad day's hunting and we followed the trail, hoping to find game. But after a while, I saw it wasn't an animal trail. It was an old, old path made by human feet; it hadn't been used in years. I wanted to turn back, but my sister kept going, curious to see where it led."

Berem's face grew strained and tense. For a moment Tanis feared he might stop speaking, but Berem continued feverishly, as if driven.

"It led to a—a strange place. My sister said it must have been a temple once, a temple to evil gods. I don't know. All I know is that there were broken columns lying tumbled about, overgrown with dead weeds. She was right. It *did* have an evil feel to it and we should have left. We should have left the evil place. . . ." Berem repeated this to himself several times, like a chant. Then he fell silent.

No one moved or spoke and, after a moment, he began speaking so softly the others were forced to lean close to hear. And they realized, slowly, that he had forgotten they were there or even where he was. He had gone back to that time.

"But there is one beautiful, beautiful object in the ruins: the base of a broken column, encrusted with jewels!"—Berem's voice was soft with awe—"I have never seen such beauty! Or such wealth! How can I leave it? Just one jewel! Just one will make us rich! We can move to the city! My sister will have suitors, as she deserves. I—I fall to my knees and I take out my knife. There is one jewel—a green gemstone—that glitters brightly in the sunlight! It is lovely beyond anything I have ever seen! I will take it. Thrusting the knife blade"—here Berem mades a swift motion with his hand—"into the stone beneath the jewel, I begin to pry it out.

"My sister is horrified. She cries to me—she commands me to stop.

" 'This place is holy,' she pleads. 'The jewels belong to some god. This is sacrilege, Berem!' "

Berem shook his head, his face dark with remembered anger.

"I ignore her, though I feel a chill in my heart even as I pry at the jewel. But I tell her—'If it belonged to the gods, they have abandoned it, as they have abandoned us!' But she won't listen."

Berem's eyes flared open, they were cold and frightening to see. His voice came from far away.

"She grabs me! Her fingernails dig into my arm! It hurts!

" 'Stop, Berem!' she commands me—me, her older brother! 'I will not let you desecrate what belongs to the gods!'

"How dare she talk to me like that? I'm doing this for her! For our family! She should not cross me! She knows what can happen when I get mad. Something breaks in my head, flooding my brain. I can't think or see. I yell at her—'Leave me be!'—but her hand grabs my knife hand, jarring the blade, scratching the jewel.

Berem's eyes flashed with a crazed light. Surreptitiously Caramon laid his hand on his dagger as the man's hands clenched to fists and his voice rose to an almost hysterical pitch.

"I—I shove her . . . not that hard . . . I never meant to shove her that hard! She's falling! I've got to catch her, but I can't. I'm moving too slowly, too slowly. Her head . . . hits the column. A sharp rock pierces her here"—Berem touched his temple—"blood covers her face, spills over the jewels. They don't shine anymore. Her eyes don't shine either. They stare at me, but they don't see me. And then . . . and then . . ."

His body shuddered convulsively.

"It is a horrible sight, one I see in my sleep every time I close my eyes! It is like the Cataclysm, only during that, all was destroyed! This is a creation, but what a ghastly, unholy creation! The ground splits open! Huge columns begin to reform before my eyes. A temple springs up from a hideous darkness below the ground. But it isn't a beautiful temple—it is horrible and deformed. I see Darkness rise up before me, Darkness with five heads, all of them twisting and writhing in my sight. The heads speak to me in a voice colder than a tomb.

" 'Long ago was I banished from this world, and only through a piece of the world may I enter again. The jeweled column was—for me—a locked door, keeping me prisoner. You have freed me, mortal, and therefore I give you what you seek—the green gemstone is yours!'

"There is terrible, mocking laughter. I feel a great pain in my chest. Looking down, I see the green gemstone embedded in my flesh, even as you see it now. Terrified by the hideous evil before me, stunned by my wicked act, I can do nothing but stare as the dark, shadowy shape begins to grow clearer and clearer. It is a dragon! I can see it now—a five-headed dragon such as I had heard nightmarish tales about when I was a child!

"And I know then that once the dragon enters the world, we are doomed. For at last I understand what I have done. This is the Queen of Darkness the clerics teach us about. Banished long ago by the great Huma, she has long sought to return. Now—by my folly—she will be able again to walk the land. One of the huge heads snakes toward me, and I know I am going to die, for she must not allow any to witness her return. I see the slashing teeth. I cannot move. I don't care.

"And then, suddenly, my sister stands in front of me! She is alive, but when I try to reach out to her, my hands touch nothing. I scream her name, 'Jasla!'

" 'Run, Berem!' she calls. 'Run! She cannot get past me, not yet! Run!'

"I stand staring for a moment. My sister hovers between me and the Dark Queen. Horrified, I see the five heads rear back in anger, their screams split the air. But they cannot pass my sister. And, even as I watch, the Queen's shape begins to waver and dim. She is still there, a shadowy figure of evil, but nothing more. But her power is great. She lunges for my sister. . . .

"And then I turn and run. I run and run, the green gemstone burning a hole in my chest. I run until everything goes black."

Berem stopped speaking. Sweat trickled down his face as if he had truly been running for days. None of the companions spoke. The dark tale might have turned them to stone like the boulders around the black pool.

Finally Berem drew a shuddering breath. His eyes focused and he saw them once more.

"There follows a long span of my life of which I know nothing. When I came to myself, I had aged, even as you see me now. At first I told myself it was a nightmare, a horrible dream. But then I felt the green gemstone burning in my flesh, and I knew it was real. I had no idea where I was. Perhaps I had traveled the length and breadth of Krynn in my wanderings. I longed desperately to return to Neraka. Yet that was the one place I knew I couldn't go. I didn't have the courage.

"Long years more I wandered, unable to find peace, unable to rest, dying only to live again. Everywhere I went I heard stories of evil things abroad in the land and I knew it was my fault. And then came the dragons and the dragonmen. I alone knew what they meant. I alone knew the Queen had reached the summit of her power and was trying to conquer the world. The one thing she lacks is me. Why? I'm not certain. Except that I feel like someone who is trying to shut a door another is trying to force open. And I am tired . . ."

Berem's voice faltered. "So tired," he said, his head dropping into his hands. "I want it to end!"

The companions sat silently for long moments, trying to make sense of a story that seemed like something an old nursemaid might have told in the dark hours of the night.

"What must you do to shut this door?" Tanis asked Berem.

"I don't know," Berem said, his voice muffled. "I only know that I feel drawn to Neraka, yet it's the one place on the face of Krynn I *dare* not enter! That's—that's why I ran away."

"But you're going to enter it," Tanis said slowly and firmly. "You're going to enter it with us. We'll be with you. You won't be alone."

Berem shivered and shook his head, whimpering. Then suddenly he stopped and looked up, his face flushed. "Yes!" he cried. "I cannot stand any more! I will go with you! You'll protect me—"

"We'll do our best," Tanis muttered, seeing Caramon roll his eyes, then look away. "We better find the way out."

"I found it." Berem sighed. "I was nearly through, when I heard the dwarf cry out. This way." He pointed to another narrow cleft between the rocks. Caramon sighed, glancing ruefully at the scratches on his arms. One by one, the companions entered the cleft.

Tanis was the last. Turning, he looked back once more upon the barren place. Darkness was falling swiftly, the azure blue sky deepening to purple and finally to black. The strange boulders were shrouded in the gathering gloom. He could no longer see the dark pool of rock where Fizban had vanished.

It seemed odd to think of Flint being gone. There was a great emptiness inside of him. He kept expecting to hear the dwarf's grumbling voice complain about his various aches and pains or argue with the kender.

For a moment Tanis struggled with himself, holding onto his friend as long as he could. Then, silently, he let Flint go. Turning, he crept through the narrow cleft in the rocks, leaving Godshome, never to see it again.

———

Once back on the trail, they followed it until they came to a small cave. Here they huddled together, not daring to build a fire this near to Neraka, the center of the might of the dragonarmies. For a while, no one spoke, then they began to talk about Flint—letting him go, as Tanis had done. Their memories were good ones, recalling Flint's rich, adventurous life.

They laughed heartily when Caramon recounted the tale of the disastrous camping trip—how he had overturned the boat, trying to catch a fish by hand, knocking Flint into the water. Tanis recalled how Tas and the dwarf had met when Tas "accidentally" walked off with a bracelet Flint had made and was trying to sell at a fair. Tika remembered the wonderful toys he had made for her. She recalled his kindness when her father disappeared, how he had taken the young girl into his own home until Otik had given her a place to live and work.

All these and more memories they recalled until, by the end of the evening, the bitter sting had gone out of their grief, leaving only the ache of loss.

That is—for most of them.

Late, late in the dark watches of the night, Tasslehoff sat outside the cave entrance, staring up into the stars. Flint's helm was clutched in his small hands, tears streamed unchecked down his face.

KENDER MOURNING SONG

Always before, the spring returned.
The bright world in its cycle spun
In air and flowers, grass and fern,
Assured and cradled by the sun.

Always before, you could explain
The turning darkness of the earth,
And how that dark embraced the rain,
And gave the ferns and flowers birth.

Already I forget those things,
And how a vein of gold survives
The mining of a thousand springs,
The seasons of a thousand lives.

Now winter is my memory,
Now autumn, now the summer light—
So every spring from now will be
Another season into night.

5
Neraka.

As it turned out, the companions discovered it was going to be easy getting into Neraka.

Deadly easy.

"What in the name of the gods is happening?" Caramon muttered as he and Tanis—still dressed in their stolen dragonarmor—stared down into the plains from their hidden vantage point in the mountains west of Neraka.

Writhing black lines snaked across the barren plain towards the only building within a hundred miles—the Temple of the Queen of Darkness. It looked as though hundreds of vipers were slithering down from the mountains, but these were not vipers. These were the dragonarmies, thousands strong. The two men watching saw here and there the flash of sun off spear and shield. Flags of black and red and blue fluttered from tall poles that bore the emblems of the Dragon Highlords. Flying high above them, dragons filled the air with a hideous rainbow of colors—reds, blues, greens, and blacks. Two gigantic flying citadels hovered over the walled Temple compound; the shadows they cast made it perpetual night down below.

"You know," said Caramon slowly, "it's a good thing that old man attacked us back there. We would have been massacred if we'd ridden our brass dragons into this mob."

"Yes," Tanis agreed absently. He'd been thinking about that "old man," adding a few things together, remembering what he himself had seen and what Tas had told him. The more he thought about Fizban, the closer he came to realizing the truth. His skin "shivered," as Flint would have said.

Recalling Flint, a sudden swift aching in his heart made him put thoughts of the dwarf—and the old man—from his mind. He had enough to worry about now, and there would be no old mages to help him out of this one.

"I don't know what's happening," Tanis said quietly, "but it's working for us now, not against us. Remember what Elistan said once? It is written in the Disks of Mishakal that evil turns upon itself. The Dark Queen is gathering her forces, for whatever reason. Probably preparing to deal Krynn a final death blow. But we can slip in easily among the confusion. No one will notice two guards bringing in a group of prisoners."

"You hope," Caramon added gloomily.

"I pray," Tanis said softly.

The captain of the guard at the gates of Neraka was a sorely harrassed man. The Dark Queen had called a Council of War and, for only the second time since the war began, the Dragon Highlords on the continent of Abanasinia were gathering together. Four days ago, they began arriving in Neraka and, since then, the captain's life had been a waking nightmare.

The Highlords were supposed to enter the city by order of rank. Thus Lord Ariakas entered first with personal retinue—his troops, his bodyguards, his dragons; then Kitiara, the Dark Lady, with her personal retinue—her troops, her bodyguards, her dragons; then Lucien of Takar with his personal retinue, his troops and so forth through all the Highlords down to Dragon Highlord Toede, of the eastern front.

The system was designed to do more than simply honor the higher-ups. It was intended to move large numbers of troops and dragons, as well as all their supplies, into and out of a complex that had never been intended to hold large concentrations of troops. Nor, as distrustful as the Highlords were of each other, could any Highlord be persuaded to enter with a single draconian less than any other Highlord. It was a good system and it should have worked. Unfortunately, there was trouble from the very outset when Lord Ariakas arrived two days late.

Had he done this purposefully to create the confusion he knew must result? The captain did not know and he dared not ask, but he had his own ideas. This meant, of course, that those Highlords who arrived before Ariakas were forced to camp on the plains outside the Temple compound until the Lord made his entry. This provoked trouble. The draconians, goblins, and human mercenaries wanted the pleasures of the camp city that had been hastily erected in the Temple square. They had marched long distances and were justifiably angry when this was denied them.

Many sneaked over the walls at night, drawn to the taverns as flies to honey. Brawls broke out—each Highlord's troops being loyal to that particular Highlord and no other. The dungeons below the Temple were filled to overflowing. The captain finally ordered his forces to haul the drunks out of the city in wheelbarrows every morning and dump them on the plains where they were retrieved by their irate commanders.

Quarrels started among the dragons, too, as each lead dragon sought to establish dominance over the others. A big green, Cyan Bloodbane, had actually killed a red in a fight over a deer. Unfortunately for Cyan, the red had been a pet of the Dark Queen's. The big green was now imprisoned in a cave beneath Neraka, where his howls and violent tail-lashings caused many up above to think an earthquake had struck.

The captain had not slept well in two nights. When word reached him early in the morning of the third day that Ariakas had arrived, the captain very nearly gave thanks on his knees. Hurriedly marshalling his staff, he gave orders for the grand entrance to begin. Everything proceeded smoothly until several hundred of Toede's draconians saw Ariakas's troops entering the Temple square. Drunk and completely out of the control of their ineffectual leaders, they attempted to crowd in as well. Angry at the disruption, Ariakas's captains ordered their men to fight back. Chaos erupted.

Furious, the Dark Queen sent out her own troops, armed with whips, steel-link chains, and maces. Black-robed magic-users walked among them, as well as dark clerics. Between the whippings, head-bashings, and spell-casting, order was eventually restored. Lord Ariakas and his troops finally entered the Temple compound with dignity—if not grace.

It might have been mid-afternoon—by now the captain had completely lost track of time (those blasted citadels cut off the sunlight)—when one of the guards appeared, requesting his presence at the front gates.

"What is it?" the captain snarled impatiently, fixing the guard with a piercing gaze from his one good eye (the other had been lost in a battle with the elves in Silvanesti). "Another fight? Knock 'em both over the head and haul 'em to prison. I'm sick—"

"N-not a fight, sir," stuttered the guard, a young goblin terrified of his human captain. "The watch at the g-gate sent m-me. T-Two officers with p-prisoners want p-permission to enter."

The captain swore in frustration. What next? He almost told the goblin to go back and let them enter. The place was crawling with slaves and prisoners already. A few more wouldn't matter. Highlord Kitiara's troops were gathering outside, ready to come in. He had to be on hand to extend official greetings.

"What kind of prisoners?" he asked irritably, trying hastily to catch up on reams of paperwork before leaving to attend the ceremony. "Drunken draconians? Just take them—"

"I-I think you should c-come, s-sir." The goblin was sweating, and sweating goblins are not pleasant to be around. "Th-There's a couple of h-humans, and a k-kender."

The captain wrinkled his nose. "I said—" He stopped. "A kender?" he said, looking up with considerable interest. "There wasn't, by any chance, a dwarf?"

"Not as I know of, sir," answered the poor goblin. "But I might have missed one in the c-crowd, sir."

"I'll come," the captain said. Hastily strapping on his sword, he followed the goblin down to the front gate.

Here, for the moment, peace reigned. Ariakas's troops were all within the tent city now. Kitiara's were jostling and fighting, forming ranks to march inside. It was nearly time for the ceremony to begin. The captain cast a swift glance over the group standing before him, just inside the front gates.

Two dragonarmy officers of high rank stood guard over a group of sullen prisoners. The captain studied the prisoners carefully, remembering orders he had received only two days ago. He was to watch, in particular, for a dwarf traveling with a kender. There might possibly be an elflord with them and an elfwoman with long, silver hair—in reality, a silver dragon. These had been the companions of the elfwoman they were holding prisoner, and the Dark Queen expected any or all of them to attempt to rescue her.

Here was a kender, all right. But the woman had curly red hair, not silver, and if she was a dragon, the captain would eat his platemail. The stooped old man with the long scraggly beard was certainly human, not a dwarf or an elflord. All in all, he couldn't imagine why two dragonarmy officers had bothered taking the motley group prisoner.

"Just slit their throats and be done with it instead of bothering us," the captain said sourly. "We're short of prison space as it is. Take them away."

"But what a waste!" said one of the officers—a giant of a man with arms like tree-trunks. Grabbing the red-headed girl, he dragged her forward. "I've heard they're paying good money in the slave markets for her kind!"

"You're right there," the captain muttered, running his good eye over the girl's voluptuous body which was enhanced—to his mind—by her chain-mail armor. "But I don't know what you think you'll get for *this* lot!" He poked the kender, who gave an indignant cry, and was instantly shushed by the other dragonarmy guard. "Kill 'em—"

The big dragonarmy officer seemed confounded by this argument, blinking in obvious confusion. Before he could reply, however, the other officer—who had been quiet and hidden in the background—stepped forward.

"The human's a magic-user," the officer said. "And we believe the kender is a spy. We caught him near Dargaard Keep."

"Well, why didn't you say so in the first place," the captain snapped, "instead of wasting my time. Yeah, go ahead and haul 'em inside," he spoke hurriedly as horns blared. It was time for the ceremony, the massive iron gates were shivering, beginning to swing open. "I'll sign your papers. Hand them over."

"We don't have—" began the big officer.

"What papers do you mean?" the bearded officer cut in, fumbling in a pouch. "Identification—"

"Naw!" said the captain, fuming in impatience. "Your leave of absence from your commander to bring in prisoners."

"We weren't given that, sir," said the bearded officer coolly. "Is that a new order?"

"No, it isn't," said the captain, eyeing them suspiciously. "How'd you get through the lines without it? And how do you expect to get back? Or were you going back? Thinking of taking a little trip with the money you'd make from these, were you?"

"Naw!" The big officer flushed angrily, his eyes flaring. "Our commander just forgot, maybe, that's all. He's got a lot on his mind, and there's not much mind there to handle it, if you take my meaning." He glared at the captain menacingly.

The gates swung open. Horns blared loudly. The captain sighed in frustration. Right now he was supposed to be standing in the center, prepared to greet the Lord Kitiara. He beckoned to some of the Dark Queen's guards who were standing nearby.

"Take 'em below," he said, twitching his uniform into place. "We'll show them what we do to deserters!"

As he hurried off, he saw with pleasure that the Queen's guards were carrying out their assignments, quickly and efficiently grabbing the two dragonarmy officers and divesting them of their weapons.

Caramon cast an alarmed glance at Tanis as the draconians grasped him by the arms and unbuckled his sword belt. Tika's eyes were wide with fear—this certainly wasn't the way things were supposed to be going. Berem, his face nearly hidden by his false whiskers, looked as if he might cry or run or both. Even Tasslehoff seemed a bit stunned by the sudden change in plans. Tanis could see the kender's eyes dart around, seeking escape.

Tanis thought frantically. He believed he had considered every possible occurrence when he had formed this plan for entering Neraka, but he'd obviously missed one. Certainly being arrested as a deserter from the dragonarmies had never crossed his mind! If the guards took them into the dungeons, it would be all over. The moment they took off his helmet, they'd recognize him as half-elven. Then they'd examine the others more closely . . . they'd discover Berem. . . .

He was the danger. Without him Caramon and the others might still pull it off. Without him . . .

There was a blaring of trumpets and wild cheering from the crowd as a huge blue dragon bearing a Dragon Highlord entered the Temple gates. Seeing the Highlord, Tanis's heart constricted with pain and, suddenly, a wild elation. The crowd surged forward roaring Kitiara's name and, for the moment, the guards were distracted as they looked to see if the Highlord might be in danger. Tanis leaned as near Tasslehoff as he could.

"Tas!" he said swiftly, under the cover of the noise, hoping Tas remembered enough elven to understand him. "Tell Caramon to keep up the act. No matter what I do, he must trust me! Everything depends on that. No matter what I do. Understand?"

Tas stared at Tanis in astonishment, then nodded hesitantly. It had been a long time since he'd been forced to translate elven.

Tanis could only hope he understood. Caramon spoke no elven at all, and Tanis didn't dare risk speaking Common, even if his voice was swallowed by the noise of the crowd. As it was, one of the guards wrenched his arm painfully, ordering him to be silent.

The noise died down, the crowd was bullied and shoved back into place. Seeing things under control, the guards turned to lead their prisoners away.

Suddenly Tanis stumbled and fell, tripping his guard, who sprawled headlong into the dust.

"Get up, slime!" Cursing, the other guard cuffed Tanis with the handle of a whip, striking him across the face. The half-elf lunged for the guard, grabbing the whip handle and the hand that held it. Tanis yanked with all his strength, and his sudden move sent the guard head over heels. For a split second, he was free.

Hurling himself forward, aware of the guards behind him, aware also of Caramon's astonished face, Tanis threw himself toward the regal figure riding the blue dragon.

"Kitiara!" he yelled, just as the guards caught hold of him. "Kitiara!" he screamed, a hoarse, ragged shout that seemed torn from his chest. Fighting the guards, he managed to free one hand. With it, he gripped his helmet and tore it off his head, hurling it to the ground.

The Highlord in the night-blue, dragonscale armor turned

upon hearing her name. Tanis could see her brown eyes widen in astonishment beneath the hideous dragonmask she wore. He could see the fiery eyes of the male blue dragon turn to gaze at him as well.

"Kitiara!" Tanis shouted. Shaking off his captors with a strength born of desperation, he dove forward again. But draconians in the crowd flung themselves on him, knocking him to the ground, where they held him pinned by his arms. Still Tanis struggled, twisting to look into the eyes of the Highlord.

"Halt, Skie," Kitiara said, placing a gloved hand commandingly on the dragon's neck. Skie stopped obediently, his clawed feet slipping slightly on the cobblestones of the street. But the dragon's eyes, as they glared at Tanis, were filled with jealousy and hatred.

Tanis held his breath. His heart beat painfully. His head ached and blood dribbled into one eye, but he didn't notice. He waited for the shout that would tell him Tasslehoff hadn't understood, that his friends had tried to come to his aid. He waited for Kitiara to look behind him and see Caramon—her half-brother—and recognize him. He didn't dare turn around to see what had happened to his friends. He could only hope Caramon had sense enough—and faith enough in him—to keep out of sight.

And now here came the captain, his cruel one-eyed face distorted in rage. Raising a booted foot, the captain aimed a kick for Tanis's head, preparing to render this meddlesome troublemaker unconscious.

"Stop," said a voice.

The captain halted so suddenly that he staggered off-balance.

"Let him go." The same voice.

Reluctantly, the guards released Tanis and fell back away from him at an imperious gesture from the Dark Lady.

"What is so important, commander, that you disrupt my entrance?" she asked in cool tones, her voice sounding deep and distorted behind the dragonhelm.

Stumbling to his feet, weak with relief, his head swimming from his struggles with the guards, Tanis made his way forward to stand beside her. As he drew nearer, he saw a flicker of amusement in Kitiara's brown eyes. She was enjoying this; a new game with an old toy. Clearing his throat, Tanis spoke boldly.

"These idiots arrested me for desertion," he stated, "all because that imbecile Bakaris forgot to give me the proper papers."

"I'll see he pays the penalty for having caused you trouble, good Tanthalasa," replied Kitiara. Tanis could hear the laughter in her voice. "How dare you?" she added, whirling to glower at the captain, who cringed as the helmed visage turned toward him.

"I—I was j-just following or-orders, my lord," he stuttered, shaking like a goblin.

"Be off with you, or you'll feed my dragon," Kitiara commanded peremptorily, waving her hand. Then, in the same graceful gesture, she held out her gloved hand to Tanis. "May I offer you a ride, commander? To make amends, of course."

"Thank you, lord," Tanis said.

Casting a dark glance at the captain, Tanis accepted Kitiara's hand and swung himself up beside her on the back of the blue dragon. His eyes quickly scanned the crowd as Kitiara ordered Skie forward once more. For a moment, his agonized search could detect nothing, then he sighed in relief as he saw Caramon and the others being led away by the guards. The big man glanced up at him as they passed, a hurt and puzzled expression on his face. But he kept moving. Either Tas had passed along the message or the big man had sense enough to keep up the act. Or perhaps Caramon trusted him anyway. Tanis didn't know. His friends were safe now—at least safer than they were with him.

This might be the last time I ever see them, he thought suddenly, with pain. Then he shook his head. He could not let himself dwell on that. Turning away, he discovered Kitiara's brown eyes regarding him with an odd mixture of cunning and undisguised admiration.

Tasslehoff stood on his tiptoes, trying to see what became of Tanis. He heard shouts and yells, then a moment of silence. Then he saw the half-elf climb onto the dragon and sit beside Kitiara. The procession started up again. The kender thought he saw Tanis look his way, but—if so—it was without recognition. The guards shoved their remaining prisoners through the jostling crowd, and Tas lost sight of his friend.

One of the guards prodded Caramon in his ribs with a short sword.

"So your buddy gets a lift from the Highlord and you rot in prison," the draconian said, chuckling.

"He won't forget me," Caramon muttered.

The draconian grinned and nudged its partner, who was dragging Tasslehoff along, one clawed hand on the kender's collar. "Sure, he'll come back for you—if he can manage to find his way out of her bed!"

Caramon flushed, scowling. Tasslehoff shot the big warrior an alarmed glance. The kender hadn't had a chance to give Caramon Tanis's last message, and he was terrified the big man would ruin everything, although Tas wasn't really certain what there was left to ruin. Still . . .

But Caramon only tossed his head in injured dignity. "I'll be out before nightfall," he rumbled in his deep baritone. "We've been through too much together. He wouldn't let me down."

Catching a wistful note in Caramon's voice, Tas wriggled in anxiety, longing to get close enough to Caramon to explain. But at that moment Tika cried out in anger. Twisting his head, Tas saw the guard rip her blouse; there were already bloody gashes made by its clawing hands on her neck. Caramon shouted, but too late. Tika struck the guard with a backhand on the side of its reptilian face in the best barroom tradition.

Furious, the draconian hurled Tika to the street and raised its whip. Tas heard Caramon suck in his breath and the kender cringed, preparing himself for the end.

"Hey! Don't damage her!" Caramon roared. "Unless you want to be held accountable. Lord Kitiara told us to get six silver pieces for her, and we won't do it if she's marked up!"

The draconian hesitated. Caramon was a prisoner, that was true. But the guards had all seen the welcome reception his friend had received from the Dark Lady. Did they dare take a chance on offending another man who might stand high in her favor? Apparently they decided not. Roughly dragging Tika to her feet, they shoved her forward.

Tasslehoff breathed a sigh of relief, then stole a worried peek back at Berem, thinking that the man had been very quiet. He was right. The Everman might have been in a different world. His eyes, wide open, were fixed in a strange stare. His mouth gaped, he almost appeared half-witted. At least he didn't look like he was about to cause trouble. It seemed that Caramon was going to continue playing his role and that Tika would be all right. For the time being, no one needed him. Sighing in relief,

---

Tas began to look with interest around the Temple compound, at least as well as he could with the draconian hanging onto his collar.

He was sorry he did. Neraka looked exactly like what it was—a small, ancient impoverished village built to serve those who inhabited the Temple, now overrun by the tent city that had sprouted up around it like fungus.

At the far end of the compound the Temple itself loomed over the city like a carrion bird of prey—its twisted, deformed, obscene structure seeming to dominate even the mountains on the horizon behind. Once anyone set foot in Neraka, his eyes went first to the Temple. After that, no matter where else he looked or what other business occupied him, the Temple was always there, even at night, even in his dreams.

Tas took one look, then hurriedly glanced away, feeling a cold sickness creep over him. But the sights before him were almost worse. The tent city was filled with troops; draconians and human mercenaries, goblins and hobgoblins spilled out of the hastily constructed bars and brothels onto the filthy streets. Slaves of every race had been brought in to serve their captors and provide for their unholy pleasures. Gully dwarves swarmed underfoot like rats, living off the refuse. The stench was overpowering, the sights were like something from the Abyss. Although it was midday, the square was dark and chill as night. Glancing up, Tas saw the huge flying citadels, floating above the Temple in terrible majesty, their dragons circling them in unceasing watchfulness.

When they had first started down the crowded streets, Tas had hoped he might have a chance to break free. He was an expert in melting in with a crowd. He saw Caramon's eyes flick about, too; the big man was thinking the same thing. But after walking only a few blocks, after seeing the citadels keeping their dreadful watch above, Tas realized it was hopeless. Apparently Caramon reached the same conclusion, for the kender saw the warrior's shoulders slump.

Appalled and horrified, Tas suddenly thought of Laurana, being held prisoner here. The kender's buoyant spirit seemed finally crushed by the weight of the darkness and evil all around him, darkness and evil he had never dreamed existed.

Their guards hurried them along, pushing and shoving their way through the drunken, brawling soldiers, down the clogged and narrow streets. Try as he might, Tas couldn't figure out any way of relaying Tanis's message to Caramon. Then they were forced to come to a halt as a contingent of Her Dark Majesty's troops, lined up shoulder to shoulder, came marching through the streets. Those who did not get out of their way were hurled bodily to the sidewalk by the draconian officers or were simply knocked down and trampled. The companions' guards hastily shoved them up against a crumbling wall and ordered them to stand still until the soldiers had passed.

Tasslehoff found himself flattened between Caramon on one side and a draconian on the other. The guard had loosened its clawed grip on Tas's shirt, evidently figuring that not even a kender would be foolish enough to try to escape in this mob. Though Tas could feel the reptile's black eyes on him, he was able to squirm near enough to Caramon to talk. He hoped he wasn't overheard, and didn't expect to be, with all the head-bashing and boot-thumping going on around him.

"Caramon!" Tas whispered. "I've got a message. Can you hear me?"

Caramon did not turn, but kept staring straight ahead, his face set rock-hard. But Tas saw one eyelid flutter.

"Tanis said to trust him!" Tas whispered swiftly. "No matter what. And . . . and to . . . keep up the act . . . I think that's what he said."

Tas saw Caramon frown.

"He spoke in elven," Tas added huffily. "And it was hard to hear."

Caramon's expression did not change. If anything, it grew darker.

Tas swallowed. Edging closer, he pressed up against the wall right behind the big warrior's broad back. "That . . . that Dragon Highlord," the kender said hesitantly. "That . . . was Kitiara, wasn't it?"

Caramon did not answer. But Tas saw the muscles in the man's jaw tighten, he saw a nerve begin to twitch in Caramon's neck.

Tas sighed. Forgetting where he was, he raised his voice. "You *do* trust him, don't you, Caramon? Because—"

Without warning, Tas's draconian guard turned and bashed the kender across the mouth, slamming him into the wall. Dazed with pain, Tasslehoff sank down to the ground. A dark shadow bent over him. His vision fuzzy, Tas couldn't see who it was and he braced himself for another blow. Then he felt strong, gentle hands lift him by his fleecy vest.

"I told you not to damage them," growled Caramon.

"Bah! A kender!" The draconian spat.

The troops had nearly all passed by now. Caramon set Tas on his feet. The kender tried to stand up, but for some reason the sidewalk kept sliding out from underneath him.

"I—I'm sorry . . ." he heard himself mumble. "Legs acting funny . . ." Finally he felt himself hoisted in the air and, with a protesting squeak, was flung over Caramon's broad shoulder like a meal sack.

"He's got information," Caramon said in his deep voice. "I hope you haven't addled his brain so that he's lost it. The Dark Lady won't be pleased."

"What brain?" snarled the draconian, but Tas—from his upside-down position on Caramon's back—thought the creature appeared a bit shaken.

They began walking again. Tas's head hurt horribly, his cheek stung. Putting his hand to it, he felt sticky blood where the draconian's claws had dug into his skin. There was a sound in his ears like a hundred bees had taken up residence in his brain. The world seemed to be slowly circling around him, making his stomach queasy, and being jounced around on Caramon's armor-plated back wasn't helping.

"How much farther is it?" He could feel Caramon's voice vibrate in the big man's chest. "The little bastard's heavy."

In answer, the draconian pointed a long, bony claw.

With a great effort, trying to take his mind off his pain and dizziness, Tas twisted his head to see. He could manage only a glance, but it was enough. The building had been growing larger and larger as they approached until it filled, not only the vision, but the mind as well.

Tas slumped back. His sight was growing dim and he wondered drowsily why it was getting so foggy. The last thing he remembered was hearing the words, "To the dungeons . . beneath the Temple of Her Majesty, Takhisis, Queen of Darkness."

6

Tanis bargains.
Gakhan investigates.

"Wine?"

"No."

Kitiara shrugged. Taking the pitcher from the bowl of snow in which it rested to keep cool, she slowly poured some for herself, idly watching the blood-red liquid run out of the crystal carafe and into her glass. Then she carefully set the crystal carafe back into the snow and sat down opposite Tanis, regarding him coolly.

She had taken off the dragon helm, but she wore her armor still—the night-blue armor, gilded with gold, that fit over her lithe body like scaled skin. The light from the many candles in the room gleamed in the polished surfaces and glinted off the sharp metal edges until Kitiara seemed ablaze in flame. Her dark hair, damp with perspiration, curled around her face. Her brown eyes were bright as fire, shadowed by long, dark lashes.

"Why are you here, Tanis?" she asked softly, running her finger along the rim of her glass as she gazed steadily at him.

"You know why" he answered briefly.

"Laurana, of course," Kitiara said.

Tanis shrugged, careful to keep his face a mask, yet fearing that this woman—who sometimes knew him better than he knew himself—could read every thought.

"You came alone?" Kitiara asked, sipping at the wine.

"Yes," Tanis replied, returning her gaze without faltering.

Kitiara raised an eyebrow in obvious disbelief.

"Flint's dead," he added, his voice breaking. Even in his fear, he still could not think of his friend without pain. "And Tasslehoff wandered off somewhere. I couldn't find him. I . . . I didn't really want to bring him anyway."

"I can understand," Kit said wryly. "So Flint is dead."

"Like Sturm," Tanis could not help but add through clenched teeth.

Kit glanced at him sharply. "The fortunes of war, my dear," she said. "We were both soldiers, he and I. He understands. His spirit bears me no malice."

Tanis choked angrily, swallowing his words. What she said was true. Sturm *would* understand

Kitiara was silent as she watched Tanis's face a few moments. Then she set the glass down with a clink.

"What about my brothers?" she asked. "Where—"

"Why don't you just take me to the dungeons and interrogate me?" Tanis snarled. Rising out of his chair, he began to pace the luxurious room.

Kitiara smiled, an introspective, thoughtful smile. "Yes," she said, "I could interrogate you there. And you would talk, dear Tanis. You would tell me all I wanted to hear, and then you would beg to tell me more. Not only do we have those who are skilled in the art of torture, but they are passionately dedicated to their profession." Rising languorously, Kitiara walked over to stand in front of Tanis. Her wine glass in one hand, she placed her other hand on his chest and slowly ran her palm up over his shoulder. "But this is not an interrogation. Say, rather, it is a sister, concerned about her family. Where are my brothers?"

"I don't know," Tanis said. Catching her wrist firmly in his hand, he held her hand away from him. "They were both lost in the Blood Sea. . . ."

"With the Green Gemstone Man?"

"With the Green Gemstone Man."

"And how did you survive?"

"Sea elves rescued me."

"Then they might have rescued the others?"

"Perhaps. Perhaps not. I am elven, after all. The others were human."

Kitiara stared at Tanis long moments. He still held her wrist in his hand. Unconsciously, under her penetrating gaze, his fingers closed around it.

"You're hurting me . . ." Kit whispered softly. "Why did you come, Tanis? To rescue Laurana. . alone? Even you were never *that* foolish—"

"No," Tanis said, tightening his grasp on Kitiara's arm. "I came to make a trade. Take me. Let her go."

Kitiara's eye opened wide. Then, suddenly, she threw back her head and laughed. With a quick, easy move, she broke free of Tanis's grip and, turning, walked over to the table to refill her wine glass.

She grinned at him over her shoulder. "Why, Tanis," she said, laughing again, "what are you to me that I should make this trade?"

Tanis felt his face flush. Still grinning, Kitiara continued.

"I have captured their Golden General, Tanis. I have taken their good-luck charm, their beautiful elven warrior. She wasn't a bad general, either, for that matter. She brought them the dragonlances and taught them to fight. Her brother brought back the good dragons, but everyone credits her. She kept the Knights together, when they should have split apart long before this. And you want me to exchange her for"— Kitiara gestured contemptuously—"a half-elf who's been wandering the countryside in the company of kender, barbarians, and dwarves!"

Kitiara began to laugh again, laughing so hard she was forced to sit down and wipe tears from her eyes. "Really, Tanis, you have a high opinion of yourself. What did you think I'd take you back for? Love?"

There as a subtle change in Kit's voice, her laugh seemed forced. Frowning suddenly, she twisted the wineglass in her hand.

Tanis did not respond. He could only stand before her, his skin burning at her ridicule. Kitiara stared at him, then lowered her gaze.

"Suppose I said yes?" she asked in a cold voice, her eyes on the glass in her hand. "What could you give me in return for what I would lose?"

Tanis drew a deep breath. "The commander of your forces is dead," he said, keeping his voice even. "I know. Tas told me he killed him. I'll take his place."

"You'd serve under . . . in the dragonarmies?" Kit's eyes widened in genuine astonishment.

"Yes." Tanis gritted his teeth. His voice was bitter. "We've lost anyway. I've seen your floating citadels. We can't win, even if the good dragons stayed. And they won't—the people will send them back. The people never trusted them anyway, not really. I care for only one thing—let Laurana go free, unharmed."

"I truly believe you would do this," Kitiara said softly, marveling. For long moments she stared at him. "I'll have to consider. . . ."

Then, as if arguing with herself, she shook her head. Putting the glass to her lips, she swallowed the wine, set the glass down, and rose to her feet.

"I'll consider," she repeated. "But now I must leave you, Tanis. There is a meeting of the Dragon Highlords tonight. They have come from all over Ansalon to attend. You are right, of course. You *have* lost the war. Tonight we make plans to clench the fist of iron. You will attend me. I will present you to Her Dark Majesty."

"And Laurana?" Tanis persisted.

"I said I would consider it!" A dark line marred the smooth skin between Kitiara's feathery eyebrows. Her voice was sharp. "Ceremonial armor will be brought to you. Be dressed and ready to accompany me within the hour." She started to go, then turned to face Tanis once more. "My decision may depend on how you conduct yourself this evening," she said softly. "Remember, Half-Elven, from this moment you serve *me!*"

The brown eyes glittered clear and cold as they held Tanis in their thrall. Slowly he felt the will of this woman press upon him until it was like a strong hand forcing him down onto the polished marble floor. The might of the dragonarmies was behind her, the shadow of the Dark Queen hovered around her, imbuing her with a power Tanis had noticed before.

Suddenly Tanis felt the great distance between them. She was supremely, superbly human. For only the humans were endowed with the lust for power so strong that the raw passion of their nature could be easily corrupted. The humans' brief lives were as flames that could burn with a pure light like Goldmoon's candle, like Sturm's shattered sun. Or the flame could destroy, a searing fire that consumed all in its path. He had warmed his cold, sluggish elven blood by that fire, he had nurtured the flame in his heart. Now he saw himself as he would become—as he had seen the bodies of those who died in the flames of Tarsis—a mass of charred flesh—the heart black and still.

It was his due, the price he must pay. He would lay his soul upon this woman's altar as another might lay a handful of silver upon a pillow. He owed Laurana that much. She had suffered enough because of him. His death would not free her but his life might.

Slowly, Tanis placed his hand over his heart and bowed.

"My lord," he said.

Kitiara walked into her private chamber, her mind in a turmoil. She felt her blood pulse through her veins. Excitement, desire, the glorious elation of victory made her more drunk than the wine. Yet beneath was a nagging doubt, all the more irritating because it turned the elation flat and stale. Angrily she tried to banish it from her mind, but it was brought sharply into focus as she opened the door to her room.

The servants had not expected her so soon. The torches had not been lit; the fire was laid, but not burning. Irritably she reached for the bell rope that would send them scurrying in to be berated for their laxness, when suddenly a cold and fleshless hand closed over her wrist.

The touch of that hand sent a burning sensation of cold through her bones and blood until it nearly froze her heart. Kitiara gasped with the pain and started to pull free, but the hand held her fast.

"You have not forgotten our bargain?"

"No, of course not!" Kitiara said. Trying to keep the quiver of fear from her voice, she commanded sternly, "Let me go!"

The hand slowly released its grip. Kitiara hurriedly snatched her arm away, rubbing the flesh that—even in that short span of time—had turned bluish white. "The elfwoman will be yours—when the Queen has finished with her, of course."

"Of course. I would not want her otherwise. A living woman is of no use to me—not like a living man is of use to you . . ." The dark figure's voice lingered unpleasantly over the words.

Kitiara cast a scornful glance at the pallid face, the flickering eyes that floated—disembodied—above the black armor of the knight.

"Don't be a fool, Soth," she said, pulling the bell rope hastily. She felt a need for light. "I am able to separate the pleasures of the flesh from the pleasures of business—something you were unable to do, from what I know of your life."

"Then what are your plans for the half-elf?" Lord Soth asked, his voice seeming—as usual—to come from far below ground.

"He will be mine, utterly and completely," Kitiara said, gently rubbing her injured wrist.

Servants hurried in with hesitant, sideways glances at the Dark Lady, fearing her notorious explosions of wrath. But Kitiara, preoccupied with her thoughts, ignored them. Lord Soth faded back into the shadows as always when the candles were lit.

"The only way to possess the half-elf is to make him watch as I destroy Laurana," Kitiara continued.

"That is hardly the way to win his love," Lord Soth sneered.

"I don't want his love." Pulling off her gloves and unbuckling her armor, Kitiara laughed shortly. "I want him! As long as she lives, his thoughts will be of her and of the noble sacrifice he has made. No, the only way he will be mine—totally—is to be ground beneath the heel of my boot until he is nothing more than a shapeless mass. Then, he will be of use to me."

"Not for long," Lord Soth remarked caustically. "Death will free him."

Kitiara shrugged. The servants had completed their tasks and vanished quickly. The Dark Lady stood in the light, silent and thoughtful, her armor half-on and half-off, her dragonhelm dangling from her hand.

"He has lied to me," she said softly, after a moment. Then, flinging the helm down on a table, where it struck and shattered a dusty, porcelain vase, Kit began to pace back and forth. "He has lied. My brothers did *not* die in the Blood Sea—at least one of them lives, I know. And so does he—the Everman!" Peremptorily, Kitiara flung open the door. "Gakhan!" she shouted.

A draconian hurried into the room.

"What news? Have they found that captain yet?"

"No, lord," the draconian replied. He was the same one who had followed Tanis from the inn in Flotsam, the same who had helped trap Laurana. "He is off-duty, lord," the creature added as if that explained everything.

Kitiara understood. "Search every beer tent and brothel until he is found. Then bring him here. Lock him in irons if you have to. I'll question him when I return from the Highlord's Assembly. No, wait . . ." Kitiara paused, then added, "*You* question him. Find out if the half-elf was truly alone—as he said—or if there were others with him. If so—"

The draconian bowed. "You will be informed at once, my lord."

Kitiara dismissed him with a gesture, and the draconian, bowing again, left, shutting the door behind him. After standing thoughtfully for a moment, Kitiara irritably ran her hand through her curly hair, then began yanking at the straps of her armor once again.

"You will attend me, tonight," she said to Lord Soth, without looking at the apparition of the death knight which, she assumed, was still in its same place behind her. "Be watchful. Lord Ariakas will not be pleased with what I intend to do."

Tossing the last piece of armor to the floor, Kitiara pulled off the leather tunic and the blue silken hose. Then, stretching in luxurious freedom, she glanced over her shoulder to see Lord Soth's reaction to her words. He was not there. Startled, she glanced quickly around the room.

The spectral knight stood beside the dragonhelm that lay on the table amidst pieces of the broken vase. With a wave of his fleshless hand, Lord Soth caused the shattered remains of the vase to rise into the air and hover before him. Holding them by the force of his magic, the death knight turned to regard Kitiara with his flaming orange eyes as she stood naked before him. The firelight turned her tanned skin golden, made her dark hair shine with warmth.

"You are a woman still, Kitiara," Lord Soth said slowly. "You love. . . ."

The knight did not move or speak, but the pieces of the vase fell to the floor. His pallid boot trod upon them as he passed, leaving no trace of his passing.

"And you hurt," he said softly to Kitiara as he drew near her. "Do not deceive yourself, Dark Lady. Crush him as you will, the half-elf will always be your master—even in death."

Lord Soth melded with the shadows of the room. Kitiara stood for long moments, staring into the blazing fire, seeking—perhaps—to read her fortune in the flames.

Gakhan walked rapidly down the corridor of the Queen's palace, his clawed feet clicking on the marble floors. The draconian's thoughts kept pace with his stride. It had suddenly occurred to him where the captain might be found. Seeing two draconians attached to Kitiara's command lounging at the end of the corridor, Gakhan motioned them to fall in behind him. They obeyed immediately. Though Gakhan held no rank in the dragonarmy—not any more—he was known officially as the Dark Lady's military aide. Unofficially he was known as her personal assassin.

Gakhan had been in Kitiara's service a long time. When word of the discovery of the blue crystal staff had reached the Queen of Darkness and her minions, few of the Dragon Highlords attached much importance to its disappearance. Deeply involved in the war that was slowly stamping the life out of the northern lands of Ansalon, something as trivial as a staff with healing powers did not merit their attention. It would take a great deal of healing to heal the world, Ariakas had stated, laughing, at a Council of War.

But two Highlords did take the disappearance of the staff seriously: one who ruled that part of Ansalon where the staff had been discovered, and one who had been born and raised in the area. One was a dark cleric, the other a skilled swordswoman. Both knew how dangerous proof of the return of the ancient gods could be to their cause.

They reacted differently, perhaps because of location. Lord Verminaard sent out swarms of draconians, goblins, and hobgoblins with full descriptions of the blue crystal staff and its powers. Kitiara sent Gakhan.

It was Gakhan who traced Riverwind and the blue crystal staff to the village of Que-shu, and it was Gakhan who ordered the raid on the village, systematically murdering most of the inhabitants in a search for the staff.

But he left Que-shu suddenly, having heard reports of the staff in Solace. The draconian traveled to that town, only to find that he had missed it by a matter of weeks. But there he discovered that the barbarians who carried the staff had been joined by a group of adventurers, purportedly from Solace according to the locals he "interviewed."

Gakhan was faced with a decision at this point. He could try and pick up their trail, which had undoubtedly grown cold during the intervening weeks, or he could return to Kitiara with descriptions of these adventurers to see if she knew them. If so, she might be able to provide him with information that would allow him to plot their movements in advance.

He decided to return to Kitiara, who was fighting in the north. Lord Verminaard's thousands were much more likely to find the staff than Gakhan. He brought complete descriptions of the adventurers to Kitiara, who was startled to learn that they were her two half-brothers, her old comrades-in-arms, and her former lover. Immediately Kitiara saw the workings of a great power here, for she knew that this group of mismatched wanderers could be forged into a dynamic force for either good or evil. She immediately took her misgivings to the Queen of Darkness, who was already disturbed by the portent of the missing constellation of the Valiant Warrior. At once the Queen knew she had been correct, Paladine had returned to fight her. But by the time she realized the danger, the damage had been done.

Kitiara set Gakhan back on the trail. Step by step, the clever draconian traced the companions from Pax Tharkas to the dwarven kingdom. It was he who followed them in Tarsis, and there he and the Dark Lady would have captured them had it not been for Alhana Starbreeze and her griffons.

Patiently Gakhan kept on their trail. He knew of the group's separation, hearing reports of them from Silvanesti—where they drove off the great green dragon, Cyan Bloodbane, and then from Ice Wall, where Laurana killed the dark elven magic-user, Feal-Thas. He knew of the discovery of the dragon orbs—the destruction of one, the frail mage's acquisition of the other.

It was Gakhan who followed Tanis in Flotsam, and who was able to direct the Dark Lady to them aboard the *Perechon*. But here again, as before, Gakhan moved his gamepiece only to find an opponent's piece blocking a final move. The draconian did not despair. Gakhan knew his opponent, he knew the great power opposing him. He was playing for high stakes—very high stakes indeed.

Thinking of all this as he left the Dark Majesty's Temple—where even now the Dragon Highlords were gathering for High Conclave—Gakhan entered the streets of Neraka. It was light now, just at the end of day. As the sun slid down from the sky, its last rays were freed from the shadow of the citadels. It burned now above the mountains, gilding the still snow-capped peaks blood red.

Gakhan's reptilian gaze did not linger on the sunset. Instead it flicked among the streets of the tent town, now almost completely empty since most of the draconians were required to be in attendance upon their lords this evening. The Highlords had a notable lack of trust in each other and in their Queen. Murder had been done before in her chambers—and would, most likely, be done again.

That did not concern Gakhan, however. In fact, it made his job easier. Quickly he led the other draconians through the foul-smelling, refuse-littered streets. He could have sent them on this mission without him, but Gakhan had come to know his great opponent very well and he had a distinct feeling of urgency. The wind of momentous events was starting to swirl into a huge vortex. He stood in the eye now, but he knew it would soon sweep him up. Gakhan wanted to be able to ride those winds, not be hurled upon the rocks.

"This is the place," he said, standing outside of a beer tent. A sign tacked to a post read in Common—The Dragon's Eye, while a placard propped in front stated in crudely lettered Common: "Dracos and goblins not allowed." Peering through the filthy tent flap, Gakhan saw his quarry. Motioning to his escorts, he thrust aside the flap and stepped inside.

An uproar greeted his entrance as the humans in the bar turned their bleary eyes on the newcomers and—seeing three draconians—immediately began to shout and jeer. The shouts and jeers died almost instantly, however, when Gakhan removed the hood that covered his reptilian face. Everyone recognized Lord Kitiara's henchman. A pall settled over the crowd thicker than the rank smoke and foul odors that filled the bar. Casting fearful glances at the draconians, the humans hunched their shoulders over their drinks and huddled down, trying to become inconspicuous.

Gakhan's glittering black gaze swept over the crowd.

"There," he said in draconian, motioning to a human slouched over the bar. His escorts acted instantly, seizing the one-eyed human soldier, who stared at them in drunken terror.

"Take him outside, in back," Gakhan ordered.

Ignoring the bewildered captain's protests and pleadings, as well as the baleful looks and muttered threats from the crowd, the draconians dragged their captive out into the back. Gakhan followed more slowly.

It took only a few moments for the skilled draconians to sober their prisoner up enough to talk—the man's hoarse screams caused many of the bar's patrons to lose their taste for their liquor—but eventually he was able to respond to Gakhan's questioning.

"Do you remember arresting a dragonarmy officer this afternoon on charges of desertion?"

The captain remembered questioning many officers today . . . he was a busy man . . . they all looked alike. Gakhan gestured to the draconians, who responded promptly and efficiently.

The captain screamed in agony. Yes, yes! He remembered! But it wasn't just one officer. There had been two of them.

"Two?" Gakhan's eyes glittered. "Describe the other officer."

"A big human, really big. Bulging out of his uniform. And there had been prisoners. . . ."

"Prisoners!" Gakhan's reptilian tongue flicked in and out of his mouth. "Describe them!"

The captain was only too happy to describe. "A human woman, red curls, breasts the size of . . ."

"Get on with it," Gakhan snarled. His clawed hands trembled. He glanced at his escorts and the draconians tightened their grip.

Sobbing, the captain gave hurried descriptions of the other two prisoners, his words falling over themselves.

"A kender," Gakhan repeated, growing more and more excited. "Go on! An old man, white beard—" He paused, puzzled. The old magic-user? Surely they would not have allowed that decrepit old fool to accompany them on a mission so important and fraught with peril. If not, then who? Someone else they had picked up?

"Tell me more about the old man," Gakhan ordered.

The captain cast desperately about in his liquor-soaked and pain-stupefied brain. The old man . . . white beard . . .

"Stooped?"

No . . . tall, broad shoulders . . . blue eyes. Queer eyes— The captain was on the verge of passing out. Gakhan clutched the man in his clawed hand, squeezing his neck.

"What about the eyes?"

Fearfully the captain stared at the draconian who was slowly choking the life from him. He babbled something.

"Young . . . too young!" Gakhan repeated in exultation. Now he knew! "Where are they?"

The captain gasped out a word, then Gakhan hurled him to the floor with a crash.

The whirlwind was rising. Gakhan felt himself being swept upwards. One thought beat in his brain like the wings of a dragon as he and his escorts left the tent, racing for the dungeons below the palace.

The Everman . . . the Everman . . . the Everman!

The Temple
of the Queen of Darkness.

"T as!"

"Hurt . . . lemme 'lone . . ."

"I know, Tas. I'm sorry, but you've *got* to wake up. Please, Tas!"

An edge of fear and urgency in the voice pierced the pain-laden mists in the kender's mind. Part of him was jumping up and down, yelling at him to wake up. But another part was all for drifting back into the darkness that—while unpleasant— was better than facing the pain he knew was lying in wait for him, ready to spring—

"Tas . . . Tas . . ." A hand patted his cheek. The whispered voice was tense, tight with terror kept under control. The kender knew suddenly that he had no choice. He *had* to wake up. Besides, the jumping-up-and-down part of his brain shouted, you might be missing something!

"Thank the gods!" Tika breathed as Tasslehoff's eyes opened wide and stared up at her. "How do you feel?"

"Awful," Tas said thickly, struggling to sit up. As he had foreseen, pain leaped out of a corner and pounced on him. Groaning, he clutched his head.

"I know . . . I'm sorry," Tika said again, stroking back his hair with a gentle hand.

"I'm sure you mean well, Tika," Tas said miserably, "but would you mind not doing that? It feels like dwarf hammers pounding on me."

Tika drew back her hand hurriedly. The kender peered around as best he could through one good eye. The other had nearly swollen shut. "Where are we?"

"In the dungeons below the Temple," Tika said softly. Tas, sitting next to her, could feel her shiver with fear and cold. Looking around, he could see why. The sight made him shudder, too. Wistfully he remembered the good old days when he hadn't known the meaning of the word of fear. He should have felt a thrill of excitement. He was—after all—someplace he'd never been before and there were probably lots of fascinating things to investigate.

But there was death here, Tas knew; death and suffering. He'd seen too many die, too many suffer. His thoughts went to Flint, to Sturm, to Laurana. . . . Something had changed inside Tas. He would never again be like other kender. Through grief, he had come to know fear; fear not for himself but for others. He decided right now that he would rather die himself than lose anyone else he loved.

You have chosen the dark path, but you have the courage to walk it, Fizban had said.

Did he? Tas wondered. Sighing, he hid his face in his hands.

"No, Tas!" Tika said, shaking him. "Don't do this to us! We need you!"

Painfully Tas raised his head. "I'm all right," he said dully. "Where's Caramon and Berem?"

"Over there," Tika gestured toward the far end of the cell. "The guards are holding all of us together until they can find someone to decide what to do with us. Caramon's being splendid," she added with a proud smile and a fond glance at the big man, who was slouched, apparently sulking, in a far corner, as far from his 'prisoners' as he could get. Then Tika's face grew fearful. She drew Tas nearer. "But I'm worried about Berem! I think he's going crazy!"

Tasslehoff looked up quickly at Berem. The man was sitting on the cold, filthy stone floor of the cell, his gaze abstracted, his head cocked as though listening. The fake white beard Tika had made out of goat hair was torn and bedraggled. It wouldn't take much for it to fall off completely, Tas realized in alarm, glancing quickly out the cell door.

The dungeons were a maze of corridors tunneled out of the solid rock beneath the Temple. They appeared to branch off in all directions from a central guardroom, a small, round, open-ended room at the bottom of a narrow winding staircase that bored straight down from the ground floor of the Temple. In the guardroom, a large hobgoblin sat at a battered table beneath a torch, calmly munching on bread and swilling it down with a jug of something. A ring of keys hanging on a nail above his head proclaimed him the head jailor. He ignored the companions; he probably couldn't see them clearly in the dim light anyway, Tas realized, since the cell they were in was about a hundred paces away, down a dark and dismal corridor.

Creeping over to the cell door, Tas peered down the corridor in the opposite direction. Wetting a finger, he held it up in the air. That way was north, he determined. Smoking, foul-smelling torches flickered in the dank air. A large cell farther down was filled with draconians and goblins sleeping off drunken revels. At the far end of the corridor beyond their cell stood a massive iron door, slightly ajar. Listening carefully, Tas thought he could hear sounds from beyond the door: voices, low moaning. That's another section of the dungeon, Tas decided, basing his decision on past experience. The jailor probably left the door ajar so he could make his rounds and listen for disturbances.

"You're right, Tika," Tas whispered. "We're locked in some kind of holding cell, probably awaiting orders." Tika nodded. Caramon's act, if not completely fooling the guards, was at least forcing them to think twice before doing anything rash.

"I'm going over to talk to Berem," Tas said.

"No, Tas"—Tika glanced at the man uneasily—"I don't

think—"

But Tas didn't listen. Taking one last look at the jailor, Tas ignored Tika's soft remonstrations and crawled toward Berem with the idea of sticking the man's false beard back on his face. He had just neared him and was reaching out his small hand when suddenly the Everman roared and leaped straight at the kender.

Startled, Tas fell backwards with a shriek. But Berem didn't even see him. Yelling incoherently, he sprang over Tasslehoff and flung himself bodily against the cell door.

Caramon was on his feet now—as was the hobgoblin.

Trying to appear irritated at having his rest disturbed, Caramon darted a stern glance at Tasslehoff on the floor.

"What did you do to him?" the big man growled out of the side of his mouth.

"N-nothing, Caramon, honest!" Tas gasped. "He—he's crazy!"

Berem did indeed seem to have gone mad. Oblivious to pain, he flung himself at the iron bars, trying to break them open. When this didn't work, he grasped the bars in his hands and started to wrench them apart.

"I'm coming, Jasla!" he screamed. "Don't leave! Forgive—"

The jailor, his pig eyes wide in alarm, ran over to the stairs and began shouting up them.

"He's calling the guards!" Caramon grunted. "We've got to get Berem calmed down. Tika—"

But the girl was already by Berem's side. Holding onto his shoulder, she pleaded with him to stop. At first the berserk man paid no attention to her, roughly shaking her off him. But Tika petted and stroked and soothed until eventually it seemed Berem might listen. He quit attempting to force the cell door open and stood still, his hands clenching the bars. The beard had fallen to the floor, his face was covered with sweat, and he was bleeding from a cut where he had rammed the bars with his head.

There was a rattling sound near the front of the dungeon as two draconians came dashing down the stairs at the jailor's call. Their curved swords drawn and ready, they advanced down the narrow corridor, the jailor at their heels. Swiftly Tas grabbed the beard and stuffed it into one of his pouches, hoping they wouldn't remember that Berem had come in with whiskers.

Tika, still stroking Berem soothingly, babbled about anything that came into her head. Berem did not appear to be listening, but at least he appeared quiet once more. Breathing heavily, he stared with glazed eyes into the empty cell across from them. Tas could see muscles in the man's arm twitch spasmodically.

"What is the meaning of this?" Caramon shouted as the draconians came up to the cell door. "You've locked me in here with a raving beast! He tried to kill me! I demand you get me out of here!"

Tasslehoff, watching Caramon closely, saw the big warrior's right hand make a small quick gesture toward the guard. Recognizing the signal, Tas tensed, ready for action. He saw Tika tense, too. One hobgoblin and two guards. . . . They'd faced worse odds.

The draconians looked at the jailor, who hesitated. Tas could guess what was going through the creature's thick mind. If this big officer *was* a personal friend of the Dark Lady, she would certainly not look kindly on a jailor who allowed one of her close friends to be murdered in his prison cell.

"I'll get the keys," the jailor muttered, waddling back down the corridor.

The draconians began to talk together in their own language, apparently exchanging rude comments about the hobgoblin. Caramon flashed a look at Tika and Tas, making a quick gesture of heads banging together. Tas, fumbling in one of his pouches, closed his hand over his little knife. (They had searched his pouches, but—in an effort to be helpful—Tas kept switching his pouches around until the confused guards—after their fourth search of the same pouch—gave up. Caramon had insisted the kender be allowed to keep his pouches, since there were items the Dark Lady wanted to examine. Unless, of course, the guards wanted to be responsible—) Tika kept patting Berem, her hypnotic voice bringing a measure of peace back to his fevered, staring blue eyes.

The jailor had just grabbed the keys from the wall and was starting to walk back down the corridor again when a voice from the bottom of the stairs stopped him.

"What do you want?" the jailor snarled, irritated and startled at the sight of the cloaked figure appearing suddenly, without warning.

"I am Gakhan," said the voice.

Hushing immediately at the sight of the newcomer, the draconians drew themselves up in respect, while the hobgoblin turned a sickly green color, the keys clinking together in its flabby hand. Two more guards clattered down the stairs. At a gesture from the cloaked figure, they came to stand beside him.

Walking past the quaking hobgoblin, the figure drew closer to the cell door. Now Tas could see the figure clearly. It was another draconian, dressed in armor with a dark cape thrown over its face. The kender bit his lip in frustration. Well, the odds still weren't *that* bad—not for Caramon.

The hooded draconian, ignoring the stammering jailor who was trotting along behind him like a fat dog, grabbed a torch from the wall and came over to stand directly in front of the companions' jail cell.

"Get me out of this place!" Caramon shouted, elbowing Berem to one side.

But the draconian, ignoring Caramon, reached through the bars of the cell and laid a clawed hand on Berem's shirt front. Tas darted a frantic look at Caramon. The big man's face was deathly pale. He made a desperate lunge at the draconian, but it was too late.

With a twist of its clawed hand, the draconian ripped Berem's shirt to shreds. Green light flared into the jail cell as the torchlight illuminated the gemstone embedded in Berem's flesh.

"It is he," Gakhan said quietly. "Unlock the cell."

The jailor put the key in the cell door with hands that shook visibly. Snatching it away from the hobgoblin, one of the draconian guards opened the cell door, then they surged inside. One guard struck Caramon a vicious blow on the side of the head with the hilt of his sword, felling the warrior like an ox, while another grabbed Tika.

Gakhan entered the cell.

"Kill him"—the draconian motioned at Caramon—"and the girl and the kender." Gakhan laid his clawed hand on Berem's shoulder. "I will take this one to Her Dark Majesty." The draconian flashed a triumphant glance around at the others.

"This night, victory is ours," he said softly.

Sweating in the dragon-scale armor, Tanis stood beside Kitiara in one of the vast antechambers leading into the Great Hall of Audience. Surrounding the half-elf were Kitiara's troops, including the hideous skeletal warriors under the command of the death knight, Lord Soth. These stood in the shadows just behind Kitiara. Though the antechamber was crowded—Kitiara's draconian troops were packed in spear to spear—there was, nevertheless, a vast empty space around the undead warriors. None came near them, none spoke to them, they spoke to no one. And though the room was stifling hot with the crushing press of many bodies, a chill flowed from these that nearly stopped the heart if one ventured too near.

Feeling Lord Soth's flickering eyes upon him, Tanis could not repress a shudder. Kitiara glanced up at him and smiled, the crooked smile he had once found so irresistible. She stood close to him, their bodies touching.

"You'll get used to them," she said coolly. Then her gaze returned to the proceedings in the vast Hall. The dark line appeared between her brows, her hand tapped irritably upon her sword hilt. "Get moving, Ariakas," she muttered.

Tanis looked over her head, staring through the ornate doorway they would enter when it was their turn, watching in an awe he could not hide as the spectacle unfolded before his eyes.

The Hall of Audience of Takhisis, Queen of Darkness, first impressed the viewer with a sense of his own inferiority. This was the black heart which kept the dark blood flowing and—as such—its appearance was fitting. The antechamber in which they stood opened onto a huge circular room with a floor of polished black granite. The floor continued up to form the walls, rising in tortured curves like dark waves frozen in time. Any moment, it seemed, they could crash down and engulf all those within the Hall in blackness. It was only Her Dark Majesty's power that held them in check. And so the black waves swept upward to a high domed ceiling, now hidden from view by a wispy wall of shifting, eddying smoke—the breath of dragons.

The floor of the vast Hall was empty now, but it would soon be filling rapidly as the troops marched in to take up their positions beneath the thrones of their Highlords. These thrones—four of them—stood about ten feet above the gleaming granite floor. Squat gates opened from the concave walls onto black tongues of rock that licked outward from the walls. Upon these four huge platforms—two to each side—sat the Highlords—and only the Highlords. No one else—not even bodyguards—was allowed beyond the top step of the sacred platforms. Bodyguards and high-ranking officers stood upon stairs that extended up to the thrones from the floor like the ribs of some giant prehistoric beast.

From the center of the Hall rose another, slightly larger platform, curling upward from the floor like a giant, hooded snake—which is exactly what it had been carved to represent. One slender bridge of rock ran from the snake's 'head' to another gate in the side of the Hall. The head faced Ariakas—and the darkness-shrouded alcove above Ariakas.

The 'Emperor,' as Ariakas styled himself, sat upon a slightly larger platform at the front of the great Hall, about ten feet above those around it.

Tanis felt his gaze drawn irresistibly to an alcove carved into the rock above Ariakas's throne. It was larger than the rest of the alcoves and—within it—lurked a darkness that was almost alive. It breathed and pulsed and was so intense that Tanis looked quickly away. Although he could see nothing, he guessed who would soon sit within those shadows.

Shuddering, Tanis turned back to the darkness within the Hall. There was not much left to see. All around the domed ceiling, in alcoves similar though smaller than the Highlords' alcoves, perched the dragons. Almost invisible, obscured by their own smoking breath, these creatures sat opposite their respective Highlords' alcoves, keeping vigilant watch—so the Highlords supposed—upon their 'masters.' Actually only one dragon in the assemblage was truly concerned over his master's welfare. This was Skie, Kitiara's dragon, who—even now—sat in his place, his fiery red eyes staring at the throne of Ariakas with much the same intensity and far more visible hatred than Tanis had seen in the eyes of Skie's master.

A gong rang. Masses of troops poured into the Hall, all of them wearing the red dragon colors of Ariakas's troops. Hundreds of clawed and booted feet scraped the floor as the draconians and human guard of honor entered and took their places beneath Ariakas's throne. No officers ascended the stairs, no bodyguards took their places in front of their lord.

Then the man himself entered through the gate behind his throne. He walked alone, his purple robes of state sweeping majestically from his shoulders, dark armor gleaming in the torchlight. Upon his head glistened a crown, studded with jewels the hue of blood.

"The Crown of Power," Kitiara murmured, and now Tanis saw emotion in her eyes—longing, such longing as he had rarely seen in human eyes before.

" 'Whoever wears the Crown, rules,' " came a voice behind her. "So it is written."

Lord Soth. Tanis stiffened to keep from trembling, feeling the man's presence like a cold skeletal hand upon the back of his neck.

Ariakas's troops cheered him long and loudly, thumping their spears upon the floor, clashing their swords against their shields. Kitiara snarled in impatience. Finally Ariakas extended his hands for silence. Turning, he knelt in reverence before the shadowy alcove above him, then, with a wave of his gloved hand, the head of the Dragon Highlords made a patronizing gesture to Kitiara.

Glancing at her, Tanis saw such hatred and contempt on her face that he barely recognized her. "Yes, lord," whispered Kitiara, her eyes now dark and gleaming. " 'Whoever wears the Crown, rules. So it is written . . . written in blood!' " Half-turning her head, she beckoned to Lord Soth. "Fetch the elfwoman."

Lord Soth bowed and flowed from the antechamber like a malevolent fog, his skeletal warriors drifting after him. Draconians stumbled over themselves in frantic efforts to get out of his deadly path.

Tanis gripped Kitiara's arm. "You promised!" he said in a strangled voice.

Staring at him coldly, Kitiara snatched her arm free, easily breaking the half-elf's strong grasp. But her brown eyes held him, drained him, sucking the life from him until he felt like nothing more than a dried shell.

"Listen to me, Half-Elven," Kitiara said, her voice cold and thin and sharp. "I am after one thing and one thing only—the Crown of Power Ariakas wears. That is the reason I captured Laurana, that is all she means to me. I will present the elfwoman to Her Majesty, as I have promised. The Queen will reward me—with the Crown, of course—then she will order the elf taken to the Death Chambers far below the Temple. I care nothing for what happens to the elf after that, and so I give her to you. At my gesture, step forward. I will present you to the Queen. Beg of her a favor. Ask that you be allowed to escort the elfwoman to her death. If she approves of you, she will grant it. You may then take the elfwoman to the city gates or wherever you choose, and there you may set her free. But I want your word of honor, Tanis Half-Elven, that you will return to me."

"I give it," Tanis said, his eyes meeting Kitiara's without wavering.

Kitiara smiled. Her face relaxed. It was so beautiful once more, that Tanis, startled by the sudden transformation, almost wondered if he had seen that other cruel face at all. Putting her hand on Tanis's cheek, she stroked his beard.

"I have your word of honor. That might not mean much to other men, but I know you will keep it! One final warning, Tanis," she whispered swiftly, "you *must* convince the Queen that you are her loyal servant. She is powerful, Tanis! She is a goddess, remember that! She can see into your heart, your soul. You must convince her beyond doubt that you are hers. One gesture, one word that rings false, and she will destroy you. There will be nothing I can do. If you die, so does your Lauralanthalasa!"

"I understand," Tanis said, feeling his body chill beneath the cold armor.

There was a blaring trumpet call.

"There, that is our signal," Kitiara said. Pulling her gloves on, she drew the dragonhelm over her head. "Go forward, Tanis. Lead my troops. I will enter last."

Resplendent in her glittering night-blue dragon-scale armor, Kitiara stepped haughtily to one side as Tanis walked through the ornate doorway into the Hall of Audience.

The crowd began to cheer at the sight of blue banner. Perched above the audience with the other dragons, Skie bellowed in triumph. Aware of thousands of glittering eyes upon him, Tanis firmly put everything out of his mind except what he must do. He kept his eyes fixed on his destination—the platform in the Hall next to Lord Ariakas's, the platform decorated with the blue banner. Behind him, he could hear the rhythmic stamp of clawed feet as Kit's guard of honor marched in proudly. Tanis reached the platform and stood at the bottom of the stairs, as he had been ordered. The crowd quieted then and, as the last draconian filed through the door, a murmur began to sweep through the Hall. The crowd strained forward, anxious to see Kitiara's entrance.

Waiting within the antechamber, allowing the crowd to wait just a few more moments to enhance the suspense, Kit glimpsed movement out of the corner of her eye. Turning, she saw Lord

Soth enter the antechamber, his guards bearing a white-wrapped body in their fleshless arms. The eyes of the vibrant, living woman and the vacant eyes of the dead knight met in perfect agreement and understanding.

Lord Soth bowed.

Kitiara smiled, then—turning—she entered the Hall of Audience to thunderous applause.

Lying on the cold cell floor, Caramon struggled desperately to remain conscious. The pain was beginning to subside. The blow that struck him down had been a glancing one, slanting off the officer's helm he wore, stunning him, but not knocking him out.

He feigned unconsciousness, however, not knowing what else to do. Why wasn't Tanis here, he thought despairingly, once more cursing his own slowness of mind. The half-elf would have a plan, he would know what to do. I shouldn't have been left with this responsibility! Caramon swore bitterly. Then, *quit belly-aching, you big ox! They're depending on you!* came a voice in the back of his mind. Caramon blinked, then caught himself just as he was about to grin. The voice was so like Flint's, he could have sworn the dwarf was standing beside him! He was right. They were depending on him. He'd just have to do his best. That was all he could do.

Caramon opened his eyes a slit, peering out between half-closed lids. A draconian guard stood almost directly in front of him, back turned to the supposedly comatose warrior. Caramon could not see Berem or the draconian called Gakhan without twisting his head, and he dared not call attention to himself. He could take out that first guard, he knew. Possibly the second, before the other two finished him. He had no hope of escaping alive, but at least he might give Tas and Tika a chance to escape with Berem.

Tensing his muscles, Caramon prepared to launch himself at the guard when suddenly an agonized scream tore through the darkness of the dungeons. It was Berem screaming, a cry so filled with rage and anger that Caramon started up in alarm, forgetting he was supposed to be unconscious.

Then he froze, watching in amazement as Berem lurched forward, grabbed Gakhan, and lifted him off the stone floor. Carrying the wildly flailing draconian in his hands, the Everman hurtled out of the jail cell and smashed Gakhan into a stone

wall. The draconian's head split apart, cracking like the eggs of
the good dragons upon the black altars. Howling in rage,
Berem slammed the draconian into the wall again and again,
until Gakhan was nothing more than a limp, green bloodied
mass of shapeless flesh.

For a moment no one moved. Tas and Tika huddled together,
horrified by the gruesome sight. Caramon fought to piece
things together in his pain-befuddled mind while even the draconian guards stood staring at their leader's body in a paralyzed, dreadful fascination.

Then Berem dropped Gakhan's body to the ground. Turning,
he stared at the companions without recognition. He's completely insane, Caramon saw with a shudder. Berem's eyes were
wide and crazed. Saliva dripped from his mouth. His hands
and arms were slimy with green blood. Finally, realizing that
his captor was dead, Berem seemed to come to his senses. He
gazed around and saw Caramon on the floor, staring up at him
in shock.

"She calls me!" Berem whispered hoarsely.

Turning, he ran down the northern corridor, flinging the
startled draconians to one side as they tried to stop him. Never
pausing to look behind him, Berem slammed into the partially
open iron door at the end of the corridor, the force of his passing nearly tearing the door from its hinges. Clanking against
the stone with a dull booming sound, the door swung crazily
back and forth. They could hear Berem's wild shrieking echo
down the corridor.

By now, the draconians had recovered. One of them ran for
the stairway, shouting at the top of its lungs. It was in draconian, but Caramon could understand it well enough.

"Prisoner escape! Call out the guards!"

In answer came shouts and the sound of clawed feet scraping
at the top of the staircase. The hobgoblin took one look at the
dead draconian and fled toward the staircase and his guardroom, adding his panic-stricken shouts to those of the draconian. The other guard, quickly regaining its feet, jumped into
the cell. But Caramon was his feet now, too. This was action.
This he could understand. Reaching out, the big man grabbed
the draconian around the neck. One jerk of the huge hands,
and the creature fell lifeless to the floor. Caramon swiftly
snatched the sword from the clawed hand as the draconian's
body hardened into stone.

"Caramon! Look out behind you!" Tasslehoff yelled as the other guard, returning from the stairway, dashed into the cell, its sword raised.

Caramon whirled, only to see the creature fall forward as Tika's boot caught it in the stomach. Tasslehoff plunged his little knife into the second guard's body, forgetting—in his excitement—to jerk it free again. Glancing at the stone corpse of the other creature, the kender made a frantic dive for his knife. Too late.

"Leave it!" Caramon ordered, and Tas stood up.

Guttural voices could be heard above them, feet scraping and clawing down the stairs. The hobgoblin had reached the stairs and was waving his hands frantically and pointing back at them. His own shouts rose above the noise of the descending troops.

Caramon, sword in hand, glanced uncertainly at the stairs, then down the northern corridor after Berem.

"That's right! Follow Berem, Caramon," Tika said urgently. "Go with him! Don't you see? 'She's calling me,' he said. It's his sister's voice! He can hear her calling to him. That's why he went crazy."

"Yes . . ." Caramon said in a daze, staring down the corridor. He could hear the draconians plunging down the winding stairs, armor rattling, swords scraping against the stone walls. They had only seconds. "Come on—"

Tika grasped Caramon by the arm. Digging her nails into his flesh, she forced him to look at her, her red curls a mass of flaming color in the flickering torchlight.

"No!" she said firmly. "They'll catch him for certain and then it *will* be the end! I've got a plan. We must split up. Tas and I will draw them off. We'll give you time. It'll be all right, Caramon," she persisted, seeing him shake his head. "There's another corridor that leads east. I saw it as we came in. They'll chase us down that way. Now, hurry, before they see you!"

Caramon hesitated, his face twisted in agony.

"This is the end, Caramon!" Tika said. "For good or for evil. You must go with him! You must help him reach her! Hurry, Caramon! You're the only one strong enough to protect him. He needs you!"

Tika actually shoved the big man. Caramon took a step, then looked back at her.

"Tika . . ." he began, trying to think of some argument

against this wild scheme. But before he could finish, Tika kissed him swiftly and—grabbing a sword from a dead draconian—ran from the jail cell.

"I'll take care of her, Caramon!" Tas promised, dashing after Tika, his pouches bouncing wildly all around him.

Caramon stared after them a moment. The hobgoblin jailor shrieked in terror as Tika ran straight for the creature, brandishing her sword. The jailor made a wild grab for her, but Tika hacked at him so ferociously that the hobgoblin fell dead with a gurgling scream, his throat cut.

Ignoring the body that slumped to the floor, Tika hurried down the corridor, heading east.

Tasslehoff, right behind her, took a moment to stop at the bottom of the stair. The draconians were visible now, and Caramon could hear the kender's shrill voice shouting taunts at the guards.

"Dog-eaters! Slime-blooded goblin-lovers!"

Then Tas was off, dashing after Tika who had vanished from Caramon's sight. The enraged draconians—driven wild by the kender's taunts and the sight of their prisoners escaping—did not take time to look around. They charged after the fleet-footed kender, their curved swords gleaming, their long tongues flicking in anticipation of the kill.

Within moments, Caramon found himself alone. He hesitated another precious minute, staring into the thick darkness of the gloomy cells. He could see nothing. The only thing he could hear was Tas's voice yelling 'dog-eaters.' Then there was silence.

"I'm alone . . ." thought Caramon bleakly. "I've lost them . . . lost them all. I must go after them." He started toward the stairs, then stopped. "No, there's Berem. He's alone, too. Tika's right. He needs me now. He needs me."

His mind clear at last, Caramon turned and ran clumsily down the northern corridor after the Everman.

8

The Queen of Darkness.

"**D**ragon Highlord Toede."

Lord Ariakas listened with lazy contempt to the calling of the role. Not that he was bored with the proceedings. Quite the contrary. Assembling the Grand Council had not been his idea. He had, in fact, opposed it. But he had been careful not to oppose it too vehemently. That might have made him appear weak; and Her Dark Majesty did not allow weaklings to live. No, this Grand Council would be anything but boring. . . .

At the thought of his Dark Queen, he half-turned and glanced swiftly up into the alcove above him. The largest and most magnificent in the Hall, its great throne remained empty still, the gate that led into it lost in the living, breathing darkness. No stairs ran up to *that* throne. The gate itself provided the only entrance and exit. And as to where the gate led—well, it was best not to think of such things. Needless to say, no mortal had passed beyond its iron grillwork.

The Queen had not yet arrived. He was not surprised. These opening proceedings were beneath her. Ariakas hunched back in his throne. His gaze went—appropriately enough, he thought bitterly—from the throne of the Dark Queen to the throne of the Dark Lady. Kitiara was here, of course. This was her moment of triumph—so she thought. Ariakas breathed a curse upon her.

"Let her do her worst," he murmured, only half-listening as the sergeant repeated the name of Lord Toede once more. "I am prepared."

Ariakas suddenly realized something was amiss. What? What was happening? Lost in his thoughts, he had paid no attention to the proceedings. What was wrong? Silence . . . a dreadful silence that followed . . . what? He cast about in his mind, trying to recall what had just been said. Then he remembered and came back from his dark thoughts to stare grimly at the second throne to his left. The troops in the hall, mostly draconian, heaved and swayed like a sea of death below him as all eyes shifted to the same throne.

Though the draconian troops belonging to Lord Toede were present, their banners mingling with the banners of the other draconians standing at attention in the center of the Hall of Audience, the throne itself was empty.

Tanis, from where he stood upon the steps of Kitiara's platform, followed Ariakas's gaze, stern and cold beneath the crown. The half-elf's ears had pricked at the sound of Toede's name. An image of the hobgoblin came swiftly to his mind as he had seen him standing in the dust of the road to Solace. The vision brought back thoughts of that warm autumn day that had seen the beginning of this long, dark journey. It brought back memories of Flint and Sturm. . . . Tanis gritted his teeth and forced himself to concentrate on what was happening. The past was over, finished, and—he hoped fervently—soon forgotten.

"Lord Toede?" Ariakas repeated in anger. The troops in the Hall muttered among themselves. Never before had a Highlord disobeyed a command to attend the Grand Council.

A human dragonarmy officer climbed the stairs leading to the empty platform. Standing on the top step (protocol forbade him proceeding higher), he stammered a moment in terror, facing those black eyes and—worse—the shadowy alcove above Ariakas's throne. Then, taking a breath, he began his report.

"I—I regret to inform His Lordship and Her D-Dark Majesty"—a nervous glance at the shadowy alcove that was, apparently, still vacant—"that Dragon Highlord To—uh, Toede has met an unfortunate and untimely demise."

Standing on the top step of the platform where Kitiara sat enthroned, Tanis heard a snort of derision from behind Kit's dragonhelm. An amused titter ran through the crowd below him while dragonarmy officers exchanged knowing glances.

Lord Ariakas was not amused, however. "Who dared slay a Dragon Highlord?" he demanded furiously, and at the sound of his voice—and the portent of his words—the crowd fell silent.

"It was in K-Kenderhome, lord," the officer replied, his voice echoing in the vast marble chamber. The officer paused. Even from this distance, Tanis could see the man's fist clenching and unclenching nervously. He obviously had further bad news to impart and was reluctant to continue.

Ariakas glowered at the officer. Clearing his throat, the man lifted his voice again.

"I regret to report, lord, that Kenderhome has been l—" For a moment the man's voice gave out completely. Only by a valiant effort did he manage to continue. "—lost."

"*Lost!*" repeated Ariakas in a voice that might have been a thunderbolt.

Certainly it seemed to strike the officer with terror. Blenching, he stammered incoherently for a moment, then—apparently determining to end it quickly, gasped out, "Highlord Toede was foully murdered by a kender named Kronin Thistleknott, and his troops driven from—"

There was a deeper murmur from the crowd now, growlings of anger and defiance, threats of the total destruction of Kenderhome. They would wipe that miserable race from the face of Krynn—

With his gloved hand, Ariakas made an irritated, sweeping gesture. Silence fell instantly over the assemblage.

And then the silence was broken.

Kitiara laughed.

It was mirthless laughter—arrogant and mocking, and it echoed loudly from the depths of the metal mask.

His face twisted in outrage, Ariakas rose to his feet. He took a step forward and—as he did so—steel flashed among his draconians on the floor as swords slid out of scabbards and spear butts thudded against the floor.

At the sight, Kitiara's own troops closed ranks, backing up so that they pressed closely around the platform of their lord, which was at Ariakas's right hand. Instinctively Tanis's hand closed over the hilt of his sword and he found himself moving a step nearer Kitiara, though it meant setting his foot upon the platform where he was not supposed to trod.

Kitiara did not move. She remained seated, calmly regarding Ariakas with scorn that could be felt, if not seen.

Suddenly a breathless hush descended over the Assemblage, as if the breath in each body was being choked off by an unseen force. Faces paled as those present felt stifled, gasping for air. Lungs ached, vision blurred, heartbeats stilled. And then the air itself seemed sucked from the Hall as a darkness filled it.

Was it actual, physical darkness? Or a darkness in the mind? Tanis could not be certain. His eyes saw the thousands of torches in the Hall flare brilliantly, he saw the thousands of candles sparkle like stars in the night sky. But even the night sky was not darker than the darkness he now perceived.

His head swam. Desperately he tried to breathe, but he might as well have been beneath the Blood Sea of Istar again. His knees trembled, he was almost too weak to stand. His strength failed him, he staggered and fell and, as he sank down, gasping for breath, he was dimly aware of others, here and there, falling to the polished marble floor as well. Lifting his head, though the move was agony, he could see Kitiara slump forward in her chair as though crushed into the throne by an unseen force.

Then the darkness lifted. Cool, sweet air rushed into his lungs. His heart lurched and began pounding. Blood rushed to his head, nearly making him pass out. For a moment he could do nothing but sink back against the marble stairs, weak and dizzy, while light exploded in his head. Then, as his vision cleared, he saw that the draconians remained unaffected. Stoically they stood, all of them staring fixedly at one spot.

Tanis lifted his gaze to the magnificent platform that had remained empty throughout the proceedings. Empty until now. His blood congealed in his veins, his breath nearly stopped again. Takhisis, Queen of Darkness, had entered the Hall of Audience.

Other names she had upon Krynn. *Dragonqueen* she was called in elven; *Nilat the Corrupter,* to the barbarians of Plains; *Tamex, the False Metal,* so she was known in Thorbardin among the dwarves; *Mai-tat, She of Many Faces* was how they told of her in legends among the sea-faring people of Ergoth. *Queen of Many Colors and of None,* the Knights of Solamnia called her; defeated by Huma, banished from the land, long ago.

Takhisis, Queen of Darkness, had returned.

But not completely.

Even as Tanis stared at the shadowy form in the alcove overhead with awe, even as the terror pierced his brain, leaving him numb, unable to feel or sense anything beyond sheer horror and fear—he realized that the Queen was not present in her physical form. It was as if her presence in their minds cast a shadow of her being onto the platform. She, herself, was there only as her will forced others to perceive her.

Something was holding her back, blocking her entry into this world. A door—Berem's words returned in confusion to Tanis's mind. Where *was* Berem? Where were Caramon and the others? Tanis realized with a pang that he had nearly forgotten about them. They had been driven from his mind by his preoccupation with Kitiara and Laurana. His head spun. He felt as if he held the key to everything in his hand, if only he could find the time to think about it calmly.

But that was not possible. The shadowy form increased in intensity until its blackness seemed to create a cold hole of nothingness in the granite room. Unable to look away, Tanis was compelled to gaze into that dreadful hole until he had the terrifying sensation he was being drawn into it. At that moment, he heard a voice in his mind.

I have not brought you together to see your petty quarrels and pettier ambitions mar the victory I sense is fast approaching. Remember who rules here, Lord Ariakas.

Lord Ariakas sank to one knee, as did all others in the chamber. Tanis found himself falling to his knees in reverence. He could not help it. Though filled with loathing at the hideous, suffocating evil, this was a goddess—one of the forgers of the world. Since the beginning of time she had ruled . . . and would rule until time ended.

The voice continued speaking, burning into his mind and into the minds of all present.

Lord Kitiara, you have pleased us well in the past. Your gift to us now pleases us even more. Bring in the elfwoman, that we may look upon her and decide her fate.

Tanis, glancing at Lord Ariakas, saw the man return to his throne, but not before he had cast a venomous look of hatred at Kitiara.

"I will, Your Dark Majesty." Kitiara bowed, then, "Come with me," she ordered Tanis as she passed by him on her way down the stairs.

Her draconian troops backed away, leaving a path for her to walk to the center of the room. Kitiara descended the rib-like stairs of the platform, Tanis following. The troops parted to let them pass, then closed ranks again almost instantly.

Reaching the center of the Hall, Kitiara climbed the narrow stairs that jutted forth like spurs from the hooded snake's sculpted back until she stood in the center of the marble platform. Tanis followed more slowly, finding the stairs narrow and difficult to climb, especially as he felt the eyes of the shadowy form in the alcove delve into his soul.

Standing at the center of the ghastly platform, Kitiara turned and gestured toward the ornate gate opening onto the far end of the narrow bridge that connected the platform with the main walls of the Hall of Audience.

A figure appeared in the doorway—a dark figure dressed in the armor of a Knight of Solamnia. Lord Soth entered the Hall, and—at his coming—the troops fell back from either side of that narrow bridge as if a hand had reached up from the grave and tossed them away. In his pallid arms, Lord Soth bore a body bound in a white winding cloth, the kind used for embalming the dead. The silence in the room was such that the dead knight's booted footsteps could almost be heard ringing upon the marble floor, though all gathered there could see the stone through the transparent, fleshless body.

Walking forward, bearing his white-swathed burden, Lord Soth crossed the bridge and walked slowly up to stand upon the snake's head. At another gesture from Kitiara, he laid the bundle of white upon the floor at the Dragon Highlord's feet. Then he stood and suddenly vanished, leaving everyone blinking in horror, to wonder if he had really existed or if they had seen him only in their fevered imaginations.

Tanis could see Kitiara smile beneath her helm, pleased at the impact made by her servant. Then, drawing her sword, Kitiara leaned down and slit the bindings that wrapped the figure like a cocoon. Giving them a yank, she pulled them loose, then stepped back to watch her captive struggle in the web.

Tanis caught sight of a mass of tangled, honey-colored hair, the flash of silver armor. Coughing, nearly suffocated by her constricting bindings, Laurana fought to free herself from the entangling white cloths. There was tense laughter as the troops watched the prisoner's feeble thrashings—this was obviously an indication of more amusement to come. Reacting instinctively, Tanis took a step forward to help Laurana. Then he felt Kitiara's brown eyes upon him, watching him, reminding him—

"If you die—she dies!"

His body shaking with chills, Tanis stopped, then stepped back. Finally Laurana staggered dizzily to her feet. For a moment she stood staring around vaguely, not comprehending where she was, blinking her eyes to see in the harsh, flaring torchlight. Her gaze focused at last upon Kitiara, smiling at her from behind the dragonhelm.

At the sight of her enemy, the woman who had betrayed her, Laurana drew herself to her full height. For a moment, her fear was forgotten in her anger. Imperiously she glanced beneath her, then above her, her gaze sweeping the great Hall. Fortunately, she did not look behind her. She did not see the bearded half-elf dressed in dragonarmor, who was watching her intently. Instead she saw the troops of the Dark Queen, she saw the Highlords upon their thrones, she saw the dragons perched above them. Finally, she beheld the shadowy form of the Queen of Darkness herself.

And now she knows where she is, Tanis thought in misery, seeing Laurana's face drain of color. Now she knows where she is and what is about to befall her.

What stories they must have told her, down in those dungeons below the Temple. Tormenting her with tales of the Death Chambers of the Queen of Darkness. She had probably been able to hear the screams of others, Tanis guessed, feeling his soul ache at her obvious terror. She had listened to their screams in the night, and now, within hours, maybe minutes, she would join them.

Her face deathly pale, Laurana turned back to look at Kitiara as if she were the only fixed point in a swirling universe. Tanis saw Laurana's teeth clench, biting her lips to keep control. She would never show her fear to this woman, she would never show her fear to any of them.

Kitiara made a small gesture.

Laurana followed her gaze.

"Tanis . . ."

Turning, she saw the half-elf, and, as Laurana's eyes met his, Tanis saw hope shine. He felt her love for him surround him and bless him like the dawning of spring after winter's bitter darkness. For at last Tanis realized his own love for her was the bond between his two warring halves. He loved her with the unchanging, eternal love of his elven soul and with the passionate love of his human blood. But the realization had come too late, and now he would pay for the realization with his life and his soul.

One look, that was all he could give Laurana. One look that must carry the message of his heart, for he could feel Kitiara's brown eyes on him, watching him intently. And other eyes were on him, too, dark and shadowy as they might be.

Aware of those eyes, Tanis forced his face to reveal nothing of his inner thoughts. Exerting all his control, he clenched his jaw, setting the muscles rigid, keeping his gaze carefully expressionless. Laurana might have been a stranger. Coldly he turned away from her and, as he turned, he saw hope's light flicker and die in her luminous eyes. As if a cloud had obscured the sun, the warmth of Laurana's love turned to bleak despair, chilling Tanis with its sorrow.

Gripping the hilt of his sword firmly to keep his hand from trembling, Tanis turned to face Takhisis, Queen of Darkness.

"Dark Majesty," cried Kitiara, grasping Laurana by the arm and dragging her forward, "I present my gift to you—a gift that will give us victory!"

She was momentarily interrupted by tumultuous cheers. Raising her hand, Kitiara commanded silence, then she continued.

"I give you the elfwoman, Lauralanthalasa, Princess of the Qualinesti Elves, leader of the foul Knights of Solamnia. It was she who brought back the dragonlances, she who used the dragon orb in the High Clerist's Tower. It was by her command that her brother and a silver dragon traveled to Sanction where—through the ineptness of Lord Ariakas—they managed to break into the sacred temple and discover the destruction of the good dragon eggs." Ariakas took a menacing step forward, but Kitiara coolly ignored him. "I give her to you, my Queen, to treat her as you believe her crimes against you merit."

Kitiara flung Laurana in front of her. Stumbling, the elfwoman fell to her knees before the Queen. Her golden hair had come loose from its bindings and tumbled about her in a shining wave that was—to Tanis's fevered mind—the only light in the vast dark chamber.

You have done well, Lord Kitiara, came the Dark Queen's unheard voice, *and you will be well rewarded. We will have the elf escorted to the Death Chambers, then I will grant your reward.*

"Thank you, Majesty." Kitiara bowed. "Before our business concludes, I have two favors I beg you grant me." Thrusting out her hand, she caught Tanis in her strong grip. "I would first present one who seeks service in your great and glorious army."

Kitiara laid a hand on Tanis's shoulder, indicating with a firm pressure that he was to kneel. Unable to purge that last glimpse of Laurana from his mind, Tanis hesitated. He could still turn from the darkness. He could stand by Laurana's side and they would face the end together.

Then he sneered.

How selfish have I become, he asked himself bitterly, that I would even consider sacrificing Laurana in an attempt to cover my own folly? No, I alone will pay for my misdeeds. If I do nothing more that is good in this life, I will save her. And I will carry that knowledge with me as a candle to light my path until the darkness consumes me!

Kitiara's grip on him tightened painfully, even through the dragonscale armor. The brown eyes behind the dragonhelm began to smolder with anger.

Slowly, his head bowed, Tanis sank to his knees before Her Dark Majesty.

"I present your humble servant, Tanis Half-Elven," Kitiara resumed coolly, although Tanis thought he could detect a note of relief in her voice. "I have named him commander of my armies, following the untimely death of my late commander, Bakaris."

Let our new servant come forward, came the voice into Tanis's mind.

———

Tanis felt Kit's hand on his shoulder as he rose, drawing him near. Swiftly she whispered, "Remember, you are Her Dark Majesty's property now, Tanis. She must be utterly convinced or even I will not be able to save you, and you will not be able to save your elfwoman."

"I remember," Tanis said without expression. Shaking free of Kitiara's grip, the half-elf walked forward to stand on the very edge of the platform, below the Dark Queen's throne.

Raise your head. Look upon me, came the command.

Tanis braced himself, asking for strength from deep inside him, strength he wasn't certain he possessed. *If I falter, Laurana is lost. For the sake of love, I must banish love.* Tanis lifted his eyes.

His gaze was caught and held. Mesmerized, he stared at the shadowy form, unable to free himself. There was no need to fabricate awe and a horrible reverence, for that came to him as it comes to all mortals who glimpse Her Dark Majesty. But even as he felt compelled to worship, he realized that—deep inside—he was free still. Her power was not complete. She could not consume him against his will. Though Takhisis fought not to reveal this weakness, Tanis was conscious of the great struggle she waged to enter the world.

Her shadowy form wavered before his eyes, revealing herself in all her guises, proving she had control over none. First she appeared to him as the five-headed dragon of Solamnic legend. Then the form shifted and she was the Temptress—a woman whose beauty men might die to possess. Then the form shifted once again. Now she was the Dark Warrior, a tall and powerful Knight of Evil, who held death in his mailed hand.

But even as the forms shifted, the dark eyes remained constant, staring into Tanis's soul, eyes of the five dragon heads, eyes of the beautiful Temptress, eyes of the fearful Warrior. Tanis felt himself shrivel beneath the scrutiny. He could not bear it, he did not have the strength. Abjectly he sank once more to his knees, groveling before the Queen, despising himself as behind him he heard an anguished, choking cry.

9
Horns of doom.

Lumbering down the northern corridor in search of Berem, Caramon ignored the startled yells and calls and grasping hands of prisoners reaching out from the barred cells. But there was no sight of Berem and no sign of his passing. He tried asking the other prisoners if they had seen him, but most were so unhinged by the tortures they had endured that they made no sense and, eventually, his mind filled with horror and pity, Caramon left them alone. He kept walking, following the corridor that led him ever downward. Looking around, he wondered in despair how he would ever

---

find the crazed man. His only consolation was that no other corridors branched off from this central one. Berem must have come this way! But if so, where was he?

Peering into cells, stumbling around corners, Caramon almost missed a big hobgoblin guard, who lunged out at him. Swinging his sword irritably, annoyed at the interruption, Caramon swept the creature's head off and was on his way before the body hit the stone floor.

Then he heaved a sigh of relief. Hurrying down a staircase, he had nearly stepped on the body of another dead hobgoblin. Its neck had been twisted by strong hands. Plainly, Berem had been here, and not long ago. The body was not yet cold.

Certain now he was on the man's trail, Caramon began to run. The prisoners in the cells he passed were nothing but blurs to the big warrior as he ran by. Their voices shrilled in his ears, begging for freedom.

Let them loose, and I'd have an army, Caramon thought suddenly. He toyed with the idea of stopping a moment and unlocking the cell doors, when suddenly he heard a terrible howling sound and shouting coming from somewhere ahead of him.

Recognizing Berem's roar, Caramon plunged ahead. The cells came to an end, the corridor narrowed to a tunnel that cut a deep spiral well into the ground. Torches glimmered on the walls, but they were few and spaced far between. Caramon ran down the tunnel, the roar growing louder as he drew closer. The big warrior tried to hurry, but the floor was slick and slimy, the air became danker and heavy with moisture the farther down he went. Afraid he might slip and fall, he was forced to slow his pace. The shouts were closer, just ahead of him. The tunnel grew lighter, he must be coming near the end.

And then he saw Berem. Two draconians were slashing at him, their swords gleaming in the torchlight. Berem fought them off with his bare hands as light from the green gemstone lit the small enclosed chamber with an eerie brilliance.

It was a mark of Berem's insane strength that he had held them off this long. Blood ran freely from a cut across his face and flowed from a deep gash in his side. Even as Caramon dashed to his aid, slipping in the muck, Berem grasped a draconian's sword blade in his hand just as its point touched his chest. The cruel steel bit into his flesh, but he was oblivious to pain. Blood poured down his arm as he turned the blade and—

with a heave—shoved the draconian backwards. Then he staggered, gasping for breath. The other draconian guard closed in for the kill.

Intent upon their prey, the guards never saw Caramon. Leaping out of the tunnel, Caramon remembered just in time not to stab the creatures or he risked losing his sword. Grabbing one of the guards in his huge hands, he twisted its head, neatly snapping its neck. Dropping the body, he met the other draconian's savage lunge with a quick chopping motion of his hand to the creature's throat. It pitched backwards.

"Berem, are you all right?" Caramon turned and was starting to help Berem when he suddenly felt a searing pain rip through his side.

Gasping in agony, he staggered around to see a draconian behind him. Apparently it had been hiding in the shadows, perhaps at hearing Caramon's coming. Its sword thrust should have killed, but it was aimed in haste and slanted off Caramon's mail armor. Scrabbling for his own sword, Caramon stumbled backwards to gain time.

The draconian didn't intend giving him any. Raising its blade, it lunged at Caramon.

There was a blur of movement, a flash of green light, and the draconian fell dead at Caramon's feet.

"Berem!" Caramon gasped, pressing his hand over his side. "Thanks! How—"

But the Everman stared at Caramon without recognition. Then, nodding slowly, he turned and started to walk away.

"Wait!" Caramon called. Gritting his teeth against the pain, the big man jumped over the draconian bodies and hurled himself after Berem. Clutching his arm, he dragged the man to a stop. "Wait, damn it!" he repeated, holding on to him.

The sudden movement took its toll. The room swam before his eyes, forcing Caramon to stand still a moment, fighting the pain of his injury. When he could see again, he looked around, getting his bearings.

"Where are we?" he asked without expecting an answer, just wanting Berem to hear the sound of his voice.

"Far, far below the Temple," Berem replied in a hollow tone. "I am close. Very close now."

"Yeah," Caramon agreed without understanding. Keeping a fast hold on Berem, he continued to look around. The stone stairs he had come down ended in a small circular chamber. A guardroom, he realized, seeing an old table and several chairs sitting beneath a torch on the wall. It made sense. The draconians down here must have been guards. Berem had stumbled on them accidentally. But what could the draconians have been guarding?

Caramon glanced quickly around the small stone chamber but saw nothing. The room was perhaps twenty paces in diameter, carved out of rock. The spiral stone stairs ended in this room and—across from them—an archway led out. It was toward this archway Berem had been walking when Caramon caught hold of him. Peering through the arch, Caramon saw nothing. It was dark beyond, so dark Caramon felt as if he were staring into the Great Darkness the legends spoke of. Darkness that had existed in the void long before the gods created light.

The only sound he could hear was the gurgling and splash of water. An underground stream, he thought, which accounted for the humid air. Stepping back a pace, he examined the archway above him.

It was not carved out of the rock as was the small chamber they were in. It had been built of stone, crafted by expert hands. He could see vague outlines of elaborate carvings that had once decorated it, but he could make nothing out. They had long ago been worn away by time and the moisture in the air.

As he studied the arch, hoping for a clue to guide him, Caramon nearly fell as Berem clutched at him with sudden, fierce energy.

"I know you!" the man cried.

"Sure," Caramon grunted. "What in the name of the Abyss are you doing down here?"

"Jasla calls . . ." Berem said, the wild look glazing his eyes once more. Turning, he stared into the darkness beyond the archway. "In there, I must go. . . . Guards . . . tried to stop me. You come with me."

Then Caramon realized that the guards must have been guarding this arch! For what reason? What was beyond? Had they recognized Berem or were they simply acting under orders to keep everyone out? He didn't know the answers to any of these questions, and then it occurred to him that the answers didn't matter. Neither did the questions.

"You have to go in there," he said to Berem. It was a statement, not a question. Berem nodded and took a step forward eagerly. He would have walked straight into the darkness if Caramon hadn't jerked him back.

"Wait, we'll need light," the big man said with a sigh. "Stay put!" Patting Berem on the arm, then keeping his gaze fixed on him, Caramon backed up until his groping hand came into contact with a torch on the wall. Lifting it from its sconce, he returned to Berem.

"I'll go with you," he said heavily, wondering how long he could keep going before he collapsed from pain and loss of blood. "Here, hold that a minute." Handing Berem the torch, he tore off a strip of cloth from the ragged remains of Berem's shirt and bound it firmly around the wound in his side. Then, taking the torch back, he led the way beneath the arch.

Passing between the stone supports, Caramon felt something brush across his face. "Cobweb!" he muttered, pawing at it in disgust. He glanced around fearfully, having a dread of spiders. But there was nothing there. Shrugging, he thought no more of it and continued through the arch, drawing Berem after him.

The air was split with trumpet blasts.

"Trapped!" Caramon said grimly.

"Tika!" Tas gasped proudly as they ran down the gloomy dungeon corridor. "Your plan worked." The kender risked a glance over his shoulder. "Yes," he said breathlessly, "I think they're *all* following *us!*"

"Wonderful," muttered Tika. Somehow she hadn't expected her plan to work quite so well. No other plans she had ever made in her life had worked out. Wouldn't you know this would be a first? She, too, cast a quick glance over her shoulder. There must be six or seven draconians chasing after them, their long curved swords in the clawed hands.

Though the claw-footed draconians could not run as swiftly as either the girl or the kender, they had incredible endurance. Tika and Tas had a good head start, but it wasn't going to last. She was already panting for breath, and there was a sharp pain in her side that made her want to double over in agony.

But every second I keep running gives Caramon a little more time, she told herself. I draw the draconians just that much farther away.

"Say, Tika"—Tas's tongue was hanging out of his mouth, his face, cheerful as always, was pale with fatigue—"do you know where we're going?"

Tika shook her head. She hadn't breath left to speak. She felt herself slowing, her legs were like lead. Another look back showed her that the draconians were gaining. Quickly she glanced around, hoping to find another corridor branching off from this main one, or even a niche, a doorway—any kind of hiding place. There was nothing. The corridor stretched before them, silent and empty. There weren't even any cells. It was a long, narrow, smooth, and seemingly endless stone tunnel that sloped gradually upwards.

Then a sudden realization nearly brought her up short. Slowing, gasping for breath, she stared at Tas, who was only dimly visible in the light of smoking torches.

"The tunnel . . . it's rising . . ." She coughed.

Tas blinked at her uncomprehendingly, then his face brightened.

"It leads up and out!" he shouted jubilantly. "You've done it, Tika!"

"Maybe . . ." Tika said, hedging.

"Come on!" Tas yelled in excitement, finding new energy. Grabbing Tika's hand, he pulled her along. "I know you're right, Tika! Smell"—he sniffed—"fresh air! We'll escape . . . and find Tanis . . . and come back and . . . rescue Caramon—"

Only a kender could talk and run headlong down a corridor being chased by draconians at the same time, Tika thought wearily. She was being carried forward by sheer terror now, she knew. And soon that would leave her. Then she would collapse here in the tunnel, so tired and aching she wouldn't care what the draconians—

Then, "Fresh air!" she whispered.

She had honestly thought Tas was lying just to keep her going. But now she could feel a soft whisper of wind touch her cheek. Hope lightened her leaden legs. Glancing back, she thought she saw the draconians slowing. Maybe they realize they'll never catch us now! Exultation swept over her.

"Hurry, Tas!" she yelled. Together they both raced with renewed energy up the corridor, the sweet air blowing stronger and stronger all the time.

Running headfirst around a corner, they both came up short so suddenly that Tasslehoff skidded on some loose gravel and slammed up against a wall.

"So this is why they slowed down," Tika said softly.

The corridor came to an end. Two barred wooden doors sealed it shut. Small windows set into the doors, covered with iron gratings, allowed the night air to blow into the dungeon She and Tas could see outside, they could see freedom—but they could not reach it.

"Don't give up!" Tas said after a moment's pause. Recovering quickly, he ran over and pulled on the doors. They were locked.

"Drat," Tas muttered, eyeing the doors expertly. Caramon might have been able to batter his way through them, or break the lock with a blow of his sword. But not the kender, not Tika.

As Tas bent down to examine the lock, Tika leaned against a wall, wearily closing her eyes. Blood beat in her head, the muscles in her legs knotted in painful spasms. Exhausted, she tasted the bitter salt of tears in her mouth and realized she was sobbing in pain and anger and frustration.

"Don't, Tika!" Tas said, hurrying back to pat her hand. "It's a simple lock. I can get us out of here in no time. Don't cry, Tika. It'll only take me a little while, but you ought to be ready for those draconians if they come. Just keep them busy—"

"Right," Tika said, swallowing her tears. Hurriedly she wiped her nose with the back of her hand, then, sword in hand, she turned to face the corridor behind them while Tas took another look at the lock.

It was a simple, simple lock, he saw with satisfaction, guarded by such a simple trap he wondered why they even bothered.

Wondered why they even bothered . . . Simple lock . . . simple trap . . . The words rang in his mind. They were familiar! He'd thought them before. . . . Staring up at the doors in astonishment, Tas realized he'd *been* here before! But no, that was impossible.

Shaking his head irritably, Tas fumbled in his pouch for his tools. Then he stopped. Cold fear gripped the kender and shook him like a dog shakes a rat, leaving him limp.

The dream!

These had been the doors he saw in the Silvanesti dream! This had been the lock. The simple, simple lock with the simple trap! And Tika had been behind him, fighting . . . dying. . . .

"Here they come, Tas!" Tika called, gripping her sword in sweating hands. She cast him a quick glance over her shoulder. "What are you doing? What are you waiting for?"

317

Tas couldn't answer. He could hear the draconians now, laughing in their harsh voices as they took their time reaching their captives, certain the prisoners weren't going any place. They rounded the corner and Tas heard their laughter grow louder when they saw Tika holding the sword.

"I—I don't think I can, Tika," Tas whimpered, staring at the lock in horror.

"Tas," said Tika swiftly and grimly, backing up to talk to him without taking her eyes off her enemies, "we can't let ourselves be captured! They know about Berem! They'll try to make us tell what *we* know about him, Tas! And you know what they'll do to us to make us talk—"

"You're right!" said Tas miserably. "I'll try."

You've got the courage to walk it . . . Fizban had told him. Taking a deep breath, Tasslehoff pulled a thin wire out of one of his pouches. After all, he told his shaking hands sternly, what is death to a kender but the greatest adventure of all? And then there's Flint out there, by himself. Probably getting into all sorts of scraps. . . . His hands now quite steady, Tas inserted the wire carefully into the lock and set to work.

Suddenly there was a harsh roar behind him; he heard Tika shout and the sound of steel clashing against steel.

Tas dared a quick look. Tika had never learned the art of swordsmanship, but she was a skilled barroom brawler. Hacking and slashing with the blade, she kicked and gouged and bit and battered. The fury and ferocity of her attack drove the draconians back a pace. All of them were slashed and bleeding; one wallowed in green blood on the floor, its arm hanging uselessly.

But she couldn't hold them off much longer. Tas turned back to his work, but now his hands trembled, the slender tool slipped out of his clammy grasp. The trick was to spring the lock without springing the trap. He could see the trap—a tiny needle held in place by a coiled spring.

Stop it! he ordered himself. Was this any way for a kender to act? He inserted the wire again carefully, his hands steady once more. Suddenly, just as he almost had it, he was jostled from behind.

"Hey," he shouted irritably at Tika, turning around. "Be a little more careful—" He stopped short. The dream! He had said those exact words. And—as in the dream—he saw Tika, lying at his feet, blood flowing into her red curls.

"No!" Tas shrieked in rage. The wire slipped, his hand struck the lock.

There was a click as the lock opened. And with the click came another small sound, a brittle sound, barely heard; a sound like "snick." The trap was sprung.

Wide-eyed, Tas stared at the tiny spot of blood on his finger, then at the small golden needle protruding from the lock. The draconians had him now, grasping him by the shoulder. Tas ignored them. It didn't matter anyway. There was a stinging pain in his finger and soon the pain would spread up his arm and throughout his body.

When it reaches my heart, I won't feel it anymore, he told himself dreamily. I won't feel anything.

Then he heard horns, blaring horns, brass horns. He had heard those horns before. Where? That's right. It was in Tarsis, right before the dragons came.

And then the draconians that had been hanging on to him were gone, running frantically back down the corridor.

"Must be some sort of general alarm," Tas thought, noticing with interest that his legs wouldn't hold him up anymore. He slid down to the floor, down beside Tika. Reaching out a shaking hand, he gently stroked her pretty red curls, now matted with blood. Her face was white, her eyes closed.

"I'm sorry, Tika," Tas said, his throat constricting. The pain was spreading quickly, his fingers and feet had gone numb. He couldn't move them. "I'm sorry, Caramon. I tried, I truly tried—" Weeping quietly, Tas sat back against the door and waited for the darkness.

Tanis could not move and—for a moment, hearing Laurana's heartbroken sob—he had no wish to move. If anything, he begged a merciful god to strike him dead as he knelt before the Dark Queen. But the gods granted him no such favor. The shadow lifted as the Queen's attention shifted elsewhere, away from him. Tanis struggled to his feet, his face flushed with shame. He could not look at Laurana, he dared not even meet Kitiara's eyes, knowing well the scorn he would see in their brown depths.

But Kitiara had more important matters on her mind. This was her moment of glory. Her plans were coming together. Thrusting out her hand, she caught Tanis in her strong grip as he was about to come forward to offer himself as escort to

Laurana. Coldly, she shoved him backward and moved to stand in front of him.

"Finally, I wish to reward a servant of my own who helped me capture the elfwoman. Lord Soth has asked that he be granted the soul of this Lauralanthalasa, that he might thus gain his revenge over the elfwoman who—long ago—cast the curse upon him. If he be doomed to live in eternal darkness, then he asks that this elfwoman share his life within death."

"No!" Laurana raised her head, fear and horror penetrating her numb senses. "No," she repeated in a strangled voice.

Taking a step backwards, she looked about her wildly for some escape, but it was impossible. Below her, the floor writhed with draconians, staring up at her eagerly. Choking in despair, she glanced once at Tanis. His face was dark and forbidding; he was not looking at her, but stared with burning eyes at the human woman. Already regretting her wretched outburst, Laurana determined that she would die before she gave way to any further weakness in front of either of them, ever again. Drawing herself up proudly, she lifted her head, in control once more.

Tanis did not even see Laurana. Kitiara's words beat like blood in his head, clouding his vision and his thoughts. Furious, he took a step forward to stand near Kitiara. "You betrayed me!" he choked. "This was not part of the plan!"

"Hush!" ordered Kit in a low voice. "Or you will destroy everything!"

"What—"

"Shut up!" Kitiara snapped viciously.

Your gift pleases me well, Lord Kitiara. The dark voice penetrated Tanis's anger. *I grant your requests. The elfwoman's soul will be given to Lord Soth, and we accept the half-elf into our service. In recognition of this, he will lay his sword at the feet of Lord Ariakas.*

"Well, go on!" demanded Kitiara coldly, her eyes on Tanis. The eyes of everyone in the room were on the half-elf.

His mind swam. "What?" he muttered. "You didn't tell me this! What do I do?"

"Ascend the platform and lay your sword at Ariakas's feet," Kitiara answered swiftly, escorting him to the edge of the platform. "He will pick it up and return it to you, then you will be an officer in the dragonarmies. It is ritual, nothing more. But it buys me time."

"Time for what? What do you have planned?" Tanis asked harshly, his foot on the stair leading down. He caught hold of her arm. "You should have told me—"

"The less you know the better, Tanis." Kitiara smiled charmingly, for the sake of those watching. There was some nervous laughter, a few crude jokes at what appeared to be a lover's parting. But Tanis saw no answering smile in Kit's brown eyes. "Remember who stands next to me upon this platform," Kitiara whispered. Caressing the hilt of her sword, Kit gave Laurana a meaningful glance. "Do nothing rash." Turning away from him, she walked back to stand beside Laurana.

Trembling in fear and rage, his thoughts whirling in confusion, Tanis stumbled down the stairs leading from the snake's-head platform. The noise of the assembly rolled around him like the crash of oceans. Light flashed off spearpoints, the torch flames blurred in his vision. He set his foot upon the floor and began to walk toward Ariakas's platform without any clear idea of where he was or what he was doing. Moving by reflex alone, he made his way across the marble floor.

The faces of the draconians who made up Ariakas's guard of honor floated around him like a hideous nightmare. He saw them as disembodied heads, rows of gleaming teeth, and flicking tongues. They parted before him, the stairs materialized at his feet as if rising out of fog.

Lifting his head, he stared up bleakly. At the top stood Lord Ariakas; a huge man, majestic, armed with power. All the light in the room seemed to be drawn into the Crown upon his head. Its brilliance dazzled the eyes, and Tanis blinked, blinded, as he began to climb the steps, his hand on his sword.

Had Kitiara betrayed him? Would she keep her promise? Tanis doubted it. Bitterly he cursed himself. Once more he had fallen under her spell. Once more he had played the fool, trusting her. And now she held all the gamepieces. There was nothing he could do . . . or was there?

An idea came to Tanis so suddenly he stopped, one foot on one step, the other on the step below.

Idiot! Keep walking, he commanded, feeling everyone staring at him. Forcing himself to retain some outward semblance of calm, Tanis climbed up another step and another. As he drew closer and closer to Lord Ariakas, the plan became clearer and clearer.

Whoever holds the Crown, rules! The words rang in Tanis's

mind.

Kill Ariakas, take the Crown! It will be simple! Tanis's gaze flashed around the alcove feverishly. No guards stood beside Ariakas, of course. No one but Highlords were allowed on the platforms. But he didn't even have guards on the stairs as did the other Highlords. Apparently the man was so arrogant, so secure in his power, he had dispensed with them.

Tanis's thoughts raced. Kitiara will trade her soul for that Crown. And as long as I hold it, she will be *mine* to command! I can save Laurana . . . we can escape together! Once we are safely out of here, I can explain things to Laurana, I can explain everything! I'll draw my sword, but instead of placing it at Lord Ariakas's feet, I will run it through him! Once the Crown is in my hand, no one will dare touch me!

Tanis found himself shaking with excitement. With an effort, he forced himself to calm down. He could not look at Ariakas, fearing the man might see his desperate plan in his eyes.

He kept his gaze upon the stairs, therefore, and he knew he was near Lord Ariakas only when he saw five steps remained between himself and the top of the platform. Tanis's hand twitched upon the sword. Feeling himself under control, he raised his gaze to look into the man's face and, for an instant, was almost unnerved at the evil revealed there. It was a face made passionless by ambition, a face that had seen the deaths of thousands of innocents as the means only to an end.

Ariakas had been watching Tanis with a bored expression, a smile of amused contempt on his face. Then he lost interest in the half-elf completely, having other matters to worry about. Tanis saw the man's gaze go to Kitiara, pondering. Ariakas had the look of a player leaning across a gameboard, contemplating his next move, trying to guess what his opponent intends.

Filled with revulsion and hatred, Tanis began to slide the blade of his sword from its scabbard. Even if he failed in his attempt to save Laurana, even if they both died within these walls, at least he would accomplish some good in the world by by killing the Commander of the Dragonarmies.

But as he heard Tanis draw his sword, Ariakas's eyes flashed back to the half-elf once again. Their black stare penetrated Tanis's soul. He felt the man's tremendous power overwhelm him, hitting him like a blast of heat from a furnace. And then realization struck Tanis a blow almost physical in its impact, nearly causing him to stagger on the stairs.

That aura of power surrounding him . . . Ariakas was a magic-user!

Blind stupid fool! Tanis cursed himself. For now, as he drew nearer, he saw a shimmering wall surrounding the Lord. Of course, that's why there were no guards! Among this crowd, Ariakas would trust no one. He would use his own magic to guard himself!

And he was on his guard, now. That much Tanis could read clearly in the cold, passionless eyes.

The half-elf's shoulders slumped. He was defeated.

And then, "Strike, Tanis! Do not fear his magic! I will aid you!"

The voice was no more than a whisper, yet so clear and so intense, Tanis could practically feel hot breath touch his ear. His hair raised on the back of his neck, a shudder convulsed his body.

Shivering, he glanced hastily around. There was no one near him, no one except Ariakas! He was only three steps away, scowling, obviously anxious for this ceremony to come to an end. Seeing Tanis hesitate, Ariakas made a peremptory motion for the half-elf to lay his sword at his feet.

Who had spoken? Suddenly Tanis's eyes were caught by the sight of a figure standing near the Queen of Darkness. Robed in black, it had escaped his notice before. Now he stared at it, thinking it seemed familiar. Had the voice come from that figure? If so, the figure made no sign or movement. What should he do? he wondered frantically.

"Strike, Tanis!" whispered once more in his brain. "Swiftly!"

Sweating, his hand shaking, Tanis slowly drew his sword. He was level with Ariakas now. The shimmering wall of the Lord's magic surrounded him like a rainbow glittering off sparkling water.

I have no choice, Tanis said to himself. If it is a trap, so be it. I choose this way to die.

Feigning to kneel, holding his sword hilt-first to lay it upon the marble platform, Tanis suddenly reversed his stroke. Turning it into a killing blow, he lunged for Ariakas's heart.

Tanis expected to die. Gritting his teeth as he struck, he braced himself for the magic shield to wither him like a tree struck by lightning.

And lightning *did* strike, but not him! To his amazement, the rainbow wall exploded, his sword penetrated. He felt it hit solid flesh. A fierce cry of pain and outrage nearly deafened him.

Ariakas staggered backwards as the sword blade slid into his chest. A lesser man would have died from that blow, but Ariakas's strength and anger held Death at bay. His face twisted in hatred, he struck Tanis across the face, sending him reeling to the floor of the platform.

Pain burst in Tanis's head. Dimly, he saw his sword fall beside him, red with blood. For a moment, he thought he was going to lose consciousness and that would mean his death, his death and Laurana's. Groggily he shook his head to clear it. He must hang on! He must gain the Crown! Looking up, he saw Ariakas looming above him, hands lifted, prepared to cast a spell that would end Tanis's life.

Tanis could do nothing. He had no protection against the magic and somehow he knew that his unseen helper would help no more. It had already achieved what it desired.

But powerful as Ariakas was, there was a greater power he could not conquer. He choked, his mind wavered, the words of magic spell were lost in a terrible pain. Looking down, he saw his own blood stain the purple robes, the stain grew larger and larger with each passing moment as his life poured from his severed heart. Death was coming to claim him. He could stave it off no longer. Desperately Ariakas battled the darkness, crying out at the last to his Dark Queen for help.

But she abandoned weaklings. As she had watched Ariakas strike down his father, so she watched Ariakas himself fall, her name the last sound to pass his lips.

There was uneasy silence in the Hall of Audience as Ariakas's body tumbled to the floor. The Crown of Power fell from his head with a clatter and lay within a tangle of blood and thick, black hair.

Who would claim it?

There was a piercing scream. Kitiara called out a name, called to someone.

Tanis could not understand. He didn't care anyway. He stretched out his hand for the Crown.

Suddenly a figure in black armor materialized before him. Lord Soth!

Fighting down a feeling of sheer panic and terror, Tanis kept his mind focused on one thing. The Crown was only inches beyond his fingers. Desperately he lunged for it. Thankfully he felt the cold metal bite into his flesh just as another hand—a skeletal hand—made a grab for it, too.

It was his! Soth's burning eyes flared. The skeletal hand reached out to wrest the prize away. Tanis could hear Kitiara's voice, shrieking incoherent commands.

But as he lifted the blood-stained piece of metal above his head, as his eyes fixed unafraid upon Lord Soth, the hushed silence in the Hall was split by the sound of horns, harsh blaring horns.

Lord Soth's hand paused in mid-air, Kitiara's voice fell suddenly silent.

There was a subdued, ominous murmur from the crowd. For an instant, Tanis's pain-clouded mind thought the horns might be sounding in his honor. But then, turning his head to peer dimly into the Hall, he saw faces glancing around in alarm. Everyone—even Kitiara—looked at the Dark Queen.

Her Dark Majesty's shadowy eyes had been on Tanis, but now their gaze was abstracted. Her shadow grew and intensified, spreading through the Hall like a dark cloud. Reacting to some unspoken command, draconians wearing her black insignia ran from their posts around the edge of the Hall and disappeared through the doors. The black-robed figure Tanis had seen standing beside the Queen vanished.

And still the horns blared. Holding the Crown in his hand, Tanis stared down at it numbly. Twice before, the harsh blaring of the horns had brought death and destruction. What was the terrible portent of the dread music this time?

IO

"Whoever wears the Crown, rules."

So loud and startling was the sound of the horns that Caramon nearly lost his footing on the wet stone. Reacting instinctively, Berem caught him. Both men stared around them in alarm as the blaring trumpet calls dinned loudly in the small chamber. Above them—up the stairs—they could hear answering trumpet calls.

"The arch! It was trapped!" Caramon repeated. "Well, that's done it. Every living thing in the Temple knows we're here, wherever here is! I hope to the gods you know what you're doing!"

"Jasla calls—" Berem repeated. His momentary alarm at the blaring trumpets dissipating, he continued forward, tugging Caramon along behind him.

Holding the torch aloft, not knowing what else to do or where else to go, Caramon followed. They were in a cavern apparently cut through the rock by flowing water. The archway led to stone stairs and these stairs, Caramon saw, led straight down into a black, swiftly flowing stream. He flashed the torch around, hoping that there might be a path along the edge of the stream. But there was nothing, at least within the perimeter of his torchlight.

"Wait—" he cried, but Berem had already plunged into the black water. Caramon caught his breath, expecting to see the man vanish in the swirling depths. But the dark water was not as deep as it looked, it came only to Berem's calves.

"Come!" He beckoned Caramon.

Caramon touched the wound in his side again. The bleeding seemed to have slowed, the bandage was moist but not soaked. The pain was still intense, however. His head ached, and he was so exhausted from fear and running and loss of blood that he was light-headed. He thought briefly of Tika and Tas, even more briefly of Tanis. No, he must put them out of his mind.

The end is near, for good or for evil, Tika had said. Caramon was beginning to believe it himself. Stepping into the water, he felt the strong current sweeping him forward and he had the giddy feeling that the current was time, sweeping him ahead to—what? His own doom? The end of the world? Or hope for a new beginning?

Berem eagerly sloshed ahead of him, but Caramon dragged him back again.

"We'll stick together," the big man said, his deep voice echoing in the cavern. "There may be more traps, worse than that one."

Berem hesitated long enough for Caramon to join him. Then they moved slowly, side by side, through the rushing water, testing each footstep, for the bottom was slick and treacherous with crumbling stone and loose rock.

Caramon was wading forward, breathing easier, when something struck his leather boot with such force it nearly knocked his feet out from under him. Staggering, he caught hold of Berem.

"What was that?" he growled, holding the flaring torch

above the water.

Seemingly attracted by the light, a head lifted out of the shining wet blackness. Caramon sucked in his breath in horror, and even Berem was momentarily taken aback.

"Dragons!" Caramon whispered. "Hatchlings!" The small dragon opened its mouth in a shrill scream. Torchlight gleamed on rows of razor-sharp teeth. Then the head vanished and Caramon felt the creature strike at his boot once more. Another one hit his other leg; he saw the water boil with flailing tails.

His leather boots kept them from hurting him now, but, Caramon thought, if I fall, the creatures will strip the flesh from my bones!

He had faced death in many forms, but none more terrifying than this. For a moment he panicked. I'll turn back, he thought frantically. Berem can go on alone. After all, *he* can't die.

Then the big warrior took hold of himself. No, he sighed. They know we're down here now. They'll send someone or something to try and stop us. I've got to hold off whatever it is until Berem can do whatever he's supposed to do.

That last thought made no sense at all, Caramon realized. It was so ludicrous it was almost funny and, as if mocking his decision, the quiet was broken by the sound of clashing steel and harsh shouts, coming from behind them.

This is insane! he admitted wearily. I don't understand! I may die down here in the darkness and for what? Maybe I'm down here with a crazy man! Maybe *I'm* going crazy!

Now Berem became aware of the guards coming after them. This frightened him more than dragons, and he plunged ahead. Sighing, Caramon forced himself to ignore the slithering attacks at his feet and legs as he waded forward through the black, rushing water, trying to keep up with Berem.

The man stared constantly ahead into the darkness, occasionally making moaning sounds and wringing his hands in anxiety. The stream led them around a curve where the water grew deeper. Caramon wondered what he would do if the water rose higher than his boots. The dragon young were still frantically chasing after them, the warm smell of human blood and flesh driving them into a frenzy. The sounds of sword and spear rattling grew louder.

Then something blacker than night flew at Caramon, striking him in the face. Flailing, trying desperately to keep from falling into that deadly water, he dropped his torch. The light vanished with a sizzle as Berem made a wild grab for him and caught him. The two held onto each other for a moment, staring—lost and confused—into the darkness.

If he had been struck blind, Caramon could not have been more disoriented. Though he had not moved, he had no idea what direction he faced, he couldn't remember a thing about his surroundings. He had the feeling that if he took one more step, he would plunge into nothingness and fall forever. . . .

"There it is!" Berem said, catching his breath with a strangled sob. "I see the broken column, the jewels gleaming on it! And she is there! She is waiting for me, she has waited all these years! Jasla!" he screamed, straining forward.

Peering ahead into the darkness, Caramon held Berem back, though he could feel the man's body quivering with emotion. He could see nothing . . . or could he?

Yes! A deep sense of thankfulness and relief flooded his pain-racked body. He *could* see jewels sparkling in the distance, shining in the blackness with a light it seemed even this heavy darkness could not quench.

It was just a short distance ahead of them, not more than a hundred feet. Relaxing his grip on Berem, Caramon thought, Perhaps this is a way out—for me, at least. Let Berem join this ghostly sister of his. All I want is a way out, a way to get back to Tika and Tas.

His confidence returning, Caramon strode forward. A matter of minutes and it would be over . . . for good . . . or for . . .

"*Shirak,*" spoke a voice.

A bright light flared.

Caramon's heart ceased to beat for an instant. Slowly, slowly he lifted his head to look into that bright light, and there he saw two golden, glittering, hourglass eyes staring at him from the depths of a black hood.

The breath left his body in a sigh that was like the sigh of a dying man.

The blaring trumpets ceased, a measure of calm returned to the Hall of Audience. Once more, the eyes of everyone in the Hall—including the Dark Queen—turned to the drama on the platform.

Gripping the Crown in his hand, Tanis rose to his feet. He had no idea what the horn calls portended, what doom might be about to fall. He only knew that he must play the game out to its end, bitter as that may be.

Laurana . . . she was his one thought. Wherever Berem and Caramon and the others were, they were beyond his help. Tanis's eyes fixed on the silver-armored figure standing on the snake-headed platform below him. Almost by accident, his gaze flicked to Kitiara, standing beside Laurana, her face hidden behind the hideous dragonmask. She made a gesture.

Tanis felt more than heard movement behind him, like a chill wind brushing his skin. Whirling, he saw Lord Soth coming toward him, death burning in the orange eyes.

Tanis backed up, the Crown in his hand, knowing he could not fight this opponent from beyond the grave.

"Stop!" he shouted, holding the Crown poised above the floor of the Hall of Audience. "Stop him, Kitiara, or with my last dying strength I will hurl this into the crowd."

Soth laughed soundlessly, advancing upon him, the skeletal hand that could kill by a touch alone outstretched.

"What 'dying strength?' " the death knight asked softly. "My magic will shrivel your body to dust, the Crown will fall at my feet."

"Lord Soth," rang out a clear voice from the platform from the center of the Hall, "halt. Let him who won the Crown bring it to me!"

Soth hesitated. His hand still reaching for Tanis, his flaming eyes turned their vacant gaze upon Kitiara, questioning.

Removing the dragonhelm from her head, Kitiara looked only at Tanis. He could see her brown eyes gleaming and her cheeks flushed with excitement.

"You will bring me the Crown, won't you, Tanis?" Kitiara called.

Tanis swallowed. "Yes," he said, licking his dry lips. "I will bring you the Crown."

"My guards!" Kitiara ordered, waving them forward. "An escort. Anyone who touches him will die by my hand. Lord Soth, see that he reaches me safely."

Tanis glanced at Lord Soth, who slowly lowered his deadly hand. "He is your master, still, my lady," Tanis thought he heard the death knight whisper with a sneer.

Then Soth fell into step beside him, the ghostly chill emanating from the knight nearly congealing Tanis's blood. Together they descended the stairs, an odd pair—the pallid knight in the blackened armor, the half-elf clutching the blood-stained Crown in his hand.

Ariakas's officers, who had been standing at the foot of the stairs, weapons drawn, fell back, some reluctantly. As Tanis reached the marble floor and passed by them, many gave him black looks. He saw the flash of a dagger in one hand, an unspoken promise in the dark eyes.

Their own swords drawn, Kitiara's guards fell in around him, but it was Lord Soth's deathly aura that obtained safe passage for him through the crowded floor. Tanis began to sweat beneath his armor. So this is power, he realized. Whoever has the Crown, rules—but that could all end in the dead of night with one thrust of an assassin's dagger!

Tanis kept walking, and soon he and Lord Soth reached the bottom of the stairs leading up to the platform shaped like the head of the hooded snake. At the top stood Kitiara, beautiful in triumph. Tanis climbed the spurlike stairs alone, leaving Soth standing at the bottom, his orange eyes burning in their hollow sockets. As Tanis reached the top of the platform, the top of the snake's head, he could see Laurana, standing behind Kitiara. Laurana's face was pale, cool, composed. She glanced at him—and at the blood-stained Crown—then turned her head away. He had no idea what she was thinking or feeling. It didn't matter. He would explain—

Running over to him, Kitiara grasped him in her arms. Cheers resounded in the Hall.

"Tanis!" she breathed. "Truly you and I were meant to rule together! You were wonderful, magnificent! I will give you anything . . . anything—"

"Laurana?" Tanis asked coldly, under the cover of the noise. His slightly slanted eyes, the eyes that gave away his heritage, stared down into Kitiara's brown eyes.

Kit flicked a glance at the elfwoman, whose gaze was so fixed, whose skin was so pale she might have been a corpse.

"If you want her," Kitiara shrugged, then drew closer, her voice for him alone. "But you will have me, Tanis. By day we will command armies, rule the world. The nights, Tanis! They will be ours alone, yours and mine." Her breath came fast, her hands reached up to stroke his bearded face. "Place the Crown on my head, beloved."

Tanis stared down into the brown eyes, he saw them filled with warmth and passion and excitement. He could feel

Kitiara's body pressed against his, trembling, eager. Around him, the troops were shouting madly, the noise swelling like a wave. Slowly Tanis raised the hand that held the Crown of Power, slowly he lifted it—not to Kitiara's head—but to his own.

"No, Kitiara," he shouted so that all could hear. "One of us will rule by day *and* by night—me."

There was laughter in the Hall, mixed with angry rumblings. Kitiara's eyes widened in shock, then swiftly narrowed.

"Don't try it," Tanis said, catching her hand as she reached for the knife at her belt. Holding her fast, he looked down at her. "I'm going to leave the Hall now," he said softly, speaking for her ears alone, "with Laurana. You and your troops will escort us out of here. When we are safely outside this evil place, I will give you the Crown. Betray me, and you will never hold it. Do you understand?"

Kitiara's lips twisted in a sneer. "So *she* is truly all you care about?" she whispered caustically.

"Truly," Tanis replied. Gripping her arm harder, he saw pain in her eyes. "I swear this on the souls of two I loved dearly— Sturm Brightblade and Flint Fireforge. Do you believe me?"

"I believe you," Kitiara said in bitter anger. Looking up at him, reluctant admiration flared once more in her eyes. "You could have had so much . . ."

Tanis released her without a word. Turning, he walked over to Laurana, who was standing with her back to them, gazing sightlessly above the crowd. Tanis gripped her arm. "Come with me," he commanded coldly. The noise of the crowd rose up around him while above him, he was aware of the dark shadowy figure of the Queen, watching the flux of power intently, waiting to see who would emerge strongest.

Laurana did not flinch at his touch. She did not react at all. Moving her head slowly, the honey-blonde hair falling in a tangled mass around her shoulders, she looked at him. The green eyes were without recognition, expressionless. He saw nothing in them, not fear, not anger.

It will be all right, he told her silently, his heart aching. I will explain—

There was a flash of silver, a blur of golden hair. Something struck Tanis hard in the chest. He staggered backwards, grasping for Laurana as he stumbled. But he could not hold her.

Shoving him aside, Laurana sprang at Kitiara, her hand

grabbing for the sword Kit wore at her side. Her move caught the human woman completely by surprise. Kit struggled briefly, fiercely, but Laurana already had her hands upon the hilt. With a smooth movement, she yanked Kit's sword from the scabbard and jabbed the sword hilt into Kitiara's face, knocking her to the platform. Turning, Laurana ran to the edge.

"Laurana, stop!" Tanis shouted. Jumping forward to catch her, he suddenly felt the point of her sword at his throat.

"Don't move, Tanthalasa," Laurana ordered. Her green eyes were dilated with excitement, she held the sword point with unwavering steadiness. "Or you will die. I will kill you, if I have to."

Tanis took a step forward. The sharp blade pierced his skin. Helpless, he stopped. Laurana smiled sadly.

"You see, Tanis? I'm not the love-sick child you knew. I'm not my father's daughter, living in my father's court. I'm not even the Golden General. I am Laurana. And I will live or die on my own without your help."

"Laurana, listen to me!" Tanis pleaded, taking another step toward her, reaching up to thrust aside the sword blade that cut into his skin.

He saw Laurana's lips press together tightly, her green eyes glinted. Then, sighing, she slowly lowered the the sword blade to his armor-plated chest. Tanis smiled. Laurana shrugged and, with a swift thrust, shoved him backwards off the platform.

Arms flailing wildly in the air, the half-elf tumbled to the floor below. As he fell, he saw Laurana—sword in hand—jump off after him, landing lightly on her feet.

He hit the floor heavily, knocking the breath from his body. The Crown of Power rolled from his head with a clatter and went skittering across the polished granite floor. Above him, he could hear Kitiara shriek in rage.

"Laurana!" He gasped without breath to shout, looking for her frantically. He saw a flash of silver. . . .

"The Crown! Bring me the Crown!" Kitiara's voice dinned in his ears.

But she was not the only one shouting. All around the Hall of Audience, the Highlords were on their feet, ordering their troops forward. The dragons sprang into the air. The Dark Queen's five-headed body filled the Hall with shadow, exulting in this test of strength that would provide her with the strongest commanders—the survivors.

Clawed draconian feet, booted goblin feet, steel-shod human feet trampled over Tanis. Struggling to stand, fighting desperately to keep from being crushed, he tried to follow that silver flash. He saw it once, then it was gone, lost in the melee. A twisted face appeared in front of him, dark eyes flashed. A spear butt smashed into his side.

Groaning, Tanis collapsed to the floor as chaos erupted in the Hall of Audience.

II

"Jasla calls—"

Raistlin! It was a thought, not spoken. Caramon tried to talk, but no sound came from his throat.

"Yes, my brother," said Raistlin, answering his brother's thoughts, as usual. "It is I—the last guardian, the one you must pass to reach your goal, the one Her Dark Majesty commanded be present if the trumpets should sound." Raistlin smiled derisively. "And I might have known it would be you who foolishly tripped my spelltrap. . . ."

"Raist," Caramon began and choked.

For a moment he could not speak. Worn out from fear and pain and loss of blood, shivering in the cold water, Caramon found this almost too much to bear. It would be easier to let the dark waters close over his head, let the sharp teeth of the young dragons tear his flesh. The pain could not be nearly so bad. Then he felt Berem stir beside him. The man was staring at Raistlin vaguely, not understanding. He tugged on Caramon's arm.

"Jasla calls. We must go."

With a sob, Caramon tore his arm away from the man's grasp. Berem glared at him angrily, then turned and started ahead on his own.

"No, my friend, no one's going anywhere."

Raistlin raised his thin hand and Berem came to a sudden, staggering stop. The Everman lifted his gaze to the gleaming golden eyes of the mage, standing above him on a rock ledge. Whimpering, wringing his hands, Berem gazed ahead longingly at the jeweled column. But he could not move. A great and terrible force stood blocking his path, as surely as the mage stood upon the rock.

Caramon blinked back sudden tears. Feeling his brother's power, he fought against despair. There was nothing he could do . . . except try and kill Raistlin. His soul shriveled in horror. No, he would die himself first!

Suddenly Caramon raised his head. So be it. If I must die, I'll die fighting—as I had always intended.

Even if it means dying by my own brother's hand.

Slowly Caramon's gaze met that of his twin.

"You wear the Black Robes now?" he asked through parched lips. "I can't see . . . in this light. . . ."

"Yes, my brother," Raistlin replied, raising the Staff of Magius to let the silver light shine upon him. Robes of softest velvet fell from his thin shoulders, shimmering black beneath the light, seeming darker than the eternal night that surrounded them.

Shivering as he thought of what he must do, Caramon continued, "And your voice, it's stronger, different. Like you . . and yet not like you . . ."

"That is a long story, Caramon," Raistlin replied. "In time, you may come to hear it. But now you are in a very bad situation, my brother. The draconian guards are coming. Their orders are to capture the Everman and take him before the

Dark Queen. That will be the end of him. He is *not* immortal, I assure you. She has spells that will unravel his existence, leaving him little more than thin threads of flesh and soul, wafting away on the winds of the storm. Then she will devour his sister and—at last—the Dark Queen will be free to enter Krynn in her full power and majesty. She will rule the world and all the planes of heaven and the Abyss. Nothing will stop her."

"I don't understand—"

"No, of course not, dear brother," Raistlin said, with a touch of the old irritation and sarcasm. "You stand next to the Everman, the one being in all of Krynn who can end this war and drive the Queen of Darkness back to her shadowy realm. And you do not understand."

Moving nearer the edge of the rock ledge upon which he stood, Raistlin bent down, leaning on his staff. He beckoned his brother near. Caramon trembled, unable to move, fearing Raistlin might cast a spell upon him. But his brother only regarded him intently.

"The Everman has only to take a few more steps, my brother, and he will be reunited with the sister who has endured unspeakable agonies during these long years of waiting for his return to free her from her self-imposed torment."

"And what will happen then?" Caramon faltered, his brother's eyes holding him fast with a simple power greater than any magic spell.

The golden, hourglass eyes narrowed, Raistlin's voice grew soft. No longer forced to whisper, the mage yet found whispering more compelling.

"The wedge will be removed, my dear brother, and the door will slam shut. The Dark Queen will be left howling in rage in the depths of the Abyss." Raistlin lifted his gaze and made a gesture with his pale, slender hand. "This . . . the Temple of Istar reborn, perverted by evil .   will fall."

Caramon gasped, then his expression hardened into a scowl.

"No, I am not lying." Raistlin answered his brother's thoughts. "Not that I can't lie when it suits my purposes. But you will find, dear brother, that we are close enough still so that I cannot lie to you. And, in any case, I have no need to lie—it suits my purpose that you know the truth."

Caramon's mind floundered. He didn't understand any of this. But he didn't have time to dwell on it. Behind him, echoing back down the tunnel, he could hear the sound of draconian

---

guards on the stairs. His expression grew calm, his face set in firm resolve.

"Then you know what I must do, Raist," he said. "You may be powerful, but you still have to concentrate to work your magic. And if you work it against *me,* Berem will be free of your power. You can't kill him"—Caramon hoped devoutly Berem was listening and would act when it was time—"only your Dark Queen can do that, I suppose. So that leaves—"

"You, my dear brother," Raistlin said softly. "Yes, I can kill you. . . ."

Standing, he raised his hand and—before Caramon could yell or think or even fling up his arm—a ball of flame lit the darkness as if a sun had dropped into it. Bursting full upon Caramon, it smote him backwards into the black water.

Burned and blinded by the brilliant light, stunned by the force of the impact, Caramon felt himself losing consciousness, sinking beneath the dark waters. Then sharp teeth bit into his arm, tearing away the flesh. The searing pain brought back his failing senses. Screaming in agony and terror, Caramon fought frantically to rise out of the deadly stream.

Shivering uncontrollably, he stood up. The young dragons, having tasted blood, attacked him, striking at his leather boots in frenzied frustration. Clutching his arm, Caramon looked over quickly at Berem and saw, to his dismay, that Berem hadn't moved an inch.

"Jasla! I am here! I will free you!" Berem screamed, but he stood, frozen in place by the spell. Frantically he beat upon the unseen wall that blocked his path. The man was nearly insane with grief.

Raistlin watched calmly as his brother stood before him, blood streaming from the slashed skin on his bare arms.

"I am powerful, Caramon," Raistlin said, staring coldly into the anguished eyes of his twin. "With Tanis's unwitting help, I was able to rid myself of the one man upon Krynn who could have bested me. Now I am the most powerful force for magic in this world. And I will be more powerful still . . . with the Dark Queen gone!"

Caramon looked at his brother dazedly, unable to comprehend. Behind him, he heard splashes in the water and the draconians shouting in triumph. Too stupified to move, he could not take his eyes from his brother. Only dimly, when he saw Raistlin raise his hand and make a gesture toward Berem, did

Caramon begin to understand.

At that gesture, Berem was freed. The Everman cast one quick backward glance at Caramon and at the draconians plunging through the water, their curved swords flashing in the light of the staff. Finally he looked at Raistlin, standing upon the rock in his long black robes. Then—with a joyful cry that rang through the tunnel—Berem leaped forward toward the jeweled column.

"Jasla, I am coming!"

"Remember, my brother"—Raistlin's voice echoed in Caramon's mind—"this happens because *I* choose it to happen!"

Looking back, Caramon could see the draconians screaming in rage at the sight of their prey escaping. The dragons tore at his leather boots, his wounds hurt horribly, but Caramon didn't notice. Turning again, he watched Berem run toward the jeweled column as if he were watching a dream. Indeed, it seemed less real than a dream.

Perhaps it was his fevered imagination, but as the Everman neared the jeweled column, the green jewel in his chest seemed to glow with a light more brilliant than Raistlin's burst of flame. Within that light, the pale, shimmering form of a woman appeared inside the jeweled column. Dressed in a plain, leather tunic, she was pretty in a fragile, winsome way, very like Berem in the eyes that were too young for her thin face.

Then, just as he neared her, Berem came to a stop in the water. For an instant nothing moved. The draconians stood still, swords clutched in their clawed hands. Dimly, not understanding, they began to realize that somehow their fate hung in the balance, that everything turned upon this man.

Caramon no longer felt the chill of the air or the water or the pain of his wounds. He no longer felt fear, despair, or hope. Tears welled up in his eyes, there was a painful burning sensation in his throat. Berem faced his sister, the sister he had murdered, the sister who had sacrificed herself so that he—and the world—might have hope. By the light of Raistlin's staff, Caramon saw the man's pale, grief-ravaged face twist in anguish.

"Jasla," he whispered, spreading his arms, "can you forgive me?"

There was no sound except the hushed swirl of the water around them, the steady dripping of moisture from the rocks, as it had fallen from time immemorial.

"My brother, between us, there is nothing to forgive." The

image of Jasla spread her arms wide in welcome, her winsome face filled with peace and love.

With an incoherent cry of pain and joy, Berem flung himself into his sister's arms.

Caramon blinked and gasped. The image vanished. Horrified, he saw the Everman hurl his body upon the jeweled stone column with such force that his flesh was impaled on the sharp edges of the jagged rock. His last scream was a terrible one, terrible—yet triumphant.

Berem's body shook convulsively. Dark blood poured over the jewels, quenching their light.

"Berem, you've failed. It was nothing! A lie—" Yelling hoarsely, Caramon plunged toward the dying man, knowing that Berem wouldn't die. This was all crazy! He would—

Caramon stopped.

The rocks around him shuddered. The ground shook beneath his feet. The black water ceased its swift flow and was suddenly sluggish, uncertain, sloshing against the rocks. Behind him, he heard the draconians shouting in alarm.

Caramon stared at Berem. The body lay crushed upon the rocks. It stirred slightly, as if breathing a final sigh. Then it did not move. For an instant two pale figures shimmered inside the jeweled column. Then they were gone.

The Everman was dead.

Tanis lifted his head from the floor of the Hall to see a hobgoblin, spear raised, about to plunge it into his body. Rolling quickly, he grabbed the creature's booted foot and yanked. The hobgoblin crashed to the floor where another hobgoblin, this one dressed in a different colored uniform, smashed its head open with a mace.

Hurriedly Tanis rose to his feet. He had to get out of here! He had to find Laurana. A draconian rushed at him. He thrust his sword through the creature impatiently, remembering just in time to free it before the body turned to stone. Then he heard a voice shout his name. Turning he saw Lord Soth, standing beside Kitiara, surrounded by his skeletal warriors. Kit's eyes were fixed on Tanis with hatred, she pointed at him. Lord Soth made a gesture, sending his skeletal followers flowing from the snake-headed platform like a wave of death, destroying everything within their path.

Tanis turned to flee but found himself entangled in the mob.

Frantically he fought, aware of the chill force behind him. Panic flooded his mind, nearly depriving him of his senses.

And then, there was a sharp cracking sound. The floor trembled beneath his feet. The fighting around him stopped abruptly as everyone concentrated on standing upright. Tanis looked around uncertainly, wondering what was happening.

A huge chunk of mosaic-covered stone tumbled from the ceiling, falling into a mass of draconians, who scrambled to get out of the way. The stone was followed by another, and yet another. Torches fell from the walls, candles dropped down and were extinguished in their own wax. The rumbling of the ground grew stronger. Half-turning, Tanis saw that even the skeletal warriors had halted, flaming eyes seeking those of their leader in fear and questioning.

The floor suddenly canted away from beneath his feet. Grabbing hold of a column for support, Tanis stared about in wonder. And then darkness fell upon him like a crushing weight.

He has betrayed me!

The Dark Queen's anger beat in Tanis's mind, the rage and fear so strong that it nearly split his skull. Crying aloud in pain, he grasped his head. The darkness increased as Takhisis—seeing her danger—sought desperately to keep the door to the world ajar. Her vast darkness quenched the light of every flame. Wings of night filled the Hall with blackness.

All around Tanis, draconian soldiers stumbled and staggered in the impenetrable darkness. The voices of their officers raised to try and quell the confusion, to stem the rising panic they sensed spreading among their troops as they felt the force of their Queen withdrawn. Tanis heard Kitiara's voice ring out shrilly in anger, then it was cut off abruptly.

A horrible, rending crash followed by screams of agony gave Tanis his first indication that the entire building seemed likely to fall in on top of them.

"Laurana!" Tanis screamed. Trying desperately to stand, he staggered forward blindly, only to be hurled to the stone floor by milling draconians. Steel clashed. Somewhere he heard Kitiara's voice again, rallying her troops.

Fighting despair, Tanis stumbled to his feet again. Pain seared his arm. Furious, he thrust aside the sword blow aimed at him in the darkness, kicking with all his strength at the creature attacking him.

Then a rending, splitting sound quelled the battle. For one

---

breathless instant, everyone in the Temple looked upward into the dense darkness. Voices hushed in awe. Takhisis, Queen of Darkness, hung over them in her living form upon this plane. Her gigantic body shimmered in a myriad colors. So many, so blinding, so confusing, the senses could not comprehend her awful majesty and blotted the colors from the minds of mortals—Many Colors and None—so Takhisis seemed. The five heads each opened wide their gaping mouths, fire burned in the multitude of eyes, as if each were intent upon devouring the world.

All is lost, Tanis thought in despair. This is the moment of her ultimate victory. We have failed.

The five heads reared up in triumph. . . . The domed ceiling split apart.

The Temple of Istar began to twist and writhe, rebuilding, reforming, returning to the original shape it had known before darkness perverted it.

Within the Hall itself, the darkness wavered and then was shattered by the silver beams of Solinari, called by the dwarves, Night Candle.

12

The debt repaid.

"**A**nd now, my brother, farewell."

Raistlin drew forth a small round globe from the folds of his black robes. The dragon orb.

Caramon felt his strength seep from him. Placing his hand upon the bandage, he found it soaked—sticky with blood. His head swam, the light from his brother's staff wavered before his eyes. Far away, as if in a dream, he heard the draconians shake loose from their terror and start toward him. The ground shook beneath his feet, or perhaps it was his legs trembling.

"Kill me, Raistlin." Caramon looked at his brother with eyes that had lost all expression.

Raistlin paused, his golden eyes narrowed.

"Don't leave me to die at their hands," Caramon said calmly, asking a simple favor. "End it for me now, quickly. You owe me that much—"

The golden eyes flared.

"*Owe you!*" Raistlin sucked in a hissing breath. "*Owe you!*" he repeated in a strangled voice, his face pale in the staff's magical light. Furious, he turned and extended his hand toward the draconians. Lightning streaked from his fingertips, striking the creatures in the chest. Shrieking in pain and astonishment, they fell into the water that quickly became foaming and green with blood as the baby dragons cannibalized their cousins.

Caramon watched dully, too weak and sick to care. He could hear more swords rattling, more voices yelling. He slumped forward, his feet lost their footing, the dark waters surged over him. . . .

And then he was on solid ground. Blinking, he looked up. He was sitting on the rock beside his brother. Raistlin knelt beside him, the staff in his hand.

"Raist!" Caramon breathed, tears coming to his eyes. Reaching out a shaking hand, he touched his brother's arm, feeling the velvet softness of the black robes.

Coldly, Raistlin snatched his arm away. "Know this, Caramon," he said, and his voice was as chill as the dark waters around them, "I will save your life this once, and then the slate is clean. I owe you nothing more."

Caramon swallowed. "Raist," he said softly, "I—I didn't mean—"

Raistlin ignored him. "Can you stand?" he asked harshly.

"I—I think so," Caramon said, hesitantly. "Can't—can't you just use that—that thing—to get us out of here?" He gestured at the dragon orb.

"I could, but you wouldn't particularly enjoy the journey, my brother. Besides, have you forgotten those who came with you?"

"Tika! Tas!" Caramon gasped. Gripping the wet rocks, he pulled himself to his feet. "And Tanis! What about—"

"Tanis is on his own. I have repaid my debt to him tenfold," Raistlin said. "But perhaps I can discharge my debts to others."

Shouts and yells sounded at the end of the passage, a dark

mass of troops surged into the dark water, obeying the final commands of their Queen.

Wearily Caramon put his hand on the hilt of his sword, but a touch of his brother's cold, bony fingers stopped him.

"No, Caramon," Raistlin whispered. His thin lips parted in a grim smile. "I don't you need you now. I won't need you any-more . . . ever. Watch!"

Instantly, the underground cavern's darkness was lit to day-like brilliance with the fiery power of Raistlin's magic. Cara-mon, sword in hand, could only stand beside his black-robed brother and watch in awe as foe after foe fell to Raistlin's spells. Lightning crackled from his fingertips, flame flared from his hands, phantasms appeared—so terrifyingly real to those look-ing at them that they could kill by fear alone.

Goblins fell screaming, pierced by the lances of a legion of knights, who filled the cavern with their war chants at Rais-tlin's bidding, then disappeared at his command. The baby dragons fled in terror back to the dark and secret places of their hatching, draconians withered black in the flames. Dark cler-ics, who swarmed down the stairs at their Queen's last bidding, were impaled upon a flight of shimmering spears, their last prayers changed to wailing curses of agony.

Finally came the Black Robes, the eldest of the Order, to destroy this young upstart. But they found to their dismay that—old as they were—Raistlin was in some mysterious way older still. His power was phenomenal, they knew within an instant that he could not be defeated. The air was filled with the sounds of chanting and, one by one, they disappeared as swiftly as they had come—many bowing to Raistlin in pro-found respect as they departed upon the wings of wish spells.

And then it was silent, the only sound the sluggish lapping of water. The Staff of Magius cast its crystal light. Every few sec-onds a tremor shook the Temple, causing Caramon to glance above them in alarm. The battle had apparently lasted only moments, although it seemed to Caramon's fevered mind that he and his brother had been in this horrible place all their lives.

When the last mage melted into the blackness, Raistlin turned to face his brother.

"You see, Caramon?" he said coldly.

Wordlessly, the big warrior nodded, his eyes wide.

The ground shook around them, the water in the stream sloshed up on the rocks. At the cavern's end, the jeweled column shivered, then split. Rivulets of rock dust trickled down onto Caramon's upturned face as he stared at the crumbling ceiling.

"What does it mean? What's happening?" he asked in alarm.

"It means the end," Raistlin stated. Folding his black robes around him, he glanced at Caramon in irritation. "We must leave this place. Are you strong enough?"

"Yeah, give me a moment," Caramon grunted. Pushing himself away from the rocks, he took a step forward, then staggered, nearly falling.

"I'm weaker than I thought," he mumbled, clutching his side in pain. "Just let me . . . catch my breath." Straightening, his lips pale, sweat trickling down his face, Caramon took another step forward.

Smiling grimly, Raistlin watched his brother stumble toward him. Then the mage held out his arm.

"Lean on me, my brother," he said softly.

The vast vaulted ceiling of the Hall of Audience split wide. Huge blocks of stone crashed down into the Hall, crushing everything that lived beneath them. Instantly the chaos in the Hall degenerated into terror-stricken panic. Ignoring the stern commands of their leaders, who reinforced these commands with whips and sword thrusts, the draconians fought to escape the destruction of the Temple, brutally slaughtering anyone—including their own comrades—who got in their way. Occasionally some extremely powerful Dragon Highlord would manage to keep his bodyguard under control and escape. But several fell, cut down by their own troops, crushed by falling rock, or trampled to death.

Tanis fought his way through the chaos and suddenly saw what he had prayed the gods to find—a head of golden hair that gleamed in Solanari's light like a candle flame.

"Laurana!" he cried, though he knew he could not be heard in the tumult. Frantically he slashed his way toward her. A flying splinter of rock tore into one cheek. Tanis felt warm blood flow down his neck, but the blood, the pain had no reality and he soon forgot about it as he clubbed and stabbed and kicked the milling draconians in his struggle to reach her. Time and again, he drew near her, only to be carried away by a surge in the crowd.

She was standing near the door to one of the antechambers,

fighting draconians, wielding Kitiara's sword with the skill gained in long months of war. He almost reached her as—her enemies defeated—she stood alone for a moment.

"Laurana, wait!" he shouted above the chaos.

She heard him. Looking over at him, across the moonlit room, he saw her eyes calm, her gaze unwavering.

"Farewell, Tanis," Laurana called to him in elven. "I owe you my life, but not my soul."

With that, she turned and left him, stepping through the doorway of the antechamber, vanishing into the darkness beyond.

A piece of the Temple ceiling crashed to the stone floor, showering Tanis with debris. For a moment, he stood wearily, staring after her. Blood dripped into one eye. Absently he wiped it away, then, suddenly, he began to laugh. He laughed until tears mingled with the blood. Then he pulled himself together and, gripping his blood-stained sword, disappeared into the darkness after her.

"This is the corridor they went down, Raist—Raistlin." Caramon stumbled over his brother's name. Somehow, the old nickname no longer seemed to suit this black-robed, silent figure.

They stood beside the jailor's desk, near the body of the hobgoblin. Around them, the walls were acting crazily, shifting, crumbling, twisting, rebuilding. The sight filled Caramon with vague horror, like a nightmare he could not remember. So he kept his eyes fixed firmly on his brother, his hand clutched Raistlin's thin arm thankfully. This, at least was flesh and blood, reality in the midst of a terrifying dream.

"Do you know where it leads?" Caramon asked, peering down the eastern corridor.

"Yes," Raistlin replied without expression.

Caramon felt fear clutch at him. "You know . . . something's happened to them—"

"They were fools," Raistlin said bitterly. "The dream warned them"— he glanced at his brother—"as it warned others. Still, I may be in time, but we must hurry. Listen!"

Caramon glanced up the stairwell. Above him he could hear the sounds of clawed feet racing to stop the escape of the hundreds of prisoners set free by the collapse of the dungeons. Caramon put his hand on his sword.

"Stop it," Raistlin snapped. "Think a moment! You're dressed in armor still. They're not interested in us. The Dark Queen is gone. They obey her no longer. They are only after booty for themselves. Keep beside me. Walk steadily, with purpose."

Drawing a deep breath, Caramon did as he was told. He had regained some of his strength and was able to walk without his brother's help now. Ignoring the draconians—who took one look at them, then surged past—the two brothers made their way down the corridor. Here the walls still changed their shapes, the ceiling shook, and the floors heaved. Behind them they could hear ghastly yells as the prisoners fought for their freedom.

"At least no one will be guarding this door," Raistlin reflected, pointing ahead.

"What do you mean?" Caramon asked, halting and staring at his brother in alarm.

"It's trapped," Raistlin whispered. "Remember the dream?"

Turning deathly pale, Caramon dashed down the corridor toward the door. Shaking his hooded head, Raistlin followed slowly after. Rounding the corner, he found his brother crouching beside two bodies on the floor.

"Tika!" Caramon moaned. Brushing back the red curls from the still, white face, he felt for the lifebeat in her neck. His eyes closed a moment in thankfulness, then he reached out to touch the kender. "And Tas . . . No!"

Hearing his name, the kender's eyes opened slowly, as if the lids were too heavy for him to lift.

"Caramon . . ." Tas said in a broken whisper. "I'm sorry. . . ."

"Tas!" Caramon gently gathered the small, feverish body into his big arms. Holding him close, he rocked him back and forth. "Shh, Tas, don't talk."

The kender's body twitched in convulsions. Glancing around in heartbroken sorrow, Caramon saw Tasslehoff's pouches lying on the floor, their contents scattered like toys in a child's playroom. Tears filled Caramon's eyes.

"I tried to save her . . . " Tas whispered, shuddering with pain, "but I couldn't. . . ."

"You saved her, Tas!" Caramon said, choking. "She's not dead. Just hurt. She'll be fine."

"Really?" Tas's eyes, burning with fever, brightened with a calmer light, then dimmed. "I'm—I'm afraid I'm *not* fine, Caramon. But—but it's all right, really. I—I'm going to see Flint. He's waiting for me. He shouldn't be out there, by himself. I don't know how . . . he could have left without me anyway. . . ."

"What's the matter with him?" Caramon asked his brother as Raistlin bent swiftly over the kender, whose voice had trailed off into incoherent babbling.

"Poison," said Raistlin, his eyes glancing at the golden needle shining in the torchlight. Reaching out, Raistlin gently pushed on the door. The lock gave and the door turned on its hinges, opening a crack.

Outside, they could hear shrieks and cries as the soldiers and slaves of Neraka fled the dying Temple. The skies above resounded with the roars of dragons. The Highlords battled among themselves to see who would come out on top in this new world. Listening, Raistlin smiled to himself.

His thoughts were interrupted by a hand clutching his arm. "Can you help him?" Caramon demanded.

Raistlin flicked a glance at the dying kender. "He is very far gone," the mage said coldly. "It will sap some of my strength, and we are not out of this yet, my brother."

"But you can save him?" Caramon persisted. "Are you powerful enough?"

"Of course," Raistlin replied, shrugging.

Tika stirred and sat up, clutching her aching head. "Caramon!" she cried happily, then her gaze fell upon Tas. "Oh, no . . ." she whispered. Forgetting her pain, she laid her blood-stained hand upon the kender's forehead. The kender's eyes flared open at her touch, but he did not recognize her. He cried out in agony.

Over his cries, they could hear the sound of clawed feet, running down the corridor.

Raistlin looked at his brother. He saw him holding Tas in the big hands that could be so gentle.

Thus he has held me, Raistlin thought. His eyes went to the kender. Vivid memories of their younger days, of carefree adventuring with Flint . . . now dead. Sturm, dead. Days of warm sunshine, of the green budding leaves on the vallenwoods of Solace . . . Nights in the Inn of the Last Home. . . . now blacked and crumbling, the vallenwoods burned and destroyed.

"This is my final debt," Raistlin said. "Paid in full." Ignoring the look of thankfulness that flooded Caramon's face, he instructed, "Lay him down. You must deal with the draconians. This spell will take all my concentration. Do not allow them to interrupt me."

Gently Caramon laid Tas down on the floor in front of Raistlin. The kender's eyes had fixed in his head, his body was stiffening in its convulsive struggles. His breath rattled in his throat.

"Remember, my brother," Raistlin said coldly as he reached into one of the many secret pockets in his black robes, "you are dressed as a dragonarmy officer. Be subtle, if possible."

"Right." Caramon gave Tas a final glance, then drew a deep breath. "Tika," he said, "stay still. Pretend you're unconscious—"

Tika nodded and lay back down, obediently closing her eyes. Raistlin heard Caramon clanking down the corridor, he heard his brother's loud, booming voice, then the mage forgot his brother, forgot the approaching draconians, forgot everything as he concentrated upon his spell.

Removing a luminous white pearl from an inner pocket, Raistlin held it firmly in one hand while he took out a gray-green leaf from another. Prizing the kender's clenched jaws open, Raistlin placed the leaf beneath Tasslehoff's swollen tongue. The mage studied the pearl for a moment, calling to mind the complex words of the spell, reciting them to himself mentally until he was certain he had them in their proper order and knew the correct pronunciation of each. He would have one chance, and one chance only. If he failed, not only would the kender die, but he might very well die himself.

Placing the pearl upon his own chest, over his heart, Raistlin closed his eyes and began to repeat the words of the spell, chanting the lines six times, making the proper changes in inflection each time. With a thrill of ecstasy, he felt the magic flow through his body, drawing out a part of his own life force, capturing it within the pearl.

The first part of the spell complete, Raistlin held the pearl poised above the kender's heart. Closing his eyes once more, he recited the complex spell again, this time backwards. Slowly he crushed the pearl in his hand, scattering the iridescent powder over Tasslehoff's rigid body. Raistlin came to an end. Wearily he opened his eyes and watched in triumph as the lines of pain faded from the kender's features, leaving them filled with peace.

Tas's eyes flew open.

"Raistlin! I—plooey!" Tas spit out the green leaf. "Yick!

What kind of nasty thing was that? And how did it get into my mouth?" Tas sat up dizzily, then he saw his pouches. "Hey! Who's been messing with my stuff?" Glancing up at the mage accusingly, his eyes opened wide. "Raistlin! You have on Black Robes! How wonderful! Can I touch them? Oh, all right. You needn't glare at me like that. It's just that they look so soft. Say, does this mean you're truly bad now? Can you do something evil for me, so I can watch? I know! I saw a wizard summon a demon once. Could you do that? Just a small demon? You could send him right back. No?" Tas sighed in disappointment. "Well— Hey, Caramon, what are those draconians doing with you? And what's the matter with Tika? Oh, Caramon, I—"

"Shut up!" Caramon roared. Scowling ferociously at the kender, he pointed at Tas and Tika. "The mage and I were bringing these prisoners to our Highlord when they turned on us. They're valuable slaves, the girl especially. And the kender is a clever thief. We don't want to lose them. They'll fetch a high price in the market in Sanction. Since the Dark Queen's gone, it's every man for himself, eh?"

Caramon nudged one of the draconians in the ribs. The creature snarled in agreement, its black reptilian eyes fastened greedily on Tika.

"Thief!" shouted Tas indignantly, his shrill voice ringing through the corridor. "I'm—" He gulped, suddenly falling silent as a supposedly comatose Tika gave him a swift poke in the ribs.

"I'll help the girl," Caramon said, glaring at the leering draconian. "You keep an eye on the kender and, you over there, help the mage. His spell-casting has left him weak."

Bowing with respect before Raistlin, one of the draconians helped him to his feet. "You two"—Caramon was marshaling the rest of his troops—"go before us and see that we don't have any trouble reaching the edge of town. Maybe you can come with us to Sanction," Caramon continued, lifting Tika to her feet. Shaking her head, she pretended to regain consciousness.

The draconians grinned in agreement as one of them grabbed hold of Tas by the collar and shoved him toward the door.

"But my things!" wailed Tas, twisting around.

"Keep moving!" Caramon growled.

"Oh, well," the kender sighed, his eyes lingering fondly on his precious possessions lying scattered on the blood-stained floor. "This probably isn't the end of my adventuring. And—after all—empty pockets hold more, as my mother used to say."

Stumbling along behind the two draconians, Tas looked up into the starry heavens. "I'm sorry, Flint," he said softly. "Just wait for me a little longer."

13
Kitiara.

As Tanis entered the ante-
chamber, the change was so startling that for a minute it was
almost incomprehensible. One moment he had been fighting to
stand on his feet in the midst of a mob, the next he was in a cool
dark room, similar to the one he and Kitiara and her troops had
waited in before entering the Hall of Audience.

Glancing around swiftly, he saw he was alone. Although
every instinct urged him to rush out of this room in his frantic
search, Tanis forced himself to stop, catch his breath, and wipe
away the blood gumming his eye shut. He tried to remember

---

what he had seen of the entry into the Temple. The antechambers that formed a circle around the main Hall of Audience were themselves connected to the front part of the temple by a series of winding corridors. Once, long ago in Istar, these corridors must have been designed in some sort of logical order. But the distortion of the Temple had twisted them into a meaningless maze. Corridors ended abruptly when he expected them to continue, while those that led nowhere seemingly went on forever.

The ground rocked beneath his feet as dust drifted down from the ceiling. A painting fell from the wall with a crash. Tanis had no idea of where Laurana might be found. He had seen her come in here, that was all.

She had been imprisoned in the Temple, but that was below ground. He wondered if she had been at all cognizant of her surroundings when they brought her in, if she had any idea how to get out. And then Tanis realized that he himself had only a vague idea of where he was. Finding a torch still burning, he grabbed it and flashed it about the room. A tapestry-covered door swung open, hanging on a broken hinge. Peering through it, he saw it led into a dimly lit corridor.

Tanis caught his breath. He knew, now, how to find her!

A breath of air stirred in the hallway—fresh air, pungent with the odors of spring, cool with the blessed peace of night— touched his left cheek. Laurana must have felt that breath, she would guess that it must lead out of the Temple. Quickly Tanis ran down the hallway, ignoring the pain in his head, forcing his weary muscles to respond to his commands.

A group of draconians appeared suddenly in front of him, coming from another room. Remembering he still wore the dragonarmy uniform, Tanis stopped them.

"The elfwoman!" he shouted. "She must not escape. Have you seen her?"

This group hadn't, apparently, by the tone of the hurried snarls. Nor had the next group Tanis encountered. But two draconians wandering the halls in search of loot had seen her, so they said. They pointed vaguely in the direction Tanis was already heading. His spirits rose.

By now, the fighting within the Hall had ended. The Dragon Highlords who survived had made good their escapes and were now among their own forces stationed outside the Temple walls. Some fought. Some retreated, waiting to see who came out on top. Two questions were on everyone's mind. The first—would the dragons remain in the world or would they vanish with their Queen as they had following the Second Dragon War?

And, second—if the dragons remained, who would be their master?

Tanis found himself pondering these questions confusedly as he ran through the halls, sometimes taking wrong turns and cursing bitterly as he confronted a solid wall and was forced to retrace his steps to where he could once again feel the air upon his face.

But eventually he grew too tired to ponder anything. Exhaustion and pain were taking their toll. His legs grew heavy, it was an effort to take a step. His head throbbed, the cut over his eye began to bleed again. The ground shook continually beneath his feet. Statues toppled from their bases, stones fell from the ceiling, showering him with clouds of dust.

He began to lose hope. Even though he was certain he was traveling in the only direction she could possibly have taken, the few draconians he passed now had not seen her. What could have happened? Was she— No, he wouldn't think of that. He kept going, conscious either of the fragrant breath of air on his face or of smoke billowing past him.

The torches had started fires. The Temple was beginning to burn.

Then, while negotiating a narrow corridor and climbing over a pile of rubble, Tanis heard a sound. He stopped, holding his breath. Yes, there it was again—just ahead. Peering through the smoke and dust, he gripped his sword in his hand. The last group of draconians he had met were drunk and eager to kill. A lone human officer had seemed like fair game, until one of them remembered having seen Tanis with the Dark Lady. But the next time he might not be so lucky.

Before him, the corridor lay in ruins, part of the ceiling having caved in. It was intensely dark—the torch he held provided the only light—and Tanis wrestled with the need for light and the fear of being seen by it. Finally he decided to risk keeping it burning. He would never find Laurana if he had to wander around this place in the darkness.

He would have to trust to his disguise once again.

"Who goes there?" he roared out in a harsh voice, shining his torchlight boldly into the ruined hallway.

———

He caught a glimpse of flashing armor and a figure running, but it ran away from him—not toward him. Odd for a draconian . . . his weary brain seemed to be stumbling along about three paces behind him. He could see the figure plainly now, lithe and slender and running much too quickly. . . .

"Laurana!" he shouted, then in elven, "*Quisalas!*"

Cursing the broken columns and marble blocks in his path, Tanis stumbled and ran and stumbled and fell and forced his aching body to obey him until he caught up with her. Grasping her by the arm, he dragged her to a stop, then could only hold onto her tightly as he slumped against a wall.

Each breath he took was fiery pain. He was so dizzy he thought for a moment he might pass out. But he grasped her with a deathlike grip, holding her with his eyes as well as his hand.

Now he knew why the draconians hadn't seen her. She had stripped off the silver armor, covering it with draconian armor she had taken from a dead warrior. For a moment she could only stare at Tanis. She had not recognized him at first, and had nearly run him through with her sword. The only thing that had stopped her was the elven word, *quisalas*, beloved. That—and the intense look of anguish and suffering on his pale face.

"Laurana," Tanis gasped in a voice as shattered as Raistlin's had once been, "don't leave me. Wait . . . listen to me, please!"

With a twist of her arm, Laurana broke free of his grip. But she did not leave him. She started to speak, but another shudder of the building silenced her. As dust and debris poured down around them, Tanis pulled Laurana close, shielding her. They clung to each other fearfully, and then it was over. But they were left in darkness. Tanis had dropped the torch.

"We've got to get out of here," he said, his voice shaking.

"Are you injured?" Laurana asked coldly, trying to free herself from his grasp once more. "If so, I can help you. If not, then I suggest we forego any further farewells. Whatever—"

"Laurana," Tanis said softly, breathing heavily, "I don't ask you to understand—*I* don't understand. I don't ask for forgiveness—I can't even forgive myself. I could tell you that I love you, that I have always loved you. But that wouldn't be true, for love must come from within one who loves himself, and right now I can't bear to see my own reflection. All I can tell you, Laurana, is that—"

"Shhh!" Laurana whispered, putting her hand over Tanis's

mouth. "I heard something."

For long moments they stood, pressed together in the darkness, listening. At first they could hear nothing but the sound of their own breathing. They could see nothing, not even each other, as close as they were. Then torchlight flared, blinding them, and a voice spoke.

"Tell Laurana what, Tanis?" said Kitiara in a pleasant voice. "Go on."

A naked sword gleamed in her hand. Wet blood—both red and green—glistened on the blade. Her face was white with stone dust, a trickle of blood ran down her chin from a cut on her lip. Her eyes were shadowed with weariness, but her smile was still as charming as ever. Sheathing her bloody sword, she wiped her hands upon her tattered cloak, then ran them absently through her curly hair.

Tanis's eyes closed in exhaustion. His face seemed to age; he looked very human. Pain and exhaustion, grief and guilt would forever leave their mark on the eternal elven youthfulness. He could feel Laurana stiffen, her hand move to her sword.

"Let her go, Kitiara," Tanis said quietly, gripping Laurana firmly. "Keep your promise and I'll keep mine. Let me take her outside the walls. Then I'll come back—"

"I really believe you would," Kitiara remarked, staring at him in amused wonder. "Hasn't it occurred to you yet, Half-Elf, that I could kiss you and kill you without drawing a deep breath in between? No, I don't suppose it has. I might kill you right now, in fact, simply because I know it would be the worst thing I could do to the elfwoman." She held the flaming torch near Laurana. "There—look at her face!" Kitiara sneered. "What a weak and debilitating thing love is!"

Kitiara's hand tousled her hair again. Shrugging, she glanced around. "But I haven't time. Things are moving. Great things. The Dark Queen has fallen. Another will rise to take her place. What about it, Tanis? I have already begun to establish my authority over the other Dragon Highlords." Kitiara patted her sword hilt. "Mine will be a vast empire. We could rule toge—"

She broke off abruptly, her gaze shifting down the corridor from which she had just come. Although Tanis could neither see nor hear what had attracted her attention, he felt a bone-numbing chill spread through the hallway. Laurana gripped him suddenly, fear overwhelming her, and Tanis knew who approached even before he saw the orange eyes flicker above the ghostly armor.

"Lord Soth," murmured Kitiara. "Make your decision quickly, Tanis."

"My decision was made a long time ago, Kitiara," Tanis said calmly. Stepping in front of Laurana, he shielded her as best as he could with his own body. "Lord Soth will have to kill me to reach her, Kit. And even though I know my death will not stop him—or you—from killing her when I have fallen, with my last breath, I will pray to Paladine to protect her soul. The gods owe me one. Somehow I know that this—my final prayer— will be granted."

Behind him, Tanis felt Laurana lay her head against his back, he heard her sob softly and his heart eased, for there was not fear in her sob, but only love and compassion and grief for him.

Kitiara hesitated. They could see Lord Soth coming down the shattered corridor, his orange eyes flickering pinpoints of light in the darkness. Then she laid her blood-stained hand upon Tanis's arm. "Go!" she commanded harshly. "Run quickly, back down the corridor. At the end is a door in the wall. You can feel it. It will lead you down into the dungeons From there you can escape."

Tanis stared at her uncomprehendingly for a moment

"Run!" Kit snapped, giving him a shove.

Tanis cast a glance at Lord Soth.

"A trap!" whispered Laurana.

"No," Tanis said, his eyes going back to Kit. "Not this time. Farewell, Kitiara."

Kitiara's nails dug into his arm.

"Farewell, Half-Elven," she said in a soft, passionate voice, her eyes shining brightly in the torchlight. "Remember, I do this for love of you. Now go!"

Flinging her torch from her, Kitiara vanished into the darkness as completely as if she had been consumed by it.

Tanis blinked, blinded by the sudden blackness, and started to reach his hand out for her. Then he withdrew it. Turning, his hand found Laurana's hand. Together they stumbled through the debris, groping their way along the wall. The chill fear that flowed from the death knight numbed their blood. Glancing down the corridor, Tanis saw Lord Soth coming nearer and nearer, his eyes seeming to stare straight at them. Frantically Tanis felt the stone wall, his hands searching for the door. Then he felt the cold stone give way to wood. Grasping the iron handle, he turned it. The door opened at his touch. Pulling Laurana after him, the two plunged through the opening, the sudden flaring of torches lighting the stairs nearly as blinding as the darkness had been above.

Behind him, Tanis heard Kitiara's voice, hailing Lord Soth. He wondered what the death knight, having lost his prey, would do to her. The dream returned to him vividly. Once again he saw Laurana falling . . . Kitiara falling . . . and he stood helpless, unable to save either. Then the image vanished.

Laurana stood waiting for him on the stairway, the torchlight shining on her golden hair. Hurriedly he slammed the door shut and ran down the stairs after her.

"That is the elfwoman," said Lord Soth, his flaming eyes easily tracking the two as they ran from him like frightened mice. "And the half-elf."

"Yes," said Kitiara without interest. Drawing her sword from its scabbard, she began to wipe off the blood with the hem of her cloak.

"Shall I go after them?" Soth asked.

"No. We have more important matters to attend to now," Kitiara replied. Glancing up at him, she smiled her crooked smile. "The elfwoman would never be yours anyway, not even in death. The gods protect her."

Soth's flickering gaze turned to Kitiara. The pale lips curled in derision. "The half-elven man remains your master still."

"No, I think not," Kitiara replied. Turning, she looked after Tanis as the door shut behind him. "Sometimes, in the still watches of the night, when he lies in bed beside her, Tanis will find himself thinking of *me*. He will remember my last words, he will be touched by them. I have given them their happiness. And *she* must live with the knowledge that *I* will live always in Tanis's heart. What love they might find together, I have poisoned. My revenge upon them both is complete. Now, have you brought what I sent you for?"

"I have, Dark Lady," Lord Soth replied. With a spoken word of magic, he brought forth an object and held it out to her in his skeletal hand. Reverently, he set it at her feet.

Kitiara caught her breath, her eyes gleamed in the darkness nearly as bright as Lord Soth's. "Excellent! Return to Dargaard Keep. Gather the troops. We will take control of the flying citadel Ariakas sent to Kalaman. Then we will fall back, regroup, and wait."

The hideous visage of Lord Soth smiled as he gestured to the object that glittered in his fleshless hand. "This is now rightfully yours. Those who opposed you are either dead, as you commanded, or fled before I could reach them."

"Their doom is simply postponed," Kitiara said, sheathing her sword. "You have served me well, Lord Soth, and you will be rewarded. There will always be elfmaidens in this world, I suppose."

"Those you command to die shall die. Those you allow to live"—Soth's glance flickered to the door"—shall live. Remember this—of all who serve you, Dark Lady, I alone can offer you *undying* loyalty. This I do now, gladly. My warriors and I will return to Dargaard Keep as you ask. There we will await our summons."

Bowing to her, he took her hand in his skeletal grasp. "Farewell, Kitiara," he said, then paused. "How does it feel, my dear, to know that you have brought pleasure to the damned? You have made my dreary realm of death interesting. Would that I had known you as living man!" The pallid visage smiled. "But, my time is eternal. Perhaps I will wait for one who can share my throne—"

Cold fingers caressed Kitiara's flesh. She shuddered convulsively, seeing unending, sleepless nights yawn chasmlike before her. So vivid and terrifying was the image that Kitiara's soul shriveled in fear as Lord Soth vanished into the darkness.

She was by herself in the darkness and for a moment she was terrified. The Temple shuddered around her. Kitiara shrank back against the wall, frightened and alone. So alone! Then her foot touched something on the floor of the Temple. Reaching down, her fingers closed around it thankfully. She lifted it in her hands.

This was reality, hard and solid, she thought, breathing in relief.

No torchlight glittered on its golden surface or flared from its red-hued jewels. Kitiara did not need the flare of torches to admire what she held.

For long moments she stood in the crumbling hallway, her fingers running over the rough metal edges of the blood-stained Crown.

Tanis and Laurana ran down the spiral stone stairs to the

dungeons below. Pausing beside the jailor's desk, Tanis glanced at the body of the hobgoblin.

Laurana stared at him. "Come on," she urged, pointing to the east. Seeing him hesitate, looking north, she shuddered. "You don't want to go down there! That is where they . took me—" She turned away quickly, her face growing pale as she heard cries and shouts coming from the prison cells.

A harried-looking draconian ran by. Probably a deserter, Tanis guessed, seeing the creature snarl and cringe at the sight of an officer's armor.

"I was looking for Caramon," Tanis muttered. "They must have brought him here."

"Caramon?" exclaimed Laurana in astonishment. "What—"

"He came with me," Tanis said. "So did Tika and Tas and . . . Flint—" He stopped, then shook his head. "Well, if they were here, they're gone now. Come on."

Laurana's face flushed. She glanced back up the stone stairs, then at Tanis again.

"Tanis—" she began, faltering. He placed his hand over her mouth.

"There will be time to talk later. Now we must find our way out!"

As if to emphasize his words, another tremor shook the Temple. This one was sharper and stronger than the others, throwing Laurana up against a wall. Tanis's face, white with fatigue and pain, grew even paler as he fought to keep his footing.

A loud rumble and a shattering crash came from the northern corridor. All sound in the prison cells ceased abruptly as a great cloud of dust and dirt billowed out into the hallway.

Tanis and Laurana fled. Debris showered down around them as they ran east, stumbling over bodies and piles of jagged broken stone.

Another tremor rocked the Temple. They could not stand. Falling on hands and knees, they could do nothing but watch in terror as the corridor slowly shifted and moved, bending and twisting like a snake.

Crawling under a fallen beam, they huddled together, watching the floor and walls of the corridor leap and heave like waves upon the ocean. Above them, they could hear strange sounds, as of huge stones grinding together—not collapsing so much as shifting position. Then the tremor ceased. All was quiet.

Shakily they got to their feet and began running again, fear driving their aching bodies far beyond endurance. Every few minutes another tremor rocked the Temple's foundations. But as often as Tanis expected the roof to cave in upon their heads, it remained standing. So strange and terrifying were the inexplicable sounds above them that they both might have welcomed the collapse of the ceiling as a relief.

"Tanis!" cried Laurana suddenly. "Air! Night air!"

Wearily, summoning the last of their strength, the two made their way through the winding corridor until they came to a door swinging open on its hinges. There was a reddish blood stain on the floor and—

"Tas's pouches!" Tanis murmured. Kneeling down, he sorted through the kender's treasures that lay scattered all over the floor. Then his heart sank. Grieving, he shook his head.

Laurana knelt beside him, her hand closed over his.

"At least he was here, Tanis. He got this far. Maybe he escaped."

"He would never have left his treasures," Tanis said. Sinking down on the shaking floor, the half-elf stared outside into Neraka. "Look," he said to Laurana harshly, pointing. "This is the end, just as it was the end for the kender. Look!" he demanded angrily, seeing her face settling into its stubborn calm, seeing her refusing to admit defeat.

Laurana looked.

The cool breeze on her face seemed a mockery to her now, for it brought only smells of smoke and blood and the anguished cries of the dying. Orange flames lit the sky where wheeling dragons fought and died as their Highlords sought to escape or strove for mastery. The night air blazed with the crackling of lightning bolts and burned with flame. Draconians roamed the streets, killing anything that moved, slaughtering each other in their frenzy.

"So evil turns upon itself," Laurana whispered, laying her head on Tanis's shoulder, watching the terrible spectacle in awe.

"What was that?" he asked wearily.

"Something Elistan used to say," she replied. The Temple shook around them.

"Elistan!" Tanis laughed bitterly. "Where are his gods now? Watching from their castles among the stars, enjoying the show? The Dark Queen is gone, the Temple destroyed. And here we are—trapped. We wouldn't live three minutes out there—"

Then his breath caught in his throat. Gently he pushed Laurana away from him as he leaned over, his hand searching through Tasslehoff's scattered treasures. Hurriedly he swept aside a shining piece of broken blue crystal, a splinter of vallenwood, an emerald, a small white chicken feather, a withered black rose, a dragon's tooth, and a piece of wood carved with dwarven skill to resemble the kender. Among all of these was a golden object, sparkling in the flaming light of the fire and destruction outside.

Picking it up, Tanis's eyes filled with tears. He held it tightly in his hand, feeling the sharp edges bite into his flesh.

"What is it?" asked Laurana, not understanding, her voice choked with fear.

"Forgive me, Paladine," Tanis whispered. Drawing Laurana close beside him, he held his hand out, opening his palm.

There in his hand lay a finely carved, delicate ring, made of golden, clinging ivy leaves. And wrapped around the ring, still bound in his magical sleep, was a golden dragon.

14
The end.
For good or for evil.

"**W**ell, we're outside the city gates," Caramon muttered to his twin in a low voice, his eyes on the draconians who were looking at him expectantly. "You stay with Tika and Tas. I'm going back to find Tanis. I'll take this lot with me—"

"No, my brother," Raistlin said softly, his golden eyes glittering in Lunitari's red light. "You cannot help Tanis. His fate is in his own hands." The mage glanced up at the flaming, dragon-filled skies. "You are still in danger yourself, as are those dependent upon you."

Tika stood wearily beside Caramon, her face drawn with pain. And though Tasslehoff grinned as cheerfully as ever, his face was pale and there was an expression of wistful sorrow in his eyes that had never been seen in the eyes of a kender before. Caramon's face grew grim as he looked at them.

"Fine," he said. "But where do we go from here?"

Raising his arm, Raistlin pointed. The black robes shimmered, his hand stood out starkly against the night sky, pale and thin, like bare bone.

"Upon that ridge shines a light—"

They all turned to look, even the draconians. Far across the barren plain Caramon could see the dark shadow of a hill rising from the moonlit wasteland. Upon its summit gleamed a pure white light, shining brightly, steadfast as a star.

"One waits for you there," Raistlin said.

"Who? Tanis?" Caramon said eagerly.

Raistlin glanced at Tasslehoff. The kender's face had not turned from the light, he gazed at it fixedly.

"Fizban . . ." he whispered.

"Yes," Raistlin replied. "And now I must go."

"What?" Caramon faltered. "But—come with me . . . us . . . you must! To see Fizban—"

"A meeting between us would not be pleasant." Raistlin shook his head, the folds of his black hood moving around him.

"And what about them?" Caramon gestured at the draconians.

With a sigh, Raistlin faced the draconians. Lifting his hand, he spoke a few strange words. The draconians backed up, expressions of fear and horror twisting their reptilian faces. Caramon cried out, just as lightning sizzled from Raistlin's fingertips. Screaming in agony, the draconians burst into flame and fell, writhing, to the ground. Their bodies turned to stone as death took them.

"You didn't need to do that, Raistlin," Tika said, her voice trembling. "They would have left us alone."

"The war's over," Caramon added sternly.

"Is it?" Raistlin asked sarcastically, removing a small black bag from one of his hidden pockets. "It is weak, sentimental twaddle like that, my brother, which assures the war's continuation. These"—he pointed at the statuelike bodies—"are not of Krynn. They were created using the blackest of black rites. I know. I have witnessed their creation. They would not have 'left you alone.' " His voice grew shrill, mimicking Tika's.

Caramon flushed. He tried to speak, but Raistlin coldly ignored him and finally the big man fell silent, seeing his brother lost in his magic.

Once more Raistlin held the dragon orb in his hand. Closing his eyes, Raistlin began to chant softly. Colors swirled within the crystal, then it began to glow with a brilliant, radiant beam of light.

Raistlin opened his eyes, scanning the skies, waiting. He did not wait long. Within moments, the moons and stars were obliterated by a gigantic shadow. Tika fell back in alarm. Caramon put his arm around her comfortingly, though his body trembled and his hand went to his sword.

"A dragon!" said Tasslehoff in awe. "But it's huge. I've never seen one so big . . . or have I?" He blinked. "It seems familiar, somehow."

"You have," Raistlin said coolly, replacing the darkening crystal orb back in his black pouch, "in the dream. This is Cyan Bloodbane, the dragon who tormented poor Lorac, the Elven King."

"Why is he here?" Caramon gasped.

"He comes at my command," Raistlin replied. "He has come to take me home."

The dragon circled lower and lower, its gigantic wingspan spreading chilling darkness. Even Tasslehoff (though he later refused to admit it) found himself clinging to Caramon, shivering, as the monstrous green dragon settled to the ground.

For a moment Cyan glanced at the pitiful group of humans huddled together. His red eyes flared, his tongue flickered from between slavering jowels as he stared at them with hatred. Then—constrained by a will more powerful than his own— Cyan's gaze was wrenched away, coming to rest in resentment and anger upon the black-robed mage.

At a gesture from Raistlin, the dragon's great head lowered until it rested in the sand.

Leaning wearily upon the Staff of Magius, Raistlin walked over to Cyan Bloodbane and climbed up the huge, snaking neck.

Caramon stared at the dragon, fighting the dragonfear that overwhelmed him. Tika and Tas both clung to him, shivering in fright. Then, with a hoarse cry, he thrust them both away and ran toward the great dragon.

"Wait! Raistlin!" Caramon cried raggedly. "I'll go with you!"

Cyan reared his great head in alarm, eyeing the human with a flaming gaze.

"Would you?" Raistlin asked softly, laying a soothing hand upon the dragon's neck. "Would you go with me into darkness?"

Caramon hesitated, his lips grew dry, fear parched his throat. He could not speak, but he nodded, twice, biting his lip in agony as he heard Tika sobbing behind him.

Raistlin regarded him, his eyes golden pools within the deep blackness. "I truly believe you would," the mage marveled, almost to himself. For a moment Raistlin sat upon the dragon's back, pondering. Then he shook his head, decisively.

"No, my brother, where I go, you cannot follow. Strong as you are, it would lead you to your death. We are finally as the gods meant us to be, Caramon—two whole people, and here our paths separate. You must learn to walk yours alone, Caramon"—for an instant, a ghostly smile flickered across Raistlin's face, illuminated by the light from the staff—"or with those who might choose to walk with you. Farewell, my brother."

At a word from his master, Cyan Bloodbane spread his wings and soared into the air. The gleam of light from the staff seemed like a tiny star amidst the deep blackness of the dragon's wingspan. And then it, too, winked out, the darkness swallowing it utterly.

"Here come those you have waited for," the old man said gently.

Tanis raised his head.

Into the light of the old man's fire came three people—a huge and powerful warrior, dressed in dragonarmy armor, walking arm in arm with a curly-haired young woman. Her face was pale with exhaustion and streaked with blood, and there was a look of deep concern and sorrow in her eyes as she gazed up at the man beside her. Finally, stumbling after them, so tired he could barely stand, came a bedraggled kender in ragged blue leggings.

"Caramon!" Tanis rose to his feet.

The big man lifted his head. His face brightened. Opening his arms, he clasped Tanis to his breast with a sob. Tika, standing apart, watched the reunion of the two friends with tears in her eyes. Then she caught sight of movement near the fire.

"Laurana?" she said hesitantly.

The elfwoman stepped forward into the firelight, her golden hair shining brightly as the sun. Though dressed in blood-stained, battered armor, she had the bearing, the regal look of the elven princess Tika had met in Qualinesti so many months ago.

Self-consciously, Tika put her hand to her filthy hair, felt it matted with blood. Her white, puffy-sleeved barmaid's blouse hung from her in rags, barely decent; her mismatched armor was all that held it together in places. Unbecoming scars marred the smooth flesh of her shapely legs, and there was far too much shapely leg visible.

Laurana smiled, and then Tika smiled. It didn't matter. Coming to her swiftly, Laurana put her arms around her, and Tika held her close.

All alone, the kender stood for a moment on the edge of the circle of firelight, his eyes on the old man who stood near it. Behind the old man, a great golden dragon slept sprawled out upon the ridge, his flanks pulsing with his snores. The old man beckoned Tas to come closer.

Heaving a sigh that seemed to come from the toes of his shoes, Tasslehoff bowed his head. Dragging his feet, he walked slowly over to stand before the old man.

"What's my name?" the old man asked, reaching out his hand to touch the kender's topknot of hair.

"It's not Fizban," Tas said miserably, refusing to look at him.

The old man smiled, stroking the topknot. Then he drew Tas near him, but the kender held back, his small body rigid. "Up until now, it wasn't," the old man said softly.

"Then what is it?" Tas mumbled, his face averted.

"I have many names," the old man replied. "Among the elves I am *E'li*. The dwarves call me *Thak*. Among the humans I am known as *Skyblade*. But my favorite has always been that by which I am known among the Knights of Solamnia—*Draco Paladin*."

"I knew it!" Tas groaned, flinging himself to the ground. "A god! I've lost everyone! Everyone!" He began to weep bitterly.

The old man regarded him fondly for a moment, even brushing a gnarled hand across his own moist eyes. Then he knelt down beside the kender and put his arm around him comfortingly. "Look, my boy," he said, putting his finger beneath Tas's chin and turning his eyes to heaven, "do you see the red star that shines above us? Do you know to what god that star is sacred?"

"Reorx," Tas said in a small voice, choking on his tears.

"It is red like the fires of his forge," the old man said, gazing at it. "It is red like the sparks that fly from his hammer as it shapes the molten world resting on his anvil. Beside the forge of Reorx is a tree of surpassing beauty, the like of which no living being has ever seen. Beneath that tree sits a grumbling old dwarf, relaxing after many labors. A mug of cold ale stands beside him, the fire of the forge is warm upon his bones. He spends all day lounging beneath the tree, carving and shaping the wood he loves. And every day someone who comes past that beautiful tree starts to sit down beside him.

"Looking at them in disgust, the dwarf glowers at them so sternly that they quickly get to their feet again.

" 'This place is saved,' the dwarf grumbles. 'There's a lame-brained doorknob of a kender off adventuring somewhere, getting himself and those unfortunate enough to be with him into no end of trouble. Mark my words. One day he'll show up here and he'll admire my tree and he'll say, "Flint, I'm tired. I think I'll rest awhile here with you." Then he'll sit down and he'll say, "Flint, have you heard about my latest adventure? Well, there was this black-robed wizard and his brother and me and we went on a journey through time and the most wonderful things happened—" and I'll have to listen to some wild tale—' and so he grumbles on. Those who would sit beneath the tree hide their smiles and leave him in peace."

"Then . . . he's not lonely?" Tas asked, wiping his hand across his eyes.

"No, child. He is patient. He knows you have much yet to do in your life. He will wait. Besides he's already heard all your stories. You're going to have to come up with some new ones."

"He hasn't heard *this* one yet," Tas said in dawning excitement. "Oh, Fizban, it was wonderful! I nearly died—again. And I opened my eyes and there was Raistlin in Black Robes!" Tas shivered in delight. "He looked so—well—evil! But he saved my life! And—oh!" He stopped, horrified, then hung his head. "I'm sorry. I forgot. I guess I shouldn't call you Fizban anymore."

Standing up, the old man patted him gently. "Call me Fizban.

———

369

From now on, among the kender, that shall be my name." The old man's voice grew wistful. "To tell the truth, I've grown rather fond of it."

The old man walked over to Tanis and Caramon, and stood near them for a moment, eavesdropping on their conversation.

"He's gone, Tanis," Caramon said sadly. "I don't know where. I don't understand. He's still frail, but he isn't weak. That horrible cough is gone. His voice is his own, yet different. He's—"

"Fistandantilus," the old man said.

Both Tanis and Caramon turned. Seeing the old man, they both bowed reverently.

"Oh, stop that!" Fizban snapped. "Can't abide all that bowing. You're both hypocrites anyway. I've heard what you said about me behind my back—" Tanis and Caramon both flushed guiltily. "Never mind." Fizban smiled. "You believed what I wanted you to believe. Now, about your brother. You are right. He is himself and he is not. As was foretold, he is the master of both present and past."

"I don't understand." Caramon shook his head. "Did the dragon orb do this to him? If so, perhaps it could be broken or—"

"Nothing *did this to him*," Fizban said, regarding Caramon sternly. "Your brother chose this fate himself."

"I don't believe it! How? Who is this Fistan—whatever? I want answers—"

"The answers you seek are not mine to give," Fizban said. His voice was mild still, but there was a hint of steel in his tone that brought Caramon up short. "Beware of those answers, young man," Fizban added softly. "Beware still more of your questions!" Caramon was silent for long moments, staring into the sky after the green dragon, though it had long since disappeared.

"What will become of him now?" he asked finally.

"I do not know," Fizban answered. "He makes his own fate, as do you. But I do know this, Caramon. You must let him go." The old man's eyes went to Tika, who had come to stand beside them. "Raistlin was right when he said your paths had split. Go forward into your new life in peace."

Tika smiled up at Caramon and nestled close. He hugged her, kissing her red curls. But even as he returned her smile and tousled her hair, his gaze strayed to the night sky, where—above

Neraka—the dragons still fought their flaming battles for control of the crumbling empire.

"So this is the end," Tanis said. "Good has triumphed."

"Good? Triumph?" Fizban repeated, turning to stare at the half-elf shrewdly. "Not so, Half-Elven. The balance is restored. The evil dragons will not be banished. They remain here, as do the good dragons. Once again the pendulum swings freely."

"All this suffering, just for that?" Laurana asked, coming to stand beside Tanis. "Why shouldn't good win, drive the darkness away forever?"

"Haven't you learned anything, young lady?" Fizban scolded, shaking a bony finger at her. "There *was* a time when good held sway. Do you know when that was? Right before the Cataclysm!"

"Yes"—he continued, seeing their astonishment—"the Kingpriest of Istar was a good man. Does that surprise you? It shouldn't, because both of you have seen what goodness like that can do. You've seen it in the elves, the ancient embodiment of good! It breeds intolerance, rigidity, a belief that because I am right, those who don't believe as I do are wrong.

"We gods saw the danger this complacency was bringing upon the world. We saw that much good was being destroyed, simply because it wasn't understood. And we saw the Queen of Darkness, lying in wait, biding her time; for this could not last, of course. The overweighted scales must tip and fall, and then she would return. Darkness would descend upon the world very fast.

"And so—the Cataclysm. We grieved for the innocent. We grieved for the guilty. But the world had to be prepared, or the darkness that fell might never have been lifted." Fizban saw Tasslehoff yawn. "But enough lectures. I've got to go. Things to do. Busy night ahead." Turning away abruptly, he tottered toward the snoring golden dragon.

"Wait!" Tanis said suddenly. "Fizban—er—Paladine, were you ever in the Inn of the Last Home, in Solace?"

"An inn? In Solace?" The old man paused, stroking his beard. "An inn . . . there are so many. But I seem to recall spicy potatoes. . . . That's it!" The old man peered around at Tanis, his eyes glinting. "I used to tell stories there, to the children. Quite an exciting place, that inn. I remember one night—a beautiful young woman came in. A barbarian she was, with golden hair. Sang a song about a blue crystal staff that touched off a riot."

"That was you, shouting for the guards!" Tanis exclaimed. "*You* got us into this!"

"I set the stage, lad," Fizban said cunningly. "I didn't give you a script. The dialogue has been all yours." Glancing at Laurana, then back to Tanis, he shook his head. "Must say I could have improved it a bit here and there, but then—never mind." Turning away once more, he began yelling at the dragon. "Wake up, you lazy, flea-bitten beast!"

"Flea-bitten!" Pyrite's eyes flared open. "Why, you decrepit old mage! You couldn't turn water into ice in the dead of winter!"

"Oh, can't I?" Fizban shouted in a towering rage, poking at the dragon with his staff. "Well, I'll show you." Fishing out a battered spellbook, he began flipping pages. "Fireball . . . Fireball . . . I know it's in here somewhere."

Absent-mindedly, still muttering, the old mage climbed up onto the dragon's back.

"Are you quite ready?" the ancient dragon asked in icy tones, then—without waiting for an answer—spread his creaking wings. Flapping them painfully to ease the stiffness, he prepared to take off.

"Wait! My hat!" Fizban cried wildly.

Too late. Wings beating furiously, the dragon rose unsteadily into the air. After wobbling, hanging precariously over the edge of the cliff, Pyrite caught the night breeze and soared into the night sky.

"Stop! You crazed—"

"Fizban!" Tas cried.

"My hat!" wailed the mage.

"Fizban!" Tas shouted again. "It's—"

But the two had flown out of hearing. Soon they were nothing more than dwindling sparks of gold, the dragon's scales glittering in Solinari's light.

"It's on your head," the kender murmured with a sigh.

The companions watched in silence, then turned away.

"Give me a hand with this, will you, Caramon?" Tanis asked. Unbuckling the dragonarmor, he sent it spinning, piece by piece, over the edge of the ridge. "What about yours?"

"I think I'll keep mine a while longer. We've still a long journey ahead of us, and the way will be difficult and dangerous." Caramon waved a hand toward the flaming city. "Raistlin was right. The dragonmen won't stop their evil just because their Queen is gone."

"Where will you go?" Tanis asked, breathing deeply. The night air was soft and warm, fragrant with the promise of new growth.

Thankful to be rid of the hated armor, he sat down wearily beneath a grove of trees that stood upon the ridge overlooking the Temple. Laurana came to sit near him, but not beside him. Her knees were drawn up beneath her chin, her eyes thoughtful as she gazed out over the plains.

"Tika and I have been talking about that," Caramon said, the two of them sitting down beside Tanis. He and Tika glanced at each other, neither seeming willing to speak. After a moment, Caramon cleared his throat. "We're going back to Solace, Tanis. And I—I guess this means we'll be splitting up since"— he paused, unable to continue.

"We know you'll be returning to Kalaman," Tika added softly, with a glance at Laurana. "We talked of going with you. After all, there's that big citadel floating around still, plus all these renegade dragonmen. And we'd like to see Riverwind and Goldmoon and Gilthanas again. But—"

"I want to go home, Tanis," Caramon said heavily. "I know it's not going to be easy going back, seeing Solace burned, destroyed," he added, forestalling Tanis's objections, "but I've thought about Alhana and the elves, what they have to go back to in Silvanesti. I'm thankful my home isn't like that—a twisted nightmare. They'll need me in Solace, Tanis, to help rebuild. They'll need my strength. I—I'm used to . . . being needed. . . ."

Tika laid her cheek on his arm, he gently tousled her hair. Tanis nodded in understanding. He would like to see Solace again, but it wasn't home. Not any more. Not without Flint and Sturm and . . . and others.

"What about you, Tas?" Tanis asked the kender with a smile as he came trudging up to the group, lugging a waterskin he had filled at a nearby creek. "Will you come back to Kalaman with us?"

Tas flushed. "No, Tanis," he said uncomfortably. "You see, since I'm this close—I thought I'd pay a visit to *my* homeland. We killed a Dragon Highlord, Tanis"—Tas lifted his chin proudly—"all by ourselves. People will treat us with respect now. Our leader, Kronin, will most likely become a hero in Krynnish lore."

Tanis scratched his beard to hide his smile, refraining from telling Tas that the Highlord the kenders had killed had been the bloated, cowardly Fewmaster Toede.

"I think *one* kender will become a hero," Laurana said seriously. "He will be the kender who broke the dragon orb, the kender who fought at the siege of the High Clerist's Tower, the kender who captured Bakaris, the kender who risked everything to rescue a friend from the Queen of Darkness."

"Who's that?" Tas asked eagerly, then, "Oh!" Suddenly realizing who Laurana meant, Tas flushed pink to the tips of his ears and sat down with a thud, quite overcome.

Caramon and Tika settled back against a tree trunk, both faces—for the moment—were filled with peace and tranquility. Tanis, watching them, envied them, wondering if such peace would ever be his. He turned to Laurana, who was sitting straight now, gazing beyond into the flaming sky, her thoughts far away.

"Laurana," Tanis said unsteadily, his voice faltering as her beautiful face turned to his, "Laurana, you gave this to me once"—he held the golden ring in his palm—"before either of us knew what true love or commitment meant. It now means a great deal to me, Laurana. In the dream, this ring brought me back from the darkness of the nightmare, just as your love saved me from the darkness in my own soul." He paused, feeling a sharp pang of regret even as he talked. "I'd like to keep it, Laurana, if you still want me to have it. And I would like to give you one to wear, to match it."

Laurana stared at the ring long moments without speaking, then she lifted it from Tanis's palm and—with a sudden motion—threw it over the ridge. Tanis gasped, half-starting to his feet. The ring flashed in Lunitari's red light, then it vanished into the darkness.

"I guess that's my answer," Tanis said. "I can't blame you."

Laurana turned back to him, her face calm. "When I gave you that ring, Tanis, it was the first love of an undisciplined heart. You were right to return it to me, I see that now. I had to grow up, to learn what real love was. I have been through flame and darkness, Tanis. I have killed dragons. I have wept over the body of one I loved." She sighed. "I was a leader. I had responsibilities. Flint told me that. But I threw it all away. I fell into Kitiara's trap. I realized—too late—how shallow my love really was. Riverwind's and Goldmoon's steadfast love brought hope to the world. Our petty love came near to destroying it."

"Laurana," Tanis began, his heart aching.

Her hand closed over his.

"Hush, just a moment more," she whispered. "I love you, Tanis. I love you now because I understand you. I love you for the light and the darkness within you. That is why I threw the ring away. Perhaps someday our love will be a foundation strong enough to build upon. Perhaps someday I will give you another ring and I will accept yours. But it will not be a ring of ivy leaves, Tanis."

"No," he said, smiling. Reaching out, he put his hand on her shoulder, to draw her near. Shaking her head, she started to resist. "It will be a ring made half of gold and half of steel." Tanis clasped her more firmly.

Laurana looked into his eyes, then she smiled and yielded to him, sinking back to rest beside him, her head on his shoulder.

"Perhaps I'll shave," said Tanis, scratching his beard.

"Don't," murmured Laurana, drawing Tanis's cloak around her shoulders. "I've gotten used to it."

All that night the companions kept watch together beneath the trees, waiting for the dawn. Weary and wounded, they could not sleep, they knew the danger had not ended.

From their vantage point, they could see bands of draconians fleeing the Temple confines. Freed from their leaders, the draconians would soon turn to robbery and murder to ensure their own survival. There were Dragon Highlords still. Though no one mentioned her name, the companions each knew one had almost certainly managed to survive the chaos boiling around the Temple. And perhaps there would be other evils to contend with, evils more powerful and terrifying than the friends dared imagine.

But for now there were a few moments of peace, and they were loath to end them. For with the dawn would come farewells.

No one spoke, not even Tasslehoff. There was no need for words between them. All had been said or was waiting to be said. They would not spoil what went before, nor hurry what was to come. They asked Time to stop for a little while to let them rest. And, perhaps, it did.

Just before dawn, when only a hint of the sun's coming shone pale in the eastern sky, the Temple of Takhisis, Queen of Darkness, exploded. The ground shivered with the blast. The light was brilliant, blinding, like the birth of a new sun.

Their eyes dazzled by the flaring light, they could not see clearly. But they had the impression that the sparkling shards of the Temple were rising into the sky, being swept upward by a vast heavenly whirlwind. Brighter and brighter the shards gleamed as they hurtled into the starry darkness, until they shone as radiantly as the stars themelves.

And then they *were* stars. One by one, each piece of the shattered Temple took its proper place in the sky, filling the two black voids Raistlin had seen last autumn, when he looked up from the boat in Crystalmir Lake.

Once again, the constellations glittered in the sky.

Once again, the Valiant Warrior—Paladine—the Platinum Dragon—took his place in one half of the night sky while opposite him appeared the Queen of Darkness, Takhisis, the Five-Headed, Many-Colored Dragon. And so they resumed their endless wheeling, one always watchful of the other, as they revolved eternally around Gilean, God of Neutrality, the Scales of Balance

The Homecoming

There were none to welcome him as he entered the city. He came in the dead of a still, black night; the only moon in the sky being one his eyes alone could see. He had sent away the green dragon, to await his commands. He did not pass through the city gates; no guard witnessed his arrival.

He had no need to come through the gates. Boundaries meant for ordinary mortals no longer concerned him. Unseen, unknown, he walked the silent, sleeping streets.

And yet, there was one who was aware of his presence. Inside the great library, Astinus—intent as ever upon his work—stopped writing and lifted his head. His pen remained poised for an instant over the paper, then—with a shrug—he resumed work on his chronicles once more.

The man walked the dark streets rapidly, leaning upon a staff that was decorated at the top with a crystal ball clutched in the golden, disembodied claw of a dragon. The crystal was dark. He needed no light to brighten the way. He knew where he was going. He had walked it in his mind for long centuries. Black robes rustled softly around his ankles as he strode forward; his golden eyes, gleaming from the depths of his black hood, seemed the only sparks of light in the slumbering city.

He did not stop when he reached the center of town. He did not even glance at the abandoned buildings with their dark, windows gaping like the eyesockets in a skull. His steps did not falter as he passed among the chill shadows of the tall oak trees, though these shadows alone had been enough to terrify a kender. The fleshless guardian hands that reached out to grasp him fell to dust at his feet, and he trod upon them without care.

The tall Tower came in sight, black against the black sky like a window cut into darkness. And here, finally, the black-robed man came to a halt. Standing before the gates, he looked up at the Tower; his eyes taking in everything, coolly appraising the crumbling minarets and the polished marble that glistened in the cold, piercing light of the stars. He nodded slowly, in satisfaction.

The golden eyes lowered their gaze to the gates of the Tower, to the horrible fluttering robes that hung from those gates.

No ordinary mortal could have stood before those terrible, shrouded gates without going mad from the nameless terror. No ordinary mortal could have walked unscathed through the guardian oaks.

But Raistlin stood there. He stood there calmly, without fear. Lifting his thin hand, he grasped hold of the shredded black robes still stained with the blood of their wearer, and tore them from the gates.

A chill penetrating wail of outrage screamed up from the depths of the Abyss. So loud and horrifying was it that all the citizens of Palanthas woke shuddering from even the deepest sleep and lay in their beds, paralyzed by fear, waiting for the end of the world. The guards on the city walls could move neither hand nor foot. Shutting their eyes, they cowered in shadows, awaiting death. Babies whimpered in fear, dogs cringed and slunk beneath beds, cats' eyes gleamed.

The shriek sounded again, and a pale hand reached out from the Tower gates. A ghastly face, twisted in fury, floated in the dank air.

Raistlin did not move.

The hand drew near, the face promised him the tortures of the Abyss, where he would be dragged for his great folly in daring the curse of the Tower. The skeletal hand touched Raistlin's heart. Then, trembling, it halted.

"Know this," said Raistlin calmly, looking up at the Tower, pitching his voice so that it could be heard by those within. "I am the master of past and present! My coming was foretold. For me, the gates will open."

The skeletal hand shrank back and, with a slow sweeping motion of invitation, parted the darkness. The gates swung open upon silent hinges.

Raistlin passed through them without a glance at the hand or the pale visage that was lowered in reverence. As he entered, all the black and shapeless, dark and shadowy things dwelling within the Tower bowed in homage.

Then Raistlin stopped and looked around him.

"I am home," he said.

Peace stole over Palanthas, sleep soothed away fear.

A dream, the people murmured. Turning over in their beds, they drifted back into slumber, blessed by the darkness which brings rest before the dawn.

Raistlin's Farewell

Caramon, the gods have tricked the world
In absences, in gifts, and all of us
Are housed within their cruelties. The wit
That was our heritage, they lodged in me,
Enough to see all differences: the light
In Tika's eye when she looks elsewhere,
The tremble in Laurana's voice when she
Speaks to Tanis, and the graceful sweep
Of Goldmoon's hair at Riverwind's approach.
They look at me, and even with your mind
I could discern the difference. Here I sit,
A body frail as bird bones.

In return
The gods teach us compassion, teach us mercy,
That compensation. Sometimes they succeed,
For I have felt the hot spit of injustice
Turn through those too weak to fight their brothers
For sustenance or love, and in that feeling
The pain lulled and diminished to a glow,
I pitied as you pitied, and in that
Rose above the weakest of the litter.

You, my brother, in your thoughtless grace,
That special world in which the sword arm spins
The wild arc of ambition and the eye
Gives flawless guidance to the flawless hand,
You cannot follow me, cannot observe
The landscape of cracked mirrors in the soul,
The aching hollowness in sleight of hand.

And yet you love me, simple as the rush
And balance of our blindly mingled blood,

Or as a hot sword arching through the snow:
It is the mutual need that puzzles you,
The deep complexity lodged in the veins.
Wild in the dance of battle, when you stand,
A shield before your brother, it is then
Your nourishment arises from the heart
Of all my weaknesses.

                When I am gone,
Where will you find the fullness of your blood?
Backed in the heart's loud tunnels?

                        I have heard

The Queen's soft lullaby, Her serenade
And call to battle mingling in the night;
This music calls me to my quiet throne
Deep in Her senseless kingdom.

                      Dragonlords
Thought to bring the darkness into light,
Corrupt it with the mornings and the moons—
In balance is all purity destroyed,
But in voluptuous darkness lies the truth,
The final, graceful dance.

                   But not for you:
You cannot follow me into the night,
Into the maze of sweetness. For you stand
Cradled by the sun, in solid lands,
Expecting nothing, having lost your way
Before the road became unspeakable.

It is beyond explaining, and the words
Will make you stumble. Tanis is your friend,
My little orphan, and he will explain
Those things he glimpses in the shadow's path,
For he knew Kitiara and the shine
Of the dark moon upon her darkest hair,
And yet he cannot threaten, for the night
Breathes in a moist wind on my waiting face.

We wish to gratefully acknowledge the following people:
Michael Williams for his splendid poetry and for being there
when we needed him.

Jeff Grubb, Douglas Niles, Laura Hickman for their advice
and for their tremendous work on related game modules.

Jean Blashfield Black for her skilled editing and her advice.

Larry Elmore for bringing our characters to life on the covers.

Jeff Butler for his fine work on the interior art.

Roger E. Moore for his articles in DRAGON® Magazine.

Patrick L. Price for assistance in editing and proofreading.

Mannheim Steamroller for their beautiful and inspirational
music, FRESH AIRE V. (American Gramaphone)

Our coworkers at TSR, INC. for their enthusiastic support.

Our families for being very patient.

And finally, we want to especially thank all of you who have
written to tell us how much you enjoy spending a few hours
of your time in our world of Krynn.

**ADVANCED DUNGEONS & DRAGONS® Adventure
Role-playing Games.**
Live the adventure you enjoyed reading!

DRAGONS OF DESPAIR
The heroes meet, the return of the ancient gods.
by Tracy Hickman

DRAGONS OF FLAME
Prisoners of the Dragon Highlord, Verminaard.
by Douglas Niles

DRAGONS OF HOPE
Fleeing into the wilderness.
by Tracy Hickman

DRAGONS OF DESOLATION
The dwarf kingdom of Thorbardin.
by Tracy Hickman and Michael Dobson

DRAGONS OF MYSTERY
Backgrounds on the characters.
by Michael Dobson

DRAGONS OF ICE
Adventures in Ice Wall Castle.
by Douglas Niles

DRAGONS OF LIGHT
The Silver Dragon of Ergoth.
by Michael Grubb

DRAGONS OF WAR
Battle of the High Clerist's Tower.
by Tracy and Laura Hickman

DRAGONS OF DECEIT
The terrifying journey into Sanction.
by Douglas Niles

DRAGONS OF DREAMS
The nightmare kingdom of Silvanesti.
by Tracy Hickman
(December, 1985)

DRAGONS OF GLORY
Lord Gunthar's Commentaries.
by Tracy Hickman and Douglas Niles
(January, 1986)

TSR, INC. Adventure Role-playing games are available at fine book and
hobby stores.

THE FURTHER CHRONICLES

Volume One, The Time of the Twins

by Margaret Weis and Tracy Hickman

The War of the Lance has been over two years. An uneasy peace exists in Krynn. But for Caramon and Raistlin, there can be no peace. Driven by ambition, Raistlin has now become the most powerful force for evil in the world—but he seeks to grow stronger. Caramon, grieving over the downfall of his twin, determines to save his brother from the shadows of darkness.

Their quests take them both on a terrifying journey back in time to the days just prior to the Cataclysm—accompanied (accidentally)—by Tasslehoff Burrfoot!

The adventure continues as one man sets out on a quest—not to save the world—but to save a soul!

January, 1986

Volume Two, War of the Twins—June, 1986
Volume Three, Test of the Twins—September, 1986

DRAGONLANCE CHRONICLES Trilogy

by Margaret Weis and Tracy Hickman

Three-Volume Gift Set

Three volumes in a beautiful boxed gift set. Artwork by fantasy artist, Larry Elmore. $9.95

SUPER ENDLESS QUEST™ ADVENTURE GAME-BOOKS:

PRISONERS OF PAX THARKAS by Morris Simon. A ranger returns to find his home in Solace occupied by draconians and his younger brother a prisoner of the Dragon Highlord, Verminaard!

THE SOULFORGE by Terry Phillips. The story of what *really* happened to the young man in the Tower of High Sorcery! (October, 1983)

DRAGONLANCE® Adventure Role-Playing Modules and Books are available at fine book, toy, and hobby stores.